Dear Target Guest:

Several years ago, my novel *The Secret Life of CeeCee Wilkes* was selected as a Target Book Club pick. It's hard to describe the thrill of seeing my books in Target stores everywhere, but the best part of that opportunity came in the form of reaching so many new readers. I'm pinching myself to learn that another of my books—*Necessary Lies*—has been chosen for the same honor. *Necessary Lies* is a meaningful book to me and I'm excited to have this chance to share it with so many readers as a Target Book Club pick.

I've spoken with many book clubs about *Necessary Lies*, either in person or via Skype or speakerphone. More than any of my other books, this story, based in historical fact, has led to remarkably rich and intense conversations. Although my characters are completely fictional, the forced sterilization program that threatens their futures was very real, existing in North Carolina from the late 1920s to the early 1970s. Many states had similar programs, but North Carolina was remarkable in that it was the only state to give social workers the ability to refer their clients for sterilization. As a former social worker myself, I was particularly stunned by this fact. What would it be like, I wondered, to have that sort of power over my clients' lives?

I knew the story I wanted to tell, but how should I tell it? I decided to set the book in 1960 to illustrate how different that era was with regard to the limited choices women had when it came to work and family. I thought it would be most intriguing to see the story unfold from the perspectives of both the powerful and the powerless, so I decided to write from two first-person points of view that would illustrate those differences. Jane Forrester is an idealistic young social worker, newly married to a man who doesn't want her to work at all, much less do the sort of tough, gritty work expected of her as a rural social worker. One of her clients is fifteen-year-old Ivy Hart. Ivy wants only two things in life: to hold the tattered remnants of her tobacco-farming family together and to one day marry and have children with the boy she's loved since she was a little girl. When Jane is tasked with referring Ivy for sterilization due to Ivy's mild epilepsy, she assumes her supervisors know what they're doing and goes along with the system. But as Jane gets to know Ivy and is touched by her goodness and her longing for children, she must decide how much she is willing to risk to do what she believes is right.

There were many "Ivies" and "Janes" during the years of the sterilization program, and I felt a deep responsibility to bring their story to light in a way that was as honest and affecting as possible. I hope I've succeeded in that.

I'm grateful to Target for again giving me this opportunity to touch and entertain so many readers. I look forward to hearing what you think of this story. I hope it gives you hours of reading pleasure and that Ivy and Jane's world stays with you for days to come.

Best wishes,

Diane Chamberlain

"Diane Chamberlain's *Necessary Lies* will steal your heart. This novel, about the courage it takes to be who you're supposed to be even when all of society's messages are telling you otherwise, is full of discoveries—for the reader as well as for the two struggling but brave protagonists. Warning: This novel will steal your time and all commitment to other obligations, too—once you open it, nothing else will matter but seeing it through to the white-knuckle, heart-racing end."

—Katrina Kittle, author of
The Blessings of the Animals

"Diane Chamberlain's *Necessary Lies* is the most important book she has ever written. Based in truth, you will be reminded how poverty is our enemy and how power is dangerous when it's in the wrong hands. I don't think I will ever forget this book or its wonderful cast of characters. Beautifully written, compellingly told. Book clubs will love it."

—Dorothea Benton Frank,
New York Times bestselling author of
The Last Original Wife

"Ms. Chamberlain brilliantly captures the feel of the early 1960s in the South. Her characters are authentic and heartfelt, the story is captivating, and her writing is lovely and compassionate. *Necessary Lies* shines!"

—Lesley Kagen, *New York Times* bestselling
author of *Mare's Nest*

"Amazing! Diane Chamberlain's *Necessary Lies* is a powerful portrait of courage and redemption, teeming with characters you won't soon forget. Chamberlain's most luminous tale to date, *Necessary Lies* expertly intertwines history and matters of the heart—love, loyalty, and choosing what is right, no matter the consequences."

—Heather Gudenkauf, *New York Times*
bestselling author of *The Weight of Silence*
and *One Breath Away*

NECESSARY LIES

diane
chamberlain

St. Martin's Griffin   New York

NECESSARY LIES. Copyright © 2013 by Diane Chamberlain. All rights reserved. Printed in the United States of America. For information, address St. Martin's Press, 175 Fifth Avenue, New York, N.Y. 10010.

Designed by Steven Seighman

The Library of Congress has cataloged the hardcover edition as follows:

Chamberlain, Diane, 1950–
   Necessary lies / Diane Chamberlain. — First Edition.
     p. cm.
  ISBN 978-1-250-01069-8 (hardcover)
  ISBN 978-1-250-01070-4 (e-book)
 1. Social workers—Fiction. 2. Friendship—Fiction. 3. North Carolina—Fiction.
4. Domestic fiction. I. Title.
  PS3553.H2485N47 2013
  813'.54—dc23

                                       2013013951

ISBN 978-1-250-06956-6 (Target Book Club Edition)

St. Martin's Griffin books may be purchased for educational, business, or promotional use. For information on bulk purchases, please contact Macmillan Corporate and Premium Sales Department at 1-800-221-7945, extension 5442, or write specialmarkets@macmillan.com.

First Target Book Club Edition: October 2014

10 9 8 7 6 5 4 3 2 1

For the women and men
who had no choice

JUNE 22, 2011

1

Brenna

It was an odd request—visit a stranger's house and peer inside a closet—and as I drove through the neighborhood searching for the address, I felt my anxiety mounting.

There it was: number 247. I hadn't expected the house to be so large. It stood apart from its neighbors on the gently winding road, flanked on either side by huge magnolia trees, tall oaks, and crape myrtle. It was painted a soft buttery yellow with white trim, and everything about it looked crisp and clean in the early morning sun. Every house I'd passed, although different in architecture, had the same stately yet inviting look. I didn't know Raleigh well at all, but this had to be one of the most beautiful old neighborhoods in the city.

I parked close to the curb and headed up the walk. Potted plants lined either side of the broad steps that led up to the wraparound porch. I glanced at my watch. I had an hour before I needed to be back at the hotel. No rush, though my nerves were really acting up. There was so much I hoped would go well today, and so much of it was out of my control.

I rang the bell and heard it chime inside the house. I could see someone pass behind the sidelight and then the door opened. The woman—forty, maybe? At least ten years younger than me—smiled, although that didn't mask her harried expression. I felt bad for bothering her this early. She wore white shorts, a pink striped T-shirt, and tennis shoes, and sported a glowing tan. She was the petite, toned, and well-put-together sort of woman that always made me feel sloppy, even though I knew I looked fine in my black pants and blue blouse.

"Brenna?" She ran her fingers through her short-short, spiky blond hair.

"Yes," I said. "And you must be Jennifer."

Jennifer peered behind me. "She's not with you?" she asked.

I shook my head. "I thought she'd come, but at the last minute she said she just couldn't."

Jennifer nodded. "Today must be really hard for her." She took a step back from the doorway. "Come on in," she said. "My kids are done with school for the summer, but they have swim-team practice this morning, so we're in luck. We have the house to ourselves. The kids are always too full of questions."

"Thanks." I walked past her into the foyer. I was glad no one else was home. I wished I had the house totally to myself, to be honest. I would have loved to explore it. But that wasn't why I was here.

"Can I get you anything?" Jennifer asked. "Coffee?"

"No, I'm good, thanks."

"Well, come on then. I'll show you."

She led me to the broad, winding staircase and we climbed it without speaking, my shoes on the shiny dark hardwood treads making the only sound.

"How long have you been in the house?" I asked when we reached the second story.

"Five years," she said. "We redid everything. I mean, we painted every single room and every inch of molding. And every closet, too, except for that one."

"Why didn't you paint that one?" I asked as I followed her down a short hallway.

"The woman we bought the house from specifically told us not to. She said that the couple *she'd* bought the house from had also told her not to, but nobody seemed to understand why not. The woman we bought it from showed us the writing. My husband thought we should just paint over it—I think he was spooked by it—but I talked him out of it. It's a *closet*. What would it hurt to leave it unpainted?" We'd reached the closed door at the end of the hall. "I had no idea what it meant until I spoke to you on the phone." She pushed open the door. "It's my daughter's room now," she said, "so excuse the mess."

It wasn't what I'd call messy at all. My twin daughters' rooms had been far worse. "How old's your daughter?" I asked.

"Ten. Thus the Justin Bieber obsession." She swept her arm through the air to take in the lavender room and its nearly wall-to-wall posters.

"It only gets worse." I smiled. "I barely survived my girls' teen years." I thought of my family—my husband and my daughters and their babies—up in Maryland and suddenly missed them. I hoped I'd be home by the weekend, when all of this would be over.

Jennifer opened the closet door. It was a small closet, the type you'd find in these older homes, and it was crammed with clothes on hangers and shoes helter-skelter on the floor. I felt a chill, as though a ghost had slipped past me into the room. I hugged my arms as Jennifer pulled a cord to turn on the light. She pressed the clothes to one side of the closet.

"There," she said, pointing to the left wall at about the level of my knees. "Maybe we need a flashlight?" she asked. "Or I can just take a bunch of these clothes out. I should have done that before you got here." She lifted an armload of the clothes and struggled to disengage the hangers before carrying them from the closet. Without the clothing, the closet filled with light and I squatted inside the tight space, pushing pink sneakers and a pair of sandals out of my way.

I ran my fingers over the words carved into the wall. Ancient paint snagged my fingertips where it had chipped away around the letters. *"Ivy and Mary was here."* All at once, I felt overwhelmed by the fear they must have felt back then, and by their courage. When I stood up, I was brushing tears from my eyes.

Jennifer touched my arm. "You okay?" she asked.

"Fine," I said. "I'm grateful to you for not covering that over. It makes it real to me."

"If we ever move out of this house, we'll tell the new owners to leave it alone, too. It's a little bit of history, isn't it?"

I nodded. I remembered my phone in my purse. "May I take a picture of it?"

"Of course!" Jennifer said, then added with a laugh, "Just don't get my daughter's messy closet in it."

I pulled out my phone and knelt down near the writing on the wall. I snapped the picture and felt the presence of a ghost again, but this time it wrapped around me like an embrace.

1960

2

Ivy

I swept the ground by the tobacco barn, hoping for a chance to talk to Henry Allen. He was on the other side of the field, though, working with the mules, and it didn't look like he'd be done soon. No point in me staying any longer. All the day labor was gone already and if Mr. Gardiner spotted me he'd wonder why I was still here. Mary Ella was gone, too, of course. I didn't want to know which of the boys—or men—she went off with. Most likely she was someplace in the woods. Down by the crick, maybe, where the trees and that tangle of honeysuckle made a private place where you could do anything. I knew that place so well. Maybe Mary Ella knew it, too. Henry Allen told me "just don't think about it," so I tried to put it out of my head. My sister was going to do what she wanted to do. Nothing me or nobody else could do about it. I told her we couldn't have another baby in the house and she gave me that hollow-eyed look like I was speaking a foreign tongue. Couldn't get through to Mary Ella when she gave you that look. She was seventeen—two years older than me—but you'd think I was her mama trying to keep her on the straight-and-narrow path to heaven. Some days I felt like I was everybody's mama.

I headed home down Deaf Mule Road where it ran between two tobacco fields that went on forever and ever. I couldn't look at all them acres and acres of tobacco we still had to get in. My fingers was still sticky with tar from that day's work. Even my hair felt like it had tar in it, and as I walked down the road, I lifted one blond end of my hair from under my kerchief and checked it, but it just looked like my plain old hair. Dried hay. That's what Nonnie said about my hair one time. My own grandma, and she didn't care about hurting my feelings. It was true, though. Mary Ella got the looks in our family. Roses in her cheeks. Full head of long wild curls, the color of sweet corn. Carolina-blue eyes. "Them looks of hers is a curse," Nonnie always said. "She walks out the door and every boy in Grace County loses his good sense."

I took off my shoes and the dust from the road felt soft beneath my feet. Maybe the best thing I felt all day. Every time I did that—walked barefoot on the dirt road between the Gardiners' two-story farmhouse and our little house—I felt like I was walking on Mama's old ragged black velveteen shawl. That was practically the only thing we had left of hers. I used to sleep with it, but now with Baby William sharing the bed with me and Mary Ella, there wasn't no room for nothing bigger than my memory of Mama, and after all these years, that was just a little slip of a thing.

I came to the end of the road where it dipped into the woods. The path got rough here with tree roots and rocks but I knew where every one of them was. I put my shoes back on before I came to the open area with the chigger weeds and by then I could hear Baby William howling. He was going at it good and Nonnie was hollerin' at him to shut it, so I started running before she could get to the point of hitting him. For all I knew she'd been hitting him all afternoon. Nonnie wasn't all that mean, but when her rheumatism made her hands hot and red, her fuse was right short. She said she raised our daddy, then me and Mary Ella, and she thought she was done with the raising. Then all of a sudden, Baby William came along.

"I'm here!" I called as I ran into our yard. The bike me and Mary Ella shared was on its side in the dirt and I jumped over it and ran around the woodpile. Baby William stood on the stoop, saggy diaper hanging halfway down his fat legs, his face all red and tears making paths through the dirt on his cheeks. His black curls was so thick they looked like a wig on his head. He raised his arms out to me when he saw me.

"I'm here, baby boy!" I said, and I scooped him up. He settled right away like always, his body shaking with the end of his crying. Now, if Mary Ella was with me, it'd be her he'd reach for—he knew his mama—but right now he was mine. "Gotcha, sweet baby," I whispered in his ear.

I looked through the open doorway of our house, trying to see where Nonnie was, but it was dark in there and all I could see was the end of the ratty sofa where the sunlight lit on it from the open doorway. Nonnie kept the shades drawn all day to keep the house cooler. Mr. Gardiner put electricity in our house when I was little, but you'd swear Nonnie hadn't figured out how to work it yet. Didn't matter. The only real light in the house was the one I held in my arms.

"Let's get you changed," I said, climbing the stoop and walking into the house. I drew up the crackling old shades at the two front windows to let some light in and the dust motes took to floating around the room. Nonnie showed up in the doorway to the kitchen. She had a bundle of folded diapers and towels in her left arm and she leaned on her cane with her free hand.

"Mary Ella ain't with you?" she asked, like that was out of the ordinary.

"No." I kissed her cheek and I could of swore her hair had more gray in it than just that morning when she spent a few hours helping with the barning. She was turning into an old lady before my eyes, with big puffy arms and three chins and walking bent over. She already had the sugar and the high blood and I had this worry of losing her. You got to expecting it after a while, things going wrong. I wasn't no pessimist, though. Mrs. Rex, my science teacher two years ago, told me I was one of them people that looked on the bright side of things. I thought of Mrs. Rex every time I started to say the word "ain't" and changed it to "isn't." "You can't get anywhere in life talking dumb," she told us. Not that I was exactly getting anywhere in life.

I took the laundry from Nonnie with my free hand, catching a whiff of sunshine from the towels. "Maybe she's getting some extras from Mr. Gardiner," I said, trying to think positive. I wanted to wipe the scowl off Nonnie's face. Once or twice a week, Mr. Gardiner, Henry Allen's daddy who owned all them acres and acres of tobacco,

gave Mary Ella things from his own personal garden—and sometimes his smokehouse—for us. He could just as easy hand them to
me, but her being the oldest seemed to mean something to him. Or
maybe it was that she was a mama now and he thought the food
should go to Baby William. I didn't know. All I knew was that we
needed them extras. Mr. Gardiner took care of us in a lot of ways. He
gave us a Frigidaire and a new woodstove so big the heat could reach
the bedroom as long as we left the door open—and since the door
didn't close all the way, that was easy. Nonnie was about to ask for indoor plumbing when Mary Ella started sprouting her belly. Then
Nonnie decided she better not ask for nothing more.

"Did Mary Ella tell him about them deer getting into our garden
again?" she asked. The deer got into our garden no matter how much
fencing I put around the little bit of good soil Mr. Gardiner let us work
for ourselves.

"Yes," I said, though it was me who told him. Mary Ella didn't like
talking to Mr. Gardiner so much. She wasn't a big talker to begin
with.

"Got your wages?" Nonnie asked, like she did every day.

"I'll give 'em to you soon as I change this boy," I said, walking to
the bedroom. Mr. Gardiner paid us pennies compared to his other
workers, but he let us live here for nothing, so we never complained.

I plunked Baby William down on the bed and started tickling the
daylights out of him because I wanted to hear him giggle. We rolled
around on the bed for a couple minutes, both of us getting the worries
of the day out of ourselves. Sometimes I just liked to stare at that boy,
he was so beautiful. Black curls like satin when you ran your fingers
through them. Black eyelashes, long and thick. Eyes so dark they was
nearly black, too. Mary Ella's hair was even lighter than mine. I didn't
like to think where Baby William might of got all that black from.

There was a rustle of the trees outside the window and Baby William looked in that direction. We worried early on he might be deaf
'cause he didn't seem to care about noises and Mrs. Werkman and
Nurse Ann said he might need a deaf school, so now every time he
heard something, I celebrated inside.

"Mama?" he asked, lifting his head to look through the window. It was about the only word he knew, which Mrs. Werkman said wasn't right. He should have more words by two, she said. I didn't like how she was always finding something wrong with him. I told her he was just quiet like Mary Ella. Not a jabbermouth, like me.

"It's just a breeze out there," I said, nuzzling his sweaty little neck. "Mama'll be home soon."

I hoped I wasn't lying.

In the kitchen, I fed Baby William on my lap while Nonnie made salad from the last of a chicken we'd been eating most of the week. It was getting near dusk and Mary Ella still wasn't home. Baby William wasn't hungry. He kept pushing my hand away and the chunks of squash fell off the spoon.

"He's always a crab at suppertime," Nonnie said.

"No he ain't," I said. I hated how she talked about him like that. I bet she talked about me and Mary Ella that way when we was little, too. "He just needs some cuddling, don't you, Baby William?" I rocked him and he hung on to me like a monkey. Mrs. Werkman said we shouldn't hold him when we feed him no more. He should sit on a chair at the table, up on the block of wood me and Mary Ella sat on when we was little, but I just loved holding him and he crabbed less on my lap. Sometimes when I held Baby William like that, I thought I could remember my own mama holding me that way.

"I doubt that," Nonnie said when I told her that one day. "She wasn't much for holding y'all."

But I remembered it. Maybe I only imagined it, but that was near as good.

Nonnie scooped Duke's mayonnaise out of the jar and mixed it into the salad, looking out the window the whole time. "Gonna be dark before you know it," she said. "You better go see if you can find your sister. That girl forgets her way home sometime."

I let Baby William eat a piece of squash with his fingers. "No telling where she is, Nonnie," I said, but I knew I had to try or we'd both be worrying half the night. I stood up, handing Nonnie the baby and the spoon, and she set him on the wooden block. He let out a howl and she clamped her hand over his mouth.

Outside, I checked the johnny first just in case, but she wasn't there. Then I walked through the woods and across the pasture, turning my head left and right, looking for Mary Ella. I walked down the lane that ran next to the tobacco, which looked spooky in the evening light. When I was little, Mama would tell me fairies lived in them tobacco plants. Nonnie said I imagined this, that Mama would never say such a fanciful thing, but I didn't care. If I had to make up memories of Mama, I'd do it. I used to think someday I'd be able to ask her myself if the things I remembered was true, but Mrs. Werkman said no good could come from me paying Mama a visit after all this time. "No good for either of you, dear," she said, and by the way she said it I knew she felt real bad about the whole thing.

Way off to my left, I could see the Gardiners' house blazing with light from just about every room. I walked faster so I could see the back of the house and the two windows I knew was Henry Allen's room. I'd been in that room. Snuck in, of course. I would of been kilt if anyone knew. Mr. or Mrs. Gardiner. Nonnie. Lord, Nonnie would have my head! But Henry Allen would keep me safe. Nobody I trusted more than that boy. Even when we was little, he'd take on anybody that said a bad word about me. Back then I couldn't of known I'd come to love him like I did.

I nearly tripped over my own feet as I watched the windows, trying to see Henry Allen's shadow move past one of them, but I was so far from the house that the windows was nothing more than rectangles of light. It was real dusky out now, so he probably couldn't see me even if he was looking. But I felt it anyway, that long invisible thread that connected me and him. It always had.

Down the lane in front of me, a light burned on the porch of the Jordans' house, the other family that lived on the farm. I knew Mary Ella wouldn't be there, so I turned around and pretty soon I could see the farmhouse windows again. I stared so hard at Henry Allen's windows that I near forgot I was supposed to be looking for my sister. I wondered if he was listening to his radio. He had one of them little

ones you could carry around with you. He brung it with him whenever we met up at the crick. We had a big old radio, of course, but you
had to plug it in. Henry Allen said he was going to get me one of the
little ones, and when I thought of having music I could carry around,
I couldn't believe it. The Gardiners even had a television and Henry
Allen promised someday he'd show it to me but it had to be a time
when his parents and the help was out of the house and I didn't know
what it would take for that to happen. A funeral maybe. I didn't want
to wish for no funeral just so I could see a television.

I looked down the lane ahead of me, wishing I brung a lantern
with me because it was getting right dark out. The moon was big,
though, and it spilled light all over the tobacco like glitter.

"What you doin' out here this time of night, Ivy?"

I jumped, and it took my eyes a minute to make out Eli Jordan
walking toward me. He was so dark he blended into the night.

I slowed my walking. "Just looking for Mary Ella," I said, casual
like, not wanting to sound worried.

"That girl's a traveler, ain't she?" We was nearly face-to-face now
and he looked off across the field like he might be able to see her. He
was seventeen, same as Mary Ella, but could of passed for twenty.
Taller than me by a hand and broad in the shoulders. Nonnie called
him a buck. "That Jordan buck can do the work of four men," she'd
say, sounding admiring, and then a breath later add, "Stay away from
him, Ivy," like I'd be fool enough to mess with a colored boy. Wasn't
me that needed that warning. Sometimes I felt like he could look out
for me. Other times, I felt scared by his power. Like the day he lifted a
giant tree stump from the ground to the back of Mr. Gardiner's blue
pickup, the muscles in his back rippling like water in the crick. He
was a boy who could be for good or evil, and I didn't know which one
he was going to pick.

"Did you see her since the barning today?" I asked.

He shook his head and started walking past me toward his house.
"Ain't seen her," he said, then over his shoulder, "She'll probly be
home when you git there."

"Probly," I said, and I started walking again, faster this time.

The moon lit up the rows of tobacco and I went back to watching the lights in the farmhouse as I walked. I put my hand in my shorts pocket and felt the scrap of paper. *"Midnight, tomorrow,"* Henry Allen had written in the note. Most every day, he left a note for me near the bottom of the old fence post where the wood was split. He could tuck the note in real deep and no one but me would know it was there. Sometimes he'd say one o'clock or two, but usually it was midnight. I liked that best. Liked the sound of it. I liked thinking someday I'd tell our grandkids, *Me and your grandpa would meet by the crick at midnight.* Of course, I'd never tell them what we did there.

I saw a lantern in the distance. Someone was walking along Deaf Mule Road where it ran between the Gardiners' house and the woods. It wouldn't be Henry Allen. Way too early. As I got closer, I saw the moonlight fall on my sister's blond hair, which was out of her braid, loose and wild, a crazy big moonlit halo around her head. She was carrying something and I knew it was her basket with the extras Mr. Gardiner gave her for us. I walked faster till I was close enough for her to hear me.

"Mary Ella!" I called out, and she stopped walking and looked around, trying to see where my voice came from. Then she must of spotted me. Instead of walking toward me, though, she ran right across the path I was on, heading for the woods and home, and I knew she was running to keep away from me. She didn't want to see me. Or me to see her. My sister was a strange one.

By the time I got home, Mary Ella was sitting on the porch rocking Baby William in her arms. Even in the dark, I could tell she was holding him so tight you'd expect him to cry, but Baby William put up with Mary Ella lovin' on him. She was the only one who could calm him when he got flustrated from not having the words to tell us what he wanted. He knew who'd carried him closest to her heart. Moments like this, they was two quiet souls cut from the same cloth.

"Where you been?" I asked, like I expected her to tell me the truth.

"Had to get the extras from Mr. Gardiner," she said.

I didn't bother arguing with her. It didn't take hours to get the extras unless she had to grow them herself. I didn't say nothing about how I saw Eli walking home about the same time she was. There was something real breakable about Mary Ella and I was always afraid if I touched her in the wrong spot, she'd crack.

Nonnie came out on the porch, rooting through the basket in the light from the house. "He gave us some of Desiree's banana pudding!" she said. "Oh sweet Jesus, I wish he'd do that every week."

"You can't have that, Nonnie," I reminded her as I sat down on the stoop. "Your sugar."

"Don't go telling me what I can and can't have," Nonnie snapped. "You seem to forget you're my granddaughter, not my mother."

I shut up. Nonnie was like a little kid about her food. You told her she couldn't have something and she'd eat it just to be ornery. You reminded her to test her pee, and she'd lie and say she already done it.

I smacked a skeeter. I wouldn't last long out here. Once you stopped moving, they was on you.

Nonnie went back in the house and came out a minute later with a spoon. She settled into her rocker and set the bowl of pudding on her lap. I couldn't watch her take that first bite. I heard her let out a sigh.

"I'm at the end of my natural working life, girls," she said. She'd been saying that for years, but lately I believed it. She didn't last but two hours at the barn today, and even chasing after Baby William seemed too much for her. It was up to me and Mary Ella to work hard enough to keep Mr. Gardiner happy so he'd let us keep the house. He could have a bunch of real workers in it. A family with a father and sons who could do five times what me and Mary Ella and Nonnie did. I was always afraid one day he'd tell us it was time to go. What we'd do without our house, I didn't know.

I watched my grandmother digging into the bowl of banana pudding and my sister holding her secrets as close as she held her baby, and I wondered how much longer we could go on this way.

3

Jane

Dr. Carson reached his hand toward me to help me sit up. I clutched the thin fabric gown against my body as I balanced on the edge of the examining table, my legs dangling uncomfortably. He rolled away from me on his stool, then folded his arms across his chest and smiled at me, his thick gray hair giving him a grandfatherly appearance.

"I think your fiancé is a lucky man," he said.

"Thank you," I said, although I couldn't imagine what on earth he was basing that on. I'd barely said a word to him during the examination, too embarrassed to do anything other than stare at the ceiling. Now, though, I had to look at him. He seemed determined to hold my gaze with his own eyes, magnified behind his black horn-rimmed glasses.

"Do you have any concerns about your wedding night you'd like to discuss?" he asked.

It was so strange to be asked that question by a man I didn't know. My own mother wouldn't ask me that question. Gloria wouldn't have, either, and she'd been my college roommate and best friend. And certainly not Robert. I felt my cheeks burn, not for the first time in the last hour. This man had touched my breasts, slipped his fingers inside me, and explored parts of my body even I had never seen. Why should a question about my wedding night feel even more intrusive?

"No," I said. "No concerns." I couldn't wait to leave his office, but there was something more I needed from him. It was now or never, and he waited as though he knew I had more to say. I cleared my throat. "I was wondering if you could prescribe that new birth control pill for me," I said.

He raised his bushy gray eyebrows. "You don't want children?" The way he said it was accusatory, and I felt his opinion of me plummet.

I pressed the gown tighter to my chest. "I'd like to put off having children for a couple of years," I said. "I plan to work for a while first."

"Surely you don't have to work." He looked at me curiously. "Not married to a pediatrician." He'd told me he'd met Robert somewhere in the Raleigh medical community, and I didn't like that connection.

"I *want* to work," I said. Dr. Carson sounded like my mother, who claimed she only worked while my father was alive because his teaching salary had never quite paid the bills, and she only continued to work after his death because the life insurance wasn't enough to see us through. I knew she loved working in the library, no matter what she said. Robert wasn't thrilled with my plan himself, though. He never out-and-out said I *couldn't* work. He did, however, say it would be embarrassing for him, since none of his friends' wives worked. Only Gloria, who taught second grade, seemed to understand.

"What do you want to do?" Dr. Carson frowned at me as though he couldn't imagine a job I might truly want.

"I just graduated from Woman's College in Greensboro," I said. "I have an interview this afternoon to be a caseworker for the Department of Public Welfare."

"Oh, you don't want to do that!" he said, as if I'd said I was going to pick up garbage in the street. "Nice-looking blond girl like you? That's so dreary. If you have the itch to work, get a job at Belk's where you can dress up and sell jewelry or smart little hats."

"I want to do something that helps people, the way Robert does."

"You could have gone into nursing, then."

"I could have, if I could stand the sight of blood." I smiled as sweetly as I could to keep my annoyance from showing.

"Well," he said, slapping his hands on his knees as he stood up. "I haven't prescribed the birth control pill yet and I won't be starting today without getting approval from the man of the house." He pulled a cigarette from the Phillip Morris pack on the ledge above the sink and I watched as he lit it with a bronze lighter and inhaled deeply. "Once you're married," he said, "have your husband call me with his permission and I'll write you a prescription."

I was twenty-two years old and having to ask Robert's permission was humiliating. Also futile. He would say no. He thought the pill hadn't been studied enough and the side effects were too dangerous. Plus, he wanted to start a family right away. I wanted a family, too. Three children sounded perfect to me, but not yet.

Dr. Carson blew a stream of smoke into the air and studied me where I sat waiting, still wrapped in the skimpy gown. "Seems like I don't see many virgins anymore," he said. "Congratulations on that. You're a smart girl."

"Thank you," I said, although I didn't like him passing judgment on me. Besides, it was a miracle I was still a virgin. Robert and I couldn't keep our hands off each other. We'd come really close to crossing the line, but we decided to wait. If it had been up to me alone, I'm not sure I could have held out.

He pulled the door open an inch or two. "Children are the greatest blessing," he said over his shoulder. And then he was gone.

Once alone in the room, I slipped out of the gown and began to dress, surprised by the sting of tears in my eyes. I hadn't gotten what I'd wanted from this visit: foolproof birth control. Instead I'd been patronized and belittled. I wished I'd had the guts to respond differently to him, but that might have gotten back to Robert. I was already wondering if Dr. Carson might call Robert to tell him about my request. I didn't want to think about any deep meaning behind the fact that I couldn't be honest with Robert about wanting to take the pill. Everything else between us was good, and thinking about him eased my heart as I sat down on the stool to attach my stockings to my garter belt. Robert and I were a wonderful team together and the one thing I was absolutely sure of was his love. Love made any problem solvable.

I was still thinking about that miserable appointment as I drove to my interview. My car had belonged to my father and I thought it still smelled faintly of his pipe tobacco, although Robert said he couldn't smell anything. It reassured me, that smell, and I tried to put Dr. Carson out of my mind. The last thing I needed was to go into a job interview upset and angry. Still, my inability to get the pill now hung over my head. Gloria's doctor had prescribed it for her months ago, even before it had been approved for birth control. Even before she was *married,* for pity's sake. I'd make an appointment with her doctor and hope I could get it in time for our honeymoon.

"Everything will work out," I said out loud to myself as I stopped at a red light. That's what Gloria said whenever I shared my doubts about fitting into Robert's social sphere. Although he and I both came from middle-class families, his fortune changed dramatically when he got that M.D. after his name. His father was an electrician and no one else in his family had graduated from college, much less medical school. He'd worked hard for years to get where he was and it meant something to him to be a part of the country club set and to play golf with some of Raleigh's most prominent citizens. I didn't care about the trappings of wealth and status, but he did. He was proud of his accomplishments and I was proud of him, and other than having babies right away, I would do all I could to make him happy.

I'd only known him for a year. He'd asked me to marry him when we'd been together six months, though it felt like forever. "Six months is only six months, no matter how long it feels," my mother had warned me when I told her we were engaged. She did like Robert, though. She particularly liked the fact that he was a doctor and I would want for nothing. As a widow, she worried about that.

We'd met at the wedding of a girl I went to college with, and we happened to be seated at the same table. It had only been a year since the accident that cost my father and sister their lives, and I was still weighed down by grief. Sitting next to Robert, though, I felt suddenly awake, as though I'd been sleepwalking through the past year. Lord, he was a handsome man! He reminded me of Rock Hudson, cleft chin and all. He said I reminded him of Grace Kelly, which was ridiculous but flattered me anyway. All my life, I'd been called plain. Teresa had been the pretty one. Suddenly, I felt beautiful. It was one of those attractions that made everyone else at the wedding disappear.

He was thirty to my twenty-one, but the age difference didn't matter. When I found out he was a doctor . . . Well, I could be just as shallow as the next girl. I was doubly attracted to him.

We crammed a lifetime of getting to know each other into that one night. He liked that I was not your typical girl. I didn't make a fuss when the woman sitting next to me accidentally dropped butter on my dress, ruining it with a greasy stain. I didn't blush when a man at the table told an off-color joke. We talked about music we liked and movies we'd seen. I'd just seen *Peyton Place* and his eyes widened at that. That movie *had* shocked me, but I didn't let on. When the band started playing, we danced and danced and danced. My feet ached in my high heels and I tossed them under our table and kept on going. I felt giddy with joy. I'd nearly forgotten how it felt to be happy.

When we parted that evening, he kissed me in a way that turned my knees to jelly. Then he asked for my number. "You're so refreshing," he told me. "So different. You're not always running to the ladies' room to powder your nose or check your hair. I love how you took off your shoes to dance. I really like you."

His extended family was huge and important to him, so I agreed to have the wedding in Atlanta, where he was from, instead of Raleigh. He'd been raised Methodist, so once we were married, we'd attend the Edenton Methodist Church instead of my beloved Pullen Baptist, where my father had been a deacon. When Robert's parents came to visit him in Raleigh, I proudly took them to my church, not realizing that a visiting colored pastor would be preaching that day. That was nothing new at Pullen, but it was far too radical for my future in-laws, who walked out during the service. To Robert's credit, he stayed with me for the service and apologized for their rudeness, but I knew he'd never set foot in Pullen again.

Leaving my church would be only one change among many. I was bidding good-bye to life as I'd known it and saying hello to the country club, where I couldn't quite get my bearings, and the Junior League, which I still hadn't applied to join. I would have Robert and that would be good enough. He'd brought me back to life when I hadn't even realized I was dead.

I found a parking place in front of the Department of Public Welfare. My dress stuck to the back of my legs as I got out of the car. I was sure my hair was a mess after the drive with the windows open, and I tried to comb it into place with my fingers as I walked into the building. My appearance wasn't going to make the best first impression and I suddenly felt nervous. I really wanted this job.

There was a fan in the office where I waited to be interviewed and I sat as close to it as I could without turning my hair into a rat's nest. The air it blew on me must have been ninety degrees, but it was better than nothing.

A woman stepped out of her office and walked toward me, smiling. "Miss Mackie?" she asked. She was very slender and wore a short-sleeved blouse tucked into beige slacks. A Katharine Hepburn sort of look.

"Yes." I got to my feet and shook her hand.

"I'm Charlotte Werkman," she said. "Come with me."

I followed her into the small office, its one window wide open, an oscillating fan in front of it fluttering the papers on her desk. "Shut the door behind you, please, and have a seat," she said.

I sat down across the desk from her, smoothing my dress over my knees. I took in everything in the tiny office: the wall calendar with its picture of the governor's mansion, photographs of children at various ages, a family picture of a young man and woman and two small children. A vase full of mixed flowers, the petals beginning to go brown at the edges but still adding a pop of color to the room. Someday, I thought, I might have an office like this.

"So." She settled behind her desk and smiled at me and I liked her instantly. Such warmth and confidence in that smile! She looked nothing like I'd imagined a social worker to look. She was striking. She had to be in her forties—maybe even her fifties—but, except for a starburst of faint lines at the outer corners of her eyes, her skin looked as if it belonged in an Ivory soap commercial. Her gray eyes were huge and her hair, which was a pale, pale blond—nearly white—was clipped into a short ponytail at the nape of her neck. But it was the smile that most impressed me, and I felt all the muscles in my body loosen as I relaxed into the chair. I wanted to be like her, someone who could put people at ease with a smile.

"This would be your first job?" she asked, and I saw she had my thin résumé on the blotter in front of her.

"Well, my first . . . professional job," I said, motioning toward the résumé, which covered my 4.0 grade point average from Woman's College. It also showed the summer jobs I'd had working at a day camp for kids and the Red Cross volunteer work I did with my father and Teresa one week each year for most of my life. I had reference letters from two of my professors, attesting to my work ethic. It was the best I could pull together. I hoped it was good enough.

"Your degree is in sociology," she said. "Did you consider a degree in social work?"

"It wasn't offered at Woman's College," I said. "I had a couple of psychology courses, though, and those in addition to my sociology courses give me a good background, I think."

She gave a slight nod. "Better than many applicants," she said. "I was intrigued with what one of your professors—Dr. Adams—said about you." She lifted one of the letters and began to read. " 'Miss Mackie's passion for her work is matched only by her desire for perfection.' " She looked at me. "What does he mean by that sentence, do you think?"

I'd read that sentence in Dr. Adams's letter many times, knowing he meant it not quite as the compliment it seemed. He thought I got carried away with my work sometimes. He said I was the only student he'd ever taught who wanted to redo a paper he'd graded an A because I thought I could make it even better.

"It's important to me that I always do my best," I said now to Mrs. Werkman.

"That can take a toll on a person, don't you think?"

"That's exactly what Dr. Adams said, but here I am." I smiled broadly.

She returned the smile. "Well, you don't look too much the worse for wear," she said. "You look sweet and perky and attractive and much younger than twenty-two. I wonder how ready you are to get your hands dirty."

"Very ready," I said. I hoped I was telling the truth.

"I want to be sure you have no illusions that this is a glamorous job," she said.

"I'm not looking for glamour," I said. "My father always said, 'True happiness comes from helping others.' I believe that, too."

She smiled again. "Tell me your strengths, then." She sat back in her chair, ready to listen.

"I'm a quick learner," I said. "I love people. I couldn't imagine ever having a job where I didn't interact with people. I'm smart." I motioned toward my résumé and its GPA again. "I communicate well. I have good writing skills. I know I have to keep good records to do this work."

"You mentioned on the phone that you're getting married in a few weeks."

"Two weeks. Yes."

"What type of work does your husband-to-be do?"

"He's a pediatrician."

"Really! With a pediatrician husband, I'm sure you won't have to work."

Here we go again, I thought. "But I want to," I said.

"I'm widowed," she said, "so I really have no choice, though I do love it. How does your fiancé feel about you working?"

"I'm sorry you lost your husband," I said. How? I wondered. My gaze moved to the photographs on her bookshelf, landing on the one of a whole family that looked like it was taken when she was much younger. The man had such a warm smile. My eyes welled.

"Oh, my dear." Mrs. Werkman leaned forward, a small smile on her lips. She reached her hand halfway across her desk as if to console me. "You may be too soft for this work."

"It's just that . . ." I smiled with embarrassment. So much for my tough exterior. "My father died a couple of years ago," I said. I wouldn't mention Teresa. Not when I was trying desperately to keep my wits about me.

"Ah," she said. "I'm sorry to hear that." She followed my gaze to the photograph. "That's not my family," she said with a laugh. "This actually isn't even my office. It's just the one I'm using for interviews. And I lost my husband a long time ago. It was terrible at first, of course, but I've adjusted. And this interview is about *you*, not me. That's something you'll have to learn very quickly, Miss Mackie."

I was confused. "What is?"

"That your work with your clients is about them, not you. You might relate to something they're going through, but you'll have to learn to put those feelings aside. Never talk about your own life. Focus on your clients and their needs or you won't be able to help them."

"I understand," I said.

"Back to my question, then. Does your fiancé support the idea of you working?"

"I know how good he feels that he can help people as a doctor and I know he'd like me to have that feeling, too." It was the best I could offer—an evasive answer.

"How about children?"

"No plans for them right now."

"You'll be in the field ninety percent of your time," she said.

I nodded. I liked the sound of that: "in the field." It made the job sound adventurous and important.

"Half your caseload will be colored." She studied me with those huge pale gray eyes to see how I'd react to that.

"That's fine," I said. I thought of the poor colored neighborhoods in Raleigh. If I was being honest with myself, there were areas I was afraid to walk in. I was going to have to develop a stronger backbone—and maybe keep it from Robert for a bit. He would never allow me in those neighborhoods.

"How do you feel about what happened in Greensboro?"

I was confused for a moment, thinking of WC, which is what we called my Greensboro college. Then I thought I understood. "Oh. Do you mean the protests at the Woolworth's lunch counter?"

She nodded. "What did you think of that?"

I hedged. I certainly knew what I thought, but I didn't know if it was the "right" answer or if it could cost me the job. Still, I couldn't lie about my feelings.

"I think they were very brave," I said of the Negro students who dared to sit at the lunch counter reserved for whites. I thought of the "colored" and "white" drinking fountains I'd passed in the hallway on my way to Mrs. Werkman's office—or whoever's office we were in. "I think all people should be treated with the same respect and have the same rights."

She smiled. "An idealist," she said.

"If that's the definition of an idealist, then I guess I am one," I said.

"I'm afraid this job could turn you into more of a realist and that would be a shame," she said, "but I agree with you. With your ideals, though, it may be too soon for the minds of the South. You're going to see what centuries of inequality have done to your Negro clients, and your white clients won't be much better off. The challenge we have is relating to people who have very different backgrounds from our own, regardless of race. It's difficult because so many of them, you'll find, are of very low intellect."

"I'd like the challenge," I said, and I meant it.

"Keep your ideals in your mind and your heart," she said. "And remember that with all of your clients, there but for the grace of God . . .'"

"I have the job?" I asked.

"Yes, Miss Mackie, you do. Salary is $185 a month. Can you start two weeks from Monday?"

I was stuck on the hundred and eighty-five dollars. Better than I'd expected. Then the "two weeks from Monday" sank in and I gave an apologetic shake of my head. "My wedding is that Saturday."

"Ah yes." She turned to look at the calendar. "And then a honeymoon, I suppose?"

"Just for a week. I could start the Monday after."

"That will have to do, then," she said. "You'll actually be taking my place in the field. Our director's retiring and I'm moving into his position."

"Congratulations." I smiled.

"Thank you, I think." She laughed. "I'll miss the field, but I hope I'll be able to make some positive changes in the department. So"—she glanced at the calendar again—"we'll begin that Monday. You'll go on home visits with me and get to know some of your clients. We'll only be able to do that for a couple of weeks, though, because we're terribly short staffed, as you'll soon find out. Dress is professional but casual. I prefer slacks for fieldwork and made the department loosen the dress code a few years ago for that reason, so you may wear them if you like. You'll want to purchase a briefcase something like this." She lifted a briefcase from the floor. Worn brown leather with a sloping top and brass clasp, very much like the one my father used to carry. I loved the idea of having my own.

"Okay," I said.

Then she gave me a look of warning. "You'll have a large caseload to balance," she said. "I have sixty cases at the moment, but I won't dump them all on you at once."

"Where?" I asked. "What part of Raleigh?"

"Not Raleigh at all," she said. "Grace County. All rural families."

Grace County. "Oh," I said. I hadn't expected that.

"Is that a problem?"

"No, just a surprise. I've never really been to Grace County, except to pass through on the way to the beach." It was a lie, but I didn't want to talk about one more thing that might make me cry.

"It will mean a lot of driving. Are you comfortable with that?"

"I *love* driving," I said. Where in Grace County? I wondered.

"I can tell you're a passionate person, Miss Mackie, as your professor wrote in his letter," she said. "I like that. Will the commute be a problem for you? Your office will be in Grace County, of course. In Ridley. That's where mine is, but it was easier to interview candidates here."

"No problem," I said. "I have a car."

"Where do you live?"

"Right now, Cameron Park with my mother, but my fiancé—husband—and I will be living in Hayes Barton."

"My," she said, eyes wide. "How lovely." She got to her feet and I stood as well. She led me to her office door.

"You remind me of myself in the early days," she said, as she opened the door for me, "But I believe you're a bit more . . . fragile than I was and that concerns me. This can be soul-searing work."

"I can be very strong," I said, wondering what had given me away. My knees had gone soft at the mention of Grace County.

"We'll see," she said. "Have a lovely wedding."

I drove home feeling both happy and anxious. I wouldn't call Robert at his office to tell him I had the job. I'd wait until I saw him tonight, and then I'd mention it in passing, as though it were no big deal. I didn't want to invite his questions about it. But I *had* to tell someone, so I drove to the library and found my mother taking a break on one of the benches out front. She was reading a book and smoking a cigarette. I sat down next to her and she looked up in surprise.

"Guess who got a job!" I said.

"You got it?" She turned the book over on her lap. "The social work job?"

I nodded and reached for her cigarette to take a drag. I was an occasional smoker. Robert didn't like it, so I never smoked around him. He loved his cigars, though.

"Well, congratulations, honey," she said, even though I knew she had mixed feelings about me working.

"I'll have my own clients," I said, handing the cigarette back to her, "*and* I'll be making a hundred and eighty-five dollars a month!"

"Where exactly will you be working?"

I shrugged. "Not sure yet," I said. "Out in the country somewhere." I smoothed a wayward lock of her salt-and-pepper hair behind her ear. I'd keep Grace County to myself for a while. Mom hadn't really been herself since the accident. I so rarely saw her smile anymore. I didn't want to bring up anything that might upset her.

She stroked my arm with her free hand. "Daddy would be so proud of you, honey," she said. "I hope Robert is, too. I hope he knows what a treasure he has in you."

"*Mother.*" I laughed at the emotion in her voice. I would have been embarrassed if anyone had overheard her, but as it was I just felt loved. I kissed her cheek. "I've got to go shopping for some work clothes. See you at home tonight?"

"So many changes," she said, as if she hadn't heard me. "You're leaving home. Getting married. Working." She shook her head. "I'll miss you so much."

"I'll only be a couple of miles away," I reassured her. The sadness in her voice worried me.

"My baby's all grown up," she said with a sigh, and maybe it was only my imagination, but I thought she was thinking of her other baby. The one who would never have the chance to grow up. I would grow up well enough for both of us.

4

Ivy

From our bed, I could see the numbers on the windup clock on the dresser, thanks to the moon. I kept my eyes on it. Eleven o'clock. Eleven-fifteen. Eleven-thirty. I was waiting for eleven forty-five and was afraid I might drift off before it came, I was so tired. I'd had to fight with Nonnie to test her pee tonight. She was getting stubborner and stubborner about it and she wouldn't boil the test tube after every time she used it because she said rinsing it out was good enough. She was no good at peeing in them tubes, anyway. The first one she dropped down the hole of the johnny. The next one she broke on the kitchen floor. Then Nurse Ann brung us two so we'd have a spare and I told Nonnie to pee in a cup and then pour it in the test tube.

It made me crazy, watching her eat that banana pudding. I reckoned her pee would turn green in the test tube in the morning. I was starting to wonder who was the grown-up in this house and who was the child. Then she left them blue testing pills right out on the kitchen table where Baby William could of got them. Nurse Ann told us them pills would burn his insides out and I had to watch Nonnie like a hawk to be sure she put them on the high shelf by the sink after she done the testing.

Eleven thirty-five. Baby William made a giggling sound in his sleep like he was dreaming about something happy and I hoped he was. On the other side of him, Mary Ella breathed so softly I couldn't hear her.

If I didn't know she was there, I'd never guess there was three human beings in this bed.

Mary Ella wore me out tonight, too, saying she didn't feel good and maybe was going to die. She hugged Baby William real close and rocked him in the living room most of the evening while I folded the laundry. Nonnie always said Mary Ella's just like our mama, and though she never did explain exactly what she meant by that, I knew it wasn't a good thing. When Mary Ella said she didn't feel good, I worried she'd done it again—gone and got herself another baby. I didn't know how I'd handle one more person depending on me.

Eleven forty-five. Finally. I got out of bed real quiet and put my pillow sideways under the covers like I did every night I snuck out—not to pretend like I was there, but to keep Baby William from rolling off the bed in his sleep. He wasn't a peaceful sleeper. Mary Ella was the same way and sometimes she woke up when I got out of bed even though I made no more noise than a butterfly. Didn't matter if she woke up. She knew where I was going. Only Nonnie didn't know. All these years—practically my whole life—I snuck out, glad Nonnie slept like the dead. The house could be burning around her and she wouldn't wake up, which was good because I had to get past her where she slept on the lumpy old sofa in the living room. Tonight, I couldn't see her for the dark, but her snoring was so loud I felt it in the soles of my bare feet on the splintery wood floor.

I had my nightgown on and not another stitch. In cooler weather, I got dressed before I snuck out or else I just wore my clothes to bed, but tonight was so hot I couldn't stand the idea of putting on shorts and a shirt that would only stick to my body with sweat. Now, sneaking out of the house with my lantern and starting down the path to the crick, I loved the feel of the thin cloth against my body. The breeze rose under the hem and up my legs and I felt naked and couldn't wait to get to Henry Allen.

I didn't really need the lantern. The moon gave me plenty of light on the path I knew by heart. All around me smelled like honeysuckle, and I pulled off some of the vines to carry with me, like I always did when they was blooming. I'd been walking that path at night since me and Henry Allen was kids. Back then, we'd haint these woods and make up monsters and scare each other with ghost stories. Nowadays, what got us excited was something altogether different.

Henry Allen was already there on the mossy bank of the crick and I could hear his radio was playing Elvis Presley singing "It's Now or Never." He had the scratchy wool blanket stretched out and I dropped down next to him. Henry Allen looked like a young version of his daddy, with that same tall, slim build and the same dark hair. Mr. Gardiner had brown eyes, though, and wore glasses. Henry Allen's eyes was blue and perfect. His hair always flopped into his eyes, like it was doing right now. I liked pushing it off his forehead. I liked any excuse to touch him. I was so in love with that boy.

"I brung you some of Desiree's cherry pie." He shined his flashlight on the pie plate, covered with wax paper.

"Won't she miss it?"

"She'll just think I got to it. Thinks I'm a pig. I got enough for you and Mary Ella and Nonnie. Maybe Baby William, too, if you slice it skinny."

"You're the sweetest boy," I said. "Nonnie can't have none of it, though. I got to hide it. She already ate the banana pudding your daddy sent over."

"Oh yeah. I forgot about her sugar."

I noticed his hand was on some kind of big flat box-looking thing on the blanket. "What you got there?" I asked, holding the lantern closer.

"I brung a new California book," he said, and I saw it wasn't a box at all, but a giant book.

"You got to the bookmobile?" He visited the bookmobile every time it passed through, but it was hard to get away during the harvest.

"Sure did." He shined his flashlight on the cover.

"It's the biggest book I ever seen." I ran my fingers over the glossy cover. The picture was of some cliffs and the sea, all of it covered in fog. It was real mysterious and beautiful and made me want to be there so bad my chest hurt. Grace County was pretty with all the trees and the fields that turned different colors depending on the time of year, but it couldn't hold a candle to California.

"Come here," he said, flopping down on his belly. "Let me show you."

I laid on my belly next to him and he opened the book, shining his flashlight on the pictures. They was the most glorious pictures I ever seen. Henry Allen visited California when he was eight and he said he never forgot it and had to live there someday, as far from Grace County as he could get. He was suffocating here, he always said, and I knew how he felt. Sometimes when I got out of bed, it felt like there was no air in my lungs at all. Our dream was to get married someday and raise up our family in California. I wasn't sure exactly when we started the dream. Seemed like one minute we was making bows and arrows in the woods and the next we was talking about getting married. It was my favorite thing to think about, living with Henry Allen and being his wife in beautiful California, where we could take our kids to Disneyland every single year. That dream got me through some mighty grim days. Nurse Ann said I should never have no babies because of the fits I used to get, though I didn't think I had them no more. I stopped taking the fit medicine long ago and I was just fine, so I wasn't worried.

"This here's the Golden Gate Bridge." Henry Allen shined the light on a gigantic orangey-colored bridge sitting in a cloud of fog.

"California's got a lot of fog." I handed him one of the honeysuckle flowers.

"Well, in this here place, San Francisco, yes they do." He pulled out the middle of the flower and sucked the honey from it. "Makes it pretty, don't ya think?"

"You been on that bridge?"

"No, but I will someday. You, too." He gave me a nudge with his shoulder and I smiled.

That "Itsy Bitsy Teeny Weeny Yellow Polka Dot Bikini" song came on the radio and we both started laughing. That song always made us laugh. "In California, you can wear one of them bikinis on the beach," he said.

"How are we ever gonna get there without a car?" I asked. Henry Allen drove one of Mr. Gardiner's trucks sometimes, but we couldn't take that.

"If we can dream up living in California, we can dream up having a car," Henry Allen said. He turned the page and it was some kind of fair, with a Ferris wheel and people walking around and eating hot dogs. Way in the distance, I could see the ocean.

"This here picture reminds me of that time your daddy took me and you and Mary Ella to the state fair. Remember that?"

"How could I forget?" I said. "I got sick on that swing ride."

"It was a good time till then," he said. "Your daddy was full of good times. Remember when he took us and the Jordans on that hay ride?"

"Mm," I said. Thinking about my daddy could make me sad.

"He did that just for fun. No other reason. I want to be a father like him. Not like my own father. Mine ain't no fun at all. Everything's about work with him."

I liked Mr. Gardiner and didn't want Henry Allen to be so mean about him. "Maybe my daddy seemed so fun because we was little when he was around, so he didn't make us do any work."

"Maybe," Henry Allen agreed. "But I swear, I got more memories of him from when I was little than my own daddy."

That was real sweet, I thought. I leaned my cheek against his shoulder. "He would of liked us ending up together," I said. I'd noticed he didn't mention my mother. No one wanted a mama like mine. I tapped the book.

"What's on the next page?" I asked.

We went through all the pages. There was trees as big around as the tobacco barns and foggy cliffs called Big Sur and rocks in the ocean covered with seals and big black birds. There was actual palm trees. How could one place have so many different beautiful parts to it? I felt that ache in my chest again as he turned the pages. I wanted to step inside the book and live that beautiful life. Henry Allen said everybody in California was rich and had swimming pools in their own yards. I wished California was right next door to Grace County and I could walk over there tomorrow.

"Which place you want to live?" Henry Allen asked.

"Any of 'em."

"No, get serious. Let's pick our top place from these here pictures."

"Someplace by the water."

He turned the pages and I stopped him. "There," I said, pointing to a pretty little tree standing all alone, way out on a cliff above the ocean. "This place."

"Monterey," he said. "Okay, then. That's our destination. Monterey, California."

"What about you, though? Which place do you want to live at?"

"Wherever you are," he said.

My throat got tight. "What if I'm here, Henry Allen? What if I can't never leave?" Me and Henry Allen used to say we'd run off after we finished school, which meant three more years for me and two for him, but I couldn't see how I'd ever be able to leave Mary Ella or Nonnie or Baby William. Everything would fall to pieces without me. I felt sad all of a sudden. All me and Henry Allen had was the dream. So we didn't talk about the *when* no more. Just the *where*.

"We're still goin'." He put his arm around me and squeezed me to him. "We'll work it out one of these days."

"They got tobacco farms in California?" I asked, letting myself back into the dream. "We have to get jobs."

"No more farming," he said. "We'll get better jobs."

"Doing what?"

"I don't know, but ones where you don't gotta ruin your hands and I don't gotta break my back."

"I still want to be a teacher," I said.

"Have to go to college for that," he said.

I groaned. Three more years of high school was bad enough, but I wasn't going to worry about that right yet.

Henry Allen rolled onto his back and pulled me on top of him, then suddenly froze up. "You ain't got nothin' on, girl!" he said.

"Do, too." I laughed. "I got my nightgown on."

"What's under it?"

"Just me."

"How am I supposed to control myself with you all naked like this?"

I laughed again. "Seems to me you stopped controlling yourself with me a long time ago," I said.

He slid his warm palms under my nightgown and up the outside of my legs and I bent over to kiss him, long and soft the way he liked it. The first time me and Henry Allen done it, I was scared in a hundred different ways. Scared of changing our friendship in a way we couldn't fix. And I was scared of ending up like Mary Ella. But doing it only made us closer and he promised me I'd never end up like Mary Ella. He always pulled out of me in the nick of time, even though it was real hard for him. He took care of me.

All day long, I worried about other people. Was Nonnie going to have to start getting shots for her sugar? Was Baby William ever going to say more words than "mama" or would he be one of them dumb boys other kids picked on? Would Mary Ella get herself in trouble again? Worry worry worry. But when I was with Henry Allen like I was right now, him slipping my nightgown over my head and pressing his body into mine, so gentle and sweet, I could forget about everything except him and me and our dreams about the future.

5

Jane

"We're waiting for one other couple," the young blond captain of our catamaran told us as he adjusted the sails. We'd been in Hawaii five days by then and I'd never been so tan or so happy. Or so in love. I sat on the catamaran's long bench seat with Robert, holding his hand as we waited. We hadn't stopped touching each other since our wedding. We'd already had a full day of swimming, snorkeling, and learning—or trying to learn—how to surf on those long heavy surfboards, and now we were looking forward to a romantic sunset cruise. At the moment, though, the catamaran rested half in the water, half on the pristine beach.

I pressed my lips to Robert's warm shoulder, breathing in the scent of suntan lotion and sweat. I couldn't get enough of him this week, and if it had been up to me, I would have skipped the boat ride altogether for a few extra hours alone in our room. We had our own little bungalow close to the beach, and it was so romantic to make love to the sound of the waves lapping the shore, the ceiling fan cooling the air above us.

Last night, he said I almost seemed to enjoy lovemaking *too* much. "I'm not complaining," he'd added quickly with a smile. "It's just unusual."

"How do you know what's usual for most girls?" I'd asked him. "You and your friends don't talk about it, do you?"

"No," he said. "Lord, no. You surprised me, that's all."

It also seemed to surprise him that I didn't bleed after we made love. I didn't understand that, either. Didn't every girl bleed the first time? I worried he'd think he wasn't my first. He most definitely was.

"This must be them," Robert said, as another couple trotted across the beach toward the catamaran.

"Hello, hello!" the man said as he and the woman scurried aboard. Even in those two words, I could hear the Yankee accent.

"Hope we didn't hold you up!" the woman said.

"Not at all." Robert rose to his feet and shook the man's hand. "Come have a seat." He motioned to the long bench seat, just big enough for the four of us. They sat down, the woman next to me. Our captain hopped off the boat onto the beach, slid us easily into the water, then hopped on again and soon we were cutting across the water into a fiery orange sunset.

The man and woman—Bruce and Carol—were from New York City and they were in Honolulu to celebrate their tenth wedding anniversary. They were garrulous and energetic and within the first three minutes of the cruise, we learned that Bruce was a stockbroker and Carol was president of the PTA. They were big fans of John Kennedy, and we talked about our hopes that he might beat Nixon in the November election. Well, *I* talked about *my* hope. Robert stayed out of that conversation, and I could tell he'd had enough of it when he abruptly said, "What have y'all done so far on the island?" The question was so out-of-the-blue that Bruce and Carol looked momentarily lost.

I picked up Robert's cue. "We learned to surf this morning," I said. I knew he didn't like conversations about politics.

"Oh, isn't that fun?" Carol said. "We did that yesterday. I was terrible at it, but Bruce was a natural."

"Wish we had those boards at Jones Beach," Bruce said. The hard edges of his accent grated on me.

"Tell them what we did this morning." Carol nudged him with her elbow.

"Skin diving!" Bruce said. "I think it was the most thrilling thing I've ever done."

"We snorkeled," I said. I'd loved how one minute you were in the regular old world, but as soon as you lowered your head, you were transported to an extraordinary new universe.

"Well, this is like that, only a hundred times better," Carol said. "You feel like you're a fish yourself."

"Isn't it a bit claustrophobic?" Robert asked.

"You get over that pretty quickly," Bruce said. "We took a lesson in a pool first. You want the name of the fella who taught us?"

"*Yes*," I said. "I'd love to try it."

Next to me, I sensed that Robert was less than enthusiastic, but Bruce pulled a notebook from his shirt pocket and wrote down the name of the instructor. He handed the sheet of paper to Robert. "You didn't mention what kind of business you're in," he said.

"I'm a physician," Robert said, and I saw their eyes pop open. I knew how Northerners thought. They didn't expect a Southern boy to have the brains to become a doctor.

"A pediatrician," I added. I wanted to say more. I wanted to tell them about the time I watched him stitch together a gash on a little girl's leg while telling her "knock-knock" jokes to keep her mind off what was happening. I wanted to talk about his compassion, how he spent one Saturday each month working for free at a clinic for poor people. But he wouldn't want me bragging about him that way.

"Well, my, my," Carol said.

Bruce leaned forward, elbows on his knees, so he could speak directly to Robert. "Our son has a cut on the side of his ankle that won't heal," he said. "Our pediatrician's tried a few things, but nothing seems to make a difference."

We spent the rest of our sunset cruise with Robert offering free medical advice, his handsome face tan and sincere, while Bruce and Carol hung on his every word. I nearly burst with pride that I could now call him my husband.

After the cruise, Robert and I had dinner on the poolside patio near our bungalow. We sat close together on one side of the table sharing an enormous pupu platter.

"I'd really like to try it," I said. "Skin diving." I nibbled a shrimp from the bamboo skewer in my hand.

Robert shuddered. "Seriously?"

"It'd be so beautiful."

"Not worth the risk of drowning or rupturing a lung."

I laughed and held a sliver of pineapple to his lips. "You're being overly dramatic," I said, as he took the pineapple from me and chewed it slowly.

He leaned over to kiss me, then wound a lock of my hair around his finger. "Every once in a while, I worry I'm too old for you," he said.

"Oh, that's silly." The nine years between us didn't bother me at all. I didn't see why it should bother him.

He let my hair spring free and smiled at me. "If you really want to skin-dive, we can skin-dive, sweetheart," he said. "I don't ever want to hold you back from something you really want to do."

"Like my job," I said, and instantly regretted it. I would start work the Monday after our return from Hawaii, and Robert wasn't happy about it.

He raised his hand to stop anything else I might say. "We've settled it about your job," he said. "You can try it for a while. I told you that, so you don't need to bring it up over and over again."

"I'll make our meals on Sundays and we can heat them up in the oven each night." We'd have a maid, of course, but cooking wasn't supposed to be one of her tasks. "I'll be sure to get home in time to do that." All his Raleigh friends had wives waiting for them at home in the evening, showered and coiffed, with dinner on the table.

"It doesn't have anything to do with the meals." He picked up something small and fried from his plate and studied it as if trying to figure out what it was. "*You* know what bothers me," he said. "If you really want to work, I'd rather you found something . . . I don't know. This is just the wrong job for my wife." He set down the food, whatever it was. "It would be one thing if you were a teacher or a librarian like your mother. You'd still be helping people, if that's what matters to you."

I swallowed another bite of shrimp. "I've always wanted to do *this*," I said.

"You won't have to work with any colored people, will you?" he asked. "They have colored social workers for that, right?"

We had one lie between us already: the pills, buried deep beneath my lingerie in the bungalow's bedroom dresser. I'd gotten them from Gloria's doctor, who promised me I'd be protected from pregnancy by my wedding night.

"I'll have some Negro clients, yes," I said.

"That's just . . . not right."

"Oh why not, for heaven's sake? They need help, too."

"They should have their own social worker."

"I don't have a problem with it."

"That left-wing church you grew up in put ideas in your head," he said. "I'm glad our kids won't be growing up there."

I bit my tongue, not wanting to argue, and we ate in silence for a while. Finally, Robert took a sip of his wine and let out a sigh. "What am I supposed to tell my friends?" he asked, setting his glass down.

"About me working?" I asked, confused.

"None of their wives work. They'll think I'm not making enough money."

"Tell them I'm obstinate and you love me so you're letting me do this." I tried to sound lighthearted and leaned over to kiss his cheek.

"I'll tell them you're involved in charitable work. That's really what it is, except you'll get paid." He laughed. "Not that a hundred and eighty-five dollars a month should really count as a salary."

That stung. "It's a lot to me," I said.

He caught my hand on the table. "Sorry," he said. "Really. I didn't mean that the way it sounded. It's just that you worry me sometimes."

"I'm sure they won't send me anyplace dangerous."

"I'm not talking about the job." He lowered my hand to his lap and held it there in both of his. "Look, darling," he said. "I love you just the way you are, you know that, right? Stubborn and full of spunk. Right?"

"I'm not stubborn."

He laughed. "Yes you are. You just admitted you're obstinate. That's all right. I love you, but you're my wife now and you need to temper it outside the four walls of our house."

"What do you mean?"

"I want people to like you, Jane. That's all. It's important for my career that we fit in."

"What do you want me to do?" I asked.

"I want you to be yourself, but just . . . tame it down a little. Don't talk politics like you did on the catamaran today. Definitely don't talk about supporting Kennedy, for heaven's sake. Especially not at the club."

"But I do."

"Oh come on, Jane. Don't be ridiculous."

"Well, I do. He cares about the little people."

"At whose expense?" he snapped, letting go of my hand and sitting back in the chair. "This is what I mean about you being stubborn. You say things like this just to shake me up."

"I honestly think he's the better choice."

He sighed. "What am I going to do with you?"

"I won't talk about it in front of your friends, if it bothers you that much." I already felt shy around his fellow physicians who looked at me as if I were a kid. We usually saw them at the country club, where no matter how many years passed with me as Robert's wife, I'd never feel as though I belonged and I was certain everyone knew it. The wives had been welcoming at first, but when they realized I was not like them— not their age or their social class—they lost interest in me. Robert said it was me. I didn't try to fit in, and maybe he was right. Now, with him telling me not to talk about my work—or politics—when I was with his friends, it was going to be even worse. "And if they ever ask me what I think about the election," I said, "I'll play coy. But at least I'd like to be able to be honest with *you*." I looked away from him. The birth control pills taunted me. Who was I to talk about honesty? Robert thought we might start a baby on our honeymoon, and I didn't say a word.

"Politics and religion," Robert said as if I hadn't spoken. "The two things we don't talk about in public."

"I told you. I'll be careful around your friends," I said, then added quietly, "But Robert . . . you knew who I was before you said 'I do.' "

"You're right." He pulled me toward him and kissed the tip of my nose, and I wondered if I'd really known who *he* was.

6

Ivy

It was Lita Jordan who started the singing, as usual, and she started early, right as me and her began looping the first load of tobacco, tying the leaves to the long sticks that would hang in the barn to cure. *"It's been a long, long time comin', but change is gonna come,"* she sang. Her voice was clear as birdsong, ringing out in the steamy early morning sun. It echoed off the tin roof of the shelter we worked under. It spread out over the field in front of us, where her two oldest boys, Eli and Devil, worked with Henry Allen and the day laborers, and it traveled behind us down Deaf Mule Road. It made my heart ache, though I couldn't of said why. It was a voice made for singing in church. When I was little and we'd walk past the AME church and I'd hear a lady singing, I'd say, "That's Lita," and Nonnie would say, "Every colored lady you hear ain't Lita," but I was sure it was her.

She could sing light songs, too, the ones that made us laugh. She could get us going with "There's a Hole in the Bucket" and the one about the old woman who swallowed a fly, but it was like she knew that this song was one to start the day. The other colored girls, the ones Mr. Gardiner brung in each day to help with the barning, they came in with the harmony and I did my bit, too. We all knew the words. It made me laugh watching Nonnie sing a few lines and then catch herself. She probably thought the song was some of that race music she hated, but sometimes you just had to give in to the feeling and sing along.

Nonnie couldn't stand on her feet for long these days, so she worked a while at the bench, then went home to rest for a bit, off and on through the day. Baby William was nothing but trouble and he ran around our feet with Lita's youngest, three-year-old Rodney, both of them getting in the way. Rodney was a good boy, but he loved Baby William like some kids love candy and together they was up to no good. We had to watch them every second.

I was already sweating in my oilcloth apron, but I didn't dare take it off till the dew was dry on the tobacco or I'd get soaked and break out in a green tobacco rash, like I did last summer. We all wore aprons, especially in the morning. Only Lita's boy Avery, who emptied the sled at the barn and carried the full sticks to the racks, refused to wear something. He was fifteen, like me, but he looked older. All three of the oldest Jordan boys looked like men already. Avery was plenty big and strong enough to work in the field with his brothers, but his eyes was so bad, that even with them thick glasses he wore, he wouldn't know which leaves was ready for priming and which needed a few more days in the sun. He hated working at the bench, except for being near Mary Ella, who was one of the handers. Sometimes he'd even help her, standing next to her as they pulled three or four leaves at a time from the bench and handed them over to me or Lita. I thought he liked how quiet Mary Ella was—how she didn't sing with the others or gossip. It was like she was peaceful and he needed some of that peace, since he was always getting picked on by his brothers and the kids at the colored school. Sometimes I'd turn and see him and Mary Ella talking quiet to each other, and I'd remind myself that my sister, for all her strangeness, could be a real nice girl. Anyway, Mary Ella's mind wasn't on the song. It was out there in the field, I was sure of it. All us gals, we was watching the field. Watching our men—Henry Allen, Eli, Devil, and the day laborers—as they walked through the rows of tall tobacco, disappearing as they bent over to snap the leaves from the stalks and pile them in the sled.

Some days the gossip came even before the singing. Other times, we'd complain about the heat or maybe worry out loud about how the machines was taking over on some of the farms. It was mostly Lita worried about that, since her boys worked the field and machines could work it much quicker. No way a machine could do what we girls was doing, though, looping the tobacco to the long sticks.

The colored day laborers liked working for Mr. Gardiner. He paid them the same as white folks and he sometimes brung all of us Desiree's pimiento cheese sandwiches for a snack in the middle of every morning. At dinnertime, we'd go home, scrub off the tar, and eat like there was no tomorrow. The Jordans went home, too. They lived in a house just like ours, but clear at the other end of the tobacco field. Their house was right out in the open. This time of year, I thought we was the lucky ones, with all the shade around us. In the winter, though, that sun warmed their place right up while we near froze to death. I liked being in their house because of the cooking smells. Didn't matter if I just ate dinner myself, I walked in that house and my mouth started watering. You could tell there was a mama living there. You could tell someone was taking care of everybody. My house never smelled like the Jordans', even if we was cooking something good.

The rest of the colored help ate dinner at tables outside the Gardiners' house. Every once in a while, Mr. Gardiner'd ask me and Nonnie and Mary Ella to eat inside with him and Henry Allen. Me and Henry Allen always acted like we hardly knew each other when we ate together. We was careful not to look straight at each other's eyes, afraid we'd start laughing. It was the same when I hitched a ride to church with them on Sunday morning. Nonnie and Mary Ella was too shamed to go to church ever since Baby William came along, but the Gardiners took me with them, and me and Henry Allen sat in the backseat of their old Ford as far apart as we could get, acting like we didn't know each other's name. I liked that nobody knew I understood that boy inside and out. Mr. Gardiner wouldn't take kindly to that news. I was a tenant on his land. Nothing more than that.

"Pay attention to your work, now," Lita said to me, quiet so Nonnie wouldn't hear and start yelling at me. I'd slowed down on my looping because I was too busy watching Mary Ella, making sure her eyes didn't light on any particular boy—or man—out in the field and give her ideas.

Then Lita started singing "Go Tell It on the Mountain," and we joined in. Nonnie liked this one and she sung it out as loud as she could, though she didn't have much of a singing voice left. I could remember when I was little, I loved listening to her. She'd sing her hymns around the house. That was before everything went wrong and she was happy and didn't have the sugar and the rheumatism and Mama and Daddy was still with us and harvesttime was me and Mary Ella running around with Henry Allen and the Jordan kids, throwing the hornworms at each other and feeling important as we made our few pennies picking up any leaves that had dropped. All of us was playmates and workmates. White and colored, didn't make no difference. But one day when I was about ten, we was at the Gardiners' store when Eli brung in a package for Mrs. Gardiner. I asked him, "You want to fish in the crick later?" in front of other shoppers and Nonnie grabbed my arm and pinched it so hard I had a bruise for a month.

"Don't you talk to that boy," she snapped in my ear, like me and Mary Ella didn't talk to him every single day. Eli understood. Didn't even look at us. Pretended he didn't hear nothin'. He'd already learned what we was only learning: colored and white didn't mix in public. Especially not colored boys and white girls. We got the message that day. We could be friends at home, but out in the world, we didn't know each other.

I watched Lita while she worked. She looked out at the field the same way we all did, and I wondered if one of the men out there was someone she knew well. *Real* well. Maybe Rodney's daddy? People said every one of her children had a different daddy. "They can't help themselves," Nonnie told us. "They're still like animals in the jungle." But Lita didn't make me think of no animal. I was jealous of all them boys having a mama they could count on.

After dinner it was so hot that Baby William was as cranky as the mules. He sat crying in the dirt or he wobbled around, hitting us on our arms to get us to pay him some attention. By then, every one of us was pretty wrung out and thirsty, and I couldn't wait for Mr. Gardiner to bring out the drinks. Baby William headed for the water bucket next to the barn. He reached for the green gourd ladle leaning up against it and Nonnie ran after him quicker than I thought she could move and swatted his hand. "That's the colored gourd!" she said, handing him the yellow gourd we used. He started hollering and no one could hear themselves sing, so we all went quiet for a while and Nonnie said, "That's enough. I'm taking him home," and she set off down the dusty road with him yanking on her arm and kicking his feet at the air.

After a while, Mr. Gardiner came around the side of the barn and up to me. "I ain't got enough Nabs for everybody," he said. "You go on over to the store and get a box full."

He hardly ever asked one of us to go to the store for him because he couldn't spare us, so I was surprised. I thought he was staring at me right hard, and I looked down at my hands, pretending to peel the tar off them. When he looked at me like that, I was afraid he knew about me and Henry Allen.

"Why're you going red in the face, girl?" he asked me now. "You ain't gonna have no heatstroke on me, are you?"

"No, sir," I said, "I'm fine. I'll be back right quick."

The bike was tossed in the dirt a ways from the barn and I climbed on and took off for the store. I wasn't sure what Mr. Gardiner'd do if he knew about me and his one and only son. Henry Allen said his parents told him, "No girlfriends till you're done with school," but what boy pays attention to that kind of thing?

I rode the bike down Deaf Mule Road to where the store stood on the corner of Deaf Mule and Gardiner Store Lane. The store wasn't much, just an old wooden place with GARDINER'S CORNER STORE painted on a board, the "Gar" near worn off the wood. Inside, the fan was going strong in the window and there was a colored woman and a white boy in there, most likely doing the same thing I was: getting afternoon snacks for the farmworkers. From behind the counter, Mrs. Gardiner waved to me. "Hey there, Ivy," she said. "Ain't you working at the barn?"

"Mr. Gardiner asked me to get some Nabs," I said.

"He probably wants a whole box, don't he?"

"Yes, ma'am. That's what he said."

"I'll get that for you. You pick yourself out a drink. Too hot to ride out here today."

"Yes, ma'am," I said, heading for the icebox. I opened it up and took out a bottle of Pepsi Cola. I wished I could of stood in front of that icebox the rest of the day, the cool air felt so good, but I closed it quick. Didn't want to get yelled at for leaving it open too long, although there was nobody around who'd yell at me. Not the boy, who I knew from seeing him at school. Not the colored woman, who wouldn't yell at no white child. And Mrs. Gardiner wasn't no yeller. "She's a saint, that one," Nonnie always said to me and Mary Ella. "A real fine Christian lady. We can all learn a lot from her, girls."

I carried the Pepsi Cola to the counter and she had a box of Nabs all ready to go. My mouth watered looking at them cheese crackers. Seemed like dinner was forever ago.

"Things going good at the barning today, Ivy?" Mrs. Gardiner asked as she put the box in a paper sack. She was so pretty. Real white skin you didn't hardly ever see around a farm. Shiny, soft dark hair in a bun at the back of her head. Blue eyes, like Henry Allen's. The only thing that kept her from being beautiful was a mean-looking scar that ran from her temple to her chin. It was a thing that was hard to look at, but you could sometimes forget about it when she smiled.

"Yes, ma'am," I said. "A little short in the field today, but it's going okay."

"That's good to hear." She handed me the bag, then leaned toward me. "Sometime you need to cool off, you just come over here and put your head in that icebox." She smiled at me, and I smiled back.

"I will. Thank you."

I walked out to my bike and fit the bag into the basket. I finished my drink, then climbed on the bike and started pedaling back to the farm, thinking about what she said and how sweet she was. You'd think she would of treated me and Mary Ella mean, but she never did, even though she sure had a right to. No one would blame her if she did, because that scar across her cheek? Our mama was the one who put it there.

7

Jane

Charlotte Werkman's car was a surprisingly dusty 1954 Chevy, and we rolled the windows down as we headed out of Ridley. It was my first day of work and I'd been twenty minutes late, because I got lost. I never would have guessed the Grace County Department of Public Welfare would be above a Laundromat, but that's where it was. Four small rooms, and a floor that vibrated with the hum of the washing machines below.

I would share an office with Charlotte for my two weeks of orientation. She introduced me to the director, Fred Price, a big, balding man who looked happy about his upcoming retirement, as well as my fellow caseworkers—a dour older woman named Gayle, who seemed very tired of the work, and an effervescent girl named Paula. I thought Paula and I actually looked a bit alike, with our blond pageboys and brown eyes, and I was excited to find someone closer to my age. She seemed equally thrilled, peppering me with questions: Where did I live? Was I married? Was my degree in social work? Hers was in English, which she called "utterly useless!"

Gayle was probably around Charlotte's age and her smile looked bored as she greeted me, as though she'd seen many staff changes over the years and this was nothing new. She was very pale, made more so by her short jet-black hair, and she wore red lipstick that was creeping into the fine lines above her lips. She was telling Paula and me about one of her clients, a newly widowed woman who wanted to put her five kids in foster care, when Charlotte called me into her office. She handed me a thick department manual full of rules and regulations. "For the nights you can't get to sleep," she said with a smile.

Now I sat in her car, my new briefcase at my feet and my purse in my lap, hoping she'd turn west and not east on Ridley Road.

She turned east, though, and my heart gave a thud. *It'll be fine,* I told myself. Charlotte was talking about the different regions I'd be covering, but I barely heard her. I remembered an earlier time on this road, a happier time when Teresa and I were kids, driving to the beach with my parents. I remembered my mother saying, "This is where Ava Gardner's from," and Teresa, next to me in the backseat saying, "She's actually from Brogden," and me kicking her leg and my father asking her how she knew that and Teresa shutting up, because she wasn't supposed to read those movie magazines. She thought Ava and Frank Sinatra had the best marriage. Teresa would never know about their divorce. There was so much she'd never know.

"Where are we headed?" I tried to sound casual, suddenly aware that being in Grace County was going to be harder than I'd thought.

"I thought we'd start with the Jordan family. Ordinarily, I'd see the Hart family at the same time because they live close together, but I don't think we'll have time for both today, since I . . . *we*"—she glanced at me with a smile—"have to pick up an elderly gentleman to get him to his doctor's appointment by noon. Besides, it's harvesttime for the tobacco, so everyone's probably at the barn. I'm hoping we can catch Lita Jordan at home since she'll be getting lunch ready for her boys." She glanced at me. "'Lunch' is called 'dinner' on the farm, by the way," she said. "The main meal of the day."

We were coming up to the Ku Klux Klan billboard. It looked even bigger than it had that terrible afternoon two years ago. Red background. Hooded man on a white horse holding a burning cross. JOIN & SUPPORT THE UNITED KLANS OF AMERICA. FIGHT INTEGRATION AND COMMUNISM. Beyond it was the stand of tall loblolly pines that haunted my dreams. In an instant, we were past it, just like that. I let out my breath. I hadn't realized I'd been holding it.

"Ava Gardner's from here," Charlotte said.

"Yes." I smiled to myself. I wouldn't argue with her. "Did you see *On the Beach?*"

"Wasn't she marvelous in that! Depressing movie, though."

On either side of us stretched tobacco fields, people toiling in a sea of green. Mostly colored. Some white. The sun beating down on all of them. The car windows were wide open and I was still perspiring. I couldn't imagine how hot it was out there in the fields.

We passed an occasional house, the yards dotted with trees and shrubs, bicycles and trucks. Every farmhouse I saw was painted white and most looked well cared for. Tall tobacco barns, many of them buzzing with activity, were tucked into stands of trees. We turned off Ridley Road onto a narrow dirt road. Dust rose up around the open windows, but it was too hot to close them. I now understood why Charlotte's car looked the way it did. I supposed mine would be just as dusty in a few weeks.

Charlotte looked at her watch. "All right now," she said, as we pulled into a long drive leading to a white farmhouse with a red metal roof. Tobacco fields stretched away from the house in all directions. "Let me give you some background on your clients here."

"I'll have clients who live in this *farmhouse?*" I asked, looking at the broad front porch. I was astounded that anyone who could afford a home this nice would need welfare.

"No, not in the farmhouse. You'll see." She pulled to the side of the road and turned off the ignition and the car immediately filled with heat. "This farm is owned by Davison Gardiner. No relation to Ava." She smiled. "Spelled differently. His family's farmed this land for generations. The Jordans and the Harts live on his land, and *they're* your clients. The Harts will almost certainly be at the barn, like I said, so tomorrow or the day after, we'll come back later in the day and you can meet them. We have too much else to do today."

"Okay," I said, wondering how late she was talking about. I'd have to make sure dinner was ready to pop in the oven as soon as I got home. Robert had been very sweet about me starting my job, even buying the briefcase for me and wishing me luck when he kissed me good-bye this morning. But last night he said I seemed more excited about the job than I was about fixing up our beautiful new—well, new to us, anyway—house, and that was true. The house was perfect just as it was. I didn't care if the drapes had been picked out by someone else or if the wallpaper in the guest bedroom was a little faded. He joked that I wasn't a normal woman. At least I hoped he was joking.

"The Jordans live in that house over there." She pointed to the end of the road where a tiny unpainted building stood out in the open. I'd thought it was some sort of outbuilding, but now I could see laundry hanging from lines strung between the house and a couple of small trees. A little building stood a ways behind it and I guessed it was an outhouse.

"No indoor plumbing?" I asked.

She looked at me kindly, the way you'd look at a child who had so much to learn about life. "Not many of your clients will have indoor plumbing," she said. "Some don't even have electricity. Mrs. Jordan has four boys and a girl. She sent the girl, Sheena, to a family up North about five years ago, so now it's just the boys."

"Six people lived in that tiny house?" I asked. Maybe it would look bigger when we got up close to it. Right now, it looked smaller than the dining room in my new house.

"Right, but Lita won't be having any more, thank goodness. I was able to get her into the Eugenics Program after she gave birth to the last one, though it wasn't easy." She looked at me. "You probably don't know what that is, do you," she said.

The only time I'd heard the word "eugenics," it had to do with Nazi Germany, and I couldn't imagine that's what she was talking about.

"Not really," I said. "It makes me think of Hitler."

"Oh, for heaven's sake." She laughed. "Get that out of your mind right now. We have a Eugenics Board we can petition to get certain of our clients sterilized. It's been a godsend to many of them and Lita Jordan's a good example, but it was rough going, getting the board to okay her petition."

"Was this something she wanted?"

"Heavens, yes. She was tired of having babies—I think she thought she was finished and then another one came along and surprised her a few years ago. She heard about the program from a friend at her church and pleaded with me to be sterilized."

"Then why was it hard to get them to okay it?"

"She didn't meet the qualifications. She needed to meet one of three criteria. Mental retardation, for one. She'd have to score low enough on the IQ test to be considered feebleminded. Do you know anything about IQ testing? What that score would be?"

I tried to remember the little I'd learned about intelligence tests in my psychology classes. "Seventy?" I said.

"That's right. You have to score below seventy to be considered feebleminded. And she scored one fifteen. A hundred and fifteen! Most of the poor folks out here barely test in the normal range, but that woman could run this farm. She graduated from the colored high school in Ridley, which is no small feat given the environment she grew up in."

"Oh, she's colored." I'd been picturing a white family. I had to alter the mental image I'd had in my mind of Lita Jordan and her children.

"Yes, colored. And definitely promiscuous. Five kids and no father in the home? Promiscuous she is, but on its own, that's not enough reason for her to be sterilized, although there are some social workers who've managed to make that case." She looked out the window away from the Jordans' house and appeared momentarily lost in thought.

"So," I prodded, "mental retardation is a yes. Promiscuity's a no."

"Well, if the case can be made that a promiscuous woman is unable to manage the children she has, then the board would consider it, but Lita Jordan's children have never been in trouble and Davison Gardiner says she's a sterling example of motherhood. So my hands were tied there. Mental illness and epilepsy are the other two reasons the board will agree to a sterilization, by the way, and she was neither mentally ill nor epileptic."

"What about birth control?" I thought of my pills and how lucky I'd been to get them.

"I had the public health nurse, Ann Laing, bring her whatever she could—condoms and diaphragms and whatever, but she still got pregnant with the littlest boy, Rodney. If we ever get access to the new birth control pill, we'll be in hog heaven, except the people out here who need it most don't have the discipline to take a pill on a regular schedule."

"So how were you able to get the Eugenics Board to say yes?"

"Ah. I finally remembered the 'one hundred and twenty' rule. You multiply her age, which was then thirty-three, by the number of children she has and if the result is more than one hundred twenty, she can be sterilized. Five times thirty-three and there you have it. I petitioned the board and she had a tubal ligation—that's where they cut the fallopian tubes—after Rodney was born. She was one grateful woman, I can tell you."

I looked toward the long clotheslines. I was too far away to tell what was hanging from them, but I could imagine all the work this Lita Jordan had to do with a house full of boys. "Shouldn't the father . . . fathers be helping out? Financially, I mean?"

"Jane," she said, "look at that field."

I did, and I suddenly saw the workers out there in a new light. They weren't just faceless field laborers—they were men who wanted a bed and a woman at the end of the day. And Mrs. Jordan's little house butted right up against the edge of the field where they worked.

"It could be one of a hundred," Charlotte said. "Or more likely five of a hundred. Life is very bleak for lots of folks out here, and you can't blame them for taking comfort where they can find it." Her tone was sympathetic. "Sometimes it's in a bed. Other times in a bottle. Whatever gives them momentary pleasure, because the future doesn't hold much promise."

I nodded, fanning my face with my hand and trying not to look too obvious about it. I was perspiring, but Charlotte's flawless skin was still powder dry.

"So." She smiled. "You'll discover we've got a lot of mothers in our caseload, and precious few fathers. Immaculate conceptions happening all over the place."

I laughed.

"Always check for a man living in the house," she said. "I don't worry about it with Lita that much, but some women hide the fact that they've got a man living with them to keep the welfare checks coming in."

I wondered how you checked for something like that. "So what do you do for these families?" I asked. "What do *we* do?"

"Plenty! We figure out how much aid they get and evaluate the family for problems that need addressing. Avery—that little Jordan boy with the vision problem—well, he's not so little anymore." She laughed. "He's fifteen, but looks older. I drive him to the itinerant Braille teacher in Ridley every week unless someone from their church can take him, so you'll be taking over that responsibility."

I pictured myself driving a blind teenaged boy. What would I talk to him about?

"How do you get people to talk to you?" I thought of the intimate conversations Charlotte must have had with Lita Jordan to get her to talk about birth control.

"You become a good listener."

"But . . . do they just automatically start talking about their personal things?"

"You feed back what they say. They say they feel overwhelmed, you say 'you feel overwhelmed?' And you'll be surprised how that opens the spigot."

"Really?" It sounded silly, but I figured she knew better than me what worked and what didn't.

"Really," she said. "I'll give you some books."

"Oh, that would be wonderful."

"If you'd had social-work training you'd have learned interviewing skills, but Fred and I are the only degreed social workers in the department. Gayle has a bachelor's in psychology, so that certainly helps, but Paula—"

"A degree in English," I said. "She told me."

Charlotte laughed. "However," she said, "Paula's been a caseworker now for six years, so she certainly knows the ropes. And she certainly knows how to manipulate them."

"Manipulate them?"

She brushed away my question. "So," she said, turning the key in the ignition and pressing lightly on the gas, "this week you just observe and next week you can take a more active role with me supervising. It will work out."

I was relieved to have air blowing into the car once more. We skirted the tobacco field and drove up the dirt lane till we reached the dilapidated house. It looked even smaller close-up. We parked on the hardpacked dirt that was the front yard. "In the office, I'm Charlotte and you're Jane," Charlotte said. "When we're in the field, though, I'm Mrs. Werkman and you are Mrs. Mackie."

"Forrester now."

"Yes. Forrester."

As we got out of the car, a woman appeared in the open doorway of the house.

"Hello, Mrs. Jordan!" Charlotte called, her voice cheerful.

"Hey, Miz Werkman. Who's this you got with you?" She was holding one hand above her eyes to block the sun and eyeing me up and down. A little boy stood at her side, hanging on to her dress.

"This is Mrs. Forrester," Charlotte said. "She's going to be taking my place. I'm moving into an administrative position."

"You don't say." Mrs. Jordan frowned, and I could tell she was none too happy about the change.

"Can we come in for a chat?" Charlotte asked. Gayle had told me it was important to see inside the house. She said she recently found a fancy television and new furniture in a client's living room and she cut off that family's welfare check.

"I ain't got nothin' to offer you," Mrs. Jordan said, adjusting the blue kerchief that covered her hair, "but you're welcome to come in."

She stepped aside while Charlotte and I walked through the doorway. I was carrying my new briefcase, which now contained both my notepad and the manual Charlotte had given me. I loved feeling the weight of it in my hand.

Charlotte bent down to greet the little boy. "Hello, Rodney," she said. "I think you've grown two inches in the last two weeks."

"Ain't that true," Mrs. Jordan said. "All my boys is like that. Growing too big too fast."

I could see the whole house from inside the front door. We stood in a small, dark living room. Beyond that, I could see a kitchen, a pot of something savory on the two-burner stove. Whatever was in that pot made my mouth water. I saw the edge of a table and the corner of a cot. Someone slept in the kitchen. Through an open door on my right, I saw a cast-iron bed. I couldn't imagine how five children and their mother ever fit into a house the size of a postage stamp. No wonder she sent one of them away.

"I was afraid you'd be at the barn and we'd miss you," Charlotte said, as we followed Mrs. Jordan and the little boy into the kitchen.

"Getting dinner ready for the boys," she said.

We sat down at the table that took up half the room and I got a good look at Mrs. Jordan. A bit of her coarse black hair poked out of the dusty kerchief, and her dark eyes slanted up at the outer corners as though she had Oriental blood. Those eyes gave her a pretty, exotic look.

I tried to be observant and study everything I could see. The cot was made up with sheets that hung to the floor. Rodney climbed onto it and bounced up and down until his mother grabbed his arm and told him to go outside. There was a hand pump above the sink. No faucet. I'd never seen that before. A narrow icebox stood next to the back door. Open shelves stretched across the wall above the counter, sagging beneath the weight of Mason jars filled with vegetables and tomatoes.

"We have some clothes for the boys in the car," Charlotte said. Then to me, "Don't let me forget them."

"That's good," Mrs. Jordan said. "Eli, he need them most. The others get the hand-me-downs, but Eli's growin' so fast and he ain't got much that fits no more. Davison . . . Mr. Gardiner . . . give him some of his old overalls."

Charlotte turned to me. "Mrs. Jordan and Mr. Gardiner have known each other since they were children."

"Oh," I said, wondering how that came to be.

"What Eli really needs is shoes. His shoes is so small we had to cut room for his toes."

"Oh my." Charlotte pulled her notepad from her briefcase. She set it on the table and wrote something on it. I assumed she was writing "get shoes for Eli." I wondered if I should pull out my own notepad.

The Jordans would be my clients, after all. I loved the sound of those words. "My clients." It filled me with a sense of responsibility that I welcomed. "What else do they need?" Charlotte asked.

Mrs. Jordan rattled off a few things, mostly clothes and linens and asthma medicine for Avery, the partly blind boy. Mrs. Jordan seemed to like and trust Charlotte. It was like watching two old friends chatting together. There was something about Charlotte's way of talking that put people at ease. Mrs. Jordan kept cutting her eyes at me like she wasn't too sure about me, though, and I sat there with a half smile plastered on my face, wondering if I could ever master Charlotte's easygoing, self-confident style.

Rodney ran into the kitchen. Around his body, he wore an old, falling-apart cardboard carton with headlights painted on it, and he ran from room to room saying, "Vroom, vroom!" I laughed, he was so cute. He barreled out the back door knocking a hole in the flimsy screen with a corner of his box, but it was one hole of many.

"We could use us a new screen door," Mrs. Jordan said, her voice tinged with irony, and we all laughed.

Rodney banged into the house again. The box was gone and now he carried a tree branch twice his size.

"Rodney, take that thing outside!" Mrs. Jordan said. "You don't bring no trees in my house."

Rodney stood still in the middle of the kitchen, clutching the branch in his hand as though trying to make up his mind whether to obey or not. He looked at Charlotte, then me, as though we could help him out.

"You hear me?" Mrs. Jordan said. "Get that nasty thing out my house."

He ran through the door again, and Mrs. Jordan rolled her eyes at us, but she was smiling. "I'm glad he's my last, but he's the best," she said. "He keeps us laughing."

Rodney popped back into the room without the branch.

"Rodney," Charlotte said. "Come over here, angel."

He marched right up to her and put his hands on her knees. Charlotte pulled a lollipop from her purse. "You sure are getting to be a big boy," she said.

He smiled, little white teeth showing as he reached for the candy. "I want that!"

"You so rude!" His mother laughed and swatted his arm. "How you ask?"

He looked at her like he had no idea what she was talking about.

"What's the word?" she asked.

"Please?"

"That's better."

But Charlotte still held the candy out of reach. "What color is this lollipop?" she asked him.

"Green," he said.

"What shape is it?" Charlotte asked. He looked perplexed.

"Is it a square or a circle?"

"Round," he said.

"That's right. A round circle. You're a smart boy." She unwrapped the lollipop and handed it to him.

"He gonna be the smartest of them all," Mrs. Jordan said. "Too smart for his own good. He's my little travelin' man." She hugged him close to her, though he only had eyes for the lollipop.

"He's your travelin' man?" Charlotte asked, and I recognized that feeding back she'd told me about. She was right. It worked like a charm.

"He goes over to the Gardiners' and bothers Desiree for sweets. Or he goes to the Harts' to play with Baby William."

"Hard to keep an eye on him," Charlotte said.

Mrs. Jordan looked like she might have said too much. "Oh, I manage," she said. "The boys help. Eli's a good help and Devil's really growed up now."

"Well, that's one thing we need to talk about," Charlotte said. "Eli's seventeen now, isn't he?"

"Don't cut him off," she said quickly. "Please, Miss Charlotte, don't cut him off. I don't know what we'd do."

"No, he won't be cut off as long as he's in school," Charlotte said. "He has one more year and if he stays in, he'll still be covered." She turned to me. "Many children Eli's age have dropped out by now, but—"

"But I won't let him. Oh, you bet there's days that boy don't want to get hisself out of bed, but I give him a talking-to while he's laying there like a lazy mule. Tell him he won't amount to nothing. That sort of thing."

"And that works?" Charlotte asked.

"Nah." She grinned. "What works is while I'm telling him all that, I poke him with a fork. Not hard, now," she added quickly. "Just enough to be a nuisance, like a fly you can't get rid of. Now, *that* works."

We laughed. She was still holding Rodney. He wriggled to get away from her arms and she let him go.

"How is Avery doing?" Charlotte asked. "I missed seeing him this week, since Pastor Freed drove him to the Braille teacher."

"They say he need new glasses again," she said with a sigh. "Wish them eyes of his would just settle."

"Is he able to help with the barning?" Charlotte asked.

"Oh, he topped the plants a few weeks ago. He could see them flowers good enough to pull them off. He wants to be out there with the other boys, but mostly he gets stuck unloading the sled and carrying the sticks. He wants to be normal so bad." Her eyes suddenly glistened and for the first time since we arrived, I felt real pain in her. I felt what her life was like and I had to look away from that raw emotion in her face. It was a tiny moment in the day. Two or three seconds. But it was my first true seed of doubt that I could do this work. It wasn't hearing about the boy so much—I knew I'd hear much worse—it was that glimpse inside her. Seeing the pain inside.

"Is he showing interest in girls?" Charlotte asked.

She shook her head quickly. "No, ma'am. He don't need no operation."

Charlotte nodded. "I do worry about it," she said. "Last time I drove him to Ridley, I could see how he's growing up. Even with those glasses, he's a handsome boy and he's gotten tall and filled out."

"All my boys is handsome," she said.

"Yes, they are," Charlotte agreed. "And the handsomer they get the more I worry."

"I know he shouldn't be no daddy, with them eyes of his. I know he can pass it on. But he don't need the operation. I keep a good eye on him."

It took me a moment to understand what they were talking about. I'd thought they meant surgery on his eyes. They meant sterilization. I hadn't realized that Eugenics Program was for boys, too. Men and boys. I didn't even know how they did it. Surely they didn't castrate them?

"I don't want him to go through the hurt of it," she said.

"We can wait," Charlotte said. "You and Mrs. Forrester can decide when the time is right."

At the mention of my name, Mrs. Jordan studied me hard. "You don't say much," she said.

I opened my mouth to speak, unsure what I'd say, but Charlotte filled the gap. "She's taking it all in right now," she said. "Next time you see her, she'll be doing all the talking." Charlotte had worked a lifetime with these people out here. How would I ever catch up?

"How are your neighbors doing?" Charlotte asked. "The Harts?"

"Mary Ella strange as ever. Like Violet." She looked at me. "That's her mama. I growed up with Violet."

I nodded even though I had no idea who she was talking about.

"Explain it to her," Charlotte said to Mrs. Jordan.

"Me and my brother growed up right here in this house. Percy Hart—that's Mary Ella and Ivy's daddy—he growed up in the house where they live now." She looked at Charlotte. "Has she met them yet?"

"Soon," Charlotte said.

"Violet—their mama—lived down the road a piece. And Davison was just a boy growing up in the farmhouse. We all knew each other. Played together. Worked the tobacca together. Just like our children do."

"I understand," I said.

"So like I said, Mary Ella's getting stranger by the day, if you ask me," she said. "Ivy's a nice girl. She sometimes plays 'school' with Rodney and Baby William, trying to teach them their numbers and things. Rodney catches on, but Baby William . . ." She shook her head. "He's a sweet baby, but he ain't right. You know that. Anyway, I think Ivy's started sneaking out at night. I seen her wanderin' a time or two like her sister does."

"Where does she go?"

She shrugged. "I just seen her on the road."

"You sure it's her?"

"Yes'm. Can tell by the hair. Mary Ella got all that wild yeller hair. Ivy don't, plus she's a bigger girl. Got more meat on her bones. Nonnie's doing poorly, too," she added, then looked at me again. "You gonna have to learn to talk to do this job," she said.

I smiled. "I'm looking forward to getting to know you better," I said, glad I'd finally managed to get a full sentence out of my mouth.

We walked back through the living room and I noticed small pictures taped to the wall in a neat line. I stepped closer. "These are your children?" I asked.

"Yes'm," she said. "This is my boy Eli." She pointed to a boy who looked more like a man to me. The pictures were all small color photographs, maybe from school. Eli wasn't smiling. He didn't look happy about having his picture taken. His eyes pulled me in, though. They were the color of clear amber.

"And this one?" I pointed to the picture of a dark-skinned cherub with a wide, white grin. "Oh my goodness, he's a cutie!" I glanced at Charlotte, worried I sounded thoroughly unprofessional, but her face gave nothing away.

Mrs. Jordan chuckled. "That's my Devil. He come by that name honest."

"Is that his real name?" I asked, touching the corner of the picture. "Devil?"

"I named him Devon James Jordan, but my oldest—my girl Sheena—she had trouble saying Devon and it come out Devil, and that stuck. He's not bad. Just full of mischief. It's a real old picture. He's growed up now." She pointed to the next photograph. "And this here is Avery."

I looked at the boy in the black horn-rimmed glasses. He had Devil's grin and my heart went out to him that his vision was as bad as it sounded.

"This was from a couple years ago, too," Mrs. Jordan said. "He's a big boy now."

"Yes, indeed," Charlotte said.

I came to the final picture. "And this must be Sheena," I said. She had her mother's exotic eyes.

"Yes, ma'am. Miss her." She tightened her lips. "I miss my baby."

I wanted to know why Sheena'd been sent away, but Charlotte touched my elbow. "We have several more families to visit," she said.

"The clothes," I reminded her.

"Ah yes," Charlotte said, as if she would have forgotten without my reminder, something I didn't believe for a second. "Let's get the clothes."

We left three bags of clothing with Lita Jordan, and then we were back in the car.

"What you did there at the end?" Charlotte said, as she turned the key in the ignition. "Talking to her about the pictures?"

"Yes?" I stiffened, bracing for criticism.

"That's the way to do it," she said. "That's the way to get them to open up. To gain their trust. You touched her where her heart is, and you've got a good natural feel for it."

I breathed a sigh of relief. "Thank you," I said. "I was wondering if I could get her some frames for those pictures," I said. "I felt sorry for her, having them just taped to the wall like that."

"Ask her if she'd like that. You never know why people do the things they do. It might be tradition in her family, for all you know, to have pictures hung plain like that." She laughed. "Though I sincerely doubt it."

I wanted to ask about the daughter, Sheena, but Charlotte pointed into the woods to our left. "The Harts live back in there," she said.

I looked into the woods, my eyes piercing the green veil as deeply as they could, but I could see nothing other than trees and shadow. Somewhere in there lived the strange girl, Mary Ella, and her wandering sister, Ivy. And I wondered what their stories would be.

8

Ivy

Wednesday was the third day of the barning and it was a long one. I was a sweaty mess by the time all the other workers left, but I stayed behind. I stood alone next to the barn, rubbing half a green tomato over my fingers to get off the tobacco gum, but really I was just hoping to see Henry Allen before I went home for the day. I knew he was working in the shed on the other side of the field. We didn't have no plans to meet up tonight and that would make three nights in a row. Last night was my fault. I was supposed to meet him at midnight, but Baby William had a coughing spell and woke Nonnie and Mary Ella up and there wasn't no way I could sneak out after that. He gave me a look this morning, asking why I didn't come and I got to tell him "Baby William was sick" but they was the only words we said to each other all day, and it made me crazy watching him carry the tobacco to us on the sled and then go out again without being able to talk to him. Anybody watching me now would know I was dawdling. The tomato was falling apart and my fingers was still stuck together.

I was rinsing the tomato juice off my hands with water from the bucket, when down the road I saw Nonnie coming toward me fast, her cane flying out behind her. That scared me. I always said I couldn't remember the day Daddy died, but I remembered the *feel* of it. The rushing around, panicky kind of feeling. Watching Nonnie run up the road toward me gave me that feeling all over again.

I dropped the tomato and started running toward her, remembering how Baby William nearly went blue in the face last night when he had his coughing fit. He was always with Nonnie this time of day but he wasn't with her now.

Nonnie stopped running and waved to me to hurry up.

"What's wrong?" I shouted as soon as I got close enough. "Is it Baby William?"

"I seen Mrs. Werkman's car," Nonnie said. She was out of breath. "She's parked on the lane. You know she'll want to see you and your sister."

"That's all?" I stopped running myself. Then Baby William popped out of one of the rows of tobacco right in front of me. I wanted to smack him for scaring me, but really it was Nonnie who deserved the smack for not watching him better. "I thought something terrible happened."

"Come on now, girl." She grabbed my arm with her fat, clammy hand.

"You shouldn't be running," I said. "And you shouldn't let Baby William run through the tobacco like that after the last time." Not two weeks ago, he got lost in the rows of tobacco and we didn't know where he was. Everyone was out looking for him. Mary Ella cried, she was so scared. It was Eli who found him, sitting on the ground, dirt smeared all over his face, playing with a fat ugly tobacco worm. When Mary Ella saw Eli come out of the field carrying her baby, she fell out on the ground sobbing, she was so relieved.

"And you should of been home by now," Nonnie scolded. "Where's Mary Ella?"

"I don't know." I didn't want to know, neither. "Mary Ella's running her own life," I said. I wanted to talk to Mrs. Werkman about the things we needed. Diapers. Underwear and clothes for me and Mary Ella. And the thing I wanted the most: a window fan. I knew people at church who had one and said it was the best thing ever invented. But Mrs. Werkman brung us little things like clothes and diapers. It couldn't hurt to ask, though.

Nonnie was holding my arm so hard her nails dug into my skin. "Don't say nothin' to Mrs. Werkman about the extras," she said.

"I ain't stupid," I said, then corrected myself in my head. *I'm not stupid.* If we told Mrs. Werkman about the extras Mr. Gardiner gave us, she'd subtract them off the money we got. And Mr. Gardiner'd been right generous with us lately, even sending Mary Ella home with half a ham the other day. I think things was going real good for him and the farm.

"I hid the ham soon as I saw her car," Nonnie said. "Hid it and come out to find you and your useless sister."

"She ain't useless," I said. I wasn't sure of the best word to describe Mary Ella, but useless wasn't right. Not the way she could calm Baby William. Not the way she loved that boy.

I'd known Mrs. Werkman as long as I could remember. She started with us after everything terrible happened and she was like a magician, the way she could get us things we needed. The most magical thing she done was the time she knew about Mary Ella's 'pendix being sick even before Mary Ella felt bad. But she had power, and it was a frightful thing to know somebody had power over your life. The money we lived on came through her and we needed to be careful around her. Never let something slip out of our mouths that could end up costing us. Mary Ella wasn't around the last time Mrs. Werkman came, either, and I was afraid she might think she had a real job and was bringing in more money than we said.

Baby William started to run back into the tobacco, but I scooped him up and carried him, ignoring his screams, though they pierced my eardrum. I looked over my shoulder at the shed one more time and saw Henry Allen standing there. He was far away but I could tell he was looking at us, and if his daddy hadn't been right there, too, he would of waved. I'd have to settle for looking at each other across the field. Sometimes you had to make do.

9

Jane

It was going to take me a long time to find my way around out here. It was late Wednesday afternoon, the end of my third full day with Charlotte, and every road still looked the same to me: acres and acres of green tobacco plants dotted with tobacco barns and white farmhouses. When Charlotte turned onto the dirt road leading to Gardiners' farm, however, I recognized the red-roofed farmhouse in the distance.

It had been an overwhelming day. We'd seen a little boy, his belly bloated from malnutrition. We drove a baby with a raging fever to the hospital because we couldn't reach the public health nurse. And we found one of our clients, a blind man, unconscious on the floor at the foot of his stairs. Who knew how long he'd been there? I shuddered to think what would have happened to him if we hadn't visited him today. I'd never felt so desperately needed.

Now we were going to visit the Hart family, and Charlotte had been telling me about them as we drove.

"Ivy and Mary Ella's father, Percy, was killed in a farming accident when they were small and their mother, Violet, was committed to Dix Hospital," she said as she drove slowly along the road. "She was a schizophrenic who decompensated after her husband's death. The girls have been cared for by their grandmother ever since, but she's marginal herself."

I tried to imagine myself ever using such jargon so easily.

"Mary Ella was kicked out of school when she became pregnant at fourteen," Charlotte said. "Once they're pregnant, that's the end of their education."

"Fourteen!" I said.

"Fifteen when she delivered."

"Who's the baby's father?" I asked.

Charlotte hesitated. "I doubt even Mary Ella knows," she said. "I have my suspicions but that's all they are. Mary Ella's blond as blond can be, but the baby's got very dark, very curly hair. His skin is fair enough, though. He'll be able to pass."

"Oh," I said, taking that in.

"Don't put anything like that in your notes," she warned. "The last thing that girl needs is for people to think she's had relations with a colored boy, and a lynch mob would find out which one it was, you better believe it. Or they'd make a guess, which could be even worse. I didn't even mention my suspicions to the Eugenics Board."

"The Eugenics Board? For her, too? Are they going to sterilize her?"

"They already have," she said. "She's feebleminded. IQ of seventy. But she doesn't know about the sterilization. Her grandmother and I agreed it was best to tell her she was having her appendix out."

My mouth dropped open and Charlotte glanced over at me. "Sometimes you have to come up with creative ways of helping people, Jane," she said.

"But it's so . . . dishonest," I said.

"It's actually a kindness. You'll realize that soon enough. She can only understand so much, and she absolutely can't handle another child. She's out of control and I worry Ivy's starting to follow in her footsteps. Mary Ella's very pretty and Ivy's a little plainer and she's a big girl. Not overweight, but not lithe, like her sister."

I instantly related to Ivy. I knew what it was like to be the "plainer" sister.

"Ivy's still in school," Charlotte said, "and my goal—now *your* goal—will be to keep her there till she finishes. The main thing is to prevent her from having a baby of her own because that'll put an end to her education."

"Is Ivy . . . feebleminded, too?" I asked. I'd rarely used that word.

"Her IQ's about eighty," Charlotte said. "Low, but not feebleminded, which is a shame because it would make it easier to petition the Eugenics Board on her behalf."

"You plan to sterilize her, too?" I asked.

Charlotte nodded. "She has petit mal epilepsy, although I don't believe she's had any seizures in recent years. But the low IQ score plus the epilepsy plus behavioral problems give us plenty of ammunition. I haven't put the petition together yet. That will be up to you. You always want to ask yourself what chance a child would have growing up in a particular household. If it's no chance at all, you have the Eugenics Board to turn to."

"You'll tell me how to do it? The petition?" I wondered if I'd have to lie to another girl about an appendectomy. I hoped not.

"Of course. Now don't get 'eugenics happy,'" she warned.

"What do you mean?"

"Oh, there are some social workers—one in our own office—who find reasons to sterilize their entire caseloads." She laughed. "That's a slight exaggeration, but only slight. It can be abusive. So always ask yourself if you have the client's best interest at heart."

I nodded, wondering which of the social workers in our office was "eugenics happy." Probably Gayle, I thought. She seemed like such a sourpuss. I doubted Fred saw many clients and I couldn't imagine the word "abusive" ever applying to that bubbly, cheerful Paula.

Now we skirted the tobacco field, driving past the Jordans' house and down the narrow dirt lane that ran between the field and the woods. Charlotte turned onto a sandy lane that ran only a short way into the woods before ending. There wasn't a building in sight. I turned to look behind us and saw trees and the tobacco field beyond, but I couldn't even see the Gardiners' white farmhouse from where we sat. "Why are we stopping?" I asked, as she gathered up her briefcase and purse.

"They live a little ways from here," she said. "There's no road." She looked down at my feet. I had on my black pumps. "You'll have to get some more sensible shoes." She pointed to the heavy black shoes she wore. "You don't want to step in a cow patty with those pretty things on."

"A cow patty?"

"That's—"

"I know what it is. I just didn't realize that would be a risk." I laughed.

"You need a sense of adventure for this job."

"I can see that."

I picked up my own light briefcase with its one notepad inside and followed her out of the car. From the trunk, we lifted a couple of bags of donated clothing we'd picked up that morning from a church. Then we set out on a path that ran through the woods, the trees and vines so thick that sunlight only penetrated the canopy here and there. I couldn't imagine walking through these woods alone. We came to an open pasture, a couple of cows at one end.

"Watch where you step," Charlotte cautioned me.

I hoped the cows would always be at the other end of the field. What would I do if I arrived here one day and had to walk past those huge animals? I'd never been much of a country girl.

Once we crossed the pasture, we were back in the woods again. The ground was uneven and my legs ached by the time an old unpainted wooden house, nearly identical to the Jordans', came into view. We walked into a dirt clearing, chickens scampering out of our way, and climbed the one step to a lopsided porch. Charlotte knocked on the open door. "Mrs. Hart?" she called.

"We're here!" a voice shouted from the woods behind us, and we turned to see a teenaged girl running from the greenery, a little boy clutched under her arm like a football. She set him down on the packed earth and he started running in our direction on wobbly legs, giggling, his dark curly hair bouncing. William, I guessed. "I just finished up at the barn," the girl said. "Nonnie's right behind me." She looked into the woods toward the path, then back at Charlotte. "We been waitin' for you," she said.

"Have you, now," Charlotte said, as we set the bags on the porch. "Why is that, dear?"

"We need diapers and clothes and a window fan." The girl spoke to Charlotte but her gaze had moved to me, clearly curious.

The little boy had reached us and he banged his palms against Charlotte's legs.

"Hello, William!" She bent over and lifted him high in the air and he laughed. A string of drool hung from the corner of his mouth, threatening to fall onto Charlotte's face, and she lowered him just in time. "How's my boy?" she asked, trying to nestle him in her arms, but he squirmed to get down and she lowered him to the ground again, where he took off after one of the chickens. I couldn't imagine myself in Charlotte's role. She was so comfortable in it. So *mature.* Playing with the toddler like she'd known him all her life. Calling the girl "dear." I was only seven years older than this girl, much closer in age to her than to Charlotte.

"This is Mrs. Forrester," Charlotte said.

Ivy nodded at me. "Ma'am," she said.

"Hello, Ivy," I said. "I'm happy to meet you."

"Is Mary Ella inside?" Charlotte asked. "We knocked but there was no answer."

"No, ma'am. She'll be home soon, I'm sure."

"William!" Charlotte called to the little boy as she pulled a lollipop from her purse. I was going to have to get a supply of those lollipops for myself.

William ignored her and I wondered about his hearing. Charlotte had told me he wasn't "reaching his developmental milestones." She was concerned he wasn't being properly cared for and that we needed to keep a close eye on him to be sure he was safe. She said we might have to consider a foster home for him. "And when he's old enough," she'd added, "I'd like to see him in a residential school for the feebleminded, where he could reach his full potential. That won't happen at home."

Now Charlotte sat down on the stoop. "William," she tried again. "Come see what I have for you."

"William, you get over here!" Ivy said sharply. "Mrs. Werkman's trying to talk to you." To me she said, "He's good but sometimes he's a mite ornery."

I nodded with a smile.

Ivy caught the little boy by the shoulder and prodded him in Charlotte's direction.

"Look what I have for you, William," Charlotte said, holding the red plastic-wrapped lollipop toward him.

William grinned at the sight of the candy. He had a bobbing little walk as he approached her. He was the cutest child I'd ever seen. His hair was thick and dark and curly, shiny as silk. His skin was definitely darker than Ivy's, but I never would have guessed he had Negro blood just from looking at him.

As she'd done with Rodney Jordan, Charlotte held the lollipop out of his reach. "What is this, William?" she asked.

He looked back at Ivy. "It's a lollipop," Ivy said.

"Let him answer, dear," Charlotte said.

"He won't," she said. "He still don't talk."

"What color is this lollipop, William?" Charlotte asked.

William stuck out his lower lip and I knew he was going to cry any second. Seeing the tears welling up in his eyes made me want to rip the lollipop from Charlotte's hand and give it to him. I was relieved when she unwrapped the candy and handed it to him. "Don't run with it," she said. "You sit right here to eat it."

Charlotte looked up at Ivy, who stood a few feet away from me, her arms locked behind her back. "Does he have any words at all?" she asked.

"He says 'mama' to Mary Ella. And he calls me 'Ibie' sometimes, and he sort of says 'Nonnie.' He's real happy, though. And he's good, most of the time. Sometimes he gets flustrated and lets out a wail, but mostly he's quiet."

"Uh-huh," Charlotte said. I could tell she wasn't happy with the answers.

"Nonnie said her brother didn't talk till he was five and then he didn't never shut up," Ivy added.

"Uh-huh," Charlotte said as she lifted up the edge of William's dirty white shirt. "How long has he had this rash, Ivy?" she asked.

"What rash?"

"Here." Charlotte held up his shirt and Ivy peered at William's side before he started fussing and pushed their hands away.

"That must of just happened," Ivy said. "Ain't seen it before. Diaper rash, maybe?"

"Not on his back," Charlotte said. "Maybe we can get you something to put on that."

"That'd be good," Ivy said, but her eyes were on the bags. "Did you bring us something?" she asked.

"I have some clothes for you and Mary Ella and William," Charlotte said.

I heard a twig snap in the woods and Ivy turned and took a few steps toward the path. "Nonnie!" she called. "Mrs. Werkman and another lady are here!"

Charlotte got to her feet, dusting off the back of her slacks as a woman emerged from the trees, leaning heavily on a cane. Charlotte leaned over and whispered to me, "It's important to talk to the parent or guardian alone. She needs to feel free to say whatever's going on with the children."

"Hello, hello!" The woman smiled at us, though it must have taken some effort because she was obviously in pain. She was overweight and missing a couple of her bottom teeth. You could tell by looking at her that she was overwhelmed by her life, and I felt sorry for her. "Good seein' you, Mrs. Werkman," she said. "Who's this?"

"Ivy," Charlotte said, "why don't you take the bags in the house and look through them while we chat with your grandmother."

"Yes, ma'am." Ivy picked up the bags, one in each arm, and called to William to follow her into the house.

"You brung them some clothes?" the grandmother asked.

"Yes. Not sure they'll fit. I believe Ivy's grown quite a bit just in the few weeks since I was here last."

"They all growin' like weeds," the woman said. She was eyeing me the same way Ivy had a few minutes earlier. She tucked a strand of her thin gray hair behind her ear. "So tell me who's this child?" she asked.

Oh Lord. She called me a child. I would be forty before anyone thought of me as a capable woman.

Charlotte pointed to a few mismatched lawn chairs under an oak tree. "Let's sit in the shade, shall we?"

We walked to the chairs, the grandmother limping the whole way.

"This rheumatism gonna be the death of me." She lowered herself into one of the rusty old chairs with a groan. "If the sugar don't get me first," she added.

"Do you have enough Bufferin?" Charlotte asked.

The woman gave her a tired look. "For all the good it do, which ain't much. If it wasn't for trying to hold this house together, I'd ask the good Lord to take me, I swear." She nodded toward me. "What's your name, honey?" she asked.

"This is Mrs. Forrester. Mrs. Forrester, I'd like you to meet Mrs. Hart."

I nodded. "Happy to meet you," I said. "I'll be taking Mrs. Werkman's place."

The woman's face fell. Every cell in her cheeks and chin literally sagged with her disappointment. *"No,"* she said. "That can't be. You need to keep on with us," she said to Charlotte. "You been with us since Violet got took away. You know everything there is to know about—"

"I know it must be a surprise," Charlotte said, "but I'm moving into another position in the department. It's time for some new blood to—"

"No," Mrs. Hart said again. "She can't take over. She's nothing but a baby!" I heard the worry in her voice and knew it was time for me to speak up with some confidence.

"Mrs. Hart." I leaned forward in the chair. I wanted to touch her, but I wasn't sure if that was allowed. There was so much I didn't know! "Mrs. Werkman is filling me in about your family, and you and I will get to know each other very well and I'll learn how I can help you. It will be all right." I smiled, but she turned her head away, a weariness in her sagging shoulders.

"Tell us how Mary Ella is doing," Charlotte said. "I wish she was here to meet Mrs. Forrester. Where is she?"

"You know as well as me I can't keep no tabs on that girl," she said. "Good thing we got her fixed, that's all I can say, and Ivy's worse every day. When can she get the operation? She flunked that test you give her, right?"

"No, no. It's not the sort of test you pass or fail. It only measures her ability to learn, and she didn't score all that low, so I'll use her epilepsy to get her the surgery. Actually"—she looked at me—"Mrs. Forrester will be taking over Ivy's case."

Mrs. Hart sank even farther down into the chair, if that was possible. "Does she know what she's doin'?" She pointed at me.

She'd picked up on my insecurity and, in doing so, fed it. I tried to smile reassuringly.

"This one's a quick learner," Charlotte said, nodding in my direction. "She'll know the ropes in no time. Don't you worry."

"Ivy's a nice girl," Mrs. Hart said to me. "Don't go thinking these girls ain't nice, 'cause they is. But there's so much evil in the world and it all just settles on their shoulders." She leaned toward me. "The devil lives in them woods." She pointed behind me in a way that sent a chill up my spine. "He lives on this here farm. Took my son—" She looked at Charlotte. "Does she know about that?"

Charlotte nodded. "Yes, I told her."

"The devil took my son," Mrs. Hart said. "Made his wife, Violet, go clear out of her head. Turned Mary Ella into a girl I don't know. Now it's doing its dirty work on Ivy. I pray to Jesus regular to watch over them, but it ain't helpin'."

I remembered Charlotte using the word "marginal" to describe Mrs. Hart. Talking with her, I thought I understood the meaning of the word.

"What's going on with Ivy now?" Charlotte asked.

"She sneaks out at night, just like Mary Ella used to."

"How do you know?" Charlotte asked.

"I hear the squeak of the front door," she said. "She thinks I sleep like the dead and most nights I do, but sometimes that squeak wakes me up like a bomb dropping next to my head."

"Do you say anything to her then?" I asked. "Do you try to stop her?"

She stared at me, then looked at Charlotte. "I thought you said she was smart?"

"Well," Charlotte said, "it's a reasonable question."

"These girls rule the roost here, I tell you," she said. "I'm just the old woman who washes their clothes and takes care of their baby. And I can't manage another one of them, so back to getting Ivy fixed. When can you do it? What's the holdup?"

"We have a long road ahead of us before we can get permission to have her—"

"I already give you my permission!"

"No, sorry," Charlotte said. "I meant the board that has to give its permission. A group of people who decide if she can have the surgery or not."

"What group? They don't know us. *You're* the one knows us."

"This is the process we went through with Mary Ella and it worked, so have some faith that it will work again. But just realize that there's no guarantee that I . . . *we* can get her approved by the board, since it's been quite a while since she's had a seizure, and—"

"Oh, you can't never tell when she gets them," Mrs. Hart interrupted. "She stares off and I think, is this one or maybe not?"

I remembered Robert telling me about a little boy he'd treated who had petit mal seizures. No one knew what they were at first, because he'd just stare into space, ignoring everybody. His parents thought he was just being difficult.

Charlotte looked at me. "We'll get you working on that petition right away," she said, and I nodded although I was thinking, what does *Ivy* want? Shouldn't that count for something? "In the meantime," Charlotte said, "has Nurse Ann talked to Ivy about preventing pregnancy?"

"Nurse Ann don't know which way her head's screwed on," Mrs. Hart said. "She don't pay no attention to Ivy. She spends all her time lookin' over Baby William and tryin' to explain about them blue testing pills to me and the test tubes and all. I got to boil them tubes like I'm some kind of scientist. Stupid, if you ask me."

"Well, if Nurse Ann says it's important to do, I'd believe her."

"She give me some new salve for my knees, but it don't work much. Got some in my eye the other day and nearly went blind."

"All right." Charlotte jotted a note on her pad, then looked at me. "You'll call Nurse Ann to tell her Ivy may need contraceptives."

I nodded.

"I hear a boy at church got his eye on her," Mrs. Hart said. "He might be the one she seein' when she sneaks out."

"We'll get Ann out here sooner rather than later."

Ivy suddenly appeared on the porch. "Mrs. Werkman, these clothes is all too small. It's nice you brung them, but even Baby William's too big for the baby ones."

"Oh my," Charlotte said. "You girls have really grown now, haven't you?" She looked worried. "When was the last time you got your monthly, Ivy?"

I couldn't believe she'd ask her straight-out like that, but Ivy didn't seem shocked.

"Just last week," she said. "I ain't doin' it, Mrs. Werkman. I know Nonnie thinks I am but I ain't. I don't want no baby."

"Who do you see when you leave the house at night?" Mrs. Hart asked.

Ivy looked alarmed. "What do you mean?"

"You think I'm stupid, girl?" Mrs. Hart said. "I know you're sneaking out."

"I don't see nobody," Ivy said. "I just have to get out sometimes."

"I'm going to ask Nurse Ann to come talk to you about ways to keep from having a baby," Charlotte said.

"I know the way."

"Just in case, all right? And bring the bags of clothes back out here, please. Mrs. Forrester and I will find you some in larger sizes." She turned back to Mrs. Hart, notepad at the ready. "Now, about how much food is Mr. Gardiner giving you these days?" she asked.

"Hardly nothin'," Mrs. Hart said, turning her head away from us as though she heard a sound, or maybe didn't want to look Charlotte in the eye when she answered. "Odds and ends from time to time. Whatever they have laying around."

"Like what, for example?" Charlotte asked. She'd told me any gifts of food needed to be subtracted from the welfare money the family received. We also needed to take their garden into account, since they could grow some of their own vegetables.

Ivy had brought the bags back to the porch and her grandmother looked at her. "What did Mr. Gardiner give us the last time, Ivy?" she asked. "Little scrap of ham?"

"Right," Ivy said. "And some turnips."

"That's about it. So don't go cuttin' our money over a couple of turnips." She motioned to where Charlotte was writing.

"And how much have you made this week?" She directed her question to Ivy.

"Twenty-five cents an hour," she said. "And I work from eight to five."

"You ain't worked that many hours!" her grandmother scolded. "Pity's sake, girl. Don't make them take more off than they have to."

I knew Ivy and Mary Ella and the Jordan family made less than the other workers, because Mr. Gardiner allowed them to stay in their houses for free. "He's a very generous man," Charlotte had told me.

"May we take a look inside?" Charlotte asked Mrs. Hart now. It was one of those questions that could only be answered with a "yes." It was clear who was holding all the cards here.

Mrs. Hart got to her feet and hobbled ahead of us into the house. The kitchen was similar to the Jordans', except there was no cot. Little William sat on the floor of the room crying his eyes out. Ivy squatted next to him, trying to comfort him, but he barely seemed to notice her.

Charlotte and I peered into their cupboards and their refrigerator, and I squirmed with discomfort at the way we were intruding into their lives. It was demeaning. I tried to imagine what it would be like to have someone like me—a total stranger—push her way into my kitchen, making judgments about how I lived and what I bought with the little money I had.

I remembered the conversation I'd had in bed with Robert the night before. He worried I might be seen as more of an intruder than a helper when I went into strangers' houses.

"We seem welcome wherever we go," I said, but that was not quite the truth. Most people did seem glad to see us coming, since we rarely showed up with empty arms. They liked and trusted Charlotte and my admiration for her was growing by the hour. But one old-timer chased us back to Charlotte's car brandishing an ax, telling us he was providing for his granddaughters and didn't need our help, and a few other people seemed wary, although they let us in their houses and talked to us. They definitely didn't trust *me* yet, though.

We were still in the kitchen when another girl appeared in the open back doorway. One look at her stopped my breath. She stood there, the fading gold sunlight illuminating her wild blond hair. Her eyes were sky blue, her perfect full lips a study in symmetry.

I stepped back against the table with a gasp. *Teresa?*

In one second, the charged, surreal moment was over as the girl walked into the room and became herself—Mary Ella Hart. She glided past me in two long strides that barely seemed to touch the floor and picked William up in her arms. She cuddled him, burying her face in his neck, and his crying stopped as if by magic.

"Mary Ella, this is Mrs. Forrester," Mrs. Hart said. "She's gonna take over for Mrs. Werkman."

Mary Ella glanced at me but I didn't think she really saw me. She had eyes for her little son only, and watching them I felt profoundly moved. *Madonna and child.* William pressed one pudgy hand to her cheek and she turned her head to kiss his palm. There was a bond between them that touched me deeply. It nearly made me want to throw away my pills and have a child of my own.

Charlotte and I walked back across the pasture, then through the darkening woods. I felt different walking away from the house than when we had walked toward it. Changed in a way no other home visit had changed me.

Charlotte was ticking off on her fingers what needed to be done for the family.

"We have to find larger-sized clothing. And call Ann Laing. That rash on Baby William . . . I bet it's the laundry soap they're using to wash his clothes. Ann needs to check it and also bring Ivy contraceptives, just in case. And we need to talk with Davison Gardiner to find out exactly how much he's supplementing their food and what he's paying them for their work on the farm."

"Charlotte . . ." I couldn't quite organize my thoughts, and she waited patiently while I tried to find the words. "What does that matter, really?" I said finally. "They have nothing. They have *less* than nothing. So what if he gives them two turnips instead of one?"

Charlotte nodded. "I felt the same way when I was new at this," she said. It was very dusky in the woods, but I could still see the small smile on her lips. "I know it seems picky, but these are your taxes and mine going to help these people. And if you multiply their need by all the other needy families in Grace County and all the extra turnips . . . well, I'm sure you can see how that adds up."

If I thought about the big picture, counting every penny made sense. But if I thought about those four unfortunate human beings in that little house . . . well, that was something else again.

"We can't take that little boy away from them," I said. It had been one thing to talk about placing William in foster care before I'd met him. Now that I'd seen him and seen the love his mother had for him, it was unimaginable.

"He doesn't stand a chance there," Charlotte said.

"Mary Ella clearly loves him."

"All the love in the world doesn't put food on the table," Charlotte said. "Those three can barely take care of themselves, much less a child. A good foster home could make a world of difference for William."

"That would kill Mary Ella," I said.

"And maybe save William," Charlotte said. "Trust me. The only member of the Hart family who stands a chance is Ivy, but not if she starts having babies."

We walked in silence for a few minutes. Just when I was wondering if we'd ever get out of the woods, she suddenly asked, "What happened back there?"

"Back . . . at the Harts' house?" I knew exactly what she meant, but not how to answer.

"When Mary Ella walked in," she said. "You seemed . . . upset or . . . I'm not sure what."

"She reminded me of someone," I said. "It surprised me, that's all. She's so beautiful."

"It's the beautiful ones who are the real problem," she said.

"What do you mean?"

"Beauty and mental retardation are a dangerous combination in a girl. They can be taken advantage of so easily. We need to help girls like Mary Ella."

We were finally to the car and I was relieved to drop the bags back into Charlotte's trunk. We drove slowly down the dirt road. Tobacco fields stretched to infinity on either side of us. There were no workers now, with sunset close upon us. I felt inexplicably sad, a heavy weight around my shoulders that made it hard to breathe.

We rode in silence for a few minutes and when we came to a corner, Charlotte pointed toward a man walking along the side of the road. He was a large man with thinning brown hair and a sluggish gait. Behind him, he dragged a small block of wood on a string.

"I've seen him before," Charlotte said. "I've seen him closer up. That block of wood has a duck face painted on it. It's his toy. He pulls it around with him everywhere."

I could hardly speak. "It doesn't even have wheels on it," I said.

Charlotte nodded. "It's only a block of wood." She looked at me. "That"—she pointed in the man's direction—"that's William Hart in twenty years if we don't get him help now."

10

Ivy

Mary Ella walked home with me from the tobacco barn on Thursday, and I was glad she wasn't going off on her own like usual. Eli'd had his eye on her every time he brung the sled to the barn today. When the day laborers looked in her direction—and they always did because there was something about Mary Ella that made them stare—Eli'd walk between them, blocking her from their eyes. Eli himself, though, looked at her like nobody's business, while Henry Allen didn't never look at me at all, which is how we planned it. We didn't want to raise no suspicion. You'd never know how deep the feelings was between us. Even Mary Ella didn't know. We wasn't the kind of sisters that told each other every thought in our heads, no, sir.

I put my hand in my shorts pocket and felt Henry Allen's note there. I picked it up from the fence post after dinner but never got a chance to open it. That note was calling my name and I wanted to pull it out and read whatever he wrote so bad, but not with Mary Ella walking beside me. She hummed a song she always sung to Baby William and she walked fast. I knew she wanted to get to him. Why some days she'd go wandering off and other days hurry home to her child was a mystery.

"Someone's here," she said, when we turned the corner of the path toward the woods. Sure enough, a white car was parked at the side of the dirt road. I didn't see the dents and rust on it till we got closer.

"That's Nurse Ann's car," I said.

"She's gonna check Baby William!" Mary Ella took off at a run. She loved when Nurse Ann came with her thermometer and scale and that thing she used to listen to our hearts. She loved it because Nurse Ann paid lots of attention to Baby William. I wasn't in no hurry to see her, though. She'd ask me personal things I didn't want to talk about. I didn't mind so much when Mrs. Werkman asked me questions about my monthly. I'd learned to say I got it a week or two ago and that would make her stop asking. Truth was, I didn't keep no track. No need with Henry Allen pulling out the way he did.

Once Mary Ella disappeared into the woods, I took the folded piece of paper from my pocket and stopped walking to read it. He wrote it in pencil. He had nice handwriting for a boy. I could always read it easy.

It's hard being around you all day and not talking to you or specially not touching you. I know your there, though. I can feel it when your around. Don't even need to see you to know your there because I feel happy and just know. I have to check the burners tonight, so meet at the green barn at midnight. Come if you can. PS did you know Monterey has an aquarium?

I started walking again, smiling now. Them was a lot of words for Henry Allen to write. Usually he just said about what time we could meet. I liked when he wrote all that about wanting to touch me. It made my body heat up, thinking about it. I didn't like meeting in one of the barns, though. It meant walking a far piece out in the open in the middle of the night, and I was afraid somebody would see my lantern.

When I got home, Nurse Ann was sitting at the table, looking inside Baby William's ears and tapping on his belly. Mary Ella held him on her lap, her chin resting on his curly black hair. Mary Ella hung on Nurse Ann's words, worshipping her, like. Nurse Ann looked at me when I walked into the room. "I want to talk with you when I'm done with William, Ivy," she said, smiling, like she couldn't wait. "So don't go away."

"I'm right here," I said, though I was eyeing the back door, wondering if I could go out there and sweep the yard or do anything to get away before she had a chance to talk to me.

Nurse Ann had really long, dark hair, almost the same color as

Baby William's. Usually she wore it in a long braid down her back but today it was just tied back kind of loose. "He's putting on too much weight," she said, wrapping her fingers around Baby William's arm. "What are you feeding him?"

"He's just naturally a big boy," Mary Ella said.

"He's gonna eat us out of house and home," Nonnie said. She sat at the other end of the table, peeling tomatoes for canning.

"How do you know he's hungry?" Nurse Ann asked. "How does he let you know?"

"He cries," Mary Ella said.

"Little boys can cry for lots of reasons besides hunger," Nurse Ann said. "This rash." She looked at the splotches on his chest. "Have you been washing your clothes with something new? Some new detergent?"

"Same old soap," Nonnie said.

"Maybe prickly heat," Nurse Ann said. "Is he scratching it a lot?"

"Yes, ma'am," I said.

"Not too much." Mary Ella looked at me like I said something mean about her baby.

"I'm gonna sweep the yard," I said.

"You stay here," Nurse Ann warned me, and I gave up on escaping and sat down at the table.

"You really need to stop calling him 'Baby William,'" Nurse Ann said. "He's two now. Not a baby any longer and you don't want folks calling him 'Baby William' when he's ten years old, now do you?"

"We'll worry about that when he's ten," Nonnie said.

Nurse Ann reached into her bag and pulled out a brown glass bottle. "Put this on his rash three times a day," she said to Mary Ella.

"I need more of that salve for my knees," Nonnie said. "It only works if I put it on thick enough and then I run out right quick."

"I have more for you," Nurse Ann said. She reached into her bag again and pulled out a tube of Nonnie's salve. "You don't need all that much. Just rub it in good."

"Only works about ten minutes," Nonnie said, "but them ten minutes is a blessing."

"I'm sorry I don't have anything better to offer. You take the Bufferin every four hours?"

"I take it regular enough."

"No more than every four hours," Nurse Ann said. "Now about your sugar. I brought more of those urine testing tablets for you. How is that working out?"

"Just fine. The pee always turns blue, so it's fine."

"Sometimes it's green," I said.

Nonnie cut me a glare. "She don't know the difference between green and blue," she said.

"Nonnie," I said. "You've got to tell the honest truth." I looked at Nurse Ann. "She don't understand how important it is."

"Well, Ivy's right, Mrs. Hart. If your urine's turning green, you need to be more careful with what you eat. And if it turns orange, then you need to be extremely careful and try to get more exercise. And call me then, because we might need to talk about changing medication. How often are you seeing the green rather than the blue?"

"Hardly never," Nonnie said.

Nurse Ann looked at me and I felt caught in the middle between them. I shrugged. I'd tell Nurse Ann the truth about Nonnie and her testing when she had her talk with me. Better to talk about Nonnie than myself, anyway. I'd tell her how Nonnie made extra biscuits to eat in the morning. I'd been eating them myself to keep her from having too many and making her sugar go up.

Nurse Ann stood up. "Ivy," she said, "let's go sit outside a bit." She picked up her nurse bag and I followed her outside, feeling like a hog going to slaughter. She led me to the old wooden bench by the side of the house, but I pointed to the chairs under the oak tree. You could hear people talking on that bench. I didn't want Nonnie or Mary Ella listening in on anything I said.

"Nonnie's not telling you the truth about them tests on her pee," I said, sitting down in one of the rickety old chairs. I'd take over the conversation right quick, I thought. Keep it off myself.

"I figured that," she said. "How often are the results green?"

"Pretty much always. Sometimes half blue and half green, but green more likely than not."

"And orange?"

"I ain't never seen it turn orange," I said. "I'm scared about it doing that. And she don't always boil them test tubes like she should. She just rinses 'em out sometimes."

Nurse Ann let out a sigh and looked back toward the house. "Do you know I couldn't find William when I arrived today? Your grandmother didn't know where he was."

"But you found him okay." I didn't want her making a big to-do about nothing.

"He needs to be watched more closely."

I shrugged. What was I supposed to say? Nonnie and Baby William couldn't last all day at the barn, and me and Mary Ella had to work. We couldn't be two places at once.

Nurse Ann opened her bag in her lap. "I have some things here for you," she said, handing me a paper bag. "Look inside and I'll explain how you use them."

I opened it up and pulled out a box that said SPERMICIDAL JELLY on the side.

"This is not the kind of jelly you eat," she said. "It kills sperm. Sperm comes from the boy and that's what makes babies."

"I know that." I wished I was someplace else.

"Now, here"—she opened the box and pulled out a long tube—"is the applicator you use to insert the jelly in your vagina." She went into a long description of how to do that and I knew my cheeks was red, listening to her. This talk was turning out worse than I expected.

She reached in the bag one more time and brought out little packages that said TROJAN on them. "These are rubbers," she said. "The boy puts these on. They're more protective than the jelly. And the best protection is using both of them together."

"You mean protection from having a baby?" I wished she'd speak plain.

"That's right."

I handed the bag back to her. "I don't need none of this. Mary Ella's the one you should be talkin' to. She already got herself a baby and any day she's gonna end up with another for sure."

"I'm not worried about Mary Ella right now. I'm worried about you."

"No need to be. I ain't doing nothing."

"Well, just in case, I want you to have these things and I can bring you more if you ever need more."

I didn't know why she wasn't giving these things to Mary Ella. I'd give them to her myself. I'd told Mary Ella about the pulling out being a way to have no more babies, and she just looked off into the blue yonder the way she always did, like she didn't hear me.

"All right," I said. Talking about this was making me think about being with Henry Allen tonight and I felt my face go hot again and turned away, not wanting Nurse Ann to see. "Are we done?"

"Yes," she said, "and I'll bring more when I come next time. Just in case."

I felt like she knew what I was thinking about Henry Allen and I stood up. "I got to sweep the yard," I said.

She looked up at me. "Are you upset about Mrs. Werkman not being your caseworker any longer?"

"Don't matter," I said, though I felt an ache inside me. It wasn't like I loved her or anything, but she knew us so well. I didn't like nothing about that new lady. Not her swingy gold hair or her nylon stockings or her smile that looked like it was painted on her face. She was a city girl who didn't know nothing. Lita Jordan met her and said she was nice, but I could tell she was worried, too. Nonnie said, "That girl ain't nothing but a little mouse all dressed up," and that was a right perfect description.

"I'm sure her replacement will be just as good," Nurse Ann said. "I hear she's young. Maybe she'll understand a young girl very well."

"She didn't say nothing when she was here."

"She's learning," Nurse Ann said. "The first time I visited patients with my supervisor, I was really quiet myself. Now you can't get me to shut up, right? And sometimes you wish I would."

I couldn't help it. I smiled. "Yes, ma'am," I said, and she laughed.

"You take good care now, Ivy," she said, and even though she'd embarrassed me clear to kingdom come, I knew she wanted the best for me, and I carried the bag of things I didn't need into the house to find a place to hide them.

11

Jane

Robert straightened his tie as he came into the kitchen. I was sliding a blueberry pancake off the griddle, and he leaned over to kiss my cheek.

"I bet my beautiful wife is tired this morning," he said.

"Why do you say that?" I asked, turning off the burners on the stove.

"I think you were up half the night reading."

"Oh," I said, "did I wake you when I got up? I couldn't sleep." I was working my way through the stack of books I'd borrowed from Charlotte. The books had the same pull on me as a bestselling novel. "Have a seat, darling." I glanced at the kitchen clock as I carried his plate to the breakfast nook. We had half an hour before either of us had to leave for work and our maid, Angeline, arrived. That was good. We needed some relaxed time together and we hadn't had much of it in the four days since I started working.

He sat down at the table and I rested one hand on his shoulder as I poured coffee into his cup. I felt like we were in a photograph in a magazine—a picture of domestic bliss.

"There's a ball at the club in a few weeks." He pulled out his wallet and laid eight twenties on the table. "Go shopping this weekend while I'm playing golf," he said. "Buy yourself something fancy. You can knock everybody's socks off at the party."

"You're so sweet," I said, sitting down across from him.

"I wish you'd shop with some of the wives from the club." He opened his cloth napkin and put it on his lap. "I know they love doing that. Shopping together."

"Maybe soon," I said noncommittally. One of the wives had stopped by the house to nudge me about joining the Junior League. I told her the truth—right now I didn't have time because I was working. Then I cringed. She would tell her husband. Her husband would tell other people. And soon the word would be out that Robert Forrester's wife had to work such long, hard hours that she couldn't even join the Junior League. "I'll make a special effort to get to know some of the wives at the ball," I promised, "but I need to ask Mom to go shopping with me this time. She's so lonely without me living there."

He swallowed a bite of pancake. "So, what have you been reading about?"

I poured syrup over my own pancakes. "Well, last night I read about how to interview clients," I said. "You know, how to put them at ease. How to accept them without judging them. That sort of thing."

"Bedside Manner 101." Robert blotted his lips with his napkin. "They should teach that in medical school, but they don't."

"I guess a doctor wouldn't have time for all that listening."

"Very true."

"I'm really enjoying it, Robert," I said. "I like getting to meet so many different people."

"I'm glad," he said. "Really."

"I'm nervous about when my two weeks with Charlotte are up, though. So much responsibility." I sipped my coffee. "I have to put together a petition for this program Charlotte told me about. Have you heard of the Eugenics Program?" Ever since meeting the Hart girls, I hadn't been able to put them out of my mind. From the eerie jolt of recognition when Mary Ella showed up in the doorway to the realization that I now held Ivy's future in my hands, they consumed my thoughts.

"I don't think so," Robert said. "I mean, I know eugenics is about improving the human race. Weeding out negative traits and encouraging the positive. But what does that have to do with your work?"

His definition didn't feel quite right to me. "Social workers can petition the Eugenics Board to get sterilization surgery for their clients," I said. "But it's not like it was in Nazi Germany," I hastened to add. "It's not like anyone's trying to improve a race of people."

Robert frowned at me. "You sound upset," he said.

He was right, and I studied my plate, trying to figure out what was making me so uncomfortable. "I think it's the way you defined eugenics," I said. "You made it sound . . . I don't know. Manipulative and controlling."

"The way *you* describe this program doesn't sound like it should be called 'eugenics,' then." He cut his pancake with his fork. "It sounds like it's just a way to help people limit the size of their families. I think that's a fine idea."

That wasn't quite right, either. "I guess it's more than that." I really felt awkward now. "One of the girls Charlotte had sterilized is only seventeen. She has a two-year-old son, and she's mildly mentally retarded. She has a fifteen-year-old epileptic sister who Charlotte wants to have sterilized, too, and I'm the person who'll have to arrange it."

"All of these people are on welfare, right?" he asked.

"Yes."

"Then this sounds like an excellent program, and you've changed my opinion of Charlotte." He drank the last of his orange juice and smiled at me. "Up till now I thought of her as someone who was simply working my wife too hard."

"Why do you think it's an excellent program?" I was relieved that he thought so, but I wanted to know why he felt that way.

"Because it prevents more children from living off the government tit, excuse my French."

I wrinkled my nose. "Robert, that's really not fair. These kids would starve without—"

"You know my background, Jane," he said. "You've seen the house I grew up in."

"There's nothing wrong with the house you grew up in." His parents still lived in the modest three-bedroom home in Atlanta.

He swallowed a bite of pancake. "I had to work hard for everything I've achieved," he said.

"I know you did."

"Nobody gave me a handout. I did it all on my own."

"I know." I felt as though I'd opened a tap I hadn't known was there. "But you can't compare where you came from to where the people I'm working with come from."

He rubbed the back of his neck, as though the conversation were tiring him. "We don't do them any favors by giving them money for nothing," he said, "and the fewer kids they have, the better."

"Why do you do your charity work every month, then?" I asked. "Why do you treat sick kids for no charge?"

"Because I can't just look the other way, but I tell you, Jane, most of those kids would have been better off if they'd never been conceived. So I think your Eugenics Program is a great idea." He looked at his watch. "And now I've got to run." He stood up and folded his napkin on the table. "*Our* children, however, can't wait to be conceived." He leaned over to give me a kiss. "Maybe tonight?"

During my first three days in the field with Charlotte, I thought I'd seen enough poverty to last a lifetime, but on the fourth day, my eyes were truly opened. We visited a family with ten people living in one room. Another in which the parents had both died of pneumonia and the seventeen-year-old son was struggling to hold the family together. Those children would have to go to foster homes, Charlotte told me as we drove away. We'd have to work on placements for them right away. "While a little boy like William Hart might benefit from a foster placement," Charlotte said, "these kids are desperate for it."

"Could we somehow get them enough money and donations to keep them together?" I asked. I hated tearing a family apart.

Charlotte glanced at me. "There you go, getting soft on me again, Mrs. Forrester," she said with a smile. "We need you, so I hope you can toughen up, but if this job is going to take too much out of you to do it right, now is the time to reconsider."

"I'll be fine," I assured her . . . and myself.

Charlotte stopped the car to check her map. We were on a thickly wooded dirt road and hadn't seen another car for twenty minutes. When we were out in the middle of nowhere like this, I wondered how I would manage alone. Charlotte had been doing this alone for a very long time, I reminded myself. If she could do it, so could I.

She drove a short distance farther and pulled to the side of the road. "This looks like as close as we're going to get to this house," she said. "I haven't been here before. The preacher of the local Baptist church told me about the family and asked me to see them. He said they have no electricity and cook in their fireplace."

"Oh my," I said, trying to imagine. "How many children?"

"A handicapped father and his wife and three little ones." She opened her car door and turned her back to me, slipping on her galoshes. I did the same. I now wore my saddle shoes to work. I'd never expected to have a job where I'd wear saddle shoes, much less galoshes, but they made sense for tromping through the fields and woods of Grace County.

"Let's see what we can see," Charlotte said, getting out of the car.

The trail reminded me of the wooded footpath to the Harts' house, until we came to a ramshackle little bridge above a small ravine.

"Good heavens!" Charlotte said, which was exactly what I was thinking. "They don't pay us enough for this work." She laughed. "Perhaps we should cross this one at a time?" she said, taking a tentative step onto the bridge. She gripped the railing which ran on only one side of the bridge and which was constructed of branches in all shapes and sizes.

"You're sure this is the right way?" I wasn't afraid of crossing the bridge—even if it collapsed, it wasn't all that far to the shallow ravine below—but I couldn't imagine a family using the bridge regularly.

"Yes, I was warned about this bridge, if you can call it that."

Charlotte was halfway across when one of the boards gave way beneath her foot. I watched in horror as her right leg slipped through the hole while her left leg twisted beneath her with a terrible crack. "Oh my God, oh my God!" she cried. "I can't move. My leg!"

I rushed forward as quickly as I dared on the uneven boards of the bridge. By the time I reached her, I knew we were in terrible trouble.

Her left leg was bent at an unnatural angle, her arms outstretched to keep her from completely falling through the gap in the bridge. She looked like a broken marionette.

"Oh, Charlotte!" I said. "Let me help you out of there."

"Don't touch my leg!" she said

"I won't," I reassured her. I could barely look at her leg. The pain had to be excruciating.

"I'm going to try to lift you out," I said, wondering how I would manage. "Try to relax and go limp."

"No, you won't be able to. You'll need to go for help."

"Let me try." I stood behind her and reached beneath her arms and pulled upward. I felt the strain in my back and worried the entire bridge would give way and toss both of us into the ravine below, but it held. I was amazed at my own strength, and I was able to get her body high enough that she could pull her right leg from the gap. I lowered her as gently as my back would allow, but she still cried out in pain. "Lie down, Charlotte," I said.

She had no fight in her at all, and she let me help her lie down.

"I need to get help," I said. "Do you know how close we are to the house?"

She didn't answer. Her face had gone absolutely white, her eyes closed, and for a frightening moment I thought I might have killed her by lifting her out of the bridge. I felt her wrist for a pulse. It was slow, but it was there. I had a terrible sense of déjà vu, remembering the accident two years ago, but I shook my head to clear it and got to my feet. I had to keep my wits about me. I forced myself to look at her leg, already swollen above her boots. I didn't dare move it.

"I'll be back as soon as I can," I said, making my way across the other side of the bridge and onto the path. The undergrowth was even thicker here, and I moved as quickly as I could, hoping I'd be able to find the family hidden in these woods.

"Help!" I called. "We need help!"

I had to slow down or risk tripping over vines and tree roots. Suddenly something leaped at me from the woods on my right and I screamed, startled. A dog! Big and yellow and friendly. The family had to be nearby. "Hello!" I shouted. "We need help!" The dog headed down the path ahead of me like a guide.

I broke out of the trees and saw the shack in front of me, but the structure barely registered in my mind. Instead, my eyes landed on the man sitting in the doorway, his shotgun aimed in my direction.

I stopped running, raising my hands over my head. "Don't shoot me!" I said.

"What you want?" he asked.

"I'm a caseworker from the Department of Public Welfare," I said. "There are two of us and my friend fell on your bridge. Her leg is broken. I need help getting her to our car so I can drive her to the hospital. Can someone help me?"

"We don't need no social work," he said. I wished he'd lower the gun. My hands were still in the air and I pictured the whole scene in an instant. Charlotte would die on the bridge. I would die from a gunshot wound. No one would ever find us. Robert would never know what happened to me.

"Please," I said. "Right now the important thing is to help my friend. I can't carry her back to the car alone."

A woman appeared at the man's side, and I felt as though I were looking at one of those old Depression-era photos of deep, inescapable poverty. Her dark hair was pulled back in a bun and she wore a faded gray dress covered by a torn apron. She carried a baby in her arms, and two little children held on to her skirt.

"My man cain't help you," she said. "Got a broke back hisself."

"Maybe you, then?" I pleaded.

The man lowered the gun to his lap. "Git the sled," he said to his wife. "Tie the little ones."

I lowered my arms and watched as she handed him the baby, then tied a rope around the waist of each of her screaming children and handed him the end of it. I was more amazed than appalled by her inventiveness. She walked around the back of the house and returned a moment later carrying an old sled, the type kids would use, one of its slats missing.

"Where's she at?" she said, walking toward me with the sled.

"On the little bridge," I said. "Thank you so much. I'm very worried about her."

"Ain't no choice, far as I can see," she said.

We walked in silence through the woods, and I remembered why Charlotte and I were there. "We can get you some money to help feed your children," I said. "Get them some clothing. Maybe other things you need."

"Don't need no charity."

I glanced at her. Her thin face was set in a determined scowl. *Think of your children,* I wanted to say, but decided I couldn't afford to alienate her right now. The first order of business was to get help for Charlotte. We could worry about the family later.

We reached the bridge where Charlotte lay still and pale.

"That leg's busted bad," the woman said, and she had the good sense to whisper it. "Never be the same. Like my man's broke back."

I knelt next to Charlotte. "Charlotte?" I said. "Can you hear me?"

She groaned, two frown lines between her eyebrows. I was glad to see her respond even if she was in agony. "We're going to lift you onto a sled and take you back to the car and then I'll drive you to the hospital. You're going to be fine," I added, though I worried I was lying. I feared the woman was right when she said Charlotte's leg would never be the same.

Together, the woman and I lifted Charlotte onto the sled, the bridge creaking and moaning beneath us as we worked. The sled was much too short, and Charlotte's legs hung from the end. One of us would have to pull the sled, while the other bent over and held her legs to keep them from dragging on the ground.

"I'll pull," the woman said.

It was slow going up the wooded path, and my back ached from trying to keep Charlotte's legs from falling. I was overjoyed to see her car come into view. Together, the woman and I managed to get Charlotte into the backseat. She'd stopped moaning by then, and when I got a good look at her on the backseat, I realized she was only partially conscious. Was this shock? People died of shock. I knew that.

"Do you know where the nearest hospital is?" I asked the woman, wiping the sweat from my forehead with my hand.

She shook her head. "Never been to no hospital," she said.

"I can't thank you enough," I said. "I don't know what I would have done without your help."

She looked in the back window of Charlotte's car. "She ain't never gonna be the same," she said again, and she turned to go back to her family.

12

Ivy

I felt right nervous walking down the lane near midnight. There was enough of a moon that I could put out my lantern, but I still felt like somebody could see me walking past the dark tobacco fields in my nightgown, nothing else on but my shoes. I hurried, trying to shake off the feeling I wasn't alone.

I didn't know why some of the barns was called what they was. The south barn—the one that was curing the tobacco right now and where Henry Allen had to check the burners—wasn't the most southern barn. And the empty green barn where we was going to meet wasn't green. The Christmas barn was the only one that made sense, since it was built around Christmastime long ago. None of them had any paint on them at all. But everybody knew which barn was which. We grew up knowing.

To my right stretched rows and rows of glittery tobacco and I thought of Mama's fairies again. Nights like this, I could believe they was truly out there and I just hoped they was good and not evil. I walked faster and was glad when I could see the barns and knew I was almost there. Once I was past the south barn a ways, I could see a light peeking out under the door of the green barn. He was there already. I started to run, my lantern banging against my leg.

Henry Allen must of heard me, because he opened the door when I got close, grabbed my hand, and pulled me inside real quick so nobody would see the light. He kissed me, his hands on my sides where I liked them, close enough to my breasts that it felt real good but not so close that we was rushing.

"Did you check the burners yet?" I asked, when we stopped kissing. I hoped he had so we could take our time. I liked when we could talk after.

"Have to check them after you go," he said. "We ain't got much time. Daddy's still up and he'll come looking if I don't get in soon." He looked in the direction of the farmhouse like he could see through the walls of the barn. "Sorry to make you come all the way out here. Ain't even got a book to show you."

"Hush up." I started kissing him again. If we didn't have much time, I wasn't wasting it talking.

I smelled smoke. Henry Allen was inside me, moving fast and wild, and I had to pull his body tight against me to get him to stop. "Henry Allen!" I shook him, but he didn't hear me. He couldn't hear nothing when he got like that.

I pushed against his shoulders. "Henry Allen!" I nearly shouted, and this time he stopped.

"What?" He could hardly get his breath.

"Do you smell that?"

He raised his head and sniffed the air, but by that time I was rolling him off me. Something was on fire.

"Damn!" Henry Allen jumped up. "Get dressed!"

I got up quick and found my nightgown where I'd tossed it on the floor. I could hear voices outside.

"Henry Allen!" his mama was calling, and her voice was loud and scared. *"Henry Allen!"* She was practically screaming it, and I put my hand over my mouth to keep from screaming myself. Something terrible was going on.

Once Henry Allen got his clothes on, he ran out of the barn with his flashlight, leaving me in the black darkness. I didn't dare go out there, not where Mrs. Gardiner could see me. I wondered if I could sneak out the other door of the barn, but I was afraid to move.

"I'm here, Mama!" Henry Allen shouted.

I peeked outside the door and could see the south barn up in flames. It had to be burning a while to look like that, and gold embers floated like fireflies in the air. Mr. Gardiner was out there now. I could see him clear as day with the light from the fire. He shouted and waved his arms, and I saw him smack Henry Allen across the face, yelling something about the burners. He looked toward the green barn and I ducked back inside, scared he might of seen me. I stood inside the door, shaking, wondering what I should do. If I left, they'd see me and know what me and Henry Allen'd been up to. But it would only take one of them gold embers to land on the roof of the green barn to set it ablaze, too.

Through the crackling sound of the fire, I heard a siren and pictured the volunteer fire truck heading up Deaf Mule Road, turning onto the lane that ran through the fields. Louder and louder the siren got until it sounded like it was inside the barn with me, and I pressed my hands over my ears. Then I heard so much shouting, I couldn't make out one word from another. Could I just sneak out of the barn while everybody was paying attention to the fire? I cracked open the door and was suddenly knocked clear across the floor, like a boulder hit me. They was spraying the green barn! The water pounded against the door and made the whole building shake, and the sound was loud enough I couldn't hear myself hollering for them to stop and let me out. Water trickled in the roof and the walls, enough that my hair was soaked in no more than a minute. I tried to move away from the water coming down, but it was too dark to see any place that was dry. I ran to the other side of the barn to try that door, but it was locked from outside. I pounded against it.

"Let me out!" I screamed. "Help!" I knew nobody could hear me over the sound of the water and the fire and the yelling, and I sat down, curled up in a ball against the wall of the barn, my hands over my head, waiting for it to be over.

The water stopped as quick as it started and then I could hear the shouting again and I figured the firemen was moving on to another barn or maybe even the house. I was soaked, my nightgown stuck like tarpaper to my body as I walked toward the barn door. It opened before I got to it and two flashlights shined in my face so bright I had to cover my eyes.

"Ivy!" Henry Allen said.

"You little tramp!" his mama shouted. *"Tramp!"* She came into the barn and grabbed my arm, yanking me around like I was a flyswatter and she was trying to kill a fly.

"Leave her alone, Mama!" Henry Allen yelled, but his mama just pulled me out of the barn so hard I tripped over my feet and would of fallen if she didn't have such a tight hold on me.

"Go home!" Mrs. Gardiner shouted, letting go of my arm. Then she started hitting me and I turned and ran. "Go home, you terrible girl!" she shouted after me.

I ran as fast as I could past the smoldering south barn, my shoes slapping the mud left by the fire hoses. I forgot my lantern in the barn, so I ran through the darkness past the fields and the fairies and then through the woods and the pasture. I let myself into the house as quiet as I could, trying to settle down my breathing, because it was loud enough to wake the dead by then.

Nonnie was asleep on the couch. Mary Ella and Baby William was still asleep, too. I was lucky they didn't get woke up by the sirens. My nightgown was stuck to my body and I worried it had turned invisible, it was so thin and wet, and Mrs. Gardiner would of seen everything. I wanted to die, thinking about it. I peeled the nightgown off and put on the only other one I had—my winter nightgown that would of been way too hot if I hadn't been wet and shaking. I climbed into bed next to Baby William, and then I started to cry. I kept it quiet, but I couldn't help it. I didn't know what would happen now that Henry Allen's mama and daddy knew about us. Did tonight spell the end of me and him?

If Mrs. Gardiner told Nonnie . . . I closed my eyes. I couldn't even think about it. For all I knew, tonight could spell the end of my life.

13

Jane

I was as tired as I'd ever been as I drove to Grace County the day after Charlotte's terrible accident. I'd spent all afternoon and evening in the hospital waiting room with her niece, a nervous girl about my age, as we waited to hear the outcome of surgery on Charlotte's shattered leg. She'd fractured her tibia and would be in the hospital at least a week and then at home for several more. The one thing she would *not* be, for the next month at least, was my supervisor.

Over supper last night, Robert went very quiet when I told him what happened. I didn't mention the man with the shotgun, or at least I didn't mention the shotgun. Nor did I tell him about the woman tying her children to her husband. It just seemed like more than he needed to hear. The rickety bridge was quite enough.

"Jane," he said gently, once I'd finished telling him about Charlotte's surgery. "This is the kind of thing I've been worried about. Please, darling," he pleaded. "Please quit this job. I hate it for you. I hate that you're traipsing around God only knows where. What if you'd been going to see that family alone and you broke your leg? You'd still be lying there. I can't stand to think about it."

That very thought had kept me awake half the night. "If I ever feel like I'm in a dangerous situation, I'll turn around," I promised. "If I come to a bridge like that one, for instance, I won't cross it. Don't worry. I'll use my head."

He set down his fork. "I just don't understand, Jane," he said. "Why are you so driven to do this?"

"It's the way I was brought up," I said with a shrug. "You're supposed to help people, even if it's hard to do. *Especially* if it's hard to do."

"You're not part of that family anymore," he said.

I bristled. "I'll always be part of that family."

He touched his napkin to his lips, set it on the table and stood up. "You know, Janie," he said, "it's not just you in this marriage. Think about that, okay?"

We didn't talk again all evening. He went to bed early, and I called my mother, suddenly missing her. I wanted to tell her everything that was going on—the horror of Charlotte's accident, the disagreement with Robert. But she said she'd been going through old photograph albums, and I could hear her sadness. There was no way I could burden her with my own problems.

I stayed up late reading more of Charlotte's books, Robert's words playing over and over in my mind. Was I being selfish? Maybe. But quitting now was unthinkable to me. Even if I wanted to quit, the department needed me more than ever with Charlotte gone.

Fred Price was waiting for me when I arrived at the office. He actually opened the main door for me as though he'd been watching for my car from the window. His face was grim. "How are you holding up?" he asked, walking with me to my office.

"I'm fine," I said. "Just worried about Charlotte."

He pointed to the two briefcases I was carrying, one in each hand. "I was hoping you had Charlotte's," he said as we reached my office. "I was able to talk with her this morning."

"Oh!" I set the briefcases down on Charlotte's desk. "She was awake? How is she doing?"

"Tremendous amount of pain, so she was quite groggy from medication. I'm sorry your orientation was cut short, but she said you'll be fine. She said you need to toughen up, but that will come with time."

I wanted to ask him if I could spend another week in the field with

Gayle or Paula. I didn't feel at all ready to be on my own, but I also didn't want to seem that weak. "At the hospital yesterday, they told me she'd be out at least a month," I said.

He nodded, running a hand over his balding head. "So much for my retirement," he said with a reluctant smile. "I'm going to divide the bulk of her caseload between Gayle and Paula, and I'll take a few cases myself. Charlotte suggested that you focus on the cases you've already dealt with for now." He pulled a piece of notepaper from his shirt pocket, unfolded it and handed it to me. "These folks," he said.

I looked down to see *"Jordan, Hart,"* and a few other familiar names written on the paper. "Okay." I nodded.

"She said you could try to see Mr. Gardiner Monday. Do you know who that is?"

"He owns the farm where the Jordans and Harts live," I said.

"She said you could get information about those two families from him and see if he has any concerns about them. She also suggested you start working on the sterilization petition for one of your clients. Ivy Hart?"

"I'm really not sure how to do that yet," I said.

"Speak to Paula," he said. "She's our resident expert when it comes to the Eugenics Board."

Ah, so Paula was the one. I'd guessed wrong.

"Sorry you're getting thrown to the wolves so soon," he said, his hand on my doorknob. "I suggest you just stay in the office today. Familiarize yourself with the cases. Speak to the public health nurse. Then Monday you can head back to the field. Good plan?"

I nodded, honestly relieved that I didn't have to go out today. Charlotte and that bridge were still too fresh in my mind. "Good plan," I agreed. I flashed him a confident smile that I managed to keep on my face until I saw him disappear down the hall. Then I shut my door and stood with my back against it. *Oh my God,* I thought. I looked at Charlotte's briefcase, then at the file cabinet next to her desk. I'd seen inside that file cabinet a few times. It was bursting with manila folders. I was glad I didn't have to tackle her whole caseload. Yet.

Sitting down at my desk, I pulled out the thick folder on the Hart family. Leafing through it, I came to the notarized permission form signed by Winona Hart, and was stunned to see the X where her sig-nature should be. She was illiterate. Did she understand what she was signing? I remembered the conversation between her and Charlotte, though, where she pleaded with Charlotte to hurry up and get Ivy sterilized. She knew. She knew exactly what she was signing.

There was a knock on my office door, and when I opened it, Paula stood in front of me, smiling, a folder in her hand. "Fred said maybe I could help you with the petition," she said. "Can I come in?"

"Yes, please!" I was relieved to see her. "I'm feeling a trifle over-whelmed right now."

"I can't believe it about Charlotte," she said. "Sounds like you saved her life."

"Well, not really." I didn't feel the least bit like a hero. "I couldn't have done it alone."

She patted my arm. "I just want to reassure you that things like that are very, very rare. We see some bad stuff, but it's not usually *life threat-ening*. Good heavens." She giggled.

I smiled myself. I liked Paula so much. Maybe it was because she looked like me or was close to my age, or maybe it was because she seemed to have a deep well of happiness inside her that made me feel good. Whatever the reason, I felt instantly calmer in her presence. I bet her clients felt the same way.

"So." She sat down in Charlotte's chair and I sat in my own. "I brought you a copy of the petition so you could see what it looks like." She handed me a short stack of papers.

I leafed through them. There were forms galore. One for the physi-cian, one for the director of the department, one for the guardian's permission, and several for me, the caseworker. "Wow," I said. "There's so much to fill out."

"It's not as bad as it looks," she said. "You just need to make sure to get the forms filled out by all the appropriate people. The main one you have to do yourself is that one." She pointed to the form I was studying. It asked me to describe the "home situation," the "client's abilities," the "community environment," and on and on and on.

I looked up at Paula. "I barely know any of this information," I said. "Just the few things Charlotte's told me."

"So, you'll learn it," Paula said with an easygoing shrug of her shoulders.

"Charlotte said you do a lot of these."

"Well, I wouldn't say a *lot*," she said with a laugh. "But I'm not afraid to use them when I think they're needed. Charlotte's really cautious, so if she says this client of yours needs it, I'd listen."

"She's only fifteen," I said.

Paula shrugged. "I petitioned for a ten-year-old last month and it was approved."

"Ten!"

"Profoundly retarded colored girl who was being taken advantage of by the boys in the neighborhood. It was only a matter of time before she got pregnant, and there was no way she'd be able to take care of a baby."

I thought of Ivy. "This girl, though . . . she's not profoundly retarded. She's not even retarded, actually. She's epileptic, and—"

"You can stop there. That's enough. They'll approve it." She looked at her watch. "I've got an appointment." She hopped up from the chair. "But I'll be in later if you need to talk." She pointed to the folder on my lap. "I'll leave that copy with you," she said. "Adios!"

"Bye," I said, as she left the office.

Once the door was closed, I sat staring at Charlotte's desk, wishing I could magically change what had happened the day before and bring her back.

You're supposed to help people, even if it's hard to do, I'd told Robert.

I reached for Charlotte's briefcase, opened it, and dug in.

14

Ivy

I hardly slept all night, and when Baby William started stirring and Mary Ella got up with him, I pretended I was asleep. I didn't want to face this day. I wasn't sure what all would happen, but it wasn't going to be good. I wished last night was a dream. What did they do to Henry Allen? His daddy was a whupper. He'd use the belt on him for sure.

Baby William was crying up a storm in the living room, drowning out Nonnie's voice and Mary Ella's and another one I could hear just faint, but I had the terrible feeling belonged to Mrs. Gardiner. I put my pillow over my head. I wanted to disappear.

I heard the front door slam and Nonnie's *thump-thump-tap* walk coming toward the bedroom, and I pulled the pillow tighter around my head.

"Fool!" she shouted, stomping into the room. "You damn, damn fool!" She started hitting on me with her cane and I was afraid she'd break one of my hands, but she smacked my hip through the covers the most and I grit my teeth together to keep from yelping. "Are you trying to get us kicked out of here?" she shouted. "Bloody stupid idiot! She told me everything. You ran around half naked and kept that boy from his duties and the barn burned down. Get up!" She cracked the cane across my hip hard enough to put tears in my eyes.

I pulled the pillow away from my face. "Stop hitting me!"

"Get up!"

"I will. Just stop hitting me."

I sat up slowly. I was a sweaty mess from trying to sleep in my winter nightgown all night and I could smell the smoke in my hair. But as bad as I was sure I looked, Nonnie looked worse. I'd seen her mad when Mary Ella turned up pregnant, but this was twice as bad. Her face was red and sweaty and her eyes was bugging out and her double chins shook. I got that worried feeling she was going to die on us, and this time it would be my fault.

"I'm sorry, Nonnie," I said.

She lifted the cane again and I covered my head with my arms and shut my eyes, but she must of changed her mind, and the hit didn't come.

"The Gardiners ain't giving you no ride to church Sunday," she said. "You have to find your own way from now on. And you better get up and get ready to go to the barn."

"To the barn?" How could I help with the barning today after what happened last night? "Nonnie, I can't go over there! They won't want me—"

"You get dressed and go over there. That's your punishment. Facing the Gardiners and facing what you made happen with that barn. You brung shame on us, Ivy Hart. Mary Ella, too, but she don't know no better. I thought you did."

She turned and stomped out of the room and I sat there feeling as low as I ever did. I didn't know how I was going to face Mr. Gardiner, but I could tell I didn't have no choice. I got up and started dressing.

We had one dresser in the room with three drawers. Mary Ella's was on top, mine was in the middle, and Nonnie and Baby William shared the one on the bottom. When I opened mine to get out my underwear, I saw a box of the spermicide jelly Nurse Ann had given me. Just one box. She gave me two. I opened Mary Ella's drawer and there it was. A box of spermicide jelly. I wasn't upset. I was glad. It wouldn't matter if a boy didn't pull out of her if she had that jelly. I'd make sure she always had some.

I walked into the living room where Mary Ella was rocking Baby

William in the old rocker my daddy made long ago, loving on him even though he was screaming.

"Why's he carrying on like that?" I asked. I wondered if she'd heard everything Mrs. Gardiner had to say to Nonnie. I supposed she did. My face felt hot, thinking about it.

"Don't know," Mary Ella said. "Why you carrying on like that, Baby William?" she asked him, but he couldn't hear her for the sound of his own screeching voice.

"Shut that boy up or I'll give him something to holler about," Nonnie said. She was standing in the door to the kitchen, eating a biscuit with jelly pouring out the middle of it. From where I stood, I could see the box of blue testing pills on the kitchen shelf and I knew it hadn't moved since the night before. I always set it just so, so I could tell if she got out the pill.

"Did you test your sugar yet this morning?" I asked her.

She looked at me like if she had a gun, she'd shoot me. "You don't tell me what to do, missy," she said. "How'd you think it feels having a lady like Mrs. Gardiner come tell me my granddaughter's nothing but trash?"

I hung my head. I didn't want to look at her no more. "Sorry, Nonnie," I said, again. I wanted to get a biscuit for myself, but didn't dare walk that close to her because I could tell she wasn't done with me yet. I'd go without breakfast this morning. My stomach was too knotted up to eat, anyhow.

"I told you, get dressed and go to the barn," Nonnie said. "Both of y'all."

"We got to get Baby William settled first," I said. If he kept carrying on like he was, Nonnie would kill him when me and Mary Ella left. "Did he eat?" I asked Mary Ella.

"He wouldn't eat nothing," Nonnie said.

I lifted him out of Mary Ella's arms and she tried to hang tight to him. "Let go!" I said to her. "Let me see that rash. Maybe that's what's bothering him."

"I already told Mary Ella to put that lotion on his rash," Nonnie said. "Did you do it, girl?"

"I done it," Mary Ella said.

I sat on the sofa and pulled Baby William's shirt over his head. His chest was fiery red, right up into his neck. "Oh, Baby William!" I was scared by the look of his chest. I pressed my hands to his skin and was shocked by how hot he felt. I didn't believe Mary Ella had put the lotion on him at all. "Bring me the lotion," I said. I'd put it on thick and if it didn't calm down by midday when we came home for dinner, we'd have to call Nurse Ann.

Nonnie came over to get a good look. "Poor boy," she said, the first sweet words out of her mouth that morning. She touched his dark curls. "Poor little baby."

Mary Ella ran into the kitchen and brung back Nonnie's knee salve. "No," I said. "Bring me the lotion Nurse Ann left for—"

"Is that what you used?" Nonnie asked her.

Mary Ella looked from me to Nonnie and then at Baby William. "This is his medicine." She held up the tube of salve.

"We need to wash that off him, quick!" Nonnie said. "That salve makes my knee feel better because it heats it up. Poor baby, poor baby!" She grabbed him from me and whisked him away, through the kitchen and out to the sink on the back porch.

I stood up. I wanted to smack my sister across her face. "How could you be so dumb?" I felt tears burn my eyes, imagining the hurt Baby William was suffering. I ran out to the porch and helped Nonnie soap him up while he screamed his fool little head off, and then I took him back in the bedroom and dressed him in clean clothes, smoothing the right lotion over his chest and back, but I was afraid the damage had been done. His skin was blistery and bright red.

Nonnie stood over me while I took care of him, and Mary Ella waited in the doorway of the bedroom, chewing her thumbnail.

"We're gonna have to call Nurse Ann to come look at him again," I said. "I don't know if this here lotion is going to be enough, now we wrecked his skin."

I looked at Mary Ella and saw tears running down her cheeks. I couldn't stand it. I gave Baby William over to Nonnie and went to my sister. I put my arms around her and she leaned against me, crying hard. "I know you didn't mean to do it," I said. "I know you thought you was doing the right thing. You just got to be more careful."

I didn't know which would be worse—going to the barn or going to the Gardiners' house to ask to use the phone. Either way, I might see Mr. Gardiner and that was the last thing I wanted to do today. I knew I'd talk better on the phone than Mary Ella, so that was the answer. As soon as we walked outside, the smoke smell I thought was just in my hair was all around us. It made me feel sick.

When we started down the lane, Mary Ella pointed to the blackened barn in the distance. "Mrs. Gardiner said you done that," she said.

"Well, I didn't light a match, but I guess it was my fault." It was too much, seeing that black mess out there. I felt like throwing up. Me and Henry Allen ruined all that tobacco, all that hard work. If only he'd checked the burners before we started up with each other. We was both so stupid.

When we got to the path that ran between the fields, I sent Mary Ella to the barn and I walked over to the farmhouse. I tried to stop my sick-to-my-stomach shakiness as I climbed the front steps.

Desiree answered the door.

"Why, hello, Miss Ivy," she said. "Ain't you working at the barn this morning?"

She didn't know about me and Henry Allen. I could tell by her smile and how nice she was. "Can I use the phone?" I asked. "Baby William got a bad rash."

"You come right in." She stood back to let me walk past her. "You know where the phone is at. Help yourself."

"Is Mr. Gardiner here?" I made my voice real quiet.

"No, Miss Ivy." She made her voice quiet right back at me, and I wondered if maybe she did know after all and just wasn't holding it against me. "He out at the barn."

The sick feeling passed and I walked toward the kitchen, where the phone was. I always liked being in this house. I liked the way one room spilled into another. There was so much space. The kitchen was big enough for a family three times the size of mine. I used to pretend me and Henry Allen would have a house like this someday. Big and roomy and waiting to be filled up with a real family. Our children would never have the kind of life I had. I thought me and Henry Allen had a chance at a good life together, but deep down I always knew his mama and daddy wouldn't let it happen. No Gardiner would ever marry a Hart. After last night, I knew that for a fact.

I had to leave a message with Nurse Ann's office, but the lady said she'd be sure to tell somebody to get out to our house to see Baby William today, because it sounded bad. I said good-bye to Desiree and headed for the barn.

Everyone was working at the green barn today, which meant I had to walk right past the south barn to get to it. The colored day laborers was all working on the burned-out building, taking apart what was left of it and tossing the charred pieces into the back of Mr. Gardiner's old pickup. It took me a minute to see that Henry Allen was one of them, his face blackened from the soot, and I guessed that was his punishment: doing the colored work. He looked up and saw me. Our eyes met for less than a second before we both looked away. My throat got real tight, but I just kept walking, right past the mess him and me made. I'd work extra hard today myself.

15

Jane

On Monday afternoon, I parked my car in front of Davison Gardiner's house. The oppressive July heat wrapped around me, but I wasn't in a hurry to get out. This would be my first solo interview. Mr. Gardiner was expecting me, and as Robert had said over breakfast that morning, I should be ready for my Ph.D. in social work with all the reading I'd been doing, but none of that eased my nerves. I pulled my pad from my briefcase and looked over the notes I'd made during a phone conversation with Ann Laing that morning. She'd been called in on Friday to check William because the Harts used the wrong medication on his prickly heat rash.

"I believe he's in danger there," she said. "When I visited the other day, they couldn't find him right away, and now this."

I didn't know what I was going to do about that. I thought of the man pulling the wooden block on a string. He haunted me, yet I wondered if there was a way to help Mary Ella be a better mother without taking her son away from her. I would have to talk to Fred about it.

"I gave Ivy some spermicidal jelly and condoms," Ann said. "She says she's not active sexually, but she's fifteen, and I'm sorry, fifteen-year-old girls living in that kind of environment . . . well, I'd be surprised if she isn't."

I hoped Ivy was telling her the truth. It made me sad to think of a fifteen-year-old having sex. At fifteen, I wouldn't have understood the connection between sex and love. I would have felt used.

"Charlotte thinks she should be sterilized," I said.

"I do, too," Ann said. "She's epileptic. I've actually filled out my part of the form, so I'll mail it to you for the petition. See if you can find out if she's running around with boys. She doesn't trust me, so I really haven't been able to get her to open up."

"We'd have to tell Ivy the truth, though, right?" I thought of Mary Ella. Of the lie told to her about her sterilization. That was simply wrong. "I mean, if the petition gets approved?"

"Just take it one step at a time," Ann had said.

So, I thought as I slipped the notepad back into my briefcase and got out of my car, talking to Mr. Gardiner would be my first step.

An acrid odor—a fire that had burned itself out, perhaps—filled my nostrils as I walked toward the house. Mr. Gardiner had the front door open by the time I'd climbed the steps to his porch. "So, you're the new social worker," he said.

"Yes." I nodded. I'd told him on the phone that I was taking Charlotte's place, and as with nearly every other person I'd met so far, he didn't sound too happy about that.

"Well, come on in. We just finished dinner and I'm about to get back to work but I've saved some time for you."

I walked into the cozy living room, which was about what I'd expected for a nice house out here. There was a large oval braided rug on the floor, and the furniture looked well-worn and comfortable, some of it covered with quilts. A spinet piano stood against one wall, above it the head of a deer. Knickknacks were everywhere.

A teenaged boy walked into the room, stopping short when he spotted me.

"This is my boy, Henry Allen," Mr. Gardiner said.

"Hello, Henry Allen." I smiled. He was a good-looking boy, nearly the spitting image of his father except for the glasses.

"You git back out there, boy," Mr. Gardiner said to him, quite sharply.

"Yes, sir." The boy nodded to me. "Nice to meet you, ma'am," he said, and then headed for what I supposed was the kitchen and the back door. I could see a maid moving around in there.

"My wife's at the store," Mr. Gardiner said. "You know where that is?"

"Yes," I said, though I wasn't sure I could find it. I remembered Charlotte driving us past it.

"Stop by and say hey to her if you can."

"I will."

"Well, have a seat." He motioned to the sofa and I lowered myself into it while he sat on the piano bench. "Desiree!" he called toward the kitchen.

A middle-aged colored woman appeared at the doorway of the kitchen. "Yes, Mr. Gardiner?"

"How about you bring some of that banana pudding out here for me and Mrs. . . . ." He raised his eyebrows at me. "Sorry, I don't recollect—"

"Forrester."

"For me and Mrs. Forrester."

"Yes, sir," she said, and disappeared into the kitchen.

"You look right young to be married," he said.

Was he flirting with me? Maybe I only thought that because he was extraordinarily handsome. He was very tan and his features were rugged and masculine. His glasses only accentuated his dark eyes.

"I'm not as young as I look." I smiled in a way that I hoped was polite but not encouraging.

"You been to the Harts' yet? You met them?"

"Yes," I said.

"Then you know we got some problems there, right?"

I nodded.

Desiree brought a tray into the room, setting it on the coffee table. "How 'bout some tea?" She smiled at me.

"No, thank you," I said. I had a big thermos of lemonade in my car and had already had a glassful this afternoon. I didn't want to have to use one of the outhouses.

"Holler if you change your mind," Desiree said, and walked back to the kitchen. Mr. Gardiner handed me a small ceramic bowl of pudding from the tray and took the other for himself.

"She makes the best banana pudding," he said, then gave a laugh. "She makes the best everything, truth be told."

I took a mouthful of the pudding, though I wasn't the least bit hungry. "Delicious," I said. I set the bowl down on the table, wondering how to begin this conversation when he began it for me.

"How long you been doing social work?" he asked.

"Not long," I said, wondering if I looked like a sparkling new penny to him. "Charlotte was orienting me to her cases when she had the accident." I'd told him about Charlotte's leg on the phone.

"Hard to step into them shoes, ain't it?" He ate a spoonful of pudding, then set the bowl on top of the piano.

"Yes," I said. "But I know she'll be keeping in close touch with me." At least I hoped she would be.

"Now, Charlotte," he said, stretching his back as though he had a crick in it, "she had plans to get the Hart girl, Ivy . . . you know, taken care of . . . like her sister, right?"

Wow, I thought. He didn't waste any time getting to the point. "That'll be my responsibility now," I said. "Mrs. Werkman had just started her evaluation so I'll continue it and that's one reason I'm here. I'll need to get your input, as someone who knows her well." I pulled a notepad out of my briefcase and set it on my lap, ready to jot down any information about Ivy that might help me make my case.

"Well, how about I paint you a picture?" he said.

I hesitated, my pen in my hand above the notepad. "I'm sorry," I said. "I don't understand."

"I'm going to paint you a picture and it ain't going to be a pretty one," he said. "You got a good imagination?"

I nodded uncertainly.

"Good. Now here's the picture." He held his hands up as though he were creating a frame, his gaze on whatever he saw inside its invisible borders. "Here's that little house the Harts live in," he said. "Can you see it?"

I nodded. I could. I could see the unpainted exterior and the lopsided front porch.

"There's Winona Hart," he said. "I knowed Miss Winona all my life. She's the mama of my buddy Percy Hart." He lowered his arms. "Percy lived in the same house, a true tenants' house back then, and I lived here in the big house, but we was good friends regardless. Anyways, back to my picture I'm painting for you here." He raised his arms again. "Winona's getting up there now," he said. "She got herself some bad health these days. She used to be able to work the farm with the best of them, but them days are sure over.

"Then we got Mary Ella." He gave a roll of his eyes but all I could picture as I looked into his invisible frame was Mary Ella standing in the doorway of her house like an angel. "What can I say about Mary Ella you don't know after a minute of meeting her?" Mr. Gardiner asked. "She's a real pretty imbecile. Agreed?"

I was stunned by the word. "I . . . I don't know her well enough to make that judgment yet." A voice inside my head snapped at me for letting him use that word unchallenged. *Be accepting,* all the books said. *Nonjudgmental.* What if he'd used the word "nigger"? If he called his maid a "nigger," would I just sit there? I had a feeling that's what I was supposed to do. *Meet your clients where they are,* the books said. "Why do you say that?" I asked.

"Oh, for the love of God." He dropped his invisible picture frame again. "Just spend five minutes talking to that girl. Now, of course you never knew her mother, Violet. Violet was never exactly right in the head, but she went plum crazy after Percy died. She did all sorts of nutty things, but the worst was when she ran into my store one day and cut my wife's cheek with a knife. That's when they locked her up."

"Oh dear," I said. "How awful."

"But back to my picture," he said, arms in the air once again. "Mary Ella got her mama's looks but she ain't too smart. Charlotte knew there was nothing worse than a pretty imbecile. They do what nature tells them to do and their looks make every man that lays eyes on them want to help nature out, if you know what I mean."

I nodded.

He dropped his arms again. "So Charlotte arranged that surgery after Baby William come along. And you know that boy's right slow. You know that, don't you?"

I licked my lips. "Mrs. Werkman believes he has some developmental milestone problems." I sounded like an idiot. Here I'd stayed up all night reading those books and I couldn't express myself any better than that?

"That's a kind way of saying he's a retard, right? He's retarded?"

"I don't know the exact nature of his problems yet," I said.

He gave me an amused-looking smile, and I thought he was seeing right through my stilted language to the quivering mass of jelly inside me. I wanted to ask him if he thought Eli Jordan was the father of Mary Ella's baby, but if he didn't already have that thought in his head, I didn't want to put it there.

"Well, you'll catch up," he said. "All I'm saying is, bottom line, Mary Ella and her sister and grandmother—their hands are already too full. The girls lost their daddy and their mama . . ." He shook his head and turned to pick up the bowl of pudding again, and I was surprised to see his eyes glistening behind his glasses. He ate another spoonful of pudding and I stayed quiet, letting him pull himself together. "Did Mrs. Werkman tell you it was my fault?" he said finally. "About Percy? Their daddy?"

I shook my head.

"It was on my land. My broke-down tractor. It was a terrible thing, what happened to that man. He was using the scoop bucket to clear weeds on a little hillside out by the shelter and he got off the tractor to do some of it by hand. The brake gave out and the tractor started rolling. The bucket pinned him down. Smashed his skull open."

I winced before I could help myself. "How terrible," I said.

"The girls, they saw it happen, though they was little. I think only Mary Ella remembers it. I guess Ivy was too young, which is a blessing, don't you think? Their mama was an ace short of a deck before the accident, but losing Percy sent her round the bend. So in some ways, I cost them both their parents."

"I think you're being hard on yourself." I suddenly liked him and felt sympathy for him.

"It's the way I feel," he said. "Can't change the way you feel about a thing, now can you?" He cleared his throat. "So back to Ivy and that picture I was painting. Add a new baby to that mess of a picture and watch that whole house of cards come tumbling down. It'd be a shame if that happened. I think the sooner you take care of Ivy, the better off for all of them."

"It sounds like you've been really kind to them. And to the Jordans."

"Oh, them Jordan boys work their behinds off around here. Even that Avery, he does his part." He smiled like he felt some affection for the boy. "They go back a long way with my kin. Back to the slave days, to be truthful. That's a hell of a long time. My great-great-granddaddy gave them their freedom and a house and some land to work and they're still here. So yeah, I treat my people good. We've got history together and that's important. People today don't appreciate how important, sometimes."

"But the Harts . . . they can't exactly work as hard for you as the Jordan boys." It suddenly worried me. He could put them out and I'd have worse problems with them than trying to find clothes that fit.

He shook his head. "I won't put them out," he said, as if he'd read my mind. "I told you, they wouldn't be in the fix they're in if it wasn't for me."

"You know," I said, "I understand why it would be good for Ivy not to have children right now, but doing something so permanent when we don't know what the future holds for her—"

"Oh, I can tell you what the future holds." He started to raise his hands again, and I was afraid he was going to paint me another picture, but he lowered them to his lap. "She'll have one baby, then another and another, all on goddamned welfare, because that's the way it happens with girls like her. She's running wild already, so it's only a matter of time."

"How do you know she's running wild?"

"Trust me on that," he said. "She's looking for trouble, that one."

"I'd like to talk to her today," I said. "I know she's probably working for you, so would that be all right? I need to drop something off at the Jordans' first. Would you mind if—"

"The sooner the better." He looked at his watch. "You take her for an hour. Spend an hour with that girl and you'll see all you need to see to know Charlotte's plans for her are right. I'll still pay her for the hour. Tell her that so she'll go with you."

I was pleased with myself as I drove around the tobacco field toward the Jordans' house. My first interview and I thought it went pretty well. Mr. Gardiner had been easy to get information from. Or at least, it had been easy to get his opinions. It would be up to me to figure out what they were worth.

I pulled into the Jordans' yard, scattering the chickens in every direction, and I got out of my car and opened the trunk. I culled through the bags of clothing until I found the two containing shoes I hoped would fit the Jordan boys. When Charlotte and I had picked them out from a pile of donated clothing, I thought they were all too big for boys, but she assured me they were the right size. I lifted the bags into my arms and crossed the dirt yard to the house. I was swimming in a pool of sweat by the time I reached the stoop, when a big black dog suddenly jumped out of nowhere, barking and snarling and snapping his jaws. I let out a yelp and dropped the bags. One of them split wide open, shoes spilling out all over the dirt.

A young man pushed open the screen door. "Shadow, git!" he shouted, while I stood stock-still, hugging my arms. I was afraid to breathe. Another man came out of the house, jumped off the porch and gave the dog a rough shove with his leg. The dog backed off, but only a step or two, and I could still hear the low growl in his throat.

A third man came out of the house—how many did she have in there? He came down the step to the ground, nodded to me, then slipped a rope around the dog's neck and tied him to a stake in the ground.

"Who are you?" he asked, as he tightened the knot around the stake.

"My name is Mrs. Forrester," I said, "I—"

"You the one taking Miz Werkman's place?" the man who'd shoved the dog aside asked me, and I realized he was not a man at all. None of them were. They were the *size* of men—Charlotte had been right about the shoes—but now that I wasn't waiting for the dog to sink his teeth into my legs, I could see the youth in their faces. The boy asking

the question wore thick glasses. Avery. I'd be driving him to the itinerant Braille teacher in Ridley once a week.

"Yes," I said, lowering my arms to my sides. "Are you Avery?"

"Yes, ma'am," he said. "You be the one to carry me to the teacher?"

"I will," I said. Avery was fairer than his brothers, a smattering of
freckles across his nose. I remembered what Charlotte said about
their different fathers.

"You brung us shoes?" One of the other men—*boys*—crouched
and began trying to pile the shoes back into the broken bag.

"Yes, I hope they fit." I still felt shaky, even with the dog tied safely
to the stake. I'd never felt quite so *white* before, surrounded by three
big Negroes. Avery seemed harmless enough, and the one gathering
up the shoes was all right, but the third leaned against the porch,
muscled arms across his broad chest, his eyes narrowed at me. Even
so, the light caught them just right and I saw their amber color. "I
believe you're Eli," I said.

"You believe right," he said, not shifting his pose even a bit.

"I'm Devil," said the boy on the ground. He was sitting down now,
trying on the shoes. His pose suggested a kid on Christmas morning.
But the muscular arms and broad back, so much like Eli's, told me he
was a young man who worked hard every day.

"Maybe you could all try them on." I looked at Eli. "Your mother
said you'd outgrown yours," I said, but I couldn't hold his gaze for
long. His was too piercing. It was like he was trying to see inside me,
and he wasn't impressed with what he saw. I wondered if he'd liked
Charlotte.

"What's all the racket?" Lita Jordan appeared behind the screen
door and I felt relieved by her presence. "Well, hey, Mrs. Forrest," she
said, pushing the screen open and stepping onto the porch. "Shadow
give you a hard time?"

I didn't correct her about my name. "You don't have to worry about
anyone sneaking into your yard, do you?" I smiled.

"No, ma'am," she said. "I see you brung some shoes. Eli, you try
them on? Yours is the worst."

"Ain't got time now, Ma," he said. "Got to git back over." He walked
past me, heading for the fields. I glanced down at his shoes where

they'd been cut to make room for his toes. "Come on," he said to his brothers.

"Nice to meet you!" I called after them.

Mrs. Jordan came down the stairs to help me gather the shoes, including the old pair Devil had left behind, and I realized only then that he'd taken a pair of the new ones. That heartened me. I'd done one small worthwhile thing today.

"That dog." She nodded toward Shadow who now lay docile near the stake. "He don't much like white folks, but he never bit no one. Only person he ever hurt was this white man, come around asking for food. Got knocked over good instead. Felt bad for him, though. Any old white man who thinks we're that good off here in this shack, he's in sad shape."

"I like dogs," I assured her. "He just came out of nowhere and gave me a start."

She glanced at me as she dropped another shoe in the bag. "You a fragile child, ain't you," she said. She pronounced "fragile" so it almost rhymed with "child." I felt about five years old.

"Not really." I tried to smile. How was it that, a few short weeks ago, I'd skin-dived in Hawaii, and here I was still trembling over an encounter with a harmless dog—and if I was being honest—over being surrounded by three young colored men I didn't know?

"Charlotte set you out on your own already?" she asked as we stood up with our bounty of shoes and my briefcase.

"She broke her leg last week," I said. "She won't be back to work for a little while."

"Oh now, that's pitiful!" she said. "You tell her I be hoping it heals up fast."

"I'll do that." I followed her into the house and through the living room to the kitchen, where plates and silverware littered the table.

"Excuse this mess," she said, setting the bag on the floor. I lowered the one I was carrying to the floor next to it. "The boys just had dinner, and Rodney's napping before we head back to the barn." She motioned to one of the chairs. "Set," she said, and I sat down.

"Must be hard to keep these growing boys fed," I said.

"Now, that's the truest thing I heard all day," she said, moving the dishes to a basin on the counter. "You like some tea?" she asked.

I thought of the outhouses again, but I was dying of thirst. "I'd love some," I said. Charlotte had told me it was good to show our colored clients that we had no problem drinking from their glasses or eating from their plates.

"Charlotte . . . Miz Werkman. She a good woman," Mrs. Jordan said as she handed me the cold glass of tea. "You got some big shoes to fill."

"I'm quickly figuring that out."

"She fought to git me that operation," she said. "Are you a fighter, too?"

"I think so," I said. I wanted to be, but her words about my fragility were going to bother me all day, if not all week.

"I didn't make it easy for her," she said, chuckling.

"How do you mean?"

"She sent me to get that test. That 'how much do you know' test with the psychology man? If I knowed I was supposed to come out dumb on that test to get the operation, I would of answered them questions mighty different. You take a test, you think you supposed to do your best, you know?"

"Yes." I smiled.

"You got to be plumb stupid to get that operation, I reckon. But I got it, and don't have to worry about having no more babies. It's a relief. You got children?"

"Not yet."

"Well, you'll see. You have two, it's good. Three, still good, but there's less food for them and they be harder to keep an eye on. Four, even worse. Five—" She shook her head. "No good for mama and no good for the babies, neither." She sipped her tea.

The mention of her five children gave me the opening I was hoping for. "Your daughter," I said. "Sheena?"

She nodded.

"She's living up North?"

"I had to get her away," she said, looking at her glass instead of at me. "She my oldest one," she said. "Nineteen. The boys around here was after her from the time she was fourteen. Real pretty little girl, Sheena. I knew I had to get her out of here or she'd end up like me." She ran her fingertip around the rim of the glass and I wasn't sure what to say. "So I got relatives up there. Cousins and my brother. And they said send her on up. She done real good up there. Going into college," she said proudly. "Got a scholarship. Not a full one, but pretty good. I miss her, though. I miss her so bad."

"I bet you do," I said.

"My cousins up there, they always after me, 'Lita,' they say, 'why you stayin' down in that pit Grace County when you could be up here a free woman? No KKK up here. No Jim Crow.'"

"Why do you?" I asked.

She leaned toward me. "Roots," she said. "I got me some deep roots here. Right here on this land."

"Mr. Gardiner told me how far back your family goes."

"Oh yes, and I can't leave, see? My brother could. He don't care. But I can't leave my folks buried in the cemetery here. I can't leave what they broke their backs for. So I stay."

"I understand," I said. I reached for my purse. "Listen, I have something I thought you might like. You don't need to take them, of course, but I just thought . . ." I pulled out a little package wrapped in tissue paper and unwrapped it to show her the five small frames I'd picked up at Woolworth's. "When I saw the pictures of your children on the wall, I wondered if you might like to frame them." She stared at the frames and I thought Charlotte might have been right about asking her first if she'd like them. Maybe I was insulting her in a way I couldn't understand. But she looked up at me. "That's right nice of you," she said. "Do you think they'll fit okay?"

"I do," I said. "But I didn't see a picture of Rodney. I brought the extra frame for when you get one of him."

"I got one, but it's a different size. Let's see if they fit."

She got to her feet and we walked into the living room. She pulled the picture of Eli from the wall and carefully peeled the tape from the corner while I opened the back of the frame. She slipped the picture on top of the glass and turned it over. Perfect fit. I watched the smile

NECESSARY LIES | 121

spread across her face. Together, we framed the other three photos and then she brought out a picture of Rodney sitting on some steps. We had to cut it down a bit to fit, and only when we'd finished framing it, did I recognize the steps as the ones leading up to the Gardiners' front porch.

"I'll get Eli to nail them up tonight." Then she smiled at me. "You all right," she said. "You real different from Miz Werkman."

I didn't know if that was good or bad or what to say.

"She's smart and full of business," she said, "and she sure knows how to get things done. You, though." She nodded. "You a real human being."

16

Ivy

I was nervous all day Monday while I looped the tobacco leaves over the sticks, waiting for Mr. Gardiner to come tell me I couldn't work for him no more and to leave his son alone. I worked faster than ever before and the handers was having trouble keeping up with me. I wanted to do everything perfect. I wished I could talk to Henry Allen. I still didn't know what happened to him after I ran home the night of the fire.

Every once in a while, I looked over at the south barn, which was pretty much gone now. One time when I looked, I saw a lady walking toward us on the path. I kept up with my looping, trying to think where I seen her before and remembered she was that social worker that came with Mrs. Werkman last week. Did Mr. Gardiner tell her about me and Henry Allen? Did he tell her to take me away someplace, like what happened to my mama?

"You messin' up," Daisy, the neighbor girl handing me the leaves, said. She pointed to the sloppy loop I'd just made, tobacco stems sticking up too high above the stick.

"Sorry." I did that loop over, paying close attention to my hands and pretending I didn't see the lady, but I knew she was coming, and she was coming for me.

Sure enough, I saw her shoes on the dirt next to where I stood. She wore clear galoshes over them saddle shoes some of the girls wore at school.

"Hi, Ivy," she said.

I looked up, pretending I was surprised. "Hi," I said, then looked right quick back at my flying fingers. I wanted to escape. Drop what I was doing and run and run and run.

"Hello, Mary Ella," she said to my sister, who was handing leaves to another looper. Mary Ella looked clear through the lady like she wasn't there. Sometimes I was jealous of how Mary Ella could get away with being so rude.

The lady turned back to me. "I'd like to speak to you for a little bit, Ivy," she said.

"I got to work," I said.

"Mr. Gardiner said it's fine for me to take you away for an hour. Just an hour. He said he'll still pay you for the time."

Now I really didn't believe a word coming out of her mouth. "Why would he pay me for not working?"

"Because he thinks it's important that we have a chat. So, can some-one take over what you're doing here and you come with me?"

"I don't want to go nowhere," I said, looping another bunch of leaves.

"Anywhere you like," she said. "You can take me to your favorite place."

"I can loop for you," Daisy said.

"I don't have to go in your car?" I asked.

"No, no," she said. "Just . . . somewhere around here where we can talk. I only want to get to know you better."

I thought of the crick. Definitely my favorite place, but that be-longed to me and Henry Allen. We was too far from it anyways.

"Okay," I said. I handed the string to Daisy and walked back up the path with the lady. I couldn't remember her name.

She was a mind reader. "I know we only met briefly the other day," she said as we walked, "so you probably don't remember my name. It's Mrs. Forrester. And my, it's hot!" She fanned her face with her hand. Here on the path through the field, right out in the sun, it was hot as blue blazes, but I was sweating from more than the heat, for sure. I didn't dare steal a look at Henry Allen when we passed what was left of the south barn.

"When did this happen?" She pointed toward the barn.

"Don't rightly know," I muttered, keeping my eyes on the path. I had the feeling she knew exactly when it happened and why and was trying to trick me somehow.

"So," she said, "where's your favorite place to sit and talk?"

"I ain't . . . I don't have no favorite place to talk. We don't do much sitting and talking around here."

She laughed like that was funny. "Well, today we will. I have a big thermos of lemonade in my car. Let's get that and take it someplace shady."

I saw her car up on the lane. I pictured her pushing me into it when she opened the door to get the thermos that probably wasn't even there. Then she'd drive me to the place where my mama was. The place they locked people up. I was sure Mr. Gardiner could make that happen.

"I don't need no lemonade," I said. We was almost to the car and I started hanging back.

"No?" She stopped walking. "Well, that's fine. Where would you like to go?"

There was only one shady spot nearby, and that was under the tin roof on the side of the empty Christmas barn. I pointed toward it and we walked over there, neither of us saying a thing. I didn't know what to say. I didn't know what she knew.

"This is perfect!" she said when we reached the shade. She sat down on the ground, leaning against the barn, her legs folded under her skirt. I sat down, too, but not close enough that she could grab me.

"Mrs. Werkman broke her leg," she said. "She and I'd been hoping we could visit you and your family a few more times together, but she won't be coming back to work for a while, so I'm trying to get to know people better on my own. That's why I wanted to talk to you today."

"Did you talk to Nonnie, too?"

"No, I don't think I'll have time to get to your house this afternoon. So for now, it's just you and me."

"Did you talk to Mr. Gardiner?" I asked.

"I did."

"What did he say?" I needed to know. Was this about me and Henry Allen or wasn't it?

She shook her head. "Not much. He told me how long your family's lived in your house. How you go way back. He told me he and your father were best friends when they were little boys."

My heartbeat was starting to settle down. "I suppose they was," I said.

She tipped her head like she was real curious. "What do you remember about your father and mother?" she asked. "I know you were quite small—just five, right?—when you . . . when your father died. Do you remember him?"

Nobody ever asked me that question. I asked Nonnie about him sometimes, but she'd just say he's gone, no point in talking about it, and her eyes would get watery. I had to remind myself he was my daddy but he was also her son and the hurt of talking about him was too much for her, so I kept my questions to myself. Mary Ella said she saw the accident and she saw his spirit fly into the sky like an angel and that's all she'd say, which was like saying nothing at all.

I was quiet so long, Mrs. Forrester leaned toward me. "I'm sorry," she said. "Is it too hard to talk about?"

"No," I said. "It's just that I ain't never talked about it. Hard to know what to say."

"Do you have any memories of him?"

I remembered Henry Allen talking about Daddy not so long ago. "He'd take us out in the pasture and play ball with us," I said.

"Really? You and Mary Ella?"

"Everybody," I said. "Me, Mary Ella, Henry Allen—that's Mr. Gardiner's son—and Eli, Devil, Avery, Sheena. Some other kids from . . . just around. I don't remember who. But lots of them. I think they all liked him because he liked to play as much as we did." I felt proud of my father, describing him like this. I could picture him. Throwing the ball. Swinging us around by our arms till we was dizzy, every kid begging for the next ride. I remembered him whupping Mary Ella once for breaking one of our windows, but I didn't remember him ever hitting me. "When it rained, he played cards with us in the house, or once on the porch under the roof." I'd forgotten that, sitting on the porch floor with him, dry and happy, listening to the rain that couldn't touch us. My throat started to close up. I didn't think I could talk. I looked down at the ground, hoping she couldn't tell.

"It hurts to think about losing someone you love very much," she said, "and it sounds like you really loved him."

I wiped the back of my hand across my eyes. "Don't do no good to remember things like this," I said. "That's what Nonnie says and maybe she's right." I looked at her. "What good's it do?" I asked.

"Well, I think when we lose somebody, maybe we owe it to that person to remember them. To hold on to the good memories."

I thought about that for a minute and liked what she said. Nobody wanted to be forgotten.

"My mama . . . it was like she wasn't there, really. She was always sickly. And then she did such a shameful thing and they took her away for good. Do you know about that? What our mama did?"

"Tell me," she said.

I wasn't sure I could. "You said hold on to the good memories about a person, but what if there ain't . . . aren't any?"

She looked away from me like she wasn't sure of the answer herself. "You don't have any good memories of your mother?" she asked.

I thought and thought. "I can't remember a single one," I said.

"I'm sorry," she said, and that made me want to cry again.

"I'll tell you the thing she did, though," I said. "The shameful thing. Mrs. Gardiner? Mr. Gardiner's wife? She works in the store. And my mama went in there with a knife out of our kitchen and walked right up to Mrs. Gardiner and cut her cheek. Cut it bad. That's why they took her away. I guess she was a terrible shameful person."

"Do you know what 'mental illness' means, Ivy?"

"Crazy?"

"Crazy is kind of a . . . mean word for it. A word like that blames a person for being mentally ill. But your mother was mentally ill. That was something she couldn't help, any more than you can help having blue eyes. Her mental illness made her dangerous, though, so they had to take her away to be sure she couldn't hurt anyone else, but also to put her someplace where she could be taken care of."

"We're not allowed to see her."

"Is that something you wish you could do?"

I shook my head. I was afraid of my mama. Afraid of how I'd feel around her. "I don't know her," I said. "Is that terrible, that I don't want to see my own mama?"

She looked out over the field of tobacco in front of us, the green barn in the distance. "Feelings are never right or wrong," she said after a moment. "They just are."

I thought of how much I loved Henry Allen. It wasn't wrong, no matter what Mr. Gardiner might think about it.

"I know what happened with William," she said. "With Mary Ella putting the wrong lotion on him."

"She almost kilt him."

"I doubt that would have happened, though I guess it was really painful for him."

"He's still hurting from it. She feels right bad, but that don't change what happened. Nurse Ann needs to come out a lot more to check on Baby William. Nonnie, too, because she don't check her sugar right."

"So you'd like Nurse Ann to check on Nonnie and William more often."

"Yes. But not me," I added quickly. The last thing I needed was to have Nurse Ann badgering me more about doing it.

"Why not you?"

I couldn't look right at her, talking about this. I looked toward the green barn, but could only see the back of it. I couldn't see none of the workers. "She brung me some things to use when you're . . . you know, doing it with a boy." I made little circles in the dirt on the ground with my fingertip, looking at them instead of her. "Mary Ella's the one that needs them things. She stole some of what Nurse Ann brung me, so it's her she should be talking to. I don't know why she's worried about me and not Mary Ella."

"Who is Mary Ella's boyfriend?" she asked.

"Who *isn't*?" I said. "You seen her. They're all after her. All the boys for miles and miles around. She's like a barn cat in heat and they all know it."

"Do you and Mary Ella get along?" she asked.

"Yes, ma'am. She's my sister," I said, like that explained everything. "I used to wish I looked like her. Awful pretty. But if that prettiness comes with being stupid, I don't want it." I looked up at her. "I worry about her," I said. "She can't take care of herself good. You going to have this talk with her, too?"

"I may."

"She won't answer nothing. She's like one of them books with a lock and key."

"Like a diary, huh?"

"Yes, ma'am. I never actually seen one of those."

"Ivy . . ." She licked her lips. "You're very pretty, too."

"I am not." I smiled and knew I was turning red like a fool.

"Yes you are. Not the way Mary Ella is. Very few girls are that beautiful. But you have a prettiness that's all your own and that I'm sure boys are attracted to. Do you have a boyfriend?"

Did Mr. Gardiner tell her? Here I'd let her talk to me about all these other things and forgot I was supposed to be worried about him. "No," I said.

She knotted her hands together and was rubbing them. "I want to be sure you're able to finish school," she said. "Not have to quit because of having a baby, like Mary Ella."

"I ain't gonna have no baby," I said. "You don't got to worry about that."

She nodded. "That's good. I was concerned because one of your neighbors said she's seen you out very late at night and she's worried—"

"Who?" I asked. Was she talking about Mrs. Gardiner and the fire or somebody else?

"It doesn't matter. The important thing to me is that you're safe and not . . . getting in trouble."

"I'm all right, ma'am," I said. "You need to spend your worries on my sister, like I said. And you can tell that to Nurse Ann, too."

"Okay," she said. She changed her legs under her from one side to the other. "What concrete things do you need now? Your family?"

"Concrete?" What was she talking about? I thought of the cement stoop on our house.

"*Things,*" she said. "More clothing? Any furniture?"

"A window fan!" I said. I'd been asking for one of them two summers in a row now.

Mrs. Forrester smiled. "I don't know if that's possible," she said. "Charlotte—Mrs. Werkman—didn't seem to think so, but I promise I'll try."

"Thank you."

"Do you have any concerns about me taking over from Mrs. Werkman?" she asked.

Yes, I thought, I had plenty. "She was sort of like a magician," I said. "We'd tell her the things we needed and she'd get them for us, like magic . . . except the window fan." I made dots around the circle I drew in the dirt. "She knew Nonnie had sugar problems before anybody else knew it," I said. "She even knew Mary Ella had a bad appendix before she felt sick. You can die if you got a busted appendix, so maybe Mrs. Werkman saved her life."

"You'll miss her," she said.

I nodded, but I was thinking how, in all the time I knew Mrs. Werkman, she never sat with me alone in the shade and asked me all these questions like I was a grown-up. Like what I thought mattered.

She never asked me one single question about my daddy.

17

Jane

I hadn't paid much attention when Charlotte was driving us around Grace County, so I shouldn't have been surprised when I faced an unfamiliar fork in the road after leaving the Gardiner farm and had no idea which way to go. Fifty-fifty chance it would be the right way, I thought, and I turned left. Ivy was on my mind as I drove. I felt a little shaky about my conversation with her. I'd rushed into asking her about her father way too quickly. Such a sensitive topic and I just dove in. I'd made her sad and hadn't meant to do that. Still, I could tell the moment she'd decided to trust me and I'd felt that trust deep in my bones. She was brighter than I'd expected. An IQ of eighty? That test had to be wrong. I wished she didn't have epilepsy. Was it so awful, having a baby if you were epileptic? Some women did it, didn't they? Plus, it seemed like she'd stopped having seizures. Yes, her children would probably end up on welfare, just like her, but I hated being the person who prevented her from ever having a family if that's what she wanted.

I came to another fork, this one even less familiar than the first. I made a right, and before I knew it, I was utterly lost, surrounded by woods so dense I could barely see the sky. I remembered the one and only time my family went camping. I'd been twelve, which would have made Teresa ten. She and I became separated from my parents in the woods. Within seconds, we were completely disoriented. I remem-

bered holding her hand, trying to be the brave, reassuring older sister
to keep her calm even though I felt panicky myself. With every step
we took, I didn't know if we were moving toward my parents or away
from them. Finally, we stopped walking and shouted for my parents,
and after what seemed like a lifetime, they found us.

I had some of that same panic now, realizing I hadn't seen another
car for at least twenty minutes. I drove another mile or two along a
narrow road before deciding I'd better try retracing my steps. I turned
around, but the road suddenly seemed full of forks and turns, and
with each one I guessed, realizing after a half mile or so that I'd most
likely guessed wrong. I finally pulled over and checked my map, only
to discover that the little road I was on was nowhere to be found on
that creased sheet of paper. I was supposed to meet Robert at his office for a dinner date at six and I wondered if I would make it—or if I'd
ever get out of the woods at all.

Far ahead of me, I saw a man and dog walk out of the trees, the
man's green jacket nearly blending into the undergrowth. I pressed
on the gas and drove forward until I was close enough for him to become aware of me. He turned and looked at me over his shoulder. His
face was weathered, and he carried a shotgun at his side.

I pulled up next to him and leaned over to roll down the passenger-
side window. "Excuse me," I said. "I'm trying to find my way to Ridley
Road."

"You're a long way from Ridley Road."

"Can you point me in the right direction?"

He told me several turns I'd need to make, and I thanked him and
began driving again, determined this time to pay attention. I looked at
him in my rearview mirror as I pulled away. He was shaking his head
slowly, and I imagined he thought a girl like me had no business driving around the back roads of Grace County.

By some miracle, I arrived at Robert's office a few minutes before six
o'clock. I parked at the curb in front, admiring the white shingle that
stood outside the small brick building. ROBERT FORRESTER, M.D., PEDI-
ATRICS. I'd hoped to have time to run home and change my clothes, but

that wasn't to be. I took off my saddle shoes and put on the black pumps I kept in the car, but I was still wearing the casual skirt and blouse I'd had on all day. I knew I was a dusty mess, especially after sitting on the dirt by that barn with Ivy.

Robert's receptionist, Sandra, greeted me when I walked into the waiting room.

"He's just wrapping up," she said. "You want to have a seat?"

The waiting room was filled with color: sky-blue walls, Kelly-green carpet, and chairs that looked like they came out of a crayon box. I sat down in an orange chair. I had the feeling Sandra was watching me out of the corner of her eye, most likely appalled that I was going out to dinner looking as though I'd been doing farmwork all day.

The door leading to the examining room opened, and I watched Robert walk into the hall with a little girl and a woman. The girl's cheeks were red as though she'd been crying, and Robert squatted down in front of her, saying something to her that made her nod and then laugh. He gave her shoulder a squeeze and I felt so much love for him. He was wonderful with his patients. Someday, he would be wonderful with our own children. He got to his feet and spotted me, acknowledging me with a nod and a smile, then he disappeared into his office. I waited until the little girl and her mother had left before walking into his office and shutting the door behind me.

He was writing notes at his desk, and he nodded toward one of the chairs.

"I love seeing you with your patients," I said as I sat down. "You're so kind with them. So good with children."

He smiled. "That little girl you saw might not agree," he said, still writing his notes. "Had to give her a booster shot today and she wasn't very happy with me." He closed the folder on his desk and sat back, a frown replacing his smile. "You're not dressed for dinner," he said.

"I didn't have time to go home and change," I said. "Sorry."

"I thought you were going to be done early today. You said you'd have time to go home and freshen up."

The way he said it made me feel as though I smelled sweaty. Maybe I did. I touched my hair, hoping I'd managed to comb it into reasonable shape. "I got lost coming home," I said. "I think I saw every road in Grace County."

He raised his eyebrows. "I don't like you driving alone in an area you don't know."

"Oh, it was nothing," I said. "I finally saw a hunter and asked him the way to Ridley Road, and—"

"A hunter? With a gun?"

"Well, yes, hunters usually have guns." I smiled, but he wasn't smiling back. He just shook his head.

"You're the craziest woman," he said. It was the sort of thing that, if he'd said it a year ago, would have sounded like a compliment. Now that I was his wife, "crazy" was not so appealing.

"Well, anyway, I found my way out but I was running late, so I'm sorry I'm not gussied up, but—"

"You look great," he said. "You always look great. Just . . . I was hoping we could go to the City Club for dinner tonight, and instead it looks like we'll be at Cooper's Barbecue."

"Sorry," I said again. "How about I treat tonight? I'm making money so I can—"

"We don't need your money, Jane." He scowled, getting to his feet. "Don't insult me that way, all right?"

"Sorry," I said for the third or fourth time. "I didn't think offering to buy you dinner was an insult."

"Let's go," he said, putting his arm lightly around my shoulders, and I hoped Sandra thought we looked like a happily married couple as we walked out of the office. I wasn't feeling like one.

"The country club ball is less than two weeks away," he said as we ate hush puppies in our booth at Cooper's. "Will you still have a chance to buy a dress and get your hair done?"

I smiled, glad the storm between us seemed to have passed. "You're really excited about that, aren't you?" I asked. He mentioned something about the ball nearly every day.

"It's my first chance to show off my new bride," he said.

"You're so sweet," I said. "Mom and I plan to shop next week and I'll make a hair appointment, I promise." I knew I was lucky to have a husband who cared about my clothes and my hair. Most wouldn't even notice. "Should I have them do my hair up or down?"

"Up," he said. "It's so sexy up." He reached across the table and smoothed his hand over the side of my head. "You have beautiful hair," he said.

"Even after a day in the field?"

"Even after," he said.

The waitress set our plates in front of us, and Robert began dousing his pork with barbecue sauce from the bottle on the table. "So what did you do today without your supervisor with you?" he asked.

"It was good," I said, sipping my sweet tea. "Really good. I was nervous at first about being on my own, but then I really enjoyed it. I took some clothes to a family. Shoes for the boys." I imagined he pictured little boys, not the three big colored boys who had intimidated me at first. I would let him hold on to his image. "I had a good talk with their mother. Before that, I met with the farmer to start evaluating one of my clients for the Eugenics Program and he was helpful." I lifted a forkful of coleslaw. "And then I met with the client herself."

"What's wrong?"

I stopped the fork before it reached my mouth. "What do you mean?"

"It's like a dark cloud passed over your face when you said the word 'client.'"

"Really?" I set down the fork, touched that he was that sensitive to my emotions. "Well." I wrinkled my nose. "I guess I'm starting to feel uncomfortable about that case."

"How come?"

"Oh, everything. Remember I told you about the seventeen-year-old girl Charlotte had sterilized?"

"Right. And you have to do something to get the sister sterilized? Is that the one you're talking about?"

"Exactly. They're so needy, Robert. The girl's only fifteen and she's running the household. At least it seems that way to me. She's the caretaker. Her grandmother is marginal. Her sister—"

"*Marginal?*" He raised his eyebrows, a half smile on his lips.

I laughed. "I guess I've picked up the lingo." It made me happy that the word slipped so easily from my tongue. "Anyhow, the family's a mess." I took a bite of the vinegary barbecue, remembering Ivy calling Charlotte a magician for knowing Mary Ella needed her appendix out. Thinking about that deception killed my appetite and I set down my fork again. I didn't want to tell Robert about that. He'd say it was unethical and then I'd have to defend Charlotte and the department and I wasn't sure I could. I probably didn't have all the facts. "The older sister's little boy has prickly heat and she accidentally put her grandmother's arthritis salve on his rash."

"You're kidding." His jaw dropped. "That poor kid."

"He might need to be removed from the home," I said. "They all love him so much, though. I hate the idea."

"Yes, but the needs of that child are paramount, Jane. Next time, the mistake could be much worse."

"I know," I said.

He added a little more sauce to his barbecue. "It sounds like everybody in that household should be neutered," he said, and I had the feeling he wasn't kidding.

"I can see how the Eugenics Program is a good thing in some cases, but I'm not sure it would be in this girl's." I toyed with my coleslaw. "I sort of see myself in her," I said, "and I wouldn't want someone else making that sort of decision about my life."

He set down the bottle of sauce. "How can you say that?" he asked. "You live in Hayes Barton, for heaven's sake. She lives in the armpit of the country with a crazy mother and wacky sister and brother—"

"No, it's the grandmother. And she has no brother. You're thinking of her nephew. Her sister's two-year-old—"

"It doesn't matter, Jane. Comparing your life to theirs is insulting to me. I'm trying to provide a good living for us. We have a beautiful home and every damn creature comfort you could want. How can you possibly compare yourself to them?"

"I'm sorry if I sounded like I don't appreciate all you do for us." I pressed my hands together in my lap. "I love our home and everything, but I wasn't talking about that. I was talking about . . ." How to make him understand? "Yes, she's very, very poor. And no, I can't relate to that. But she's a human being. All these people I'm working with are human beings. Just like me."

"Not just like you."

I was getting angry. "*Just* like me," I said, "and like you, too, in that they're *people*. We're all people. I don't care how much money they have or we have or what color anyone's skin is or how smart they are or aren't. When I say I see myself in her, I mean I see a teenage girl with a sister she loves and worries about and I see her trying to figure out who she is and what she wants and—"

"Listen to me, Jane." His voice was much quieter and controlled than mine and I realized I'd been loud. "This is all wrong," he said. "*You* are all wrong for this job. If you don't believe me, talk to your supervisor or someone in charge over there. They'll say just what I'm saying—that you're relating too much to these people." Red splotches had formed high on his cheekbones. I couldn't remember ever seeing that in his face before. "You're a sweet person," he said, "and that allows you to get too caught up in their problems. It's not good for you. It's not good for *us*."

"Look," I said, trying to make my voice as reasonable as his, "this was my first day alone, so maybe I got carried away. It will be *fine*. I'll be fine."

"There's no reason on God's green earth why you need to be doing this."

"I'll be fine," I repeated. I would keep everything about my job to myself from now on. It wasn't safe to talk about it with him. It only led to bad feelings on both our sides. "Let's talk about something else."

"Good idea," he said.

But neither of us seemed to have anything to say, and we ate the rest of our meal in silence.

18

Ivy

I knew what the words "playing with fire" meant and I knew that's what me and Henry Allen was doing. I sat by the crick at ten to nine, waiting for him, the note he left me that morning scrunched up in my hand. *"They're going to a church supper,"* he wrote. *"Crick at 9."* So here I was, feeling like him and me was risking everything to be together. For the past week, we didn't even dare look at each other. I didn't think I could take it anymore and when I saw that little scrap of white at the bottom of the fence post, I could of jumped for joy.

I tossed a twig into the crick, but it was too dark to see it land in the water. *"Ivy."* He said my name in a whisper I hardly heard, but I turned around and there he was, coming through the path in the woods, pointing his flashlight toward the ground. I ran to him and threw my arms around his neck, kissing him all over his face. He laughed, dropping the blanket and his radio and flashlight. "Yeah, I missed you, too," he said, and then he gave me a good long kiss like the one in the barn that started the whole mess.

I ducked out of his arms. "Let's not do that right off," I said, bending down to pick up the blanket. "I want you to tell me everything." I opened the blanket over the mossy ground above the crick and he helped me lay it out. "What did they do to you? What did they say?"

He picked up his flashlight and radio. "First things first," he said, holding out the radio. "See this radio?"

It looked like the same radio he brung every time we met. "What about it?" I asked.

"It's yours."

I sucked in my breath. "Honest?"

"Honest. I bought it for you yesterday when me and Mama went to Ridley. Had to sneak away from her to get it."

I took it from him like it was made of glass. "You're the sweetest boy." I kissed him. "I love you, Henry Allen Gardiner."

"So, put on a station," he said, sitting down on the blanket.

I sat next to him, my body right up against his. "Show me how."

I shined the flashlight on the dial while he found the station we always listened to on his radio. WKIX. "Sixteen Candles" was playing, and Henry Allen started singing along with the part about being his "teenage queen." His voice wasn't real good and it made me laugh. I felt like I hadn't really laughed in a year.

"I can't believe it's mine," I said, taking it back from him. "I never had nothing so special before."

"You should have plenty of special things," he said.

I looked at him, wishing I could see him better. "What did they do to you?" I asked. "What did they say?"

"Lie back and I'll tell you everything," he said.

I put the radio on the blanket next to me and then we laid down on our backs, looking at the million stars God put in the black sky. The tops of the trees made a picture frame around them and it was the most beautiful thing. Henry Allen held my hand and after a week of terrible things happening, I finally felt some peace.

"Did you get in trouble?" he asked. "I didn't know if they told your grandma or not."

"Oh, they told her for sure. She beat me with her cane."

"Oh no."

"It wasn't too bad. I was in bed, so she did it through the cover and I had on my winter nightgown plus she ain't—isn't—so strong."

"Why'd you have on your winter nightgown?"

I knew he'd seen me after the water made my nightgown invisible. It sure wasn't the first time he saw me like that, but I still didn't want to bring it up and put that picture of me in his mind, with his mama standing right there. I didn't want to remember it, neither. "I just did," I said. "Lucky, too, 'cause it didn't hurt so much. Then she yelled and called me 'trash' and—"

"You ain't trash," he said.

"And she said your mama and daddy wouldn't take me to church no more."

"That's true," he said.

"They think I'm trash, too, don't they," I said. "They look down on me now."

He was quiet long enough that I knew it was true. "I don't care what they think. I know better."

"I don't like seeing your daddy now," I said.

"He's mad, all right, but Mama's worse," he said.

"Did your daddy whup you?" I asked.

"With his belt. He ain't done that since I was twelve. I just stood there and took it to get it over with. The real punishment was seeing that barn gone," he said. "All that work for all them months, gone up in the blink of an eye. It was insured and so was the tobacco, but that ain't—"

"What's that mean? Insured?"

"Daddy gets some money back on it, but he would of much rather had the crop."

"I know. It was terrible. *We* was terrible."

"Wasn't your fault." His voice was real quiet and I knew he felt bad about the whole thing.

"A new social worker came to see me Monday," I said, "and I was sure she was going to take me away. She came to the barn and—"

"I saw her. I didn't know who she was. You went off with her."

"I thought she was going to lock me up, like my mama."

"I was wondering the same thing. I thought maybe my daddy called that mental hospital to come take you away. I was real glad when you came back looking okay."

I smiled up at the sky. He'd been keeping a good eye on me from the south barn. "I like her," I said. "She's real nice. I felt like I could tell her just about anything."

"You didn't tell her about us, did you?" He sounded so worried, and I poked him with my elbow.

"'Course not," I said. "I thought your daddy might of told her, but it didn't seem like it. But your parents know now, so what's it matter?"

"Be careful you don't tell nobody. I promised my parents we wouldn't get together no more, or else they'll send one of us away."

"What do you mean?"

"Ain't exactly sure. I guess they'd either kick your family out or send me to my uncle's in Jacksonville."

They'd never send Henry Allen away. They needed him on the farm too much. My family, though? We was getting to be more trouble than we was worth.

We watched the stars a while, being quiet together. The radio played that song "Why Must I Be a Teenager in Love," which seemed perfect except the words didn't fit us too well. I could of stayed like that all night, but I knew we didn't have all night. After a while, I leaned up on my elbow and kissed him. He kissed back, but then held me away.

"I don't want to do it tonight," he said.

"You ain't got to pull out," I said. "The nurse gave me something to keep me from having a baby."

"What?" he asked.

"Special jelly medicine. I put it inside and you ain't got to pull out." When I got his note this morning, I decided to try out the spermicide jelly. I made a mess trying to get it in me, but figured it'd be worth it if Henry Allen didn't have to worry about pulling out in time.

"I like the sound of that," he said.

I couldn't see him real good but I could hear that he was smiling. I kissed him again.

"I mean it, Ivy," he said, "I don't want to do it tonight."

"Why not?"

He didn't talk right away and I felt nervous, waiting. "I don't know, exactly," he said, "but after last week . . . I just want to be sure you know it ain't all about doing it for me."

"I know that, silly," I said, relieved that was all that was bothering him. "Me, neither."

"Just wanted to be sure you know that," he said, and then he kissed me and I knew we'd be doing it after all, and that was right fine by me.

19

Jane

I'd worried needlessly about how I'd make conversation with Avery Jordan when I drove him to Ridley each week for his Braille lesson. He loved to talk. It took us fifteen minutes to get to Ridley and another five for me to find the colored school where the teacher would meet us, and in that time I said, perhaps, ten words to his ten thousand. It seemed that way to me, anyway. He was sweet and unintentionally funny, and he wasn't the least bit shy about telling me what it was like to have his eye disease.

"Like looking through a long pipe," he said. He leaned toward me in the front seat of my car, trying to make a pipe in front of my eyes with his hands.

"Avery." I gently moved his hands aside, laughing. "I have to see to drive."

"I can't see nothing outside the pipe," he continued, unfazed, "but I can see what's at the end of it pretty good." That explained why he turned his head constantly as we drove to the school. He could only see what was at the end of that pipe.

He told me everything I could ever want to know about his brothers, and he didn't censor himself, as far as I could tell. I found him, frankly, refreshing. Everyone else tiptoed around sensitive topics, but Avery dove right in.

"Devil got a girlfriend at school, but he got another summer one," he said. "The summer one don't know nothing about the school one, but he gets them mixed up sometimes. He calls one by the other name. Things like that. So he makin' up ways of remembering. The school one's called Belinda and she got a big behind, so that's how he remembers. Belinda and behind, get it?"

I nodded, smiling. "And how does he remember the summer one?" I asked.

"She got big, you know"—he raised his hands and I was certain he was going to demonstrate big breasts, but instead he tapped against his front teeth—"a big space between her teeth."

"So . . ." I glanced at him, trying not to laugh. "How does that help him remember her name?"

"It don't, far as I know."

"Ah." I couldn't help but laugh now. I was quickly getting used to the mind-tangling nature of a conversation with Avery.

"Does Eli have a girlfriend?" I asked, thinking of Charlotte's suspicions about Baby William's father.

"No, ma'am," he said with a vigorous shake of his head. "Eli done with girls. That's what he always say. Girls is too much trouble, is what he say."

"And how about you?" We were at a light, getting close to the school, and I looked at him.

He grinned like a little kid with a secret, and he was fair enough I thought he might be blushing. I loved those freckles across his nose. His glasses made his eyes look bright and big. He was so cute. How I wished I could magically fix his eyes for him! He was looking straight ahead, so I knew he couldn't see my curious expression. "Well?" I prompted him, smiling at his coyness.

"No, ma'am," he said. "I got a made-up girlfriend, but she ain't real."

"Ah," I said again. I believed him, and I was glad. If he'd had a girlfriend, I was afraid Ann Laing or someone would say it was time for him to be sterilized. I decided right then and there I wouldn't ask him that question ever again.

I had an hour to myself while Avery was with the teacher. Gayle had given me the number for a church in Ridley where she'd managed to track down hard-to-find donated items in the past, and sure enough, they had two old window fans. Only one was in working order but the woman I spoke with promised me the other was repairable. I was discovering that Gayle knew the resources better than anyone else in the office. She was quiet and serious, but she knew how to get a job done.

I drove to the church and picked up the fans. I'd take the broken one to a repair shop near our house. By next week, I hoped I'd be able to surprise both the Harts and the Jordans with them. Then I picked Avery up at the school and we headed back to the farm.

"Ma'am?" Avery said, when we turned onto Ridley Road. "Guess why I like learning Braille?"

"Why?" I asked.

"'Cause my brothers don't know it," he said. "I can do something they can't do at all."

I nodded. "I bet that's nice," I said, "having something to yourself."

"Yes, ma'am. I ain't got nothing to myself. I sure ain't got no bed to myself."

"No, I imagine it's pretty crowded in that bedroom. How about your mother? Where does she sleep?"

"She sleep in the kitchen."

I remembered the cot in Lita's kitchen.

"Sometime she goes missing, though."

"What do you mean, she 'goes missing'?

"Sometime I wake up and she ain't there."

"Probably in the johnny," I said.

"No, ma'am," he said. "She just ain't there."

I wasn't sure what to say or what questions to ask, so I let it rest. But when I dropped him off at his house, Lita came to my car window.

"Thank you, Mrs. Forrester," she said. "He likes riding with you."

"He's a very sweet boy," I said. "He said something . . . odd to me as we were driving home, though."

"Did he now? What's that?"

"He said sometimes you go missing. At night, he meant. He said he'd wake up and you'd be gone."

She hesitated a split second too long before laughing. "That boy!" she said. "If I sit out on the porch, he thinks I'm on the moon or something. You can't pay him no mind, Mrs. Forrester. He got an imagination. That's all."

I smiled. "Yes, I know he does," I said, then I waved and put the car in gear. "I'll see y'all next week," I said, and pulled out of their yard. In my rearview mirror, I saw her watching me drive away. She wasn't laughing anymore.

Gayle was getting ready to leave the office when I arrived. She stood by our receptionist Barbara's empty desk in the main office, studying herself in her compact mirror as she applied her too red lipstick.

"Thanks for telling me about that church," I said, setting my brief-case on Barbara's desk. "I got the fans."

"Very good." She pressed her lips together, then tilted her head to check her short, dark hair in the small mirror. "You have the office to yourself," she said, snapping the compact shut. "I'm on my way to see a client. Fred and Paula are in the field and Barbara has a doctor's appointment. You'll be all right?"

"Oh, I'm fine," I said. "I have a petition to work on."

"Good," she said, heading for the door. "See you tomorrow."

I carried my briefcase to my own office, then headed back into the main room. Paula had helped me with Ivy's petition the day before, but I'd made a mess of one of the forms and needed to find a blank one to work on. I remembered her telling me the forms were kept in one of the cupboards by Barbara's desk. I squatted down in front of the cupboard and opened it, instantly overwhelmed by the stacks of teetering paper threatening to spill onto the floor. I sat on the floor, hiking my skirt up, glad no one else was around. How was I ever going to find the form I needed in this mess?

I began pulling stacks of paper from the cupboard, planning to take a stab at organizing them. Soon, I was surrounded by piles of forms and booklets and memos and address lists.

A few blue pamphlets were tucked into a stack of other papers. I pulled one of them out and leafed through it. It was full of simple drawings that looked like they'd been done by a kindergartener, but it was the message behind the pictures that made me uncomfortable. *You wouldn't expect a moron to drive a train or a feebleminded woman to teach school,* the pamphlet read. *Then why should we expect them to be good parents? Voluntary sterilization saves taxpayer dollars and protects the community.*

How voluntary would it be in Ivy's situation if no one told her what was happening to her? Or Avery's, for that matter?

At the back of the pamphlet, someone had tucked a magazine article, folded in thirds. I unfolded it and read the title: "Better Human Beings Tomorrow." The first line read, "Tomorrow's population should be produced by today's best human material." I scanned the article, which advocated sterilizing "mental defectives." All I could think about was Hitler and his master race. How was this any different?

I heard the door to the main office open, and Paula shouted, "Hello!"

"Paula!" I said. "I'm over here. Come here and see what I found!"

"Yikes, what a mess!" she said as she spotted me sitting on the floor in a sea of paper. She leaned against the side of Barbara's desk. "What are you doing?"

"I was looking for a blank form for my part of the petition," I said, "and this cupboard was such a mess that I decided to clean it out. And, Paula, I found things that . . . Well, they give me the creeps."

"Like what?"

"This, for example." I handed her the pamphlet on sterilization. "Tell me this doesn't remind you of Nazi Germany."

She sat on the corner of Barbara's desk and paged through the pamphlet. "Oh my God." She laughed. "This is so ridiculous. Look at these drawings! I think this was *written* for morons."

"But don't you find it upsetting?"

"I find it silly," she said. "Is there a date on this thing?" She turned it over to check the back cover. "Nobody uses this anymore," she said. "I've never even seen it before."

"What about this article?" I handed it to her.

She scanned it as I had, shaking her head and smiling as though she couldn't believe I was upset. "Did you see the date on this?" she asked. "It's 1947! Thirteen years ago. We don't think this way anymore,

Jane." She looked at me. "You haven't been comfortable with the program from the start, have you?"

"I can see the benefit in some cases," I said. "I have a client who really wanted to be sterilized and I know it's helped her. Ivy, though"—I shook my head—"she needs to have a say in this."

Paula leaned toward me. "E-pi-lep-sy," she said. "That's all you need to think about. Plus her IQ."

"She's normal," I said.

"Not by much."

"I think that IQ test is off."

She let out a sound of exasperation, throwing her arms up in the air. "I don't have time for this," she said, standing up. "IQ tests don't lie." She handed the pamphlet and article back to me. "Charlotte thought you might be a problem," she said.

"What do you mean?"

"You're unprofessional," she said. "You get too involved. That's what she was afraid of. It's easy to lose objectivity when you get too involved."

I didn't like that they had talked about me.

"You need guts for this work," Paula said. "I hope you'll get some, because we need you. Obviously. We need you badly right now, with Charlotte gone. Just keep working on the petition," she said. "I think as you work your way through it you'll understand why it's the best thing for your client."

She picked up something from her office and called good night to me as she left, and I sat there on the floor surrounded by messy stacks of paper. I thought of taking the pamphlet and article home to Robert, but I was frankly afraid of his opinion. I suddenly felt alone, surrounded by eugenics propaganda and forms I wish I didn't have to fill out, and all I could think about was the teenaged girl who was only now starting to trust me.

20

Ivy

"That lady's here," Mary Ella said. She stood in the doorway of the kitchen where me and Nonnie was canning. We was all hot and sweaty and I was tired after looping all day, but the canning had to be done while the tomatoes was still good. "I seen her come out of the woods."

"What lady?" Nonnie asked, but I had a feeling right away who it was, and I ran into the living room and pulled open the door. Sure enough, Mrs. Forrester was coming onto the porch carrying some big metal thing and sweating up a storm.

"Hi, Ivy." She set the metal thing down on the porch and dusted off her hands. "Guess what I have for you?"

I took a closer look. "Is that a *fan*?" I asked.

"It certainly is. I just left one with the Jordans, too."

I couldn't believe it. I ran back in the house. "Nonnie! Mary Ella! Come look what Mrs. Forrester brung us!"

Nonnie hollered something about not being able to leave her jars, but Mary Ella came out and looked down at the fan. "Do it work?" she asked.

"How about we find out," Mrs. Forrester said. "Let me talk to your grandmother. See what window she'd like it in."

We all walked into the kitchen, Mrs. Forrester carrying the fan again.

"We got a window fan, Nonnie!" I said.

"Hello, Mrs. Hart," Mrs. Forrester said, "I hope you don't mind me visiting this late in the day, but I just dropped Avery Jordan off and thought I'd stop by."

"You work night and day, now don't you," Nonnie said, not even looking up from her steamy pot on the stove. Her dress and hair were wet with sweat and it dripped down her shiny face.

"Looks like you're working pretty hard yourself," Mrs. Forrester said.

"Ain't no choice here." Nonnie could be right ornery when she was hot.

"What window should it go in?" I asked.

"I'd suggest we try it out right here." Mrs. Forrester pointed to the window at the end of the kitchen. "See if we can get some circulation in this room while your grandmother's cooking."

"She ain't cooking," Mary Ella said. "She's canning."

"Oh," Mrs. Forrester said. "I've never canned anything. I'd love to see how you do it."

Nonnie looked at her like she was the dumbest lady she'd ever seen. "Oh, it's exciting, all right," she said.

"Would it be okay if I try to install it?" she asked Nonnie. "I'll have to take out the screen." The screen was old and full of big holes and not doing much good anyway.

"Do what you please," Nonnie said.

"Can I help?" I asked.

"You go outside and just make sure it doesn't fall through while I'm putting it in the window," she said.

I ran outside and helped steady it while Mrs. Forrester stretched out the sides of the fan to fit the window. I came inside and she was plugging it in.

"Everybody ready?" she asked, as she held her finger above the knob to turn it on.

"Ready!" Mary Ella said. I could tell she was excited. "Baby William!" she called. "Come watch."

Mrs. Forrester turned the switch and a breeze blew into the room and changed everything like magic. Nonnie smiled. Mary Ella laughed. Baby William came running from the other room to see what the fuss was about. And I looked at Mrs. Forrester where she was playing with the knob and a feeling come over me that was real good and real warm. I couldn't remember the last time I had that feeling, but I knew exactly what it was. *Hope.* She cared enough to bring us a fan. Mrs. Werkman never did nothing like that in all the years I knowed her. Mrs. Forrester could make things change for the good. Ever since that day she talked to me, I been talking to her in my head, telling her every little thought that came into it. I wished I could talk to her every minute. I was bursting with things to say to her, except for anything about Henry Allen. I wouldn't tell nobody about me and him.

"What do y'all think?" she asked, standing back to feel the breeze.

"Mary Ella," Nonnie scolded. "You're standing right in front of it, blocking it for everybody else."

Mary Ella *was* standing right in front of it, arms stretched out, head tipped back, hair blowing wild all around her head. Sometimes she didn't seem like a regular everyday kind of girl.

I took her arm and moved her to the side. "It's real nice," I said to Mrs. Forrester.

Baby William was hanging on to my leg.

"You've got to make sure William doesn't get his fingers near it." She looked worried.

"He ain't that stupid," Nonnie said. She was facing the fan and the sweat was starting to dry on her face.

"How's his rash?" She leaned over and lifted the edge of Baby William's shirt.

"Near gone," Nonnie said.

"A lot better," Mrs. Forrester agreed. She stood up straight and looked at her hands. They had a little grease on them from the fan. "May I wash my hands?" she asked.

"Sure," Nonnie said, and Mrs. Forrester went to the sink, looked at the pump a minute, then lifted the handle and pressed it down and nothing happened.

"Just needs priming," I said, pointing to the cup of water we kept on the windowsill.

She looked like a little girl seeing a toy she didn't know how to play with. Then she laughed. "Sorry," she said. "I don't know how to do it."

"You ain't never primed a pump?" Nonnie asked, like she never seen a girl so stupid.

"Here." I took the cup and poured it in the top of the pump. "Now it'll work," I said. "Just make sure to put more water in the cup for next time."

She laughed as she scrubbed the greasy marks on her fingers with the cake of soap. "Well, this is a first for me," she said, holding one hand under the pump, then the other.

"Guess what I got?" I said. "A transistor radio!" I ran into the living room to get it to show her.

"She must of stole it," I heard Mary Ella say. She'd been saying that since I brung it home. She and Nonnie didn't believe I just found it, like I said. One of the day workers must of dropped it by the fields, is what I told them.

I looked at Mrs. Forrester as I came back in the kitchen. "I found it," I said, and she nodded like she believed me.

I turned it on and put it on the table. "Oh! I love this song," I said as "Cathy's Clown" played, but it was almost at the end. Then the radio man said Chubby Checker was coming on next, singing "The Twist."

"Do you know that song?" Mrs. Forrester asked. "'The Twist'?"

"No, ma'am," I said, though I thought I heard it once on Henry Allen's radio.

"It's a new dance," Mrs. Forrester said as the music started.

"Race music." Nonnie shook her head. She thought everything was race music unless it had the word "Jesus" in it.

Mrs. Forrester didn't pay her no mind. She started moving funny, shaking her hips around and holding her arms up. "This is the dance," she said. "The twist. Can you do it?"

Mary Ella laughed, putting her hands over her mouth. "That ain't no dance!" she said, and she leaned back against the wall, watching Mrs. Forrester do the twist dance.

"It *is*," Mrs. Forrester said. "Want to try it?"

"Sinful is what it is," Nonnie said, but she was almost laughing herself.

I tried it, moving my hips and arms the way Mrs. Forrester done, and pretty soon, we was all twisting, even Baby William, who couldn't do it good at all. Even Nonnie. We was twisting around the kitchen, first smiling, and then laughing. When the next song came on, Mrs. Forrester took Nonnie's hands and started teaching her another dance, but Nonnie's face got red like she was ashamed she was dancing. She let go of Mrs. Forrester's hands. "Nothin' but race music," she said, returning to her pot on the stove. Mrs. Forrester took Baby William's hands then, and we was all still dancing and twisting and moving whatever way felt good around our kitchen.

"It's actually called 'beach music,'" Mrs. Forrester said. "They play it on the coast."

"I ain't never been to no beach," I said.

"Really?" she said. "You've never seen the ocean?"

"Never."

"Me, either," Mary Ella said.

"Have you seen the beach, Mrs. Hart?" Mrs. Forrester asked Nonnie.

"Oh yes, ma'am. All that sticky sand. No point to it, really."

Mrs. Forrester looked at me and then Mary Ella. "Well, I hope you get to go someday," she said. "There *is* a lot of sticky sand, like your grandmother says, but it's also very beautiful and fun."

I suddenly realized that was what we was having right then: fun. I thought the only time I could have fun anymore was when I was with Henry Allen. I thought being with him was the only time I could feel as good as I felt right that minute.

I was sad when Mrs. Forrester stopped dancing and looked at her watch. "I'd better get going," she said. "But"—a worried look came to her face—"may I use your . . . your outhouse before I go?" she asked, picking up her purse from the kitchen table.

"It's a johnny," Mary Ella said.

"Sure," I said. "Thank you for the fan."

"You're so welcome." Her face was all pink and pretty and I felt like hugging her, but of course I didn't. She left through the back door and I watched her step around the chickens as she walked toward the johnny.

"If she ain't used no pump," Nonnie said, lifting a jar out of the pot with the tongs, "she ain't used no johnny, neither."

152 | Diane Chamberlain

I thought of the bathroom at school and how different it was from our johnny. It had soft paper to use.

I pushed open the screen door and ran after her.

"Mrs. Forrester!" I called.

She was almost to the johnny and she turned around. "Yes, Ivy?" she said.

"Do you know about the johnny?" I asked. "About the . . . paper?"

"Paper? You mean toilet paper?"

I nodded. "We ain't got none," I said. "Use the pages from the catalog. Not the shiny pages, though. Crinkle them up a bunch of times to make them soft." I knew I was blushing, but she didn't seem embarrassed.

"Thank you, Ivy. I wouldn't have known."

"Yes, ma'am," I said, happy I could help her. I twisted all the way back to the house, dancing to the music in my head.

21

Jane

"You look beautiful," Robert said, as I took his arm to walk into the country club.

"Thank you." I leaned into him a little. Tonight was the night I would not think about my job. I'd promised myself that. Tonight was my gift to Robert. I'd give him all my attention. I'd make friends with the wives of his friends. I'd try my best to be the wife he wanted me to be.

I'd told all that to my mother when she went shopping with me for my dress the day before, and her response was "Good luck."

"Why do you say that?" I stopped sorting through the rack of dresses to look at her.

"No reason," she said. "I shouldn't have said anything. Sorry."

"Mother!" I said. "Now you have to tell me." I thought I'd been careful to keep my problems with Robert from her.

"Well"—she kept her eyes on the dresses rather than on me—"it's just that sometimes he seems to want you to be someone you're not," she said, and she took a deep blue sequined sheath-style gown from the rack. "How about this one?" she said.

I knew she was right, but then I could say the same about myself, I thought. Sometimes I wanted him to be someone he wasn't. I guessed that was typical of ninety-nine percent of all marriages.

Robert loved the blue sequined dress the moment he saw it. I spent the afternoon at the beauty parlor getting my hair styled into a French twist, little white pearls somehow hooked through the tresses. Robert said my hair looked even prettier than it had for my wedding.

The room was a sea of white and gold. Dozens of round tables, some with white tablecloths, others with gold, filled the entire space except for the dance floor, and each table was decorated with beautiful yellow and white floral centerpieces.

Robert seemed to know everyone—or at least all the men—and he introduced me as we made our way to our table at the edge of the dance floor. I found my place card, and took my seat between Robert and a man who quickly introduced himself and his wife. Gavin and Lois Parker. They were the oldest couple at the table. Early thirties, I guessed. Gavin's light brown hair was already starting to recede. The other two couples were closer to my age, and I recognized one of the girls. Beverly Ann Somebody. She was the one who'd stopped by the house just after we moved in to tell me about the Junior League, and now I suddenly remembered I was supposed to get back to her. She smiled across the table at me, but it was not the warmest of smiles.

Five minutes into sitting at the table, I knew the men's occupations—two pediatricians, one psychologist, and one attorney—and their golf scores. And I knew without asking that none of the three girls worked and they all knew each other. They talked about their children and the Junior League and an upcoming charity event. I kept a smile on my face and tried to make conversation with them, with little success. I was sitting next to the best conversationalist at the table in Gavin, the lawyer, though. He was one of those people who asked lots of questions and looked sincerely interested in my answers.

"Are you in the Junior League, too?" he asked. He had the most beautiful eyes, a pale translucent blue.

Robert spoke across me, answering quickly. "Jane hasn't had time to join yet," he said. "She's very involved in charitable work." I knew I was not to say anything about my job. I tried to imagine how it felt to Robert to have his wife employed when all the other girls at the table—maybe in the *room*—were not.

"Tell me about your charitable work," Gavin said.

I glanced at Robert, who gave me a resigned look and a nod. "I'm working for the Department of Public Welfare," I said. Ten minutes into the evening and the cat was already out of the bag.

Gavin's eyebrows lifted. "Office work?" he asked.

"No," I said, "in the field."

"What on earth does that mean?" Beverly Ann asked. "'In the field'?"

"I go to my clients' homes and evaluate their needs."

"You mean, people getting welfare?" Deborah, the psychologist's wife, asked.

"Yes."

I felt everyone's eyes turn to Robert. Whether they were asking why he'd allow his wife to do such a thing or if his practice was going that poorly, was anyone's guess.

"I'd love her to stay home," he said with a smile it must have taken him some effort to produce, and he put his arm around my shoulders, "but I learned early on you don't tell this girl what to do."

"You don't have to go into colored homes, do you?" Beverly Ann asked.

I nodded. "Sometimes."

She looked at Deborah. "Can you imagine?" she asked, and Deborah shook her head, a horrified expression on her face. Really, I was starting to hate them.

"Why?" Beverly Ann asked me. "You don't need to work, do you?"

"You mean financially?" I gave a look of mock surprise. "No, of course not. I just want to work for a while before we have a family. I've always wanted to have a career of my own. Haven't you ever felt that way?"

The two girls laughed. "The only career I want is as a wife and mother," Deborah said.

"I'm secretary of the Junior League," said Beverly Ann, "and trust me, that's as much work as anyone can handle. And the Junior League is all about charity," she added. "If helping the needy is so important to you, you can do it without getting your hands dirty."

Gavin's wife, Lois, had been quiet through much of the conversation. Now she leaned across her husband to touch my hand in what felt like a show of support. "I admire you," she said. "I was a teacher for a few years before I had our daughter. It was very satisfying."

"Thank you," I said, grateful.

"What sort of law do you practice?" I asked Gavin, desperate to get the topic off myself.

"Family," he said. "Divorce. Child custody. That sort of thing."

"It must be very interesting," I said. "You must hear some stories."

"You, too, with the sort of work you're doing."

"Well, yes," I admitted. Somehow, the topic was back on me. "It's been eye-opening."

"Are you working in Raleigh?"

"Grace County."

"Oh my," he said, "I can just imagine the stories! So rural. Were you raised on a farm?"

"Me? Oh no. Cameron Park. No, this is all new to me. I feel as though I've been shot into space and landed on another planet."

"I bet it's interesting."

"It is. And I'm dying to ask David a question about one of my clients," I said quietly, as if asking Gavin's permission to talk to the psychologist sitting next to Lois.

"Go ahead," Lois said. "David loves to talk. *Loves* it."

"Did I hear my name?" David asked.

"Do you mind if I ask a question related to my work?" I had to speak up to be heard; the room was full of chatter and the band had started to play.

"Darling," Robert said, "this is a social event."

"You're right." I sat back in my chair, remembering my promise to him. "Sorry," I said to David.

"Would you like to dance, Jane?" David smiled at me. He touched Deborah's shoulder. "Do you mind, dear?" he asked, and she shook her head, but I was afraid she minded very much and he'd be in the doghouse later. David turned to Robert. "May I dance with your wife?" he asked.

"Of course," Robert said. What else *could* he say?

Once on the dance floor, we fox-trotted to a Sinatra song. "So," he said, "what's your question?"

"Do you do psychological testing?" I asked.

He groaned. "That's all I do these days," he said. "I work for Wake County Schools. Do you need someone tested?"

I shook my head. "No, I was just wondering if it's possible that the results of an IQ test can be affected by, say, a child's environment." I had to lean close to his ear for him to be able to hear me. "For example, many of my clients test very low—"

"How low?"

"Well, all over the place, but I'm thinking of a particular fifteen-year-old girl who tests eighty. She seems smarter to me than that."

"She wouldn't be considered retarded at eighty," he said. "Dull normal, yes, but not retarded."

"I know," I said, nearly shouting so he could hear, "but I think—"

He held up a hand to stop me, then took me by the arm and led me off the dance floor to the side of the room where we could hear each other more easily.

"To answer your question," he said, "there's a lot of controversy about this. I believe the environmental and cultural factors do come into play. The tests were created for white middle-class children, so you add in poverty and cultural differences, and it makes sense that the results would be different, though not everyone would agree with me. There are a few studies that show that poor children who scored low and were then adopted into good middle- or upper-class families later tested higher. But Jane, here's the thing," he said. "We have to work with the tools we have. This isn't a perfect world. What's your concern with this girl? So she tests eighty. So what? How is that affecting her? Is it holding her back in school, or—"

"No, that's not it. They—the Department of Public Welfare—plan to sterilize her."

"Really?" He looked surprised.

I nodded. "I'm in charge of putting together a petition to have her sterilized." I'd actually finished the petition, but couldn't bring myself to send it to the board yet.

"Are there other factors being considered?" he asked. "As I said, eighty is not retarded."

"Yes, she's epileptic—"

"Ah," he said, as though that explained everything.

"But it's petit mal," I said. "And I don't think she's had a seizure in a long time. Maybe years."

"Colored?"

"White."

"How about her parents?"

I felt Robert's eyes on us. Maybe Deborah's, as well, although I may have been imagining that.

"Her father is dead and her mother . . . her mother's insane. She's at Dix Hospital. My client and her sister are being raised by their grandmother."

"And of course they're on welfare."

"Yes."

"How are they making out?"

"You mean . . ." I wasn't sure what he was asking. "What do you mean?"

"In general. What's your assessment of the family and how it's functioning?"

I looked away from him, formulating my answer. Making things seem better than they were would do me no good. "Not well," I said. "The grandmother's diabetic. The older sister has a toddler and he's not getting the best care. The girl I'm talking about, though . . ." I looked away again, and felt my eyes begin to sting. "She's really the one taking care of everything. She's the only one who seems able to manage and she's pretty overwhelmed."

"Hmm," he said. "Too bad you can't see her out of her environment. Might be interesting. She might look high functioning to you only because she's someplace where she knows exactly what's expected of her."

I thought of my inept use of the kitchen pump, and I would have been lost in the outhouse if she hadn't told me about the Sears and Roebuck catalog. I would have thought it was there to read, the way my mother kept a *Reader's Digest* in our bathroom at home. In Ivy's world, *I* was the retarded one.

"Her grandmother's signed the petition and all I have to do at this point is turn it in," I said. "But as I get to know her, I'm having trouble doing that."

"Well, you said it yourself, Jane. She's overwhelmed. What will another baby do? Make her less overwhelmed? And the baby will most likely inherit some of the problems you just described. Perhaps the mother's mental illness. Epilepsy. Low intelligence. Maybe even the grandmother's diabetes. If it were up to me, I'd get her sterilized sooner rather than later. I'd want to lighten her load and the load on the welfare system."

I nodded, not happy with the answer. "Thanks for talking to me about it."

He smiled. "My pleasure," he said.

We walked back to the table in silence. Deborah sent me a look of blue-eyed daggers across the table but I turned away. I felt depleted. All the people—Robert, Charlotte, Paula, Fred, Gayle, Ann—who'd told me Ivy should have the surgery had made similar arguments. Not one had agreed with me. Maybe I was the one who was wrong.

Gavin leaned over and whispered in my ear, "Well, that looked rather intense."

I smiled uncomfortably, not looking at him. I felt Robert's disapproval of me and thought I had been rude, monopolizing another girl's husband, bending his ear for so long. The next time Deborah looked my way, I was ready and caught her eye. "Thanks for letting me borrow your husband," I said across the table. "He helped me figure out a problem I'm having at work." She didn't smile, but turned toward Beverly Ann, and I knew the look they exchanged was enough to keep me out of their circle for the rest of my life.

The band started playing "The Twist," and nearly everyone got to their feet, Robert included. He reached his hand toward me and we joined the mob on the dance floor. I loved that dance. Loved how it made me feel—young and free. I'd never again be able to do the twist without thinking of the Hart family and the few precious, lighthearted minutes in their kitchen last week, when even Winona Hart couldn't help but smile.

When we returned to our seats, the other three wives excused themselves to go to the ladies' room. None of them looked in my direction with an invitation to join them and that, maybe more than anything else that had happened during the evening, made me aware I was an outsider.

I stood up, and Robert looked at me in surprise. "Going to powder my nose," I said, and I followed the three girls, tagging along behind them, carrying my sequined purse with its lipstick and powder.

The restroom was large, and I stood next to Deborah in the mirrored lounge as we each reapplied our lipstick.

"I really am sorry I monopolized your husband like that," I said. "It was rude. I had a question about psychological testing regarding one of my clients and he was able to explain a few things to me. I had no idea it would take so long."

She cut her eyes at me, then pressed her lips together around a tissue. "You think you're above us, don't you," she said, tossing the tissue into the can below the counter.

"No," I said. "Why on earth would I think that?"

"We all have university degrees. Beverly Ann, Lois, and I. You're not the only one."

"I never thought I was," I said, "and what does it matter, anyhow? I don't care who has a degree and who doesn't."

"Leave her alone." Lois approached us, pulling a comb from her purse. To me, she said, "Don't listen to her."

"I'd like us to be friends," I said to both of them. "Our husbands are all connected through the club, and we're going to be seeing each other throughout our lives, so please. Can we try to be friends?"

"Of course we can." Lois ran the comb through her short brown hair. She was the only girl in the lounge who wasn't wearing a fancy hairstyle.

"I don't see the point," Deborah said. "You refuse to join the Junior League, and you're working, so the only time we'll ever see you is events like this."

"I can do things with all of you, just not in the daytime," I said. "I'm really not sure why you're freezing me out like this."

"You have no idea how hard *we* work," Deborah said. "Taking care of a household and two children, plus working in the thrift shop and—"

"Oh, for Pete's sake, Deborah," Lois said. "You have a full-time maid. When is the last time you did a load of laundry?"

"You've frozen *yourself* out." Beverly Ann appeared in the mirror behind me, smoothing her hair carefully into place. "Come on, Deb," she said.

I bit my lip as I watched them leave the lounge. Lois touched my elbow. "Let's sit for a minute," she said, nodding toward the two chairs near the door.

I was all too ready to sit. "I never got back to Beverly Ann about the league," I admitted. "My mistake."

"Most of the wives are lovely, and I think you'd enjoy the Junior League," Lois said. "Tonight, we just got stuck sitting with two of the prunes. I've been ill off and on for the last couple of years and—"

"Oh, I'm so sorry." Perhaps that explained her pallor.

She shrugged off my sympathy. "They . . . Deborah and Beverly Ann . . . they cut me out. When I couldn't make league meetings or help with a baby shower or whatever, they stopped calling. So it's not just you. It's anyone who doesn't fit neatly into their mold."

"Thank you for telling me that."

"They're threatened by you," she said. "You chose to do something they'd never have the gumption to choose for themselves. Being their own person. When I was teaching, it upset Gavin at first because he thought it reflected badly on him, but then he realized how much I loved it. How it made me a happier person. I hope Robert understands that, too."

"Oh, he does," I said, a tiny bit envious.

"That's what it's all about, isn't it?" she asked. "Being able to choose what we want to do."

I walked with her back to our table, thinking not about her or myself or Beverly Ann or Deborah, but about Lita Jordan and Ivy and Mary Ella Hart and all the other women and girls I was seeing who didn't have many choices in their lives at all.

Robert was quiet in the car on the way home and I felt the tension between us. The evening had definitely gone downhill and I knew it was my fault. He'd had such high expectations. I remembered him saying he wanted to show me off. Now, he probably wanted to hide me.

"The band was great," I said, taking a stab at a neutral conversation. "I loved how they played something for everyone. You know, for all the age groups."

"You don't even try to get along with them." His hands clenched the steering wheel, eyes on the road.

"What are you talking about?"

"The wives. You don't have any problem talking to the *men,* though, do you." He glanced at me. "No problem there at all. But you look down your nose at the girls. You're never going to fit in."

"I do not look down my nose at them!" I said. "Why do you think I followed them to the powder room? Except for Lois, they were intentionally rude to me, so I went with them to the powder room to talk to them directly about trying to be friends."

"Well, there's your problem." He shook his head. "You don't talk *directly* about things like that. I swear, Jane, you have no social graces whatsoever."

"Why not be direct?" I said. I was pulling the silly pearls out of my hair and dropping them in my purse. "Isn't it better to be honest? Lois understood. At least I have one friend in that group."

His nostrils flared, the way they did when he got angry. "You've changed so much since you started working," he said.

"I haven't changed." I pulled the bobby pins out of my hair and tried to let it down, but it was sprayed into place. "It's just that the things you loved about me when we were dating are the things that seem to bother you now," I said. "I'm the same person. You loved that person as your *girlfriend,* but not as your *wife.*"

"We're in that beautiful club tonight, surrounded by successful people who've worked hard to get where they are—and all you could think about was those . . . *people* you work with." He made the word "people" sound like something dirty. "Do you have to throw it in their faces? That you work with Negroes and poor white trash?"

"Don't talk about my clients that way, all right?" I snapped. "Just don't!"

"You better start caring about your marriage as much as you care about them."

"Is that supposed to be some kind of threat?" I stared at him. I wished he'd look at me. I wanted him to see the fury in my face. But he focused on turning into our driveway, parking next to my car. Then he finally turned to me.

"Lois will be dead in a year," he said.

"*What?*"

"She has cancer. So if she's your only friend in our social circle, you're in trouble."

He got out of the car and walked around to my side to open my door for me, but I brushed away his hand when he reached for mine to help me out.

"Just leave me alone," I said.

I didn't need to ask him twice. He slammed the door so hard that I jumped.

I rolled down the window to catch the breeze and sat there for what seemed like hours. How Robert had looked forward to this night! I played back the evening, remembering my determination to be light and fun and attentive to him all evening, a plan that fell apart within minutes of our arrival.

My fault.

No one else to blame.

I got out of the car and went into the house to apologize to my husband.

22

Ivy

Mrs. Forrester popped out of the woods while I was hanging sheets on the line. Baby William'd peed all over them last night because Mary Ella was right sloppy with diapers sometimes. It was Sunday. What was Mrs. Forrester doing here on a Sunday? Couldn't be good.

"Good morning, Ivy!" she said, like seeing me was the best thing that ever happened to her.

"It's Sunday, Mrs. Forrester," I said, thinking she might of got her days confused. I was happy to see her, though. Even Nonnie still laughed when we talked about doing the twisting dance in the kitchen and we loved the fan. We moved it into the bedroom and I never slept so good on a summer night before.

"That's why I'm here," she said. "You don't work on the farm on Sunday, right? I thought I could take you and Mary Ella and Nonnie and Baby William on a little trip to the beach."

I just stared at her. Had she lost her mind?

"The beach?" I shook out Nonnie's raggedy old slip and hung it up. "What are you talking about?"

"I think y'all need a getaway," she said. "Just for the day. Would you like that?"

"I ain't never been," I said.

"I know. That's why I thought it might be fun. Do you have a bathing suit?"

"No, ma'am. When we go to the pond, we just wear shorts."

"Well, let's talk to your grandmother and Mary Ella and see if y'all can take time off from your household duties and have a relaxing day."

I slipped a clothespin over one of Baby William's dingy-looking diapers and started toward the house. "Mary Ella ain't here right now," I said. "Nonnie sent her to a church friend to get some of the cookies they give out after the service." I was embarrassed to let Mrs. Forrester know how far Nonnie would go for sweets, sending Mary Ella two miles away on the bike just for a few cookies.

"When will she be back?"

"I don't rightly know," I said. You never did know with Mary Ella. She might of been doing one of her disappearing acts.

I looked up at the blue sky, a few puffy clouds right over my head. I didn't know why Mrs. Forrester came up with this idea, but Lord, it was a beautiful day and I wanted to see the ocean. I didn't think Nonnie would say yes, though. She had chores lined up for me and Mary Ella that would take us all day.

"Well, we'll start with your grandmother, then."

We found Nonnie in the kitchen, eating the biscuit I told her not to eat at breakfast. Smeared with jelly, of course. I wanted to rip it out of her hand, but knew better than to do that in front of somebody. I just gave her the eye and she gave it right back to me.

"Mrs. Forrester wants to take all of us to the beach," I said. Mrs. Werkman would never do anything like that. Never.

"That's the craziest thing I ever heard," Nonnie said. "You supposed to be home with your own family on Sunday."

"My husband's playing golf today," she said, "and I thought it would be nice to drive out to the beach, and since I knew the girls had never been, I'd invite you all to come along."

"Sticky sand." Nonnie said the same thing she did the other day, licking the jelly from her fingers and probably making her sugar go sky-high. "Ain't been since I was a child, but I remember."

"Well, then you must also remember how special it is," Mrs. Forrester said. "Let's all take a day off and go."

"I got too much to do," Nonnie said, "but you can take the girls and the baby."

I squealed. What a surprise! "Thank you, Nonnie!" I said, giving her a hug, even though I knew why she was letting us go: She was going to eat the cookies and anything else she could find, all day long, starting as soon as we left the house. Nobody home to tell her she shouldn't.

"Great," Mrs. Forrester said. "Get some clothes you can swim in and whatever you need for William. Do you have any extra towels? I have some, but we could use a few more if you have them. I have suntan oil and an umbrella." She looked around the room. "Where *is* William?"

"Where's he at?" I asked Nonnie, and she shrugged.

"Baby William!" I hollered. I poked my head in the bedroom. "You want to see the ocean, Baby?" But he wasn't there.

"Could he be outside?" Mrs. Forrester looked worried.

"That boy could be anywhere," Nonnie said.

"He's only two," Mrs. Forrester said. "He really needs all of you to keep a more careful eye on him." She was peeking behind the sofa like he might be hiding there. I was pretty sure where he was: under the porch, watching for Mary Ella to come home.

"I know where he is," I said, hoping I was right so Mrs. Forrester wouldn't think we wasn't watching him right. I walked out the front door, hopped down the step and peeked underneath. Sure enough, there he was. "Come on outta there," I said, grabbing him and yanking him out, but not before I pulled a lizard from his hand. I hoped he wasn't going to stick that thing in his mouth. "We're going to the beach."

He let out a howl at how rough I was being with him. Mary Ella would of smacked me if she saw me pull him out that way, but I had to show Mrs. Forrester I could be tough with him. I knew she thought we wasn't doing right by him. She didn't understand you couldn't keep an eye on a little boy on a farm any more than you could keep an eye on a dog or cat.

When we got back inside, Nonnie was already getting the towels and some clothes ready for us. She was fired up to get us gone so she could dig into the jar of jelly by the spoonful.

"Now we just got to wait for Mary Ella," I said.

"We could drive to the church friend's house," Mrs. Forrester said. "Give her a ride back."

"All right. Can you change Baby William and get some extra diapers for us while we're gone?" I asked Nonnie.

Nonnie nodded. "Don't let Mary Ella forget what I sent her for," she warned. "That girl forgets her own name sometimes."

We drove up Deaf Mule Road. Mary Ella'd been gone long enough she should be coming home by now, but there wasn't no sign of her yet. I spotted a truck coming toward us and could tell from a long ways away it was Eli driving it.

"Here comes Eli Jordan," I said.

"He has a truck?" She sounded . . . suspicious? Like how could a colored boy have a truck. That made me disappointed with her. It was all about money with them social workers, even Mrs. Forrester, I guessed. You had a truck or a car—where'd you get the money for it? Did you take it out of your babies' mouths?

"It's Mr. Gardiner's old truck," I said. "He lets Eli use it for farmwork sometimes. He's slowing down. Can you stop?"

Mrs. Forrester pressed on the brake real slow and we stopped right next to the truck. Devil and Avery were sitting in the bed and Avery stood up and waved. "Hey, Mrs. Forrester!" he shouted.

"Sit down, Avery," she said. "It's dangerous."

Eli looked at Mrs. Forrester and then past her to me. "Where you going?" he asked.

"We're looking for Mary Ella Hart," Mrs. Forrester said, using Mary Ella's last name like she was a stranger to Eli instead of a girl he knowed all his life. "She went on an errand for her grandmother."

"You seen her?" I asked. "She's on her bike."

Eli didn't answer right away. Then he called out his open window. "Mary Ella!"

Mary Ella's head popped up from the bed of the truck and I knew she'd been hiding back there so no one would see her with colored boys. "We saw her on the bike," Eli said. "Gave her a ride home." He was staring at Mrs. Forrester like he was waiting for her to say he done something wrong. It *was* wrong. I didn't want to think what Mary Ella might have been doing in the bed of the truck with Devil and Avery. I didn't know my sister no more.

"Mary Ella, get out of that truck," I said. "You know better. Nonnie'll shoot Eli if she sees you riding with him." I looked at Eli. "We'll take her home," I said.

He looked at me again. "Everything all right?" he asked.

"We're going to the beach with Mrs. Forrester," I said.

"Ain't that dandy," he said.

Mary Ella looked around to be sure no one was watching, then jumped out of the back of the truck carrying the basket she always had on her arm. She reached up for the bike Devil was handing down to her, but Eli told him to leave it. "I'll carry it home for you," he said to Mary Ella.

Mary Ella got in the backseat of Mrs. Forrester's car, and Eli took off.

"What do you mean about the beach?" Mary Ella asked.

"I have a free day," Mrs. Forrester said, "so I stopped by to see if you girls and William would like to take a little trip to the beach." I was so glad she didn't say anything about Mary Ella being in the truck with the boys. Mrs. Werkman would have preached a whole sermon.

"We can swim?" Mary Ella asked.

"Yes," Mrs. Forrester said.

"But it ain't like the pond," I told Mary Ella. "You've seen pictures of them big waves in the ocean." I thought of the pictures in Henry Allen's California book, the ones with them boys on the boards, but I knew the Atlantic Ocean didn't have no waves like that. "We have to keep a good eye on Baby William." I wanted Mrs. Forrester to know I heard her. I wanted her to like me; it was dumb how much. I didn't usually care that much about being liked, except by one handsome boy I hardly ever got to see these days.

"Hopefully, it will be calm today," Mrs. Forrester said. She kept looking in her mirror at Mary Ella.

"What did you get for Nonnie?" I asked her.

"Oatmeal cookies."

"She's gonna collapse and die on us," I said.

"Maybe Nurse Ann needs to talk to her some more about what to eat," Mrs. Forrester said.

"She knows what," I said. "She just gets real hungry and can't stop herself."

"It must be very hard for her," Mrs. Forrester said, and I thought that was real kind of her. More kind than I would be, and Nonnie was my own flesh and blood.

We got back to the house and Mrs. Forrester told us to pee and get a fresh diaper on Baby William. Then she went in the johnny herself and then we put on the clothes Nonnie got out for us. I'd outgrowed mine already. I had to stop eating Nonnie's biscuits. I didn't have nothing to wear to swim in, so Nonnie gave me one of her old housedresses. It would have to do. She said we could take a few cookies with us, but Mrs. Forrester said she had sandwiches in a cooler and a big thermos full of lemonade, so we was set.

The drive took a long time. No wonder we never got to the beach before! It took forever and Baby William cried half the way there, then finally calmed down and fell asleep on Mary Ella's lap in the backseat. Mrs. Forrester asked us lots of questions, which seemed like her favorite thing to do. What subject did I like best in school? I said history. Then she asked Mary Ella what subject did she like back when she was in school and Mary Ella said, "Nothing." If we could live anywhere, where would we like to live? That was her next question. For me, that was easy. California, of course. Mary Ella had a harder time answering. She didn't like questions. She didn't like nobody seeing inside herself. Not even me, her own sister. When she didn't answer, Mrs. Forrester just asked it again. "Where would you most like to live, Mary Ella?" she asked. "If you could live anywhere in the whole wide world?"

"California," she said.

"What?" I said. "You ain't never said nothing about California before. You just said that because I did. She don't even know where California is," I said to Mrs. Forrester.

"Do you really want to live in California, Mary Ella?" Mrs. Forrester asked, looking in her mirror. I knowed what she was seeing. My sister, her hair blowing all around her head from the open window, looking at the countryside, thinking how to answer.

"No," she finally said. "I just want to live away. Far away. Baby William and me."

"Far away . . . some place in particular?" Mrs. Forrester asked.

"Any place. Long as it's far away."

"Who else would live there?" Mrs. Forrester asked, and I knew even before the last word was out of her mouth that she'd pushed Mary Ella one question too far. Sure enough, my sister shut up and didn't speak another word for the rest of the drive.

Mary Ella turned out to be afraid of the ocean. I understood. When we got out of the car and climbed over the little sandy hills, I felt dizzy myself. When you see a picture of the ocean, it's cut off at the edges. You know it goes on and on to the right and on and on to the left, but you never really know how it feels to see that until you actually do see it. Mary Ella climbed over the sandy hill and couldn't take another step. She just stood there, Baby William in her arms, yellow hair blowing all around.

"It's too big," she said.

Mrs. Forrester laughed, but just a little. Not like she was making fun of Mary Ella. "It's a shock at first, isn't it?" she said. "You'll get used to it quickly. Baby William is used to it already. He wants to get down and play." Baby William was squirming in Mary Ella's arms. Mrs. Forrester took him from her and set him on the sand. He started doing his wobbly run toward the water. "Don't go in yet!" Mrs. Forrester called after him. "Wait for us."

I laughed. Let her see how easy it was to keep an eye on that boy.

There was other people on the beach, but not too many. I could hear music from transistor radios and wished I brung mine. Mary Ella and me rubbed suntan oil on each other's arms and backs and we set out the two blankets Mrs. Forrester had and the cooler and thermos and towels and took off our shoes and then we walked into the water. The waves seemed big to me but Mrs. Forrester said they were tiny. Mary Ella stayed up near the beach, the water just splashing around her legs, but me and Mrs. Forrester held Baby William's hands and swung him through the waves. I never saw that boy smile and laugh so much. I wished we lived right next to the ocean. When I said that, Mrs. Forrester said you could ruin a thing by wishing for something else. She asked me if I understood what she meant, but I thought she was talking gibberish. So she said, "If you're having fun at the beach, like we are, but you spend all your time here wishing you could be here all the time, you're wasting the time you're here." She asked me if I understood that, and I said yes but I still thought she was talking some other language.

When we came out of the water, Mrs. Forrester went back to her car to get a big umbrella and she put it up over us. The truth is, Mary Ella and me are pretty brown from working on the farm all summer, but Mrs. Forrester is sickly pale and she put a lot of the suntan oil on her skin. I tried to keep Baby William under the umbrella as much as I could because when his skin gets brown, people think he's colored. Little colored-looking boy with a blond mama? Didn't look so good.

After we ate, Mary Ella and Baby William went to sleep on the blanket, but Mrs. Forrester and me sat watching the waves.

"I could watch the ocean forever and ever," I said. "Don't think I'd ever get tired of it."

"I agree," Mrs. Forrester said. "Wouldn't it be fun to have a house right on the water?"

"Like a floating house?"

"No, no. A house up on the dunes. Where you'd be on safe ground—at least until a hurricane came—but you'd have this view every single day."

I tried to remember what she'd said to me about wishing for something and how that wasted the time you had now, but I couldn't think exactly how she said it, so I just thought it to myself.

"Is the Pacific Ocean just like this?" I asked.

"You're very interested in California," she said.

"I seen pictures. You ever been there?"

She shook her head. "It does sound beautiful," she said.

I wanted to tell her about Henry Allen so bad. I never got to tell nobody about him. We sat there quiet for a few minutes, me almost shaking while I got up the courage. "You asked me if I had a boyfriend," I said. "I do. I got one."

She just looked out at the waves and I didn't think she heard me, but then she said, "Tell me about him."

The way it took her a few seconds to answer made me change my mind about telling her. "Please don't tell," I said. It was stupid I said anything. She'd tell Nonnie and Nonnie would kill me. "Promise you won't tell nobody?" I asked.

"Yes, I promise," she said. "How do you know this boy?"

"I just do," I said. "Me and him talk about living in California someday. We both want to be teachers."

"So . . . to be a teacher you have to stay in school."

"I know that." Did she think I was dumb?

"What I mean is, you need to be very careful about not getting pregnant so you don't get kicked out of school."

"We already talked about this, ma'am." I tried to sound as polite as I could but I wasn't going to tell her about personal things. It was bad enough with Nurse Ann.

"I just worry, that's all."

"He has a book on California and we spend hours looking at the pictures. That's all we do."

She smiled at me. Her nose was pink and she looked real pretty. "He sounds like a nice boy," she said.

"Yes, ma'am, he is."

"When do you get to see him?"

"Oh, hardly never now school's out." I'd let her think I knew him at school.

"It's very hard to be a teacher and have a family at the same time," she said. "Have you thought about that?"

"My favorite teacher, Mrs. Rex, done it. She got two children and she's a teacher."

"Do you want children, Ivy?"

"Don't everybody?" I asked. Sometimes she asked the stupidest questions.

"Well, no," she said. "Every girl in the world doesn't want to have

NECESSARY LIES | 173

children. Some of them only have them because they feel society says they should."

"What does that mean? Society says?"

"Other people. Other people judge you if you don't have children. As if there's something wrong with you. But for some women, it can be the right choice because they want to do other things with their lives."

"Like what?"

"Oh, have a career—that means a job—that doesn't mix well with raising a family. That sort of thing. So no, every woman doesn't want to have children."

"That's not me," I said. "I can't imagine having no children. That's crazy. That's what life's about." Then I thought maybe she was one of them ladies who didn't want children and I just made her feel bad, because she went quiet again.

"Do you want to have children?" I asked.

She nodded, but real slowly. "Someday," she said. "Not yet."

We walked back to the car, and we was hot and the dunes steep. I didn't feel so good and Mrs. Forrester said maybe I had too much sun. I was out of breath by the time we got to the car and really, really tired. Everyone was quiet and when I got into my seat I thought Mrs. Forrester had tears in her eyes. She turned her face away from me real quick.

"What's the matter?" I asked.

She shook her head and smiled at me but it was one of them weak smiles, not a real smile at all. "Nothing," she said. "It was just a good day." She looked over her shoulder at Mary Ella and Baby William, already almost asleep.

"Why don't you nap while I drive home?" she said. She reached over and put her palm on my forehead like she was checking me for a fever. She was acting strange, but I liked that she touched me. Her hand felt real soft. "Would you like some lemonade before we start driving?" she asked.

"I don't need nothing," I said.

She started the car and pulled into the street and I closed my eyes and before I knew it, I was asleep, dreaming of all that water.

23

Jane

"Welcome back!" I smiled as I walked into my office . . . well, the office that had been mine alone for the past month while Charlotte recovered from her fall. Now Charlotte sat at her desk, with her leg, still in a cast, propped up on a stool and her crutches leaning against the wall. She still had that polished, clear-skinned look I'd come to associate with her, though there was a tightness around her mouth that made me think she was in pain. "How are you feeling?" I set my briefcase on the floor near my desk. "And how on earth did you get up the stairs?"

"It took me about twenty minutes with lots of help from Fred and Gayle," she said. "But I couldn't stay home another day. I was going stir-crazy."

"I bet." I sat down at my desk. "You look wonderful."

She brushed aside the compliment with a small groan. "I still relive that fall every time I close my eyes," she said.

"It was terrible. I'm so glad you're doing all right."

"Obviously, I won't be working in the field for a while," she said. "Fred will stick around another month until I'm at full strength. And actually"—she looked at her watch—"he'll be here any minute. We need to talk to you."

Her tone told me they didn't have good news for me, and I immediately thought of my clients. Had something happened to one of them?

"What's wrong?" I asked.

Fred walked into the room at that moment. He stood just inside the doorway and pointed at me. "You," he said, "are a loose cannon."

"Me?" I said. "I don't understand."

Fred sat down in the only unoccupied chair in the room, a straight-backed chair against the wall by the door. "I got a call from Ann Laing this morning," he said. "She was out to check on the Hart family and learned you took them to the beach yesterday."

"Yes, I did."

"*Jane.*" Charlotte's voice registered disappointment and disbelief. "You can't go carting your clients around willy-nilly at off-hours," she said. "It's against regulations."

Fred looked at her. "Does she have the manual?" he asked.

"I gave her one," Charlotte said, talking about me as if I weren't sitting right there. She looked at me. "Didn't you read it? Your manual?"

"Yes, of course I did, but I—"

"These people are not your best friends," Fred said. "You had no authority to take them on a *road trip* with you."

"I didn't realize I was doing something wrong." I'd remembered what David, the psychologist at the country club, had said about seeing Ivy in a different environment. "I thought it would be helpful to see Ivy someplace unfamiliar to her," I said. "I'm so convinced that she's brighter than her test shows and thought—"

"You're treading on very thin ice," Charlotte said.

"You've been at this job how long?" Fred asked.

"Five weeks," I said.

"And you know better than Charlotte and the testing psychologist and the nurse who've been working with this girl—and others like her—for decades?"

I thought of what I'd learned on the beach trip. It had been valuable, but perhaps only to reinforce Charlotte and Ann's case. I now knew Ivy had a boyfriend, so there was greater potential for her to have sex. But I also knew how much she wanted a family. I knew she had what the books I'd read called "native intelligence"—common sense—and I was sure her IQ was higher than 80, though perhaps not by much. But the thing I'd learned that had truly shaken—and depressed—me, had happened in the last few minutes of our time on the beach. As we climbed over the dune to go back to the car, Ivy suddenly stopped walking. When I looked at her, she was staring into space, blinking a mile a minute. Her eyes rolled up and I knew what I was seeing even before Mary Ella said, matter-of-factly, "It's a fit. It'll be over in no time."

It *was* over in no time and Ivy picked up walking right where she left off, unaware of what had just happened, but for me, everything had changed. She was still epileptic. She hadn't outgrown it, as I'd hoped. That family she wanted? It would be much harder to come by now. By the time we reached my car, my eyes had stung with tears. I'd already planned to talk to Ann about the weight Ivy was putting on. She needed some guidance to know what she should eat and what she shouldn't. After that seizure, though, I knew I had something much more serious to talk to Ann about, and I also knew what Ann would say.

If Ivy were my neighbor, though, no one would think of sterilizing her. That was the thing. The petition was because she was poor. Poor and on welfare and unable to speak for herself.

"Ivy wants children," I said. "If she doesn't get pregnant now and gets good medical care for her epilepsy and good care once she's married and pregnant, she could have a chance at the family," I said.

"That's a hell of a lot of ifs," Fred said.

"Unrealistic ifs," Charlotte added. "I was shocked this morning when Paula told me you haven't turned the petition in yet," she said. "She said you're getting cold feet about the Eugenics Program. I thought we'd talked about that and you understood the benefits."

"I—"

"How far along are you with the petition?" Fred asked.

"It's almost finished," I said.

"Then finish it and turn it in," Charlotte said.

Barbara appeared at my office door. "There's a call for you, Jane," she said. "A Davison Gardiner? He said it's urgent."

I turned away from Charlotte and Fred, glad to escape their angry eyes. I picked up the phone. "Mr. Gardiner?" I said. "This is Jane Forrester."

"Hey, Mrs. Forrester," he said. "I'm afraid we got a situation here."

24

Ivy

I was looping at the Christmas barn, trying to watch Henry Allen at the same time. He was driving the mule in front of the sled out in the field, and I couldn't wait till the sled was full and he'd bring us the leaves. Then he'd be close enough for me to touch. Or at least to get a good look at. We was so careful about not looking at each other when people was around—which was always—and we never talked in front of nobody. It'd been almost three weeks since the last time we was together and I missed him so bad I felt crazy. How we was ever going to work things out, I didn't know. Once school started in September, though, I'd get to see him more. Nobody could keep us apart at school.

It was nearly time for our morning break and I hoped Desiree'd bring us some of her deviled eggs. We'd been working extra hard that morning because Lita was home with Rodney, on account of him not feeling good, and Nonnie never did make it to the barn today herself, her hands and feet hurting too much.

"Here comes Lita." Mary Ella handed me five leaves instead of three or four, which she did a lot when she wasn't paying good attention. I handed a leaf back to her and looked up to see Lita coming up the path to the barn at a good clip. I had that sick-to-my-stomach feeling that something was wrong.

"Baby William's gone missin'!" she said, when she was close enough we could hear. "Nonnie says she been looking for him all morning."

Mary Ella dropped the leaves she was holding and took off running toward home. I stopped looping. "Did she look under the porch?" I asked Lita.

"I suppose, but I don't rightly know," Lita said. "It's almost break time. Stop work now and get everybody looking."

I knew Mr. Gardiner wasn't going to be too happy about us stopping, but right then I didn't care. I took off running to the house, while Lita let the boys in the field know what was going on.

Mary Ella must of run like the wind, because I didn't see her anywhere ahead of me, but then, I couldn't run as fast as usual. It was so hot and I was sweaty and out of breath by the time I got home. I found Nonnie sitting at the kitchen table, chewing the side of her finger like she always did when she was a nervous wreck.

"Did you look under the porch?" I couldn't catch my breath and had to lean against the wall.

"I looked everywhere," she said. Her eyes was red. "I thought maybe he tried to go to Lita's to see Rodney, but he ain't nowhere. He disappeared."

"Don't say that!" I said. "Where's Mary Ella?"

"Out looking. She came home just a minute ago and went back out. Lita told me just stay here," she said. "I ain't much good out there, and I'll be here if he comes back."

"How'd he go missing?" I got a glass of water from the pump and drank it all in one big gulp.

Nonnie looked away from me, still chewing on her finger. "I was so tired," she said. "I took some Bufferin and fell asleep. I woke up and he was gone."

I felt bad for her and mad at the same time. "Don't worry, we'll find him," I said. "Most likely he's in the tobacco." I headed for the door. "That's where he always hides." I hoped I was right. He could be lost in the tobacco field for days, but at least he'd be safe. "Maybe by now someone's found him." I went out the back door and started to run toward the woods, but my body told me it was done running for the day and I slowed down. I didn't know what was wrong with me. I was getting a taste of how tired Nonnie felt all the time.

I hunted through the woods, hollering for Baby William. Nonnie told me I got lost once when I was real little. She said how they looked for me everywhere. My daddy and mama and her plus Lita and Lita's mama and daddy. "Too many places to look," Nonnie'd told me. "Just too many. So we waited for you to come home, and you did. Like a dog. We never did find out where you went or what you did." I didn't know, either. I had a lot of fits back then and they left big empty gaps of time in my head. Getting lost that day was just one more big gap. I didn't remember being afraid, and I hoped Baby William wasn't afraid, neither. He'd be okay in the tobacco, if that's where he was. *He's okay, he's okay.* That's what I kept saying to myself as I searched the woods. Mary Ella, though. She had to be scared. She'd be beside herself looking for him.

Coming out of the woods and walking across the pasture, I heard other people shouting for Baby William. Everybody was out looking for him, it seemed. I looked all around me as I walked through the wide-open pasture, but all I could see was the cows that was always there. I came to the patch of woods that led out to the road, and saw somebody walking through them toward me. Mrs. Forrester? I stopped walked. Sure enough, that's who it was.

"Have you found him?" she asked when she saw me.

"How did you know about him being gone?" I asked.

"Mr. Gardiner called me," she said. She pulled a hankie from her purse and pressed it to her forehead. "He said he's been missing all morning."

"Oh, it ain't been that long," I said, like I wasn't worried. "I think he's just messing with us. Sometimes he plays hide-and-seek in the tobacco, so I'm heading that way."

She started walking next to me. "Has he run off like this before?" she asked.

This was one time I wasn't happy to see Mrs. Forrester. I wished she didn't come. I didn't like her thinking we wasn't keeping an eye on Baby William. Social workers took kids away for things like that. "Like I said, he plays hide-and-seek sometimes." I wouldn't tell her about the other time he went missing and Eli found him rolling in the dirt with a tobacco worm. "He's probably hiding in the tobacco and just fell asleep."

"He doesn't know the meaning of hide-and-seek," Mrs. Forrester said. "He really needs to be watched more carefully, Ivy."

"We watch that boy good, ma'am," I said. "I'm telling you. Wherever he is, he's just fine."

I hoped I was telling the truth.

25

Jane

Oh dear God, I thought as Ivy and I entered the second hour of our search for William. *How do these people tolerate the heat out here?* I thought my office was bad, with the little oscillating fan blowing a hot breeze into the room, and I complained regularly at home that we only had one window air-conditioning unit in the whole house, but out here in the open, the sun was simply brutal. The day laborers were still working in the field, but Lita and the Jordan boys, the Hart girls and the Gardiner boy, Henry Allen, had all abandoned the tobacco to look for William. Everyone was searching, but no one was finding.

Ivy and I hadn't spoken much. The heat was sapping our strength as we walked across the fields or down Deaf Mule Road or through parts of the woods I'd never seen before. Plus, I had a lot on my mind. Although I was upset that William was missing, I'd honestly been glad for an excuse to leave the office, where I was suddenly very unpopular. Word was out that I'd broken several rules by taking the Harts to the beach, and I guessed it had been stupid even though it had also been illuminating. Fred and Charlotte had nothing positive to say to me and I had the distinct feeling as I talked with them this morning that my job was in jeopardy. Paula passed me in the hall and said only "What were you thinking?"—a question I knew she really didn't expect me to answer. Even Gayle, who rarely spoke to anyone, asked me if I was trying to get fired. I knew Fred and Gayle and Paula were overworked and tired and grouchy and that Charlotte was probably in a lot of pain, but I felt as though everyone was taking their frustrations out on me this morning.

I watched Ivy as we searched. A couple of times I caught her crying. She hadn't expected William's disappearance to become so serious. I was also watching her for another seizure, wondering if the heat and exertion had triggered the one she had on the dunes. How often did she have them? Mary Ella's cavalier acceptance of it—*It's a fit. It'll be over in no time*—told me they were not all that rare.

I didn't know what I was going to do about that petition. It *was* finished. I'd written my sections as honestly and objectively as I could, although that hadn't been easy. All I had to do now was put it in an envelope and hand it to Barbara to mail to the board. It was beginning to look as though I had no choice. Now, to make matters worse, William Hart had gone unsupervised long enough to vanish into thin air, and Charlotte would badger me to have him removed. Maybe she was right. Maybe they were all right.

We crisscrossed paths with the other searchers during the afternoon, and every time I saw Mary Ella, Eli was close by. We'd see Henry Allen or Devil or Avery and they'd always be searching on their own. But if I spotted Mary Ella or Eli, I knew that within seconds, I'd see the other. They didn't touch each other. Not that I saw, anyway. But they seemed for all the world like two parents desperate to find their little boy. It made me uncomfortable, watching them together. Mary Ella was such an ethereal wisp of a girl and she'd only been fourteen when she conceived William. Had Eli forced himself on her? I shuddered. He was bigger than most men, with that broad back and those powerful arms. I thought of the way he could cut his eyes at me and make me look away. If he could intimidate *me* that way, what could he do to a delicate girl like Mary Ella? She didn't seem afraid of him, though. Had she welcomed it, being with him? Maybe she even loved him.

Ivy and I were scouring a neighbor's tobacco field across Deaf Mule Road from the farm, when I spotted Davison Gardiner walking through his front yard.

"I'm going to talk to Mr. Gardiner," I said to Ivy.

She looked across the street in silence, a dazed expression on her face.

"You should get some shade and water, honey," I said.

"I just want to keep looking," she said.

I crossed the road. I hadn't bothered with galoshes this morning, since the weather had been dry for so long, and I looked down to see my saddle shoes covered with dust.

Davison Gardiner was spraying water from a hose on the sparse shrubbery next to his house. "Hello, Mr. Gardiner," I called, shading my eyes to see him better.

He turned the water off at the spigot on the side of his house. "Hey, Mrs. Forrester," he said. "Any news on the Hart boy?"

I shook my head. "I think it's time we called the police," I said. "May I use your phone?"

He set down the hose and stuffed his hands in his pockets. "Don't want them out here," he said. "This is private farm business."

"Well, actually, it's not," I said. I felt my youth, talking to him. I was twenty-two and he was probably close to forty and had lived here his whole life. He must have thought I had some nerve, disagreeing with him about something that happened on his own property. "William could be anywhere by now."

"That boy should be took away," he said. "Charlotte once told me she was working on getting him fostered out. Someplace they'd watch him better. It'd be too bad, but he ain't getting supervised, you know what I mean?"

"I do. I'll have to look into it as well. I don't like taking a baby from his mother unless there's no other way." I listened to myself with disbelief. I sounded like an experienced social worker who'd seen this situation many times before, but I sure didn't feel like one.

"No," he said, "that ain't never good, but in this particular case, maybe for the best."

I wondered if he was trying to tell me he knew Eli was William's father.

"Mary Ella loves him so much," I said.

Lita Jordan walked across the yard toward us, little Rodney running ahead of her. She looked worn out and I knew she'd been doing her part in the search.

"Hello, Mrs. Jordan," I said. "Any sign of William?"

"No, ma'am." She pulled her green kerchief lower over her hair. "That boy just plum disappeared into thin air."

"Rodney." Mr. Gardiner squatted down on the ground and Rodney approached him. "I heard you wasn't feeling so good," he said.

"I ate something that don't agree on me," Rodney said, and Davison Gardiner laughed. He put his hand on the little boy's forehead and I was surprised by that gentleness in him. I didn't know his son Henry Allen well at all, but I had the feeling he was lucky to have Mr. Gardiner as his father.

"He's feeling better now, ain't you, Rodney?" Lita said as Mr. Gardiner stood up again.

"They found him!" Devil ran around the corner of the house toward us. "He's all right!"

"Hooray!" I said, clapping my hands together, and I realized I hadn't expected a happy ending to this day. I put my hands to my mouth as a megaphone and called across the street. "Ivy! Ivy!" I had to call a few times before she heard me. She looked up from the field and I waved, and she started running toward the road.

"We got him!" Henry Allen shouted. He was walking next to Mary Ella, Eli not two steps behind her, and she cuddled William in her arms, covering him with kisses. William rested his head on her shoulder, looking exhausted.

Next to me, Davison Gardiner sighed. "One of these times, they ain't gonna be this lucky," he said, loud enough for me alone to hear.

Everyone seemed to get the word at once. Avery came running from one direction, almost falling when he tripped over a tree root he couldn't see with his tunnel vision. He was his usual bright-eyed, happy self, though. "They found him, they found him!" he said, to no one in particular.

"Where was he at?" Lita asked Mary Ella.

"Down the crick a ways," Eli said, pointing toward the woods on the other side of the fields. "Trying to catch them little fishes."

How deep was the creek? I wondered. I'd read that a child could drown in a few inches of water.

"I'll take him home," Mary Ella said. "He needs a good nap."

"He needs a good *scrubbing*," Lita said, holding up his grubby arm. But she was smiling. Everybody was smiling, myself included. I'd worry about William's future later.

"You boys go help Mr. Gardiner now," Lita said. "He done lost a day of work here. I'll be right behind you."

I watched Eli and his brothers and Henry Allen follow Mr. Gardiner to the path leading to the barn. Then Lita and I looked after Mary Ella and Ivy as they walked toward the woods and home. At one point, they turned to face each other, Ivy brushing something off William's face.

"I better be gettin' to work myself," Lita said, "I'll have to take over Ivy's loopin', I guess." But she didn't move. She stared after the girls, then dusted off her hands, and gave me a pointed look.

"That Ivy," she said, "she sure has packed on a lot of pounds, now hasn't she?"

26

Ivy

Nonnie cried when we brung Baby William home. "Thank you, Jesus! Thank you, Jesus!" she shouted when she saw us come out of the trees. She always acted like she didn't care about him and he was nothing but a bother, but she loved him like we all did. She grabbed his little face between her swole-up hands and kissed him all over his cute little pudgy cheeks. He smiled, but he was too tuckered out to laugh. Mary Ella was right. That boy needed a nap.

"Don't you go putting that filthy baby in that clean bed," Nonnie said.

"I'll take him." I could see it was Mary Ella needed a lie-down the most. She'd been running all over kingdom come all day looking for him.

Usually I'd just wash him in the kitchen sink, but he was getting too big for that now, and with him being this dirty, I thought I'd better use the tub outside. I pumped water into it and then took off his filthy clothes and sat him down in the cool water. He splashed his hands up and down, but only for a second. He was too tired to play.

"Ivy?"

I turned to see Mrs. Forrester walking across the yard.

"Hey," I said. "I thought you left."

"I was going to, but then I realized I need to talk to you. Are you alone?"

"Do I look like I'm alone?" I laughed. I rubbed the soap through Baby William's black curls.

"I mean . . . where are your grandmother and Mary Ella?"

"Nonnie's inside and Mary Ella's taking a nap."

"Good." She was talking real quiet. "I wanted to talk to you alone."

"Why?" I soaped Baby William's grimy neck. He was a mess.

"Ivy . . ." she said, "when was your last period?"

"Just last week," I said, as usual.

"Really?" She looked relieved and I suddenly felt bad for lying to her.

"Nah, I don't rightly know," I said. "They've always been all over the place. I always got to be ready for it. It'll come on at school, and one time on the bus."

"I'm worried you're pregnant." She blurted it out like she couldn't hold it in no more.

"I *ain't* pregnant," I said, talking as quiet as her now. The kitchen window was open and I sure didn't want Nonnie to hear none of this.

"I noticed today that you've put on weight. Here." She touched her own stomach, but she was looking at mine. "Haven't you noticed that?"

"I just been eatin' too much. I try to eat the biscuits so Nonnie don't get to 'em."

"Please tell me the truth, Ivy," she said. "This is so important. Have you had intercourse—sex—with someone? That boy you told me you liked, maybe?"

I looked down at Baby William, who was nearly falling asleep in the tub. It would have been easy to lie to her if she didn't look so serious and if she wasn't so nice. "Yes, I done it," I said, "but I can't be pregnant because he always pulls out except one last time when I used that spermicide jelly Nurse Ann give me."

"I see." She reached over and started rinsing the soap off Baby William's back, using her hand like a cup. "Maybe he forgot one time? That's all it would take."

"He always pulls out except that last time."

"And this boy . . . he's the only one you've been with?"

"Yes, ma'am." I hated she could even think that. "I love him."

"Well, I'm not sure how it happened, honey, but I'm pretty sure you're pregnant."

I put my hand on my belly. It *was* big. Bigger than yesterday. And for sure, bigger than last week. I thought it was the biscuits. "You telling me I'm gonna have a baby?" I whispered.

"I think so. We need to have Nurse Ann come see you."

I tipped Baby William back and used a cup to rinse the soap out of his hair. I wasn't paying no attention and got some of the soap in his eyes and he started hollering. Mrs. Forrester was fast, getting clean water from the pump, washing the soap out of his eyes. He was too tired to keep up the screaming for long, but his little bottom lip shivered like he might start again any minute. I could hardly stand it when he looked sad like that.

"Can you tell me who it is?" she asked. "The father?"

I shook my head, rubbing Baby William's back to settle him down. "No, ma'am," I said. "I mean, there's only one choice, but I can't tell."

"All right."

I lifted Baby William out of the tub, and Mrs. Forrester grabbed a towel off the line and helped me wrap him up in it. I hugged him to me, all clean and sleepy. My arms felt rubbery and strange. Me having a baby wasn't sinking in yet. It was like we was talking in a dream.

"What about school?" I asked, remembering when they kicked Mary Ella out. Mary Ella's teacher figured it out before anyone. "They'll kick me out."

She nodded. "You know you can't go if you have a baby, honey." She touched my shoulder. The way she said "honey," it wasn't the way other people did. Not like Nonnie or Lita. She said it like she didn't say it to just anybody.

"I *got* to go to school, Mrs. Forrester," I said. That was the plan. Me and Henry Allen would graduate and then go to California.

"I know you wish you could," she said, but she didn't say there was some way I could do it. I felt trapped.

"Don't tell nobody," I whispered. "Please." I knew she talked to Mr. Gardiner sometimes. That would be the worst. That would be the end of me.

"I'll wait until Nurse Ann has a chance to see you and we know for sure," she said. "But then, Nonnie will have to know."

I shook my head.

"You're a minor, sweetheart," she said. "She'll have to know."

27

Jane

The next morning, I sat in my car in the parking lot of the Laundromat for the longest time, putting off going upstairs to the DPW offices. There were voices in my head. Charlotte's and Ann's, primarily, telling me in one way or another that I was both naïve and foolish. They were right.

I could see Ivy's future mapped out in front of me now. She'd become one of the tired, worn-down women I saw every day, half a dozen children clamoring for food and love. This pregnancy wasn't my fault, though. I'd known her little more than a month, and she had to be four or five months along. I hadn't missed her weight gain, but I *had* missed the cause of it. Yesterday, though, it had been impossible to miss.

I got out of my car and climbed the outside steps to the second floor, preparing myself for what lay ahead. I was disappointed to find Fred in Charlotte's and my office, sitting in my chair. I hadn't wanted to tell them both at once. I hadn't wanted to tell Fred at all, actually, although I knew it was inevitable—he was still the director of the department, and his signature would have to be on the petition.

"May I speak with the two of you?" I asked.

"Have a seat." Charlotte pointed to the straight-backed chair against the wall. Fred made no move to get out of my own chair.

I sat down, my briefcase on my lap like a shield. "I think . . ." I began, "or actually, I'm quite sure that Ivy Hart is pregnant."

They stared at me in total silence.

"I think she's pretty far along," I said. *This baby is not my fault.* "She must have been pregnant before I started working with the family."

Charlotte sighed with a shake of her head. "I knew I should have gotten that petition in long ago," she said. "Is it ready for Fred to sign?"

"I'll have to rewrite my part now," I said. "And I guess Ann Laing will have to rewrite hers, too." I thought about Fred reading what I'd written. The weak, unconvincing way my portion of the petition was currently written, he'd probably refuse to sign it. Now I'd be able to make a much stronger case, whether I wanted to or not.

She nodded, and I thought I saw some of the old sympathy and understanding in her eyes. "We all get a wake-up call at one time or another, Jane," she said. "Ivy Hart is yours."

I hugged my briefcase, leaning forward. "I have to tell her, though, Charlotte. I won't be a party to a lie. Another appendectomy."

Fred shook his head. "Maybe you should go into the ministry," he suggested, "where that 'holier than thou' attitude might be an asset."

That stung. Did I sound like that much of a prig?

"Ivy won't understand," Charlotte said. "If you're right about this, she's been pregnant for months without so much as an inkling. She probably doesn't even know how she got that way."

"She knows," I said. "She was trying not to get pregnant, but—"

"Do you honestly think she'd understand the sterilization procedure?" she interrupted me, and I knew it was a rhetorical question. "It would just make her very anxious, knowing what lay ahead of her. In my opinion, that would be cruel. Her grandmother's her guardian. We have her permission and I'm sure now that Ivy's expecting a baby, Winona would sign that paper five times over. That poor woman. This is the last thing she needs."

"I just . . . even if she doesn't completely understand, I can't be that dishonest."

Fred got to his feet and headed for the door. He looked down at me.

"Your self-righteousness is getting in the way of your duty to your clients, Mrs. Forrester," he said as he left.

I looked at Charlotte. "He really doesn't like me," I said.

"He's under the gun right now, Jane," she said. "He hates being back in the field. He has a lot of fires to put out with his clients at the moment, and yes . . . he wishes you wouldn't try to change the way this department's been run for years. Frankly, so do I. We need you to work *with* us and not against us."

"I'm trying," I said weakly.

"I don't think you are," she said. "Give me the permission form. The one the patient's supposed to sign." She motioned impatiently for me to hand it over.

My hands felt clammy as I opened the briefcase and leafed through the petition papers for the Consent of Patient form. I pulled it out and handed it to her.

She lowered her leg in its cast from the stool and turned her chair toward her desk, slipping the form into her typewriter. I waited while she typed a single sentence.

"Call Ann Laing," she said, pulling the paper from the typewriter. "Let's get her out there and make sure your hunch is right. Plus you need to look into finding a foster placement for Mary Ella Hart's son."

She handed me the form. I looked down at what she'd typed: "Patient is a minor; not consulted."

"*Charlotte* . . ." I pleaded.

"I need to make some phone calls," she said. "And so do you."

28

Ivy

It was the first time I wrote the note to Henry Allen instead of the other way around. *"I got to see you tonight. You got to find a way to get out. Midnight."*

We was finishing up the morning break. Me and him didn't even look at each other on break no more, but somehow I had to get the note to him and it was now or never. Him and Eli was walking toward the field and I stepped away from Mary Ella and took the risk, handing him the tiny little piece of paper as quick as I could.

"Hey!" Mr. Gardiner shouted from the path. I hadn't seen him there and he was looking right at me. "What'd you give him?"

My eyes must have been big as griddlecakes and my heart skipped two or three beats. Henry Allen looked just as scared, standing there with his hand wrapped tight around the note.

"Nothin'," I said. "I don't know what you—"

"Hey, Mr. Gardiner!" Eli walked between me and Henry Allen real fast, heading toward Mr. Gardiner. "I got to show you somethin' right quick." He touched Henry Allen's hand as he passed him, like he was taking something from him, then held his hand out flat when he got close to Mr. Gardiner. "These screws is poppin' out the side of the Christmas barn," he said. "I give one to Ivy to show you and I guess she was turnin' it over to Henry Allen. This is just one of 'em. They's a bunch comin' out." He handed the screw—at least I guessed that's what it was—to Mr. Gardiner, who seemed as mixed up as me and Henry Allen. He looked at the screw in his hand, then started walking toward the Christmas barn with Eli at his side. Eli turned his head just long enough to shoot me and Henry Allen a grin.

"Eli knows about us?" I whispered.

"Eli knows every damn thing there is to know about anything," Henry Allen said. "I swear. Boy's got eyes in the back of his head." He wiped the sweat off his forehead. "I thought we was doomed there for a minute."

"Me, too."

He walked away from me in case his father turned to look, and I saw him read the note. He looked over at me and nodded. I didn't know how he'd get out with his parents keeping such a close eye on him these days, but he had to. I needed to tell him.

I was at the crick by midnight, alone on the moss, worrying he couldn't get out. Lying there on my back, I wondered how I couldn't of known I had a baby inside me. My belly was so big. I could almost feel the shape of a little critter beneath my hands. What I thought was my belly acting funny from eating too many biscuits was a little live person in there, moving around.

I spotted the moon, round and silvery, behind the branches of the trees and that little person in my belly suddenly seemed more important than school and being a teacher and everything else I could think of. I remembered the preacher saying we couldn't always understand the reason God did something, but we could be sure he had a good one. I wished I knew what his reason was for me having a baby.

I reached my arms up to the sky. "Thank you for this little baby," I whispered. "I'll take good care of it."

I didn't know what Henry Allen would say, though. He thought the pullin' out would work and he was careful about it because he sure didn't want no babies. Not yet, anyways. I didn't think he'd be thanking God for one of them.

I heard him coming through the woods. I got up—not as quick as I used to—and helped him spread the blanket.

"They're watching me like a hawk," he said, as he flattened a corner of the blanket. "Sorry I'm late. You got me worried with that note."

"I'm gonna have a baby," I said.

I didn't mean for it to pop out like that. We wasn't even lying down yet.

He stared across the blanket at me. "That ain't possible. We was real careful."

"You're the only one, Henry Allen. Mrs. Forrester figured it out."

"You *told* her?"

I couldn't see him good but I could hear he was mad. "*She* told *me*," I said. "She figured it out."

"You sure she's right?"

"I think so."

He sat down real heavy on the blanket, facing the crick. "Damn," he said.

I sat next to him. "Feel it," I said. We hadn't been together in so long and I could see his eyes go big when he touched my belly. He pulled his hand away right quick, but I grabbed it and pressed it flat on my big belly again.

"Damn," he said. "This ain't good, Ivy. This is about the worst thing I could think of to happen."

I forgot all about my little thank-you talk to God from a couple of minutes ago. He was right. This was the worst thing. But it was going to happen, terrible or not. No way I could get out of having a baby now. Henry Allen could just say "It ain't mine" and walk away. He could keep going to school, maybe on to college and then California, like he planned. Me, I didn't have no choice. I was done with school. I was going to be a mama whether I liked it or not. The way Henry Allen was acting, maybe I was going to be a mama all by myself, same as Mary Ella.

We sat and stared at the moonlight glittering on the crick. I talked to Jesus in my head while we sat, asking him to make Henry Allen act different than he was. Jesus was a baby once, so maybe he'd understand.

After a while, Henry Allen put his arm around me. "We got to get married," he said. "Give this here baby a name. Not like Baby William.

My baby ain't gonna be no Hart baby. He's a Gardiner. We're gonna make him a Gardiner."

"But how?" I asked. "Your parents will . . . I don't know what they'll do."

"Me, neither," he said. "Give me a while to think about it, all right? I got to figure some things out. But you ain't gonna be alone with this, Ivy Hart. Don't you fret about that."

I looked up at the stars again. *Thank you, Jesus,* I thought to myself. He was working right quick tonight.

29

Jane

I pushed the cart through the aisles of the Piggly Wiggly, checking the list in my hand and mechanically putting peaches and corn and cherries into the basket. Robert had a poker game with his friends from the club and I was frankly relieved to have this evening to myself. I'd spent the afternoon unhappily working on Ivy's petition and I was still bristling from my conversation with Charlotte and Fred that morning. Maybe I'd call my mother when I got home. I missed having her to talk to every night, even though when we spoke these days, our conversations were superficial. She seemed so fragile to me, still grieving for my father and sister.

"Jane?"

I looked up to see Lois Parker pushing her cart in my direction.

"Lois!" I was taken aback by how gaunt she looked. *She's dying,* Robert had said. My problems were small and petty. "It's good to see you," I said. "How are you feeling?"

"I'm still up and at 'em," she said. "And you? Honey, your eyes are red." She held my shoulder to get a better look at me. "What's wrong?"

I looked down at my cart, trying to get my emotions under control. "Oh, just . . . some things at work are piling up and I—" My voice locked up and nothing else would come out.

"Do you have anything frozen in there?" Lois peered into my cart, and I looked at the produce, confused by her question. "No, you don't," she said. "Leave your cart. Let's go over to the Pharmacy and Grill for a cup of coffee and a chat."

"Oh, I really should get the shopping done."

"I think you need to talk to a friend more," she said.

Oh, how right she was! I didn't feel as though I had any friends at the moment. And I had to go to the pharmacy anyway. I needed some of that special Breck Banish shampoo. For the first time in my life I had dandruff, but I wasn't about to tell Lois—or anyone—about that. I wondered if too much stress could cause a case of dandruff.

We moved our carts to the side of an aisle and left the store. "I'll drive," she said. I loved her take-charge attitude—even though she was clearly losing her battle with cancer. That horrible word.

"Robert must be at the poker game," she said as she drove the short distance to the Hayes Barton Pharmacy and Grill. "That's where Gavin is."

"Yes," I said. "I'm glad. It helps him get rid of his stress."

"Gavin, too. I'm so glad he has friends to do things with. Golf especially. He's being both mother and father to our little girl these days, in addition to managing his law practice."

Oh my God. I'd nearly forgotten about their little girl. How painful it had to be to know you were dying, leaving behind a motherless child you would never get to see grow up.

"You need a hobby, too, I think," she said. "Something fun. You work just as hard as our men do, and then you're expected to grocery shop and run a household at the same time."

I cleared my throat. "Well, I don't know how I'd fit a hobby into my life right now."

"That's how I felt when I was teaching. Working all day, then grading papers all night."

"Did that bother Gavin?"

She shook her head. "I saved the weekends for him. That's an important thing to do," she said. "Also, he knew I loved what I was doing."

"I don't think Robert would mind so much if I was a teacher," I said, although actually, I was pretty sure he would. He didn't want me to work, period. "He doesn't like the kind of work I'm doing. Social work."

"Gavin really enjoyed talking to you about it at the ball," she said. "You impressed him."

"I did?"

She nodded. "He said, 'That Jane Forrester's a sharp cookie.'"

I laughed, hugely flattered. I wished Robert felt that way.

Lois parked in front of the pharmacy and we walked inside and sat at the counter. I ordered coffee, but she ordered a chocolate sundae. She laughed at the look of surprise on my face.

"I eat whatever I want whenever I want it these days," she said. "What does it matter? I lose weight no matter what I put in my mouth. My doctor's amazed I still have a good appetite. I guess I'm lucky, at least as far as that goes."

"Lois . . . I'm so sorry you're ill." I put my hand over hers where it rested on the counter. Although I'd only met her a little over a week before, I felt completely at ease with her and I wasn't surprised when she seemed pleased by my touch. She took her hand away only because her sundae had arrived, and I liked seeing her eyes light up as she dug in.

"I've been sick with this for two years," she said, between bites. "Ever since my little girl was born. They took everything out." She rested a hand on her stomach, and I guessed she meant a hysterectomy, though I didn't want to ask. "They thought they got it all. But I guess there was some little bit of cancer waiting to get another toehold."

"I'm sorry," I said again. I wanted to know how she could sit here and tell me what she just did and not be reduced to a puddle of tears.

"I suspected this was how things would go right from the beginning," she said, "because my mother had the same thing."

"Oh no."

"Yes, and I know what it's like for a child to lose her mother. I don't remember her, my mother. It makes me sad to think my daughter won't remember me."

"She's two?" My heart broke for her.

"Just."

"Gavin can keep your memory alive for her," I said. It was the best I could do.

"I hope so." She ate another spoonful of ice cream, while my coffee was still untouched and growing cold. "I know he'll try."

"I think you're amazing, Lois," I said. "And it amazes me that you can talk about this so openly with me."

"Well, I don't with everyone," she said. "But as I said, I've come to grips with this. And you're a very good listener."

"Anytime you feel like talking, you can call me." I was sincere. I wanted to help her somehow. "Even in the middle of the night."

"How sweet you are," she said. "Robert certainly got lucky when he found you."

"Thank you," I said, although I doubted Robert was feeling very lucky about that these days.

She swallowed another bite of her sundae and I took my first sip of the cold coffee. For a moment, neither of us spoke.

"What was troubling you in the grocery store?" she asked. "When I saw your face, I knew something was really wrong."

I looked at the reflection of the overhead lights shimmering in my coffee. "It's just a case I'm working on. Two teenaged girls I've come to care about, which is a no-no."

"Oh, that's bull," Lois said. "It's impossible to care too much."

"Tell that to my supervisor."

"I will. Give me her phone number."

I had the feeling she meant it and I smiled. "I took them to the beach," I said. "They'd never seen the ocean and their lives are . . . well, they're not much fun. I honestly didn't know I was breaking the rules. I read the manual, but I guess that part didn't sink in."

"There are too many silly rules in our lives," she said, "and our lives are far too short to pay attention to them." She'd finished her sundae and pushed the empty dish a couple of inches toward the back of the counter. "I wish I'd broken more of them," she said. "So that's what I'm doing these days. I eat sundaes whenever I want, and I chat with a friend instead of grocery shopping. Maybe I'll even run naked through Cameron Village."

I laughed. "You've got guts," I said.

"And so do you." She patted me on the shoulder. "Those girls will remember that beach trip for as long as they live."

30

Ivy

Nonnie opened the kitchen door and there was Nurse Ann, standing on the porch ready to knock. My heart dropped smack to my toes. It was too soon for her to come. I didn't figure out how to tell Nonnie about the baby yet. I stood in the middle of the kitchen like I was stuck to the floor.

"You was just here," Nonnie said to her. "I told you I'd stop eating so much. I'm just about starved to death already."

"I'm not here to see you, today," Nurse Ann said. "I'm here to check on Ivy and the baby."

Nonnie looked good and confused. "He's outside somewhere with his mama," she said. "Mary Ella's been keeping a better eye on him, so you don't need to be coming around all the—"

"Not Baby William," Nurse Ann said. "*Ivy's* baby."

"What are you talking about?" Nonnie looked from her to me.

"I didn't tell her yet," I said to Nurse Ann.

Nonnie catched on. Her eyes got big and her face went red. "No!" she hollered, and she came at me, her hands flying, ready to swat me good. I covered my face with my arms and Nurse Ann tried to grab Nonnie.

"Winona!" she said, her long braid flying all over the place. "Stop it! Stop!" But Nonnie was too riled up.

"You whore!" she said, smacking my head. "You're just like your sister. What are we gonna do with another baby in the house?"

I dropped down next to one of the kitchen chairs and ducked under the table like a scared dog. She still tried to get to me, but she was tuckered out and had no wind left.

"Sit down!" Nurse Ann barked at her. "You're going to have a stroke if you don't get a handle on yourself."

Nonnie was breathing hard and I got out from under the other side of the table, glad to have it between me and her. Nurse Ann had her fingers on Nonnie's wrist and was looking at her watch. Nonnie's face was redder than I ever seen it.

"You're a disgrace," she said to me.

"Hush," Nurse Ann said. She let go of Nonnie's wrist and wrote something in that notebook she always carried. "Now you listen to me, Winona. I'm going to take Ivy in the bedroom and examine her and when I come out we can talk. Till then I want you to just sit here at the table and rest."

"Can you get her one of them abortions?" Nonnie asked.

Did she mean give my baby away? I'd never do that.

"No, ma'am, I certainly cannot," Nurse Ann said. She waved her hand toward the bedroom. "Let's go, Ivy," she said.

I didn't want to go with her but it was better than staying with Nonnie, so I did. Nurse Ann shut the door behind us as far as it would go.

"Why didn't you tell her?" she asked.

"Why'd you think?" I asked. "I don't want to get kilt. She would of done me in if you wasn't here."

"Sit down," she said, pointing to the bed, and I sat. "Mrs. Forrester said you had no idea you were pregnant."

"He always pulled out."

"Well, you learned your lesson there, now didn't you? That doesn't work. Why do you think I gave you that spermicidal jelly, Ivy?"

I looked out the window, remembering Mary Ella taking one of the boxes of jelly. "Mary Ella took some of it," I said. "You better give her some more before it's too late for her, too."

"Who's the boy?" she asked, opening up her medicine bag.

"Nobody."

She made a disgusted face at my answer. "I need you to take off your underwear and lay back on the bed so I can check inside you," she said.

"What?" I said. "No!"

I remembered how she'd come in the bedroom a time or two with Mary Ella in the months before Baby William was born. Was she checking inside her then? I thought she was just listening to Mary Ella's heart and looking at her eyes and throat. Nurse Ann was supposed to bring Baby William into the world until Mrs. Werkman told us about Mary Ella's appendix and sent her to the hospital instead.

"It won't hurt," she said. "I'm just going to feel inside you. Make sure the baby's healthy and—"

"You can feel it?" If she could feel it up there, what was to keep it from falling out of me?

"I can feel your uterus."

"What's that?"

"Your womb," she said. "You'll see. Just take off your underwear now."

I stood up and reached under my dress and pulled off my stretched-out old drawers. I laid them on the bed and sat down again.

She put a rubber glove on her hand. "Now move back a little and put your feet on the bed and spread your legs open wide."

I put my feet up but I wasn't doing any spreading. "Don't want to," I said.

"Well, Ivy, I know this isn't the first time you've spread your legs open or else you wouldn't be in the state you're in, isn't that true? Come on now."

I done like I was told and closed my eyes while she put her fingers inside me and moved them around and pressed all over my belly. "You are good and pregnant," she said, pulling out her hand. She took off the glove and told me I could sit up. I pulled my dress down. My knees was shaking.

"Every time I asked you about your period, you told me you were keeping track of it."

"I thought I was," I lied. I didn't know what else to say.

"Do you actually know when your last period was?"

I shook my head.

"Well, I'd say you're somewhere between five and six months," she said. "Closer to six, I'd say. That means you'll have a baby around Thanksgiving time. The baby's small, so it's hard to tell. Might be epilepsy or poor nutrition causing that or you might not be as far along as I think you are. Did you have any morning sickness a while back? Any throwing up in the morning?"

I thought of one week in the spring when I felt like throwing up every day while I waited for the bus. I never did, though. "No," I said. Outside the door, I could hear Mary Ella's voice. Then Nonnie's. Then both together. And then one more voice I couldn't place right away. Mrs. Forrester? Yes, that was it. I was glad she was here.

"Have you been taking any of that medicine you used to take for your seizures? Your fits?"

"No, ma'am." I hated that medicine. It made me feel dizzy and strange.

"Well, if you're doing all right without it, that's probably best for now," she said. "It could hurt your baby. I'm going to leave you some special vitamins and I want you to take one every single morning. I know you aren't very religious about taking medication, but this is important."

"What's religion got to do with it?"

She sighed. "Absolutely nothing. I'll leave these on the shelf next to Nonnie's pills, okay?" She leaned over and took my hands. "Ivy, you're not a bad girl. You help Nonnie remember to take her medicine and test her urine. She's told me that. You know how to take care of other people. Now take care of you, okay? Take care of yourself because it's not just you anymore. It's that little baby, too."

I nodded. "Should I take two of them pills instead?" I asked. "Would that be better?"

She shook her head. "Just one. Too much of a good thing is no good at all."

I walked behind her into the living room, afraid Nonnie was going to come at me again, but she was wore out and sitting on the sofa now, the sheets still on it from when she slept there last night. Mrs. Forrester stood inside the front door, real quiet. Mary Ella, though, was squealing and jumping up and down and she hugged me. "We gonna have another Baby William!" she said.

I hoped my baby was a girl, but didn't say nothing.

"I have something for you," Nurse Ann said to Mrs. Forrester. She wasn't friendly to her at all. It was like she was mad. She sat on the edge of the sofa and wrote something real fast on a piece of paper on top of her notebook. Then she stood up and shoved the paper at Mrs. Forrester, who took it from her. "Tear up the petition form you already have from me and type this one up instead," she said.

She called me into the kitchen and put a big bottle of pills next to Nonnie's little one and her testing pills on the shelf. "Here's those vitamins I told you about," she said to me. "Just one a day."

"I know," I said.

She left by the kitchen door, and when I went back into the living room, I saw Mrs. Forrester still standing by the door, reading the paper Nurse Ann gave her. Then she stuck it in that case she always carried.

"How are you?" she asked me.

"She said it's gonna be a Thanksgiving baby," I said. I knew that wasn't what she'd said but I couldn't remember her exact words and I liked how "Thanksgiving baby" sounded.

Mary Ella was rocking Baby William in the rocker and he was babbling his words that wasn't really words. "This is a happy day," she said.

"Lord." Nonnie put her head in her hands. "She thinks this is a happy day! I'm living with two imbeciles, Mrs. Forrester. Lord, help me, please. Three of 'em, you count Baby William. And now a fourth coming."

"It's my dream," said Mary Ella.

"No more school for me," I said to Mrs. Forrester, hoping she might have some way to fix that. I knew she had the only clear-thinking brain in the house.

She nodded. "I'll talk to them," she said. "Maybe there's a way you can continue your schoolwork from home."

"Ain't no way," Nonnie said, like Mrs. Forrester was stupid.

My knees was still jittery, and I sat down on the sofa, as far from Nonnie as I could get.

"This is my dream," Mary Ella said again, and Mrs. Forrester looked at her.

"What's your dream, Mary Ella?" she asked.

"Me and Ivy having babies together. I dreamed about it and now it's a dream come true."

Mrs. Forrester went in the kitchen and brung out one of the chairs and put it right next to Mary Ella's rocking chair. She rubbed her hand over Baby William's back. "It's really not good to have babies when you're not married, though," she said. "Too hard to do it on your own."

"Now, that's the first true thing anybody's said in this house today," Nonnie said.

"I know," Mary Ella said. "I didn't mean we should have a lot of babies right *now*. When we're married we can. I want five. Baby William and four more."

"Is there someone you wish you could marry, Mary Ella?" Mrs. Forrester was almost whispering to her. I leaned forward to hear because I wanted to know the answer myself, but Mary Ella only rested her cheek on Baby William's curls.

"Nobody yet," she said. "But someday I'll meet the right boy."

"Five children," Mrs. Forrester said. "That's a handful."

I knew what she was thinking: Mary Ella couldn't keep a good eye on even one little boy.

"It's a handful," I said, "but now that I'll be out of school, I can help her."

Mrs. Forrester stood up. "I think I'd better get going," she said. She looked at me. "I just wanted to make sure Nurse Ann got here to see you today."

"Well," I said, "she sure did." I was afraid of Mrs. Forrester leaving, but I got up and opened the door for her and went out on the porch to watch her walk across the yard to the woods. I wished I could just walk away myself. I didn't want to go back in the house.

I had the feeling Nonnie wasn't done with me yet.

31

Jane

I'd parked my car between the woods and the tobacco field, and now I sat behind the steering wheel in the heat, rereading the form Ann had handed me to go with the petition. I'd type it up when I got back to the office. It was time to send the petition to the board. I couldn't put it off any longer.

I looked toward the fields where the Jordan boys were helping Henry Allen with the mule. So, Mary Ella wanted five children, I thought, remembering her happiness over Ivy's pregnancy. It was her dream and she had no idea it was impossible. Maybe it was right to prevent her from having more, but it wasn't right that she had that dream. I didn't care if she was deemed feebleminded. I didn't care.

I felt angry as I turned the key in the ignition. I wouldn't deceive these girls I'd come to care about. I'd hope and pray the board would turn down Ivy's petition, but if they didn't I would tell her. And I was going to tell Mary Ella as well. If she was capable of understanding that she could have those five children, then she was capable of understanding that she couldn't.

32

Jane

Form No. 1-Petition For Operation of Sterilization or Asexualization

NORTH CAROLINA

Grace COUNTY

IN RE: STERILIZATION OR
~~ASEXUALIZATION~~ OF

Ivy Hart

Before the
EUGENICS BOARD OF NORTH CAROLINA

Petition for Operation Of
Sterilization

TO THE EUGENICS BOARD OF NORTH CAROLINA: Greetings—

YOUR PETITIONER, **Frederick F. Price** Director of Public Welfare

of **Grace** County, having made a full study of the case of

Ivy Hart ,hereinafter designated as the

patient, who resides at **Gardiner's Farm, Deaf Mule Road, Almore, NC**

AND WHEREAS, It appears to your Petitioner that (1) it is for the best
interest of the mental, moral, and physical improvement of the patient that
he (she) undergo an operation for sterilization ~~or asexualization~~; (2) that
it is for the public good that such patient undergo such operation; or (3)
that said patient would be likely to procreate a child or children who would
have a tendency to serious physical, mental, or nervous disease or
deficiency;

NOW THEREFORE, Your Petitioner prays that an order be entered by the
Eugenics Board of North Carolina requiring your Petitioner to perform, or to
have performed by some competent physician or surgeon as may be designated by
the Board in such order, upon **Ivy Hart** the patient named in this
Petition, one of the operations specified in Section 36, Chapter 35, of the
General Statutes of North Carolina, which in the discretion of the Board,
shall be best suited to the interests of said patient or to the public good.

Signed *Frederick F. Price*

Director of Public Welfare ~~or Sup't of Institution~~

This **17** day of **August, 1960**

Personal and Family History

Name **Ivy Hart**   Age **15** Race **white**   Sex **F**

Home address **Gardiner's Farm, Deaf Mule Road, Almore, NC**
County of **Grace**

Date of birth **March 18, 1945** Place of birth **Almore**
Born in wedlock: Yes **X** No

Marital status: Single **X** Married   Widowed   Separated   Divorced

Education **9th grade**

Father's name   **Percy Hart**   Address

If dead give: Age at death **27**   Cause of death   **accident**

Mother's name   **Violet Hart**   Address   **Dorothea Dix Hospital**

If dead give: Age at death   Cause of death

If father and mother are dead and subject is not married: Next of kin
Winona Hart

Relationship to patient **grandmother** Age **58** Address **same**

Has patient been given a mental examination? **yes** If so: Name of examiner
Dr. Stuart Vass

Result of examination **IQ 80 dull normal** Date of examination **2-11-60**

Public Health Nurse's ~~Physician's~~ Statement

How long have you known patient? **3 years**   Date of last examination **8-16-60**

General physical condition   **Pt is illegitimately pregnant, approximately
25 weeks gestation. Did not realize she was pregnant.
Poor understanding of reproduction and pregnancy.**

If patient is epileptic specify type and indicate to what degree this
interferes with every day activities **Petit Mal epilepsy, frequent
seizures in childhood, frequency now unknown, pt. refused
to take medication.**

Is there any known contraindication to the requested surgical procedure? **no**

Ann Laing, RN
~~(Physician)~~/public health nurse

Form No. 6-B-Consent for operation of sterilization
NORTH CAROLINA,

Grace COUNTY

In Re: Sterilization

}

Before the
EUGENICS BOARD OF
NORTH CAROLINA
Consent of Patient

of **Ivy Hart**

Patient is a minor; not consulted.

I, the undersigned _____ patient, do hereby give
my permission
to _____
(Name and title, as Director of Public welfare or Supt. Of State Institution
where patient is an inmate.)
to institute proceedings before the Eugenics Board of North Carolina for my
sterilization; and I do hereby give my consent to the performance of such
operation, said operation to be performed in accordance with the
authorization of said Board.

Signed: _____
(Signature of patient)

Form No. 6-A-Consent for operation of sterilization
NORTH CAROLINA,

Grace _____ COUNTY
In Re: Sterilization

of ____ **Ivy Hart** _____

}

Before the
EUGENICS BOARD OF NORTH CAROLINA

Consent of Parent,Guardian
Spouse, or Next of Kin

I, the undersigned _____ **Winona Hart, grandmother**, do hereby petition
(Name and relationship to patient)
Frederick F. Price, Director of Public Welfare, Grace County
(Name and title, as Supt. of Public welfare or ~~Supt. Of State Institution where patient is an inmate.~~)

to institute proceedings before the Eugenics Board of North Carolina for the
sterilization of **Ivy Hart** _____ ; and I do hereby give my consent
to the performance of such operation, said operation to be performed in
accordance with the authorization of said Board.

Signed: _____ **X** _____
(Signature of parent, guardian, spouse or next of kin)

FORM NO.7-SUPPLEMENT TO FORM NO.1 PETITION FOR STERILIZATION-SOCIAL INFORMATION

Name **Ivy Hart**   Date first known to DPW **1951**

Family members known to DPW **sister,17; grandmother and 2 yr old nephew**

In making a comprehensive analysis of individual functioning, it is necessary to consider, in addition to the specific diagnosis required by law, other aspects of the individual's social, emotional, mental, and physical development, as well as environmental factors.

1. Home situation. Describe the home in terms of its adequacy for the family and how it is kept. Explain the ability of the spouse, parents, or other relatives to give supervision and protection. Give their attitude toward the client.

The family lives in a one bedroom tenants' house on the property of a tobacco farmer. While the house itself is run-down, the interior is fairly clean and sanitary. The grandmother has health problems (diabetes, arthritis, high blood pressure) which limit her ability to provide care. The sister is feebleminded and her son, born out of wedlock, shows signs of retardation as well. The family relies on welfare checks and donations of clothing. The 2 year old is not well supervised and has wandered off at least once. The grandmother seems to love her grandchildren but is overwhelmed and can use more support.

2. Client's abilities. Describe the kind of responsibility individual can take for the home and children (including training and supervision). Describe any work experience (giving the quality of performance).

Client loves children and is capable of providing care such as feeding, washing, and loving a child, but may not have the family support to adequately supervise a child. Client completed 9th grade and hoped to continue her education, which is now cut short by her pregnancy. She and her sister work on the farm as payment for their home. Client expresses herself fairly well, but sometimes requires explanations of more complicated concepts.

3. Reason for the decision to petition for sterilization. Describe

individual's inclinations toward opposite sex, indications of sex experience,

promiscuity, etc.

Others in the community (the farmer who owns the house and property as well as a neighbor and the client's grandmother) seem concerned that the client is sneaking out to see boys, although the client herself says she has only one boyfriend. With little supervision from the grandmother and poor understanding of reproduction and access to reliable birth control, it's likely she could become pregnant again. The household is cramped and chaotic, a situation with little hope of improvement in the future. The 2 year old child already in the household does not have enough supervision and care. In addition, the client's seizure witnessed by this case worker indicates she is still suffering from petit mal epilepsy, putting her children and herself at risk.

4. Attitude of the individual and relatives toward sterilization, including

their ability to understand the procedure.

It's the feeling of this department that the client cannot adequately understand the benefits of sterilization and given that she is only fifteen, this has not been discussed with her. Her grandmother fully understands the surgery and is anxious to have it performed. The sister was sterilized after the birth of her son.

Form completed by Jane Forrester   Date of completion 8-17-60

Title case worker, Grace County Department of Public Welfare

33

Ivy

Three days passed since Nurse Ann was here, and Nonnie hadn't spoke one word to me. The only time she looked at me it was like she wanted to shoot me dead, so I tried my best to stay out of her way. When me and Mary Ella got back from the barn today, though, all of a sudden Nonnie started screaming at me. I'd ruined her life, she yelled. I'd ruined everybody's life. She wanted to know who the boy was, and when I wouldn't say, she yelled, "Well, he better be white, that's all I can say!" We got into a shouting match so loud it made Baby William scream his head off and Mary Ella start to cry. All of a sudden, in the middle of a sentence, Nonnie ran out the back door. Was she going out there to cool off? I hoped so.

"I never seen her so mad," Mary Ella said. She stood in a corner of the living room like she was trying to hide from all the noise, hugging Baby William to herself.

"I know," I said, though I *had* seen her that mad once before— when Mary Ella turned up pregnant three years ago.

Mary Ella walked over to the rocker and sat down, Baby William in her lap. I flopped down on the sofa, trying to cool off after all the hollering. My baby was doing somersaults inside me and ever since Nurse Ann said she could feel it up in there I worried about it falling out, so I tried to sit as much as I could when I wasn't at the barn.

"There's Mrs. Forrester again." Mary Ella pointed through the front door and I stood up to see her walking toward the house.

"Today ain't her day for Avery," I said. That was usually when she'd stop by. Either way, I was glad to see her. I started walking to the door when all of a sudden Nonnie came rushing at me from the kitchen, carrying a switch, and I knew she hadn't gone outside to cool off at all. She just went to find something worse than her cane to hit me with.

I ran behind the one big chair in the room. "Mrs. Forrester's coming!" I pointed to the door. "Don't hit me!"

"I don't care if Jesus Christ hisself is coming!" Nonnie yelled at me, waving the switch through the air. She couldn't reach me and I kept the chair between me and her.

"Don't hit her, Nonnie!" Mary Ella shouted from her chair. She was covering poor Baby William's ears with her hands.

"What's going on here?" Mrs. Forrester stood in the doorway and I saw what she was seeing: a house full of crazy people.

"This child needs a whupping!" Nonnie said.

"That won't change anything." Mrs. Forrester said exactly what I'd been thinking. A whupping might work if you stole a biscuit off somebody else's plate, but it wasn't gonna change me having a baby.

"Don't matter." Nonnie sliced the switch through the air, hitting the seat of the chair with a whack, and I sure was glad I wasn't sitting there. "She needs it for what she's done. How am I gonna feed another child?" Her voice cracked like she was about to cry, and I suddenly knew she was more scared than mad. I felt sorry for being the cause.

"Mrs. Forrester will give us more money, won't you?" I looked at Mrs. Forrester. Every baby meant more money. Not much, but everybody knew they wouldn't let a new baby starve.

"Please, Mrs. Hart." Mrs. Forrester walked into the room. I thought she was awful brave to do that. "Please put that stick down," she said. "Hitting her won't solve anything."

"Why are you here?" Nonnie asked.

"I need to talk to Mary Ella about something."

"Me?" Mary Ella sounded surprised.

"What about?" Nonnie asked. She was still holding the switch and I wasn't moving from behind the chair.

"I want to talk to her in private," Mrs. Forrester said. "Mary Ella, can you come outside with me for a few minutes?"

"Okay." Mary Ella put Baby William on the floor and stood up. Baby William stuck his thumb in his mouth and sat down right where she put him.

Nonnie looked suspicious. "She's a minor child," she said. "I should be there."

"I can speak to her privately."

"What do you want to say to her?" Nonnie looked like she wanted to take the switch to Mrs. Forrester now, and I was glad she wasn't looking at me no more.

"It's between Mary Ella and me," Mrs. Forrester said. "But please hand me the stick first." She reached her hand toward Nonnie, who gave up so easy I felt bad for her. She didn't hand the stick to Mrs. Forrester, though. Just put it on the floor, then looked at me.

"Go change that boy," she said, pointing at Baby William. "He's stinkin' up the house."

Mrs. Forrester put her arm around Mary Ella and turned her toward the door. "Let's sit outside," she said. Mary Ella looked over at me and smiled. She liked Mrs. Forrester. She liked her paying attention to her. I wished she was talking to me instead, like usual. I was jealous.

I didn't smell nothing coming from Baby William's diaper, but I was glad to get out of the room. I shut the door of the bedroom as far as it would go and dropped Baby William onto the bed. He was tired out from all the fuss and just laid there with his thumb in his mouth. I got a diaper from the dresser and was taking the old one off him when I heard Mrs. Forrester's voice coming in the window right next to me.

"Do you remember when you had your appendix out after William was born?" she asked.

Baby William started to babble and I pressed my fingertip over his lips. "Hush," I whispered. They must have been sitting on the old bench by the side of the house, because I could hear every word real good.

NECESSARY LIES | 215

"No, ma'am," Mary Ella said. "I was asleep."

"But I bet you were sore afterward," Mrs. Forrester said. "You remember that? You remember when it happened?"

I did. When she came home, she had a cut on her belly with black thread sticking out of it.

"Yes, ma'am," Mary Ella said.

I put the clean diaper underneath Baby William, glad he'd shut up. My hands was working real slow so I could listen.

"Well, I want to be honest with you, Mary Ella," Mrs. Forrester said. "The doctor didn't take your appendix out. Instead, he did an operation that would keep you from having more babies. He thought that would be a good thing for you, and I think he was right. It's hard for you to even take care of Baby William, even though I know you love him very much. But I *don't* think it was right for you not to know the truth about what happened."

I held the safety pin frozen in the air. I couldn't believe my ears. Mary Ella didn't say nothing. She must of been as shocked as me.

"Do you understand what I'm saying?" Mrs. Forrester asked.

Baby William grabbed at the safety pin and I moved his hands away and started pinning the diaper, but my mind was outside the window.

"You saying I can't have no more babies?" Mary Ella asked.

"That's right. Not every woman . . . every girl . . . should have a lot of children. You have one beautiful little boy. I hope that once you really think about it, it'll be a relief to you to know you'll never have to worry about getting pregnant again."

"How do I get my five children, then?" Mary Ella asked.

I kept real quiet, waiting for Mrs. Forrester to answer. It took her a while. "You won't be able to have them yourself," she said. "But there will always be children around. Ivy's little one is coming. Your neighbors will have babies. People at church. You can go back to church, Mary Ella. I'm sure you miss it and I know they'll welcome you. I spoke to your preacher a few weeks ago, and he said you're always welcome there. So you can have children in your life, just not your own."

"I want my own," Mary Ella said. "I dreamed about my five children."

"I know, but sometimes our dreams aren't really what's best for us."

"I want my *own*!" Mary Ella suddenly shouted.

I peeked out the window just as she jumped up from the bench and started running.

"Mary Ella!" Mrs. Forrester took off after her, and I heard Mary Ella come in the house.

"Nonnie!" She was crying. "She said I can't have no more babies!"

I picked up Baby William and headed for the door. When I came out of the bedroom, Mary Ella grabbed Baby William from my arms. "She said they lied!" she said to me.

I could hardly stand how much hurt was in her face. I looked past her to where Mrs. Forrester stood in the doorway, looking right pale.

"They lied about doing that appendix operation?" I asked her, like I didn't already know everything Mrs. Forrester told her.

"Now, now." Nonnie hobbled out of the kitchen, heading straight for Mary Ella. She was all a bunch of nerves, twisting her apron in her hands. She looked at Mrs. Forrester. "Why'd you go and do that?" she asked. "*Why?* That child was doing just fine."

"It wasn't fair." Mrs. Forrester pressed her hands together in front of her, like she did sometimes. "She had a right to—"

"What's a right got to do with it?" Nonnie snapped at her. "You probably live in a big house and gone to fancy schools and you ain't got no idea what it's like to try to raise up these motherless girls." She picked up the switch from the floor again and started toward Mrs. Forrester, who didn't have the brains to get out of the house, but I grabbed Nonnie's arm before she could do something stupid.

"I want five babies!" Mary Ella squeezed Baby William so hard he let out a screech.

"Put him down!" I said, sharp enough that I surprised her, and she opened her arms so fast he just slid to the floor and sat there hollering even louder.

Mrs. Forrester rushed to him, squatting down to help him to his feet.

"He ain't hurt," Nonnie said. "Just surprised hisself."

I was still holding Nonnie's arm and she didn't try to stop me when I took the switch out of her hand. "Why'd they lie?" I asked Mrs.

Forrester. "How'd they do it? How'd they fix it so she couldn't have no more babies?"

"They . . ." Mrs. Forrester got to her feet. She sounded out of breath. "It's a simple surgery," she said. "They just cut something inside that keeps a girl from getting pregnant. She can still have . . . intercourse, but—"

"Don't use that word in my house!" Nonnie shouted. "I want Mrs. Werkman back. You ruin things." She hugged Mary Ella, who cried against her. "Look what you done to this child!" she said.

"Mary Ella." Mrs. Forrester tried to talk to her, but she had her head buried on Nonnie's shoulder. "You'll be healthier and better able to take care of—"

"You git!" Nonnie said to her. "You're welcome to come back here with the clothes and the food, but don't you mess with my family no more!"

I could tell Mrs. Forrester was trying to figure out what to do. Finally she put her hand light on Mary Ella's back. "I'll be in touch," she said, and she left without even looking in my direction.

Nonnie and Mary Ella stayed in the living room while I carried the switch into the yard. I looked toward the woods where Mrs. Forrester had already disappeared. I didn't know what I thought of her right now. Whether I still loved her or hated her.

I went back in the house to start making supper for Baby William, and I was cutting up a carrot when I suddenly thought about my own baby. Would I wake up after it was born with that black thread coming out of my belly? Were they going to lie to me, too?

34

Jane

Oh dear God, what have I done?

I drove home from Grace County in a fog of guilt and confusion, my temples throbbing and my stomach roiling. I kept playing my talk with Mary Ella over and over in my head, unable to get her face out of my mind. I thought of the way she'd stared at me when she finally understood what I was telling her, her mouth open in surprise, her blue eyes wide and disbelieving. I'd wanted to look away from that shock and sorrow. No one could tell me she wasn't smart enough to understand. She knew exactly what I was saying. She had a right to know, damn it! I pounded the steering wheel with my fist. I didn't know how else I could have told her, but the one thing I knew for certain was that I'd handled it all wrong.

I pulled into our driveway, but didn't get out of the car. I sat there, staring blindly at our garage, hoping and praying I wouldn't need to have the same conversation with Ivy. I'd made my part of the petition as weak as I dared, knowing it had to be damning enough to get Fred's signature. He made me rewrite it. Twice. When I read the final version before putting it in the envelope, I was appalled at how convincing an argument I'd made for sterilization, but I also knew that every word was the truth.

Robert's car pulled up behind mine and he tapped his horn in greeting. This was the first week we'd had Angeline make dinner for us. She'd prepare it during the afternoon and all I had to do was heat it in the oven. Robert wasn't thrilled with the idea, but having Angeline do the cooking was the only way we could eat before eight at night. I had no idea what she'd made for us tonight and it didn't matter. I wouldn't be able to eat a bite.

I ran my hands through my hair and gave my temples a quick massage that did nothing to ease the pain. Then I put a smile on my face and got out of my car.

"Hi, darling," I said, greeting him with a kiss as he got out of his own car.

"Hi," he said, and we started walking side by side to the back door. "You're just getting home?" he asked.

"I needed to see one of my families at the end of the day," I said. "It was a little rough." How I wished I could talk to him about it! There was really no one I could confide in these days. Charlotte was the natural candidate, but she was way too judgmental. Lois was too ill for me to bother with my problems and I didn't want to worry my mother. I missed college, when I'd been surrounded by Gloria and my other girlfriends. Now we were all scattered to the winds.

Robert sighed as we neared the back door, and I could tell he was debating whether to ask me why it was rough. I didn't wait for him to make up his mind. I was desperate to talk to someone about what I'd done.

"You know that family with the seventeen- and fifteen-year-old sisters?"

"How could I forget," he said.

I ignored his tone. "I told the older one that's she's sterile and she got very upset. Everyone had told her that she had an appendectomy instead of a tubal ligation, and I thought—"

"Why did you tell her?" he asked as we walked into the kitchen. The room was filled with the aroma of Angeline's cooking, but it turned my stomach. "Hey! It smells like heaven in here, doesn't it?" he asked.

"Yes, it really does," I agreed absently, turning on the oven. The sooner I had dinner on the table, the happier my husband would be. "I told her because she thought she could still have children," I said.

"She was talking about wanting five. How could I let her go through her life believing she could have four more children?"

"Five little welfare babies?" Robert set his briefcase on the bench of the breakfast nook. "Who cares if she wants them? She shouldn't have children she can't support."

"I just think it was so wrong to lie to her."

He loosened his tie and stared at me. "You know what, Jane?" he asked. "I'm sick to death of talking about your work." He looked as tired as I felt. "Sick . . . to . . . death."

"I haven't talked to you about my work in weeks," I said, my hand on the refrigerator door.

"Oh come on." He laughed, but it wasn't a happy sound.

"I haven't!" I dropped my hand from the refrigerator. I felt wrongly accused. "I know you hate it so I've avoided talking to you about it, even though I really, really wish I could."

He rubbed his forehead. "Would you make me a drink, please?" He slumped onto the bench, facing the room instead of the table.

I let out my breath in a huff and reached into the cupboard where we kept the liquor. We'd have to talk about this, but now was obviously the wrong time. "Did you have a hard day, too?" I asked, shaking the gin and vermouth together. I knew I had a way of putting my problems first in this marriage. I needed to be better about that.

"Diagnosed a boy with polio," he said.

"*Polio?*" I stopped the shaker.

"His parents had refused to have him vaccinated. They broke down in my office. I spent an hour with them while other patients waited, but I had to take the time."

"Of course you did," I said. "I'm so sorry, Robert." I poured the drink into a cocktail glass and dropped in an olive.

He stood up and I handed him the glass. "Why don't you relax while I get dinner in the oven," I said, "and then we can talk about it."

He nodded. The orange sunlight coming through the window of the breakfast nook illuminated the side of his face, and I saw tiny lines around his eyes. I could see how he'd look when he got older. So distinguished. I reached up to touch his cheek, but he suddenly grabbed my hand. He was staring at my hair.

"Come over here," he said, and he pulled me toward the door and turned on the overhead light. He touched my hair and I was embarrassed.

"Oh, don't look," I said, trying to cover my hair with my free hand. "I've got dandruff. I never had it before, so I've been using—"

"Jesus H. Christ!" He backed away from me as though my hair had burned him. "You've got lice!"

I thought—I *hoped*—I'd misunderstood him. *"What?"*

"Damn it!" he said, setting down his drink. "I must have them, too. My head itches, but I thought it was that new shampoo you bought. Damn it, Jane!"

"No!" I said. "I think it's just dandruff." My scalp suddenly itched like mad, but I didn't dare touch it.

"It's lice," he said. "I've seen lice." He looked at his watch. "The pharmacy just closed but I'll see if I can catch the pharmacist before he leaves. I'll tell him the shampoo is for . . . a neighbor or . . . I'll make up something. You stay here and strip the bed. Hot water. Sheets. Towels. Our clothes. Everything!" He grabbed his keys from the counter where he'd tossed them. "You're quitting!" he said. "You are finished with this job."

"How do you know *you* didn't bring them home?" I asked. "You just said you've seen them. You could just as easily have—"

"Go strip the bed!" he shouted, his back to me as he stormed out the door, and I heard him mutter under his breath, *"Goddamn it."*

I stood there, stupidly staring at the back door, afraid to move. Afraid the lice would fall off my head and onto my shoulders. Onto the kitchen floor. It wasn't dandruff I had. It was nits. I climbed the stairs to our bedroom slowly, holding my head perfectly still, although I knew the dandruff—the *infestation*—had started weeks ago; it hardly mattered if I moved my head now.

I wrapped a towel around my head, then started to strip the bed, but the thought of the tiny insects was too much for me and I rushed to the bathroom to be sick.

I sat on the bathroom floor for a few minutes after I threw up, my head against the cool tile wall. I thought of the houses I went into, some of them more like shacks. Some of them filthy and crawling with vermin. I'd brought them home, almost certainly. He was right about that.

I pulled myself together and got weakly to my feet. He'd be angry if I didn't have the bed stripped and the laundry going by the time he got home. I could hardly blame him.

35

Ivy

"Set aside some of these for supper tonight," Nonnie said, as me and her shelled peas at the kitchen table to get them ready for canning.

"We probably only need enough for me and you and Baby William," I said. "Mary Ella won't eat nothing."

Nonnie sighed. "She's gonna save us money that way, but that ain't the way to do it."

"She ain't never getting over this," I said. Nonnie knew what I meant. Ever since Mrs. Forrester told Mary Ella about the operation, it's all we thought about.

"Oh, she will." Nonnie popped open a peapod with her thumbnail and scraped the peas into the bowl in front of her. "She'll see the rightness of it one of these days."

"Did you say it was okay for them to do that to her?" I asked. I'd wondered about that.

Nonnie took a while to answer. "I thought it was best," she said. "I still think so."

I stopped shelling. "You *told* them to do it?" I asked.

"I didn't *tell* them, but Mrs. Werkman brung it up and I said 'Yes, ma'am.'" She looked across the table at me. "It was like a miracle, Ivy. I was worried how I'd keep her from having a whole run of babies and there was the answer. So yes, I done it and it was the right thing."

I went back to shelling the peas. I didn't know why I couldn't get my next question out right away, but I sat with it for two or three minutes, trying to get my courage up. "You wouldn't let them do that to me, would you?" I asked finally.

Nonnie kept on working. "Why would I let that happen to you?" she asked. "You getting married and all."

"That's right," I said. I'd told Nonnie and Mary Ella me and my baby's father would get married before the baby came. I'd make sure I didn't have no little bastard like poor Baby William. When I told them, Nonnie just gave me a look like I'm a fool, and Mary Ella didn't give me no look at all. Mary Ella was too sad to care about me or anything else except Baby William.

The problem was, I told Henry Allen about the baby three weeks ago and hadn't been able to talk to him since. The barning was over, but I knew he was still working in the pack barn. I wished I could walk over and see him, but I didn't dare. I was sure Mr. Gardiner knew about the baby—all he had to do was catch a look at me; I was getting mighty big. So far, he didn't say nothing to me about it, but I worried he'd kick us out and I knew that was Nonnie's worry, too. He put up with one Hart girl having a baby. Would he put up with two? Especially when one of them babies might be his bastard grandchild? I was glad Nonnie wouldn't let me go nowhere, especially not to the store, because I was afraid of seeing Mrs. Gardiner. What she must think of me, dragging her boy down!

"Here comes Lita again," Nonnie said, looking through the kitchen window. She got up to open the door.

Lita walked into the kitchen, smiling at me. She carried a brown paper bag in one arm and a glass jug of her special tea in the other. "Hey, Miss Winona," she said to Nonnie. "Hey, Ivy."

I was glad to see her. This was the second time she paid me a visit this week—a bad week in every way—and I'd already drunk a whole jug of her tea. She made it out of some leaves she found in the woods and said it would make my baby strong. Nonnie didn't want me to drink it, but I did anyway because the one thing them Jordan boys was was strong.

She put the jug on the counter. "I brung some of Rodney's baby things for you," she said, nodding to the bag. "Let's set in the living room and I'll show you."

"Don't keep her long." Nonnie sat down at the table again. "I can't shell all these peas by myself."

"I'll be back in a few minutes, Nonnie," I said, and me and Lita went in the living room. I moved Nonnie's sheets into a bundle at one end of the sofa and we sat down.

"How're you feeling, baby?" she asked. Lita'd been real nice to me since I been pregnant. Real nice. She never used to call me "baby" and I liked when she said it. I got the feeling she understood how I felt: alone. I ain't never felt so alone before. School would start next week and I wouldn't be on that bus. Wouldn't see my friends. Wouldn't see Henry Allen every day. That was the worst part of all.

"Let me show you what I got in here." Lita started pulling little teeny clothes out of the bag. They was so cute and I tried to picture a baby of mine in them, but it was hard. I knew Nonnie would make me wash them before I put them on my baby on account of a colored baby wore them. So I'd clean perfectly clean clothes, but I wouldn't make a fuss about it because Nonnie was too tired and miserable to fight with these days.

"This one's really special," Lita said, handing me a little blue sweater.

"It's real pretty," I said, taking it from her and resting it on my knees to look at. It made a crinkly sound and I lifted one side of the sweater to see a bit of that notepaper Henry Allen always used for his notes. "Oh!" I said, and closed the sweater up real quick.

I looked at Lita, and she nodded toward the sweater with a smile. "Go ahead," she said. "Read it."

I glanced at the kitchen door, worried Nonnie might come out. Then I quickly opened the note.

I ain't forgot we're getting married. Just got to figure it out.

I folded it back up and tucked it in the pocket of my dress. I felt like crying and laughing at the same time.

Lita was still smiling. "That's the best thing in this bag, ain't it?" she whispered.

I nodded. "I was beginning to think he forgot about me," I whispered back. I didn't know Lita knew about me and Henry Allen. He must of trusted her to do this. It made me trust her more. I didn't know how me and Henry Allen would work it all out, getting married. I didn't think I could leave Nonnie and Mary Ella and Baby William. They needed me too much. Me and him sure couldn't move into the Gardiners' house, although when I thought of living in a nice place like that—well, I just couldn't picture myself there. We'd have to have our own place and how could we afford it? Henry Allen would have to quit school and try to find work and that's how people started going downhill, when they quit school. I'd seen it happen to lots of people. But I trusted he was figuring it all out, like he said. One day, he'd come over and say, "I got it figured out, Ivy," and he'd tell me the plan and it would all be fine.

Lita pulled out a pair of pants, way too big for a baby. "Rodney's outgrown these, so I thought maybe Baby William could use them." She looked around. "Where is he? Where's Mary Ella?"

"Napping, I think. She ain't good, Lita." I'd told Lita all about Mrs. Forrester's visit. I didn't know who to be mad at—Mrs. Werkman, because she's the one that made it happen, or Mrs. Forrester for making Mary Ella so upset. I was mad at both of them, really. Mary Ella wasn't right these days. She was either in bed or in the rocker all day long, holding Baby William or just by herself. "She ain't talking at all," I said to Lita. Mary Ella was never much of a talker, but now she was plum silent, all wrapped up in herself. When she was home, she loved on Baby William like she always did, but nearly every evening, she went wandering again. She didn't bother taking my spermicide jelly now. The past two years, I been so worried about her having another baby and now I knew she never could of. She still remembered to get us them baskets of extras from the Gardiners, but I worried someday she'd be out wanderin' and forget and then I'd have to go over and ask for it and . . . well, there just wasn't no way I could do that.

I wanted to ask Lita to keep Eli away from Mary Ella, but what did it matter now, really? She couldn't have no more babies and everybody already thought she was trash. Now I guessed they was thinking the same about me.

"Do you know why I sent Sheena up North, Ivy?" Lita asked, folding up them little pants again.

I shook my head. Sheena'd been gone five years. I hardly remembered her no more.

"I sent her up there because Mrs. Werkman started talking about her having the operation. She said she was feebleminded." Lita unfolded the pants again and spread them out smooth on her lap, running her hands over them again and again, and I thought she wasn't really seeing them. Maybe she was seeing Sheena in her mind instead. "If she was so feebleminded, how come she's starting college right this minute?" she asked.

I shook my head. "Don't make sense," I said.

"That's right. It don't. I got her out of here before she either got pregnant or had the operation. One or the other was headed her way. They say you have to give permission before they do it, but a lady at church refused to sign them papers and they told her she wouldn't get no more welfare if she didn't. So I had to get her away."

I nodded. "It's good you sent her," I said.

"Ivy!" Nonnie hollered from the kitchen. "I ain't doing this alone!"

"I'll go," Lita said. "You drink that tea, now, okay?"

I nodded. "I like it once I put sugar in it."

"Good," she said.

Me and Lita walked back in the kitchen and suddenly heard a terrible howl from outside. It was the kind of sound that made your heart stop cold.

"What on earth?" Nonnie started getting to her feet, but me and Lita was already running out the door.

Baby William stood in the yard, holding on to the corner of the porch, his mouth opened wide as he let out another howl.

"What's the matter, Baby William?" I ran down the steps. "I thought you was sleeping with your mama."

"His mouth!" Lita said. "What's around his—"

"Oh no!" The skin around his mouth was blue. "No!" I shouted. "It's Nonnie's testing pills!" I grabbed him and carried him up the stairs to the pump on the porch, holding him sideways as I pumped water over his mouth. Already there was blisters coming up on his lips. "Did you eat one?" I shouted at him.

"How many was in this box?" Lita asked. She was on the ground, picking up the pills.

"I don't know!"

"Here's one looks like he just got a lick of, maybe."

"What's going on?" Nonnie slammed the screen door behind her.

"He got into them testing pills!" I said. "You didn't put them on the shelf!" I hoped he didn't swallow one. I tried to see inside his mouth to check if the pills burned him there, but he was screaming and squirming and I couldn't get a good look.

"I did, too!" Nonnie said. "I thought I did."

"Well, you didn't! Pump this water for me!"

She started pumping and I was nearly drowning Baby William, trying to clean off the blue.

"He needs to go to the hospital," Lita said. "I'll get Davison to drive you. Take the pills with you." She slipped them in the pocket of my dress, the pocket with Henry Allen's note. "I'll be right back!" she said, taking off for the woods.

I didn't have time to think about how bad it would be to ride in a car with Mr. Gardiner. I set Baby William on the porch. He was still screaming and I saw little bubbles at the corners of his lips.

"I'll get Mary Ella," Nonnie said, running back into the house. "I thought she was watching him. I thought I put them pills . . ."

Whatever she said got swallowed up by Baby William's screams and I just hugged him to me, scared we'd ruined him for all time.

For once, not even Mary Ella could settle Baby William down. We rode to the hospital in Mr. Gardiner's car. I wished Lita could of come with us, but they wouldn't let her in the white hospital, plus she had to get home to her own boys. Mary Ella and Nonnie sat in the back with Baby William, who hadn't stopped screaming for one single second since me and Lita found him. I was in front with Mr. Gardiner, wishing anybody else in the world was driving us—except *Mrs.* Gardiner.

Nobody said nothing in the car. We couldn't of heard each other anyway. In the emergency room, Mr. Gardiner told the nurse, "The boy ain't watched right," and then the nurse took Mary Ella and Nonnie and the box of pills into a back room with Baby William, but she said there wasn't enough room for me. That left me in the waiting room with Mr. Gardiner. We sat next to each other, Henry Allen's note nearly burning my thigh through my dress.

For the longest time, we stared straight ahead, like we didn't know each other was there. Then finally, he said, "You ain't wrecking my boy's life, Ivy."

I wanted to get up and move to the other side of the room, but I had to remember he held our lives in his hands. So I didn't move and I didn't say nothing and some time passed and he got up and talked to the lady who was checking in people at a desk and she took him someplace I couldn't see. Maybe the bathroom? And after a while, he came back and then we sat some more. One hour passed. Then two, and I thought of all kinds of things they might be doing to Baby William and I started to cry. Mr. Gardiner handed me his handkerchief, but didn't say nothing.

Suddenly he stood up, and I saw why. Mrs. Forrester! There was a policeman next to her. She spotted us and we met her halfway across the room.

"How is he?" she asked. She rested her hand on my arm just for a minute, but it was long enough to make me feel like I loved her again.

"We ain't heard nothing," Mr. Gardiner said.

She nodded. "All right." She glanced toward the lady at the desk. "I'll see what I can find out."

I wanted to stay with her, but Mr. Gardiner took my arm and walked me back to our seats again while Mrs. Forrester talked to the lady. The lady got up and took her and the policeman down a hallway.

"Why is she here?" I asked Mr. Gardiner. "Why is there a policeman with her?"

"Because that boy needs to be took away."

"*What*? What do you mean?"

"He ain't safe with you folks."

"Yes he is!" I stood up and started running down the hall after them.

"Ivy!" Mr. Gardiner called, but he didn't try to follow me.

I couldn't find the room they was in right away. I walked in a room with an old lady lying on a stretcher and then a big room with a bunch of beds in it. Finally, I found the room where Mrs. Forrester was talking to Nonnie and Mary Ella. The policeman stood just inside the door.

"Ivy!" Mary Ella hollered. She was crying.

"You can't come in," the policeman said.

"It's all right," Mrs. Forrester said to him. "She's part of the family. Come in, Ivy."

I went right to Mary Ella and put my arm around her. "Where's Baby William?" I asked.

"They're still treating him," Mrs. Forrester said, "but the doctor says he's going to be all right. He was very, very lucky. This could have been much worse."

"The doctor said he could of died," Mary Ella said.

"I thought I put them pills on the shelf," Nonnie said. She looked old and sad and fat to me. I was so mad at her, but I didn't like seeing that scared face on her.

"He could have died, that's right," Mrs. Forrester said. "And given the fact that this happened because he was unsupervised on top of the time he was missing for nearly half a day and the time the wrong lotion was put on his rash, the department feels he should be in a foster home, at least temporarily."

"What's that mean?" Mary Ella whispered to me.

"Please," I said, "don't take him away from us. That's so wrong. We're his kin."

"I know this is very difficult." She was doing that hand-rubbing again like she did sometimes. "We need to be absolutely sure he's safe while we decide the next step. I'm going to work on allowing y'all to visit him, but I can't promise that."

"It's my fault," Nonnie said. Tears was coming down her cheeks. "It's all my fault, so don't blame these girls. Don't blame Baby William."

"We're not blaming anyone," Mrs. Forrester said. "We just need to keep him safe and healthy, and putting him in a foster home is the best way to do that."

A nurse stuck her head in the door and looked at Mrs. Forrester. "He's ready," she said.

Mrs. Forrester took in a big breath like she was getting ready to dive underwater. "It's best if the three of you stay here in this room," she said. "I'll ask the doctor to come in and tell you about his injuries. And then I'll be in touch. I'll come over next week and we can talk more about this."

"I want to see my baby!" Mary Ella said. I could tell she didn't understand what was happening. Nonnie sure did, though, and her legs couldn't hold her another minute. She sat down in the chair against the wall, her face in her hands.

I put my arms around Mary Ella. "Mrs. Forrester needs to take him to another family for a little while," I said. I stared at Mrs. Forrester while I talked, deciding I hated her after all. She wasn't on our side. She was our enemy.

"What other family?" Mary Ella asked. "He needs to come home with us!"

The policeman touched Mrs. Forrester's elbow. "Let's go," he said.

She looked like she wasn't sure if she should stay with us or go with him. "I'll come over next week," she said again, and then left with the policeman.

When the door closed behind them, Mary Ella all of a sudden seemed to understand what was happening. She ran to the door and tried to open it, but someone must of been holding it shut from the other side. "Baby William!" she hollered, pounding on the door.

I went to her, meaning to put my arms around her and hold her real tight, but instead I started pounding on the door myself, hitting it with the sides of my fists, pounding as hard as I could. It felt like the only thing I could do. It felt like I was pounding on God.

36

Jane

I drove into work Monday morning with a sense of dread and a weariness I couldn't shake. I'd barely slept all weekend. Every time I closed my eyes, I saw the trusting, hopeful faces of the Hart family disintegrate into masks of hurt. I knew I'd done the right thing in removing William Hart from his home. He was now in an attentive foster home and receiving medical treatment for the blisters in his mouth and on his lips, and I felt good knowing that he was safe. He was probably scared and miserable and would suffer psychological scars that might haunt him forever, but he would live. Sometimes, though, you could do the right thing and still feel sick with doubt.

I'd just sat down to dinner with Robert on Friday evening when the call came from the hospital. Robert and I had finally gotten past the misery of the lice infestation. For two weeks, we'd shampooed with the smelliest medicinal shampoo imaginable and washed so many loads of laundry that I'd started dreaming about suds filling all the rooms of our house. When I answered the phone Friday evening and told him I had to go back to Grace County for an emergency, he simply waved good-bye to me without looking up from his pork chop.

Charlotte was already in our office this morning. Her cast was off now, but she still rested her bruised and swollen leg on the stool, and a cane had taken the place of the crutches. She looked up when I walked in.

"You finally got that child out of there," she said in greeting.

I set my briefcase on my desk and sat down. "It was terrible," I said.

She nodded. "I'll never forget my first time," she said. "The only thing more painful would be doing nothing and then hearing later about the disastrous result. You had a close call with this one, and I blame both of us. I should have gotten him out of there before turning the case over to you. You weren't ready to face what had to be done."

I bristled, but tried not to show it. The last thing I wanted today was an argument with Charlotte. She was still furious with me for telling Mary Ella the truth about her surgery—which I admitted to her before Ann Laing had a chance to tell her—and she was never going to let me forget about the beach trip, either. "I'm going to go over to the Harts' house this week to see how they're doing," I said.

"You have other cases to attend to," she said.

"I know, but—"

"This arrived for you this morning." She reached for a large envelope on her desk and handed it to me. "The board approved your petition."

Oh no. This was terrible timing. I took the envelope from her reluctantly.

"Even if they hadn't approved it on this first round, they would now that a child's been removed from the home."

She watched me as I opened the envelope and read the form giving the board's permission.

I looked up. "I can't lie to her," I said.

"Then say nothing."

"She's not going to believe she had an appendectomy."

"We'll cross that bridge when we come to it."

"I'll lose all credibility with her."

"Better with her than with me, don't you think?"

I looked down at the form again, my cheeks hot.

"Your actions are bordering on insubordination, Jane." Charlotte leaned forward as if trying to get me to look at her. "You've overattached yourself to a family. You've broken rules. You dragged your feet when a child's welfare was at stake. And you *specifically* went against my orders not to tell Mary Ella Hart about her sterilization. You, yourself, realized that was a mistake. I hope you won't make the same mistake with her sister."

I couldn't think of a thing to say that wouldn't get me in more trouble.

"We'll have to seriously discuss removing Ivy's baby when it's born, as well," she said. "We can't put another child into a home that's known for neglect."

I shook my head and looked at her. "You have to give her a chance to be a good mother to her baby," I said.

"She was right there when William got into those pills. Even if she proves herself to be mother of the year, she can't control what her grandmother and Mary Ella do. It's more than her ability. It's the environment."

"One thing at a time," I said, turning away from her. I picked up my briefcase and feigned searching through it for something. "I have some work I need to get done right now," I said.

"So do I," Charlotte said, carefully moving her leg from the stool to the floor so she could face her desk. "We can talk more about this later."

"All right," I said, but I knew I would tell Ivy.

Even if it meant losing my job.

Form No. 4-Order For Operation of Sterilization

NORTH CAROLINA	Before the
.... COUNTY	EUGENICS BOARD OF NORTH
IN RE: STERILIZATION OF	CAROLINA
	Order for Operation
Ivy Hart	Sterilization

WHEREAS, on **August 19, 1960** ...., a Petition for Operation

of Sterilization or ~~Asexualization~~ to be performed upon .... **Ivy Hart**

............was instituted with this Board by .... **Frederick F. Price** ,the

Petitioner, (WHEREAS, on **August 19, 1960** , the Secretary of the

Eugenics Board of North Carolina having received written consent by **Winona Hart**

Patient's **grandmother**

as provided for in Section 44 (d) of Chapter 35 of the General Statutes of North Carolina, a hearing is unnecessary; and

WHEREAS, this Board at the time and place designated in the aforesaid Notice of Hearing, did consider the said Petition and did hear consider evidence duly offered in support of and against said Petition, and patient not being present nor represented.

AND it being the opinion and the judgment of this Board that this case fall within the intent and meaning of one or more of the circumstances mentioned in Section 39, Chapter 35, of the General Statutes of North Carolina, and that an operation of sterilization will be for the best interest of the mental, moral and physical improvement of the said patient, and/or for the public good.

NOW THEREFORE, IT IS ORDERED THAT THE PETITIONER, **Frederick F. Price**,

proceed to have performed upon **Ivy Hart** , patient, the operation of **sterilization**

such operation to be performed by **staff surgeon of hospital where patient delivers**, on any day between the **19th** day of **August 1960**, and the **19th** day of **February 1961**;

Provided, that nothing in this order shall prevent or interfere in any manner with the right of the patient, guardian, spouse, or next of kin of such patient to select competent physicians of their own choice to perform such operation at the patient's expense.

Provided further, that nothing contained in this order shall be construed to authorize the interruption or termination of pregnancy in any case where the same is known to exist.

SIGNED *Peter Simon*

Rosemary D. Carmas

This **19th** day of **August** 19 **60** *David J. Pyle*

Members of the Eugenics Board of North Carolina

37

Ivy

For the first time, I wasn't happy to see Mrs. Forrester coming out of the woods into our yard. I was hanging the wash, feeling empty as could be since there wasn't any of Baby William's diapers in the basket. I wished I could take back all the times I complained about having to wash all them diapers. I was home alone. Nonnie was visiting the one old church friend she still had and Mary Ella was . . . well, who knew where she was. She'd spent the whole past week in our bed, staring at the ceiling. Not even crying, though she sure cried a lot the first day or two. I couldn't get her to eat nothing or talk to me.

The house felt real empty without Baby William in it. Felt like a house hardly worth living in. Even Nonnie was real quiet and I knew she felt bad about leaving them pills where Baby William could get them.

"Ivy," Mrs. Forrester said as she walked toward the clothesline.

I didn't look up from what I was doing. I had nothing to say to her.

"I know you all must be very upset with me," she said when she got close. "I checked with the foster home this morning and Baby William is fine. His mouth is healing very well."

I pulled another clothespin from my apron and stuck it on one of the towels, acting like I didn't see her standing next to me.

"Is Mary Ella here?" she asked. "I wanted to see how she's doing."

"How do you think?" I asked, sticking another clothespin on the line. I was mad at her even though I knew she wasn't the only one to blame. I blamed the doctor in the emergency room, too, and Mr. Gardiner, since I knew he talked to somebody at the hospital about us. I turned to face her.

"Ever since they took Baby William, Mary Ella's just stayed in bed. She don't talk and she don't eat. Today she's gone out who knows where."

"This must be terrible for her," she said. "For all of you. I'd really like to talk to her."

"Well, if you can find her, you can try, but good luck."

"Is Nonnie inside?"

"She's gone visiting."

"Well, maybe it's best I have you alone," she said. "I wanted to talk to you about something."

"Talking to you always goes bad," I said. "All you bring us is bad news."

"I guess it must seem that way lately."

I hung another towel on the line. "You got more of it, don't you," I said.

"Can we go inside?" she asked.

Might as well get this over with, I thought. I had a handful of clothespins and I dropped them back in my apron pocket. They must of tickled my baby, because it started moving around inside me. I kept my hand in my pocket a minute, feeling the somersaults. Nobody was taking my baby away from me.

I walked ahead of Mrs. Forrester into the house. I didn't say "you want some tea" or nothing. Just walked through the kitchen and sat on the sofa and said what was weighing heavy on my mind. "You ain't taking my baby away."

She sat down in Mary Ella's rocker like she owned it, and that made me even madder at her. I looked at her blond hair—how it always curled under just perfect. She must of spent lots of money at the beauty parlor to get it to do that. I looked at her perfect white blouse and her perfect, probably brand-new, stockings. She was nothing but a phony double-crosser, how she pretended to care about us.

238 | Diane Chamberlain

"As long as he or she is cared for," she said, "I don't think that will happen."

"Baby William was cared for!" I felt my eyes fill up. "We love him!"

"I know," she said. "I know you do."

"He was doing just fine," I said. "Everybody makes a mistake like with them pills. People don't take their babies away."

"Everybody doesn't make a mistake that serious," she said in a calm voice I didn't like. She didn't sound much like herself today.

"Can we get him back?" I asked.

"I don't think so," she said. "Not right away, anyhow."

"Then why'd you bother coming? Why'd you want to see me alone?"

She moved to the edge of the seat like she could get closer to me that way. "Before I became the caseworker for your family, Mrs. Werkman had started the process to have you . . . to get you the same operation Mary Ella had."

"What are you talking about?" I didn't know what she meant about the "process." I sure did know what the operation was, though, and I hoped I wasn't understanding her right.

"After you have your baby, the doctor is going to make it so that you'll never have to worry about getting pregnant again," she said.

"Oh no." I shook my head. "No he won't. I ain't letting that happen to me, too. I won't go to the hospital. I'll have the baby right here with Nurse Ann."

"Nurse Ann knows about it," Mrs. Forrester said. "She'll make sure you go to the hospital."

I stood up. "You can't do this!" I shouted. "People can't cut up other people when they don't want it."

"You're only fifteen, Ivy, and your grandmother signed the permission form for you to have the surgery."

"She said she didn't. She wouldn't. She said because I'm getting married."

"You are?" Mrs. Forrester looked surprised. She looked *hopeful.* "To the baby's father? When?"

I flopped down on the sofa again, not knowing how to answer because it was a dream, wasn't it? Marrying Henry Allen? He hadn't sent me no more notes, and I only seen him once—getting off the school bus with the other kids. He didn't see me because I was hiding in the trees, wishing I could still be on that bus. I missed school something awful, but I missed Henry Allen worse. It seemed like he'd forgot all about me and the baby now.

But I wouldn't let Mrs. Forrester and Mrs. Werkman and Nurse Ann and the doctor do to me what they done to Mary Ella. "I want children, Mrs. Forrester!" I pleaded. "You got to let me do that."

"Can you see anything good about this, Ivy? You'll have one precious baby and then not have to worry about—"

It was the same kind of thing she'd said to Mary Ella and it was all wrong. "No. There ain't nothin' good about it!" I shouted. "Just one baby ain't natural. You said Mrs. Werkman came up with this idea, right? Don't you have some say? Can't you stop them?"

She shook her head. "Please think about it," she said. "Think about the good things that can come from having just one child to—"

"Get out of my house!" I stood up again, not caring how rude I sounded. "I hate you!"

"I know you feel that way now—"

"Get out. You're a horrid person."

"I want to check on Mary Ella to see—"

"Don't bother!" I wanted to push her out the door, but going to jail was the last thing I needed. "She don't want to see you no more than I do."

She stood up. "All right," she said as she walked to the front door, "but I'll be in touch."

I slammed the door behind her as hard as I could, wishing it would hit her and I could say it was an accident, but she was too fast. She wanted to get away from me as much as I wanted her to go.

38

Jane

I pulled my car to the side of Deaf Mule Road, unable to see to drive. I put my head in my hands. I'd made such a mess of things. I'd wanted to help Ivy see why this could be a good thing for her, but I'd bungled it, just as I had with Mary Ella. How could I *not* bungle it? It was just wrong. The whole damn thing was wrong! There was no way to be honest with a girl about sterilization without making a mess . . . unless you took the Charlotte Werkman approach of not telling at all. Charlotte was going to kill me. She was right: I couldn't keep an emotional distance from the people I worked with. Or at least, not from these particular people.

I looked over my shoulder down Deaf Mule Road. I could go back to Ivy. I imagined her crying now, terrified as she tried to understand what would happen to her. I pressed my fist to my mouth, imagining how scared she was right this minute. I wanted to hold her. Comfort her. But the truth was, she probably wouldn't let me near her right now.

I blotted my eyes with a tissue, then started driving again. I was a couple of miles from the farm when my car suddenly began slowing down. I pressed the gas pedal harder, but it made no difference. I looked at the gas gauge in disbelief. Empty. The needle was actually below the E. *Stupid, stupid.*

I was able to pull to the side of the narrow road before the car came completely to a stop. The tires sank into the sand on the shoulder and I wondered if I'd just given myself two problems instead of one.

I got out of the car and turned in a circle to plan my next move. I couldn't see another car on the road in either direction. Fields surrounded me. A few tobacco barns stood here and there, and in the far, far distance, I could see a farmhouse. At least I hoped it was a farmhouse. It had a red roof. A good sign.

I got my purse and briefcase from my car and started walking. At least this hadn't happened to me in the heat of July or August, I thought. The temperature still had to be close to eighty degrees, but it was bearable. And anyway, it wasn't the weather that was troubling me most today.

I heard the sound of a vehicle a distance behind me, and turned to see a truck approaching. I started to lift my hand to wave, but something about the appearance of the truck kept my hand at my side. As it got closer, I could see that one of its front fenders was missing and the body was rusting through the fading green paint. The right side of the front window was a spiderweb of cracked glass. I suddenly felt very exposed walking alone down the road. I faced forward, my gaze on that little farmhouse, willing the truck to pass me by, but I heard it slow until it was even with me.

"Where you goin', blondie?" a man asked. "Need a lift?"

I looked up to see two men in the cab of the truck. I guessed the man leaning on the windowsill closest to me was the one who had spoken. He looked like every stereotypical depiction of a backwoods nutcase—goofy grin, toothpick jutting from the side of his mouth, graying hair askew, and three days' worth of whiskers. Against the window behind his head, I could see a gun rack holding two shotguns.

I ignored him, facing forward again, but my heart had sped up. *Just go away*, I thought. *Leave me alone.* I wouldn't get in a truck with those two if my life depended on it. I had the feeling my life depended on *not* getting in the truck with them.

"I *said*, need a lift?" the man asked again.

"No, thank you," I said.

"She got manners," one of them said. "Her mama raised her right."

I kept walking, faster now, keeping my eyes straight ahead, and they continued driving right along next to me. Then I heard them stop. The squeak of a door opening. I wanted to run, but I'd never make it to that farmhouse before they caught me.

The man from the truck started walking behind me and to my left, enough out of my line of sight to make me paranoid.

"Please leave me alone," I said, without turning around.

"What you got in that there case you're carryin'?" he asked.

I ignored him. I was walking as quickly as I could, getting nowhere fast.

"Come on now, blondie," he drawled. "Where you headed? We can take you to the garage if that's what you want." He pronounced it "gay-roj." I heard another set of footsteps and knew they were both behind me now. At least one of them was close enough that I thought I could smell his whiskey breath. Any second, he could grab me, and then what? I felt sweat trickle down my neck.

In the distance, I saw another truck coming toward us and I ran into the middle of the road, waving my free arm. Maybe I'd be jumping from the frying pan into the fire, but right then I didn't care, and as the truck grew closer I saw the color: pale blue. Mr. Gardiner's truck? Could I possibly be that lucky? I lifted my arm to wave again, and one of the men reached out and touched my breast.

"Get the hell away from me!" I smacked his face with my briefcase.

"Oh, she's a live one!" he said, his hand to his cheek.

The truck neared and I realized it wasn't Mr. Gardiner at all. A colored man was behind the wheel, but as he slowed to a stop, I recognized Eli. For the first time, I was happy to see him.

"Get in," he called to me through the open window.

"You get in that nigger's truck, he's one dead nigger," one of the men said. The other was heading for his own truck, and I remembered the guns.

I had no choice. I ran around the other side of the truck and climbed in, and Eli took off before I even closed the door. Getting in a truck with Eli Jordan seemed just one step up from being with those two drunks back there, and I sat close to the door. I'd never been comfortable around him. I always felt as though he were studying me, seeing something inside me that I didn't want anyone to see. Something even I didn't know was there.

"I'm getting you in trouble," I said.

"We'll lose them," he said, looking in the rearview mirror as he took a turn onto another road. "Matter fact, we done lost them already."

"Is there a chance they'll find you, though? Come looking for you?" I tried to look behind us, but Eli was driving so fast, everything was a blur. I felt conspicuous riding with him. If we passed another truck or car, I'd crouch down and hide.

"You mighty worried about me all of a sudden, ma'am," he said.

"I've always been concerned about your family."

"I s'pose. Mama says you all right."

It burned me that he was passing judgment on me when it should be the other way around. I didn't know the real story between him and Mary Ella, but I did know he'd taken advantage of her and was taking no responsibility for William. Did he even care about the little boy?

Eli made another turn and then another, and I was relieved that I knew where we were now. The farm was no more than a half mile from here. My heartbeat returned to normal and I suddenly felt brazen.

"Are you upset William Hart was taken away?" I asked. I couldn't help myself.

He didn't look at me. He kept those amber eyes of his on the road ahead, and soon we turned into the long drive leading up to the farmhouse and the barns and shelter beyond.

"Baby William ain't my concern, ma'am," he said. "Why you aks me that?"

"Eli, let's talk straight, all right?" I said. "I've seen how you act around Mary Ella. I know you're . . . close to her. And I've had a good look at William."

He stopped the truck next to the farmhouse and shot me a quick, hard look. "You call that talkin' straight?" he asked, then faced forward again. "You can get out here, ma'am," he said. "I'm sure Mr. Gardiner'll help you with your car."

I didn't know what else to say, and that look he gave me told me the less I said right now, the better.

I got out of the cab and shut the door behind me, then said through the open window, "Thank you for picking me up." I wasn't sure what he'd saved me from, but I was glad I never had to find out.

"You know"—he leaned across the front seat to look at me—"I may be plum broke, and I may not be smart as you with your schoolin' and all, but I can tell you one thing, and this is for sure"—he glanced ahead of him, toward the barns and the fields, then back at me—"I wouldn't *never* do my own sister."

He pressed on the gas and took off toward the shelter where the other truck and the tractor were parked. I stared after him, trying to make sense of what he'd just said. To my right, I heard the screen door slam and turned to see Mary Ella walk onto the porch from the Gardiners' house.

"Mary Ella!" I started toward her as she walked down the stairs, but when she saw me, her face registered absolute panic, and she took off at a run in the direction of the path leading to her house. "Mary Ella!" I called again. "Please wait! I want to talk with you!"

She kept running without looking back, the basket over her arm swinging with each step. I wouldn't chase her. There was no way I could catch up to her now, anyway.

"Hello, there!" Mr. Gardiner came out of the house. "Didn't see your car."

I was still watching Mary Ella run toward the path through the woods, and it took me a moment to shift my attention to Mr. Gardiner.

"Hello." I set my briefcase on the ground and tried to smooth down my hair. I was sure I was a sweaty mess after the last half hour. "That's just it," I said. "I ran out of gas on . . . I'm not sure the name of the road. I can't believe I didn't check the gauge before I left home this morning. Eli happened to be driving by and he gave me a ride here."

He chuckled. "That's the kind of thing you only let happen once," he said.

"Could I use your phone to call a garage?" I looked toward the woods again. Mary Ella had disappeared inside them.

Mr. Gardiner followed my gaze. "She came over to see if there was a way I could get her boy back for her." He shook his head. "Sad situation there."

"It is," I agreed. "There are no winners."

"I appreciated your help with it. It needed to be done."

I nodded.

"That poor boy," he said. "He'll have some mental scars from it all, don't you think?"

"I hope not," I said.

"I know Mary Ella and her folks are tore up about him being took away, but the next mishap might have been the last, if you know what I mean."

"Exactly," I said, relieved to talk to someone who understood why William had to be removed.

"Well, come on now," he said, nodding toward his car, where it was parked at the side of the house. "You don't need no garage," he said. "I've got a gas can in the shelter and we'll fix you up good as new."

"Oh, that's really kind of you, but I don't want to put you to any trouble."

"No trouble at all."

We got in his car and he drove to the shelter, where Eli was unloading whatever he'd had in the truck. Mr. Gardiner got out of the car, and I heard him say something to Eli about the gas can. Eli looked in my direction, but not for long. In a moment, Mr. Gardiner returned with the can. He put it in the trunk and we turned around and headed back toward Deaf Mule Road.

"Mr. Gardiner," I said, as he turned onto the road. "Eli said something disturbing to me."

"Eli did? He's a good boy. Ain't the type to do no harm. I'll have a word with him."

"No, no. I don't mean anything . . . like that. I mean, I jumped to the conclusion based on some things Charlotte . . . Mrs. Werkman had said that Mary Ella's little boy was . . . well, his. Eli's."

He chuckled again. "I can tell you that ain't the truth."

"I said something to him about it, and he said . . . well, he *implied* that Mary Ella is actually his sister. He was angry at my accusation, I think, so maybe he was just saying—"

"No, that's true." He turned onto the road where my car had run out of gas. I could see it in the distance. "They're half sister and brother," he said. "But don't go spreading that around now, all right? No need to write it in your little notebook there." He motioned to my briefcase. "Eli shouldn't have said it."

"How can that be?" I asked.

"Let's have a look-see at your car." He pulled up behind my car and we both got out of his. I watched as he poured gas into my empty tank. Then he checked the tires on the right-hand side to be sure I wasn't stuck in the sand on the shoulder.

"You're good as new and can be on your way now," he said, putting the gas can back in his trunk.

"I can't thank you enough," I said, "but Mr. Gardiner, please explain to me about Eli and Mary Ella . . ." My voice trailed off.

He looked toward the fields in the direction of his house. "You ain't got to be no scholar to figure it out, now do you? Their daddy, Percy, and Lita Jordan and me . . . we all knowed each other since we was little. Percy had it bad for Lita, right from when we was kids. Of course, he couldn't marry her, so he married Violet, who even back then was crazy as a loon, but pretty, too. Looked a little like Mary Ella. The thing was, Violet started suspecting Percy of messin' around, only she guessed the wrong woman. Thought it was my wife." He glanced over at me, and I'm sure I looked as shell-shocked as I felt. "When Percy got killed, that's when Violet cut my wife," he said. "Violet blamed her. Said he was thinking about her instead of his work."

"My God," I said. "So . . . Eli is Percy Hart's son? He's truly Mary Ella's . . . and Ivy's . . . half brother?"

"Not just Eli. Him, Sheena, Devil, and Avery. All four of 'em. Only one's not Percy's and that's little Rodney."

I thought of Lita Jordan, who everyone thought had five illegitimate children with five different fathers. "Did she love him? Lita?"

"Yes, ma'am, I sure believe she did. I told him many a time he was looking for trouble, but—" He looked worried all of a sudden. "Now look," he said, a warning finger in the air, "this don't go no further than me and you here. I don't want no more trouble on my farm. We got enough already."

"Who else knows?" I asked. "Do Ivy and Mary Ella know?"

"Hell no. But Winona, she knows. Percy was her son, and she knew he was pining for Lita from when we was young. She'd smack him around when she'd catch him looking at her. She didn't figure it out for sure, though, until after Percy was dead and Avery got that eye disease. Winona's daddy had it, too. It runs in families, so she knew, but she won't ever admit to nothin'. You could tie her to the tractor and drive her through the tobacco and she wouldn't say nothin'. My wife . . . she bears the scar of that misbelief in more ways than one, but we all just keep it quiet." He gave me a warning look. "And you will, too."

"There's no need for me to ever say a thing about it," I said. "But . . . I do wonder now who William's father is? I thought it was Eli."

"What does it matter? Mary Ella . . . she's different, in case you ain't noticed. She got her pick of boys. And she's fixed now, so we don't got to worry about her having another one. Way I look at it, let her enjoy herself. She don't have much pleasure in her life."

"No, she doesn't," I said. "But it's not good for her to be so . . . pro-miscuous, whether she can get pregnant or not. She could get a vene-real disease or just . . . it's not good for her self-esteem."

"Her self-esteem?" He laughed and I knew it was at me. "When you're wondering if you'll have enough food for dinner, you ain't thinking about your self-esteem."

I smiled. "I guess you're right," I said, "although everyone feels one way or another about themselves, don't they?"

"It's the other one I worry about now," he said. "You'll get Ivy fixed after she has this baby, right?"

I was suddenly uncomfortable talking about Ivy with him. Here we'd talked about the most intimate details of people's lives, and we'd certainly spoken about Ivy before, but there was something almost desperate in the way he asked the question, and I felt like saying, "What business is it of yours, really?" I felt protective of the little bit of privacy she had left.

But he was the one who controlled their lives, who could snatch their house right out from under them.

"Yes," I said. "It'll be taken care of."

39

Ivy

I had to be real careful sneaking out of the house this time. If Nonnie caught me, I didn't know what she'd do. I'd gone to bed in my clothes, sneaking under the covers so Mary Ella wouldn't see, but it probably didn't matter. Mary Ella got a blank look in her eyes these days and she don't care about nothing. She keeps running her hand over the big empty space in our bed that Baby William used to fill. I missed him kicking me during the night. Funny how you could miss something like that. I thought about him all the time. We had to get him back, but I didn't know how. We didn't even know where he was and nobody would tell us.

Nonnie was on the sofa like usual, snoring up a storm, and I tiptoed past her and out the door. It was chilly out tonight, so I had to close the front door and I pulled it shut slow and quiet. I didn't think she heard a thing.

Lita brung over the note with my tea that afternoon, slipping it in my pocket when she pretended she was feeling the baby doing its somersaults. Nobody but me and her was in the kitchen, but she was being real careful about Nonnie finding out, and I 'preciated it.

"Midnight, crick," was all he wrote, but they was the two most beautiful words I'd read in the three weeks since his last note. Three weeks since he wrote me anything and six weeks since we got to be alone. Last time was when I told him I was having a baby. He'd seen me

around the farm since then, but not up close. I wondered what he'd think of how fat I was now. All of it baby fat, though. His baby. I thought of him going to school every day, seeing the other girls there, and I felt right jealous. It was like the whole world was moving forward, taking Henry Allen with it, while I was holding still.

He was there before me, sitting on the ground in the dark, his flashlight pointing across the crick at the other bank. I couldn't see no blanket or his radio and I didn't hear no music, either. He stood up fast when he saw me coming. He rushed up to me and hugged me tight, then he took a step back and touched my belly through my sweater. "Is it okay?" he whispered. "Did I hug you too tight?"

"No," I said. "You can hug me tight as you want."

"Listen." He seemed real nervous. "I only got a few minutes."

"Where's the blanket?" I asked.

"I didn't bring it. We don't have time. They check on me all night long, Ivy. It's like I'm in jail. I told them I got a new girlfriend at school, so if you hear anyone say that, it's not true. Okay?"

It wasn't really okay. I hated hearing him even say them two words, "new girlfriend." "Why'd you tell them that?" I asked.

"So they won't be spying on me every minute," he said. "I don't want them to think I still care about you."

"Do you?" I'd never wondered that before, but too much time had passed now for me to know for sure.

"Ivy! Don't even ask me that! Of course I do, and I've been trying to figure out how we can get married, but we—"

"But what?" I felt so scared. *But what?*

"I found out we can't do it without permission. Not till we're eighteen."

"Henry Allen!" I clung to his hands where they was between us, right above our baby. I didn't want to cry. That wouldn't solve anything.

"Mama and Daddy won't never say yes," he said. "I can't push them. If they knew we was here right now, they'd kick you and your grandma and sister off the farm to get you away from me. They're ready to do it at the drop of a hat. So we still got to act like we don't mean nothin' to each other no more."

"We can't wait, Henry Allen!"

"I know, I know."

"No, you don't know! You don't know what they done to Mary Ella and they're going to do to me!"

"Sh." He squeezed my hands real tight. I'd never seen him so shook up. "What're you talking about?

"They fixed it so she can't have no more babies, and—"

"Who did?"

"Mrs. Werkman. And now Mrs. Forrester's going to do the same to me."

"You got to be wrong. How can they do that?"

"They just can. When they said she had that appendix operation . . . that was a lie. I don't want them to do it to me, Henry Allen! Please."

"Sh." He pressed his fingertips to my lips to shut me up. "When would they do it?" he whispered.

"When I have the baby."

"Don't worry," he said. "I'm saving money for bus tickets to California. We'll pretend like we're married when we get there. No one'll know."

"But when—"

"Sh, Ivy. I got to get back. You just got to trust me, okay?"

He kissed me quick and picked up his flashlight and went back into the woods, leaving me standing there all alone. I watched the light from his flashlight jump around in the trees and then everything went dark and I knew he'd turned it off in case anybody might see him.

We couldn't get married. I was sure Nonnie would give permission—she didn't want another bastard grandbaby. But his parents never would. I knew he wasn't lying about that. We needed some kind of miracle. He didn't understand how soon this baby was coming. Thanksgiving was only two months away.

40

Jane

Lois died over the weekend. I'd visited her twice while she was in the hospital. The first time she was almost cheerful, asking me questions about my work and my life, listening attentively to my answers. She didn't want to talk about herself or her husband or her little daughter, so I did as she wanted and filled the half hour with my own life. She asked me if I'd made friends with any of the other country club wives and I had to admit that I hadn't, but I promised I would try.

The second time I visited, she was weak and quiet but peaceful, as though she were finished with this life and looking toward the next. Now she was gone, and I felt the loss in my bones. I wished I'd had the chance to know her longer. I had the feeling she would have understood me. Nobody else seemed to these days. I wasn't even sure I understood myself anymore.

Robert and I sat together through the Monday afternoon funeral and then drove to the country club for a reception.

"I've made my plane reservations for the medical conference in Atlanta," Robert said as we drove. "Are you sure you'll be okay with me gone all week?"

"I'll be fine," I said. His family was in Atlanta, so he planned to attend the medical conference during the week and then spend the weekend with his parents. I didn't want to admit, even to myself, how much I was looking forward to the time alone. I wouldn't have to worry about getting home late or saying something that might annoy him. The littlest things could set him off. We hadn't been getting along very well before the lice, but since that fiasco, I was walking on eggshells.

The reception was quite casual, despite the country club setting. People milled around the room nibbling hors d'oeuvres from the buffet table and balancing glasses of iced tea or punch. As usual, I felt like a fish out of water. I watched the other girls in the room. They all seemed so connected to one another, while I stayed close to Robert's side.

When it was time to leave, Robert and I still hadn't had a chance to speak to Gavin. He'd been surrounded by family and friends all afternoon, and as we approached him, I felt awkward. *Normal*, I thought. Nobody knew what to say to someone who'd just lost the love of his life, for that's what I was certain Lois had been to him.

Gavin was holding his and Lois's sleepy little two-year-old daughter in his arms, so Robert didn't try to shake his hand. Instead, he patted his shoulder. "Please accept our condolences," he said, sounding a little stiff, but there was warmth behind the words. I knew he liked Gavin.

"I'm so sorry, Gavin," I said. "I was glad I got to know Lo—"

The little girl suddenly reached for me. Instinctively, I raised my arms to her and she moved into them.

"Brenna!" Gavin said with a laugh, then to me, "I'm so sorry. She's very tired."

"Oh, it's fine," I said. Brenna rested her head on my shoulder, and I patted her back. Her brown hair was soft against my cheek and it smelled sweetly of baby shampoo. Gavin reached forward as if to extract her from my arms, but I turned away. "She's fine," I said. "I've got her." I felt Robert's hand on the small of my back.

"This is all very confusing to her," Gavin said. "I probably should have left her home with a sitter, but . . . I wasn't sure what to do, really."

"I'm glad she's here," I said. "Someday she'll ask about today and you can tell her she was here. That she got to say good-bye to her mother."

Gavin's blue eyes filled, and Robert squeezed my elbow and I had the feeling he thought I'd said too much. "We should go," he said.

I gently handed Brenna back to her father and his eyes locked warmly with mine. "Thank you," he said quietly. "Thank you."

In the car, Robert was quiet while I talked about how lovely the service had been and how much I would miss Lois, but I was sure that what was on our both our minds were those last few minutes with Gavin and his daughter.

"It was so amazing how she went right to you," Robert said finally. "It made me realize what a great mother you'll be. You took her into your arms so easily, like you did it every day."

We were driving straight into the setting sun—a ball of red fire. I leaned my head against the car window, remembering how light and precious Brenna had felt in my arms. "She's darling, poor little thing," I said.

"Jane," Robert said in a voice that made me sit up straight again, "I think I'd like you to see an ob-gyn guy I know. I'm worried you haven't gotten pregnant yet."

"It hasn't even been three months," I said.

"Well, I just want to make sure there's nothing wrong."

I leaned against the window again, and all at once, I realized how wrong I was to deceive him. I'd thought it was so unfair not to tell Mary Ella and Ivy why they wouldn't be able to have more children, yet I'd left my husband in the dark about our own inability to conceive. I pressed my fist to my mouth, horrified with myself. What was wrong with me that I could sympathize with the feelings of near strangers and not with my husband?

"Robert . . ." I bit my lip and he glanced at me.

"What?"

"I haven't been honest with you about something."

He hesitated. "You can have children, right?" he asked. He sounded afraid of my answer.

"Oh yes. As far as I know, anyway. But . . . I knew I wanted to work a while before we had children, and when the birth control pill was approved, I was able to get some. I've been taking them."

He pressed on the brake and I flew forward, nearly cracking my head against the dashboard. "What are you *doing*?" I shouted.

"What the hell are *you* doing? I told you I didn't want you taking the pill. And now you tell me that not only did you ignore my wishes, you've been lying to me about it?"

The car behind us honked and Robert began driving again, but only to pull to the side of the road.

"I should have talked to you more about it first," I said. "I knew how you felt, though, and . . . you never actually said I couldn't."

"And your feelings came first. As usual."

"That's not fair."

"Isn't it? I want children, you don't. I want a wife at home when I get there, but you never are."

"That's not true. I'm there most of the—"

"You are not the girl I thought I was marrying."

"I thought I could be that girl. I wanted to be her. I love you." Even as I said those three words, I was no longer sure they were true. "I was wrong to keep it from you," I said. "Very, very wrong. And I'm sorry."

He didn't speak for a full minute, and I wasn't sure what to say myself. In front of us, I watched the red sun drop below the tops of the trees.

"I think I'll take the week after the Atlanta conference off," he said finally. "I'll spend the whole week with my family instead of just the weekend. I think it'll be good for you and me to have some time apart."

"I agree," I said. "And again, Robert, I'm really sorry. It was so wrong of me not to tell you."

"If you'd told me that was your plan, I never would have married you," he said bluntly.

I nodded, wishing I could turn back the clock and start our relationship over.

This time, I would have told him.

41

Ivy

Walking with Mary Ella to the store was like walking with a statue. I couldn't get her to talk no matter what. Of course, there wasn't no easy topics for me to bring up. I couldn't talk about any of the things on our minds, like Baby William or the operation she had. I couldn't talk about what Henry Allen said to me about saving money for California. I wanted to tell her I was sad for her, but I didn't know what to say. As we got closer and closer to the store, the only thing on my mind was that I couldn't go in there. How could I face Mrs. Gardiner with her grand-baby inside me? I'd been staying out of her way the best I could. I hadn't gone to the store all month.

Nonnie'd told me to wear my raincoat, even though it was pretty warm outside. "Covers up that baby," she said. "Don't want nobody seeing you like that."

I was surprised she was even letting me go to the store, much less pushing me out the door. She was practically keeping me locked up in the house now, with me looking so big. I knew she just wanted to get Mary Ella out of the house. Every time she saw Mary Ella's sad face, she'd say, "It's the best for Baby William," and I guessed she'd be saying that for the rest of our lives, while Baby William grew up without his mama. I thought Mrs. Forrester had Nonnie good and brainwashed now. She'd come over the days she drove Avery and talk to Nonnie, but I didn't have nothing to say to her and Mary Ella didn't talk to nobody.

Even though I was big as a house, Nurse Ann said I wasn't big as I should be. "You don't eat enough of the right food," she said. I was scared my baby would have problems like Baby William, that it'd be slow and not talk and get took away from me. I ate one of them vitamins Nurse Ann gave me every single day and hoped that would make the difference. Of course, I was hoping me and Henry Allen would be gone before the baby came, but Henry Allen was taking his own good time saving the money to get us out of here.

I slowed down when we got close to the store. "I can't go in there," I said to Mary Ella. "You got to do it."

She didn't say nothing, not yes or no, but when we got to the front of the store, she went on in while I sat on the stoop, catching my breath. Everything made me out of breath these days.

I was watching two turkey vultures pecking at something in the street, when all of a sudden Mrs. Gardiner flew out of the store. I quick jumped to my feet and took a step back from the porch. Her face was red and wild looking, and strands of her black hair was out of her bun.

"You disappoint me, Ivy Hart!" She shook her finger at me. "You trying to ruin my boy's life?"

"No, ma'am," I said. "I'd never do that."

"We been nothing but good to your people, even after your mama done what she did to me." She touched the scar. Her red cheeks made it stand out white as bone. "But now you've gone too far. Davison always said we should keep you on, on account of what happened to your daddy on our land, but that was long ago now. Some people at church told me about a big colored family who'd be happy to have your house and would break their backs to help Davison so they could keep it."

"Mrs. Gardiner," I said, "please don't throw us out. Nonnie's sick and you can see Mary Ella ain't herself and I'll work for you in the store or on the farm after the baby comes. Nonnie and Mary Ella can watch it and I'll work every day, whatever you need." But inside, I was thinking I'd be thousands of miles away by then. I hoped with me being gone, they'd let Nonnie and Mary Ella stay, but why should they if they could put a big family with strong backs in our house?

"I don't want you working for me!" she said. "Do you think I want you anywhere near my house and my family?"

"No, ma'am, I suppose not."

Mary Ella came out the door carrying a sack of flour. She handed Mrs. Gardiner a dollar bill and headed straight for me.

"Get the change," I whispered to her.

"Don't need it," she said. She turned the corner and started walking.

From the porch, Mrs. Gardiner yelled, "Leave my boy alone, Ivy Hart!"

I blocked out her voice and caught up to Mary Ella. "What do you mean, we don't need it?" I asked.

She just kept walking and I had to move faster than was easy for me to keep up.

"She said she might kick us out," I said, knowing I shouldn't bring up anything bad, but right now there was nothing good to say and I wanted my sister to talk. Maybe that would do the trick, but she didn't say a word back to me.

Up in the distance, I could see one of Mr. Gardiner's blue trucks coming in our direction.

"Oh no," I said. I hated seeing Mr. Gardiner as much as I hated seeing his wife. With any luck it'd be Eli driving it, but then I remembered Eli would be in school at this hour.

Mary Ella suddenly handed me the sack of flour. "Here," she said.

"Can't you carry it?" I asked. "I'm already carrying this baby."

Mary Ella didn't answer me. She looked hypnotized by the blue truck, her eyes just staring at it. I looked from her face to the truck. It was Mr. Gardiner, for sure. I wished we was walking someplace where it'd be easier to hide, but here we were, out in the open. The truck was coming on fast, dust flying up behind it. He was going to pass us at a good clip, and that was fine with me.

When he got almost even with us, Mary Ella suddenly ran into the road, right in front of him. I dropped the sack of flour and let out a scream, and even though the truck squealed and tried to swerve, it swallowed my sister whole. I screamed again. Screamed and screamed, but then everything went black and quiet in my head. It was like wherever Mary Ella went, I was trying to go with her.

42

Jane

I was typing case notes when I heard a commotion outside my office door. Raised voices and shouting and clatter. Charlotte was at a doctor's appointment and Paula, Gayle, and Fred were all in the field, so I had the office to myself with the exception of Barbara. I got to my feet and was reaching for the doorknob when the door suddenly flew open. Ivy burst into my office, fists flying. One of them connected with my cheek before I managed to catch both her wrists in my hands.

Barbara was close behind her. "I'll call the police!" she said.

"No, don't." I held Ivy away from me as I tried to dodge her kicks. She managed to land one on my shin, and I nearly lost my grip on her.

"Ivy!" I tried to get her to look at me, but her hair covered her eyes and she fought like a caged animal. "Settle down!" I said. "Talk to me!" Her cheeks were wet with tears and smeared with dirt, and she was so big! I hadn't seen her in several weeks, although I'd been to her house. She hadn't *let* me see her.

"Really, Mrs. Forrester," Barbara said, "I think I'd better call."

Without thinking, I pulled Ivy closer instead of holding her at a distance, and she went limp against me, sobbing. I shook my head at Barbara.

"It's all right," I said. "Please close my door."

I looked away from Barbara's worried face while she left the room, shutting the door behind her. I stood there holding Ivy as she cried, feeling her swollen belly between us, wondering how she'd gotten to the office. She'd been upset over the petition and William when I last saw her, but not like this. Something more was wrong, and I thought of her grandmother.

"Is it Nonnie?" I asked. "Tell me what's wrong."

"Mary Ella," she murmured against my shoulder, and then another word that sounded like "deaf."

"Mary Ella's deaf? What do you mean?"

She stepped back from me. "She's *dead!*" she said, and I thought she was going to hit me again. "You might as well of took a gun and shot her."

My chest felt suddenly empty and I dropped into my chair. "Sit down," I said to Ivy.

Ivy sat in the straight-backed chair and pressed her hands over her face.

"Tell me what happened." I tried to hand her a tissue, but she didn't seem to see it and I placed it on her knee.

She dropped her hands to her lap. "She ran in front of Mr. Gardiner's truck," she said, her eyes hard and angry. "On *purpose.*"

"*Why?*" I asked. "Why would she do that?"

"Because you ruint her life!" she shouted, tears spilling down her cheeks again. "You took Baby William away! And you made it that she can't have no more babies."

Oh God. I gripped the arms of my chair. I'd really missed something. Something terrible. I'd been so focused on Ivy that I hadn't seen the depth of Mary Ella's depression. I never should have told her the truth about her operation. I should have realized she couldn't handle it.

"How did you get here?" I asked.

"Eli brung me."

"Where is he?" I needed to talk to him. Make sure he'd keep an eye on her.

"None of your business. I hate you so much." Her voice broke and I leaned forward, my fingertips on her knee.

"I understand," I said. "I'd feel the same way, but Mary Ella was—"

"You can't *do* it to me!" Ivy stomped her foot and my fingers fell from her knee. "The operation. You can't or I'll do what she done. I swear I will."

"No you won't. You'll have a little baby who needs you, and—"

"Bullshit! You'll just take it away from me."

I opened my mouth to argue, but I was afraid she might be right. I had so little power here.

"I'll help you make sure he has the care he needs so that doesn't happen," I promised, not believing the promise even myself. I'd told them I'd try to get them visitation rights with William, and I'd failed. I'd told Ivy I'd try to arrange for her to continue school at home, and I'd failed there, too. Why should she trust me this time?

"I can't believe my sister's gone!" She started to cry again. "I'll go home and she won't be there."

Oh, how I knew that feeling!

"She won't be *nowhere*. She won't even be in heaven. God don't forgive people who kill themselves."

"I don't believe that," I said.

"You don't know nothing." She shook her head at me. "That's one thing I figured out about you now. You don't know nothing but you act like God anyway." Her chin trembled. "Please don't do it to me!" she pleaded. "Please don't do the operation."

I couldn't bear the fear in her eyes. "All right," I said, surprising both of us. Somehow, I would withdraw that petition.

She stopped crying abruptly and stared at me. "Promise?" she asked. There was no trust at all in her face, but a promise from me was the best she could hope for and she knew it.

"Yes, I promise," I said.

This time, I would find a way.

43

Jane

There were only a couple of cars and Mr. Gardiner's truck parked along the road that ran through the old graveyard, and in the distance I could see a small group of people standing in a circle around what I guessed was Mary Ella's grave. I parked behind the truck and gripped my steering wheel, wondering if I could do this. The last time I'd watched a coffin being lowered into the ground, it had contained the body of my sister. Did both of them die because of me? I would never be able to shake that guilt.

I got out of my car, smoothed the skirt of my black dress, and started walking across the rutted grass. I could make out Winona and Ivy and Lita and a number of colored men, probably the Jordan boys. A tall white man, most likely Mr. Gardiner, stood a short distance behind the others, and I spotted Mrs. Gardiner standing at his side as I got closer. Would Mary Ella be laid to rest next to her father, I wondered, the way Teresa had been laid next to our father?

A preacher was speaking, hands raised in the air, and I could hear the rise and fall of his voice on the crisp October air, although I couldn't make out what he was saying. What would he say about Mary Ella? No one thought much of her. The preacher probably saw her as a sinner. Most likely, he'd never seen the pure love in her eyes for William. The only joy I'd ever seen in her came from her baby—the baby we'd taken away from her. The baby we *had* to take away.

I'd been spotted, and I saw some of the faces turn in my direction. Eli started walking toward me with a determined stride that didn't look welcoming. As he neared me, he held up a hand like a stop sign and I stopped walking.

"You ain't wanted here," he said, as he got closer.

"I'd like to pay my respects," I said.

"Is you a fool, girl?"

I was shocked that he'd speak to me that way and yet I felt as though I deserved it. "I cared about Mary Ella," I said.

He narrowed his eyes at me and shook his head. "You got a funny way of showing caring," he said.

I glanced past him. Everyone had turned back toward the preacher, obviously leaving Eli to deal with me.

"Please let me go to them." I nodded in the direction of Ivy and her grandmother.

"No, ma'am. It's best you turn around and drive on out of here."

"I can't leave without speaking to them."

"They ain't got nothing to say to you."

"I know they must be very hurt and angry, but—"

"You don't know *nothin'* about them." Eli bit off every word. "Or about me and my kin, neither. You only know what we let you know." He looked down at my neatly pressed dress, my black pumps, my leather purse, and my nylons. "And you sure don't know nothing about being poor. I bet you live in a mansion, don't you?"

"No," I said, but my house *was* a mansion compared to theirs.

"Well, let me tell you what it's like," he said. "You do anything you got to do to get by." His nostrils flared. "You break the law if you got to. I ain't sayin' I do, but I would if it was the only way my brothers and mama could get food. I surely would."

"I understand," I said, mostly to get him to stop talking and step away from me. I didn't like how close he was. I could see the anger boiling in those gold eyes of his, waiting to spill over.

"You do things you don't want to do," he said. "Things that mess with your soul." He glanced over his shoulder at the group, then lowered his voice a decibel or two. "Why you think Mr. Gardiner gave Mary Ella extra food every week, did you ever ask yourself that?"

"Because . . . he feels guilty about what happened to her fa—"

"It ain't got nothing to do with guilt!" he said. "That man ain't got no guilt in him. Ask yourself! Why didn't he give them extras to Nonnie. Or Ivy?"

I shook my head. "I just figured—"

"Them extras ain't free," he said. "You don't see no price tag on them, but it's there. A big one." He looked over his shoulder again, and I saw Mr. Gardiner watching us. And Lita. "He ruint that girl, and now he got the balls to come out here and act like he cared about her."

I felt numb. "Eli," I said, "you can't make accusations like that. I mean, you don't know for sure that—"

"Her word ain't good enough?"

"She talked to you about it? She told you that he . . ." I couldn't finish the sentence. I remembered seeing Mary Ella come out of the Gardiners' house the day I ran out of gas. I remembered the panicky look on her face. *She came over to see if there was a way I could get her boy back,* he'd said.

"I'd kill him if I could get away with it," Eli said.

"Don't even think that," I said. "Mary Ella . . . she was troubled, Eli. And you have no proof, really."

He scoffed at me. "You snatched the proof away from her," he said.

Oh God. "Baby William?" I asked. Behind him, I could see Lita breaking away from the group and walking toward us. I leaned a little closer to him. "Are you saying he . . . that he raped her?"

"There's things worse than rape." Eli looked away from me, out toward the road and my car. "When you go along with it like she had to, it kills you slow inside. She put up with it. Lived with it." He looked at me again. "Everybody sayin' Mary Ella's a whore. This and that. She put up with it to get them extras for her family and a place to live."

"She actually told you all this?" I asked.

"She got no reason to tell me tales." He glanced over his shoulder, then said to me in a near whisper, "And where you think Rodney come from?"

The shock of his words stopped my heart for a moment.

"What's going on here?" Lita had reached us and she took her son's arm, looking from him to me.

"I came to pay my respects," I said, and my voice had a tremor that it didn't have a few moments earlier.

"Fine," Lita said, drawing her son away from me. "I'll pass them along, but you should go."

I hesitated, looking past her to Winona and Ivy. "All right," I said, taking a step backward. "Please tell Winona and Ivy they're in my prayers," I added, but Lita and Eli had already turned away from me and were walking back to the gravesite. Only Mr. Gardiner was watching me now. He lifted a hand in a wave that looked hesitant, as if he weren't sure if I was now friend or foe.

I thought of driving back to the office, but changed my mind and drove to the farm instead. I turned down the long dirt driveway to the Gardiners' house, parked in front of the porch, and marched up the front steps. I sat down in one of the rockers. I would wait. My hands were knotted into fists on the broad arms of the chair. I was seething. If only I'd known, I could have done something. If only Eli had told me earlier. Mary Ella would never have dared to tell me herself. She just accepted what was dished out to her for the sake of her family. Ivy didn't know. Winona, either. I was sure of it. They would never have allowed it.

The front door suddenly opened and Desiree took a step onto the porch. "Miz Forrester?" She looked surprised to see me sitting there like I owned the place. "They ain't home."

"I know," I said. "I'm just going to sit here and wait for them to come back."

"Well, I believe Miz Gardiner's gonna work at the store, so it'll just be the mister."

"That's fine." I tried to smile, but my lips felt like wood. "That's who I want to see."

"All right, then. Can I bring you something to drink?"

"No, thank you, Desiree. I'm fine."

She gave me a look that told me I didn't look fine at all, then nodded and walked back into the house.

Moments later, Mr. Gardiner turned into the driveway, dust rising up around the truck as he drove in the direction of the shelter beyond the house, but the truck suddenly slowed and I knew he'd noticed my car—and perhaps, me. He parked behind my car and waved as he got out of the truck.

"Sad day," he said as he walked up the porch steps. "I'm sorry Eli didn't let you come mourn with the rest of us. He was broke up. You know"—he lowered his voice to a whisper—"her being his sister and all." He gave me a knowing look, as though he were mentioning some piece of information only the two of us were privy to.

"Why did you always give the basket of extra food to Mary Ella?" I asked.

He shrugged like my question made no sense. "They need it," he said.

"But why not to Ivy or Winona?"

He folded his arms and leaned against the porch railing and I thought I should stand to be on more equal footing with him, but I was afraid my legs wouldn't hold me. "What are you getting at?" he asked.

"You've been taking advantage of her," I said.

He frowned. "Have you lost your mind? What kind of nonsense did Eli fill your head with?"

"This has nothing to do with Eli," I said. "I just need to know . . . Are you William's father?"

He let out a laugh so sharp it made me jerk back in the chair. "Now, look, miss," he said, "if you're set on hanging me, you just keep telling lies like that one. I never laid a hand on that girl. William's daddy could be one of a hundred. I never held that against her like other people did. I treated that girl right."

I shook my head in disgust. "You used her," I said. "She was so vulnerable, you knew she'd do anything you asked to help her family." I thought of what Eli'd said about Rodney. It was too crazy. Yet Lita needed a house for her and her boys, too, didn't she? Suddenly I remembered Avery telling me how she sometimes went missing in the night.

"I told you," Mr. Gardiner said, "Mary Ella Hart was a messed-up girl. Ain't you figured that out by now, you being a high-and-mighty

social worker and all? Don't they train you to recognize craziness
when you see it? Maybe she said something to Eli. I don't know. I
don't have no crystal ball into their conversations. But I can tell you, if
she said I done something like that it was just her sick mind doing the
talking."

This was going nowhere, but what had I expected? That he would
confess? Even if he did, so what? She was gone. Nothing was bringing
Mary Ella back. My throat tightened, but I refused to break down in
front of him.

"I'll . . ." I started to say that I'd be speaking to Charlotte about it
when I saw her in the office the next day, but the lump in my throat
cut off the words and I walked past him in silence. I was grateful that
the tears waited until I got to my car.

I drove out of his driveway in a cloud of dust, full of hatred for the
man I'd so recently respected. Eli had no reason to lie to me, and Mary
Ella had no reason to lie to him. I was sure it was the truth. It fit together as neatly as the pieces of a jigsaw puzzle.

Or did I just need someone to share my guilt?

44

Ivy

"Okay, Ivy, you can sit up now." Nurse Ann stepped away from the bed and pulled off the glove she always used when she examined me. I locked my knees together and sat up. It took me a minute because my belly was getting so big and my legs was shaking. Every minute she was checking me, I was afraid she was going to do the operation. I kept an eye on her the whole time. If she pulled out a knife or something that looked like it could cut me, I'd get off the bed and out of the room so fast she wouldn't know what hit her. She handed me my underwear and I put it on fast.

"Now listen," she said, while I let Nonnie's housedress fall over my knees. They was all I could wear these days—Nonnie's big shapeless dresses. "Your grandmother tells me you've had a couple of minor seizures, so—"

"She says that, but I ain't had any. I don't know why she says it." Nonnie told me I had one the other day when I was getting dressed to go to Mary Ella's service and that I might of had one when Mary Ella got hit by the truck, but Mr. Gardiner said I just fainted then.

"They've always been the sort of seizure that you're not aware of yourself, isn't that true?"

"No," I argued, because I was afraid of what it might mean if I was really having fits again. "I used to know when they happened. I'd get this mixed-up feeling, like I didn't know where I was. I ain't had that feeling since I was little."

"Petit mal seizures can happen without you being aware of them," she went on, like I didn't say nothing. "And it sounds like they're happening when you exert yourself, so I need you to rest between now and when your baby's born. I also think he or she is going to be born earlier than we expected."

"Why do you think that?"

"From the way you feel inside." She wiggled her hand in the air like she was feeling inside me. "Have you had any bleeding or contractions? Pain in your belly?"

"No, ma'am. I been fine," I said, even though I never felt so un-fine in my life. How could I be fine? Everything was wrong. William was gone. My sister was in the ground. I couldn't see Henry Allen and it felt like maybe I'd never see him again. Nonnie's pee turned orange in the tube this morning and Nurse Ann told her she'd have to get shots if she didn't eat right, which Nonnie wasn't ever going to do. And Mrs. Forrester. I thought she was wonderful but turned out she was the worst person ever to come into my life. I didn't believe her that she'd stop the operation. She promised, but why should I believe her when she already hurt us so much?

I was afraid to say anything about the operation to Nurse Ann in case she forgot about it, but I had to know.

"Did Mrs. Forrester get the operation stopped?" I asked.

"Don't worry about that right now. Do you understand what I'm saying about resting? Not doing anything that makes your heart beat fast or makes you breathe fast?"

"What about the operation?"

"Oh, Ivy." She made a sound like she was tired of me, while she put her things away in her big nurse bag. She swung her long black braid over her shoulder. "You need to think of one thing at a time, please!" she said. "Just think of getting this baby into the world healthy and strong, okay?"

"You're not answering my question!" I shouted.

"I haven't spoken to Mrs. Forrester in several days," she said, "so I don't know what the current plan is."

"Well, I want to know," I said.

She smiled at me. "Of course you do. Hopefully I can tell you next time I see you."

I watched her walk out of the room, then I laid down on the bed and stared at the ceiling. I could hear Nurse Ann talking to Nonnie in the living room and I tried to listen but couldn't hear what they was saying.

I reached out across the bed, where Mary Ella and Baby William belonged, but all I felt in their place was the empty air.

45

Jane

On Monday morning, Robert stood by the front door, waiting for his cab to the airport. Two suitcases sat at his feet—one with his suits for the medical conference, the other with more casual clothes for the week in Atlanta with his family. I knew there was something very wrong with our young marriage that I wanted him gone . . . and that he wanted to go. Last night in bed, after I'd told him every detail of my talk with Eli and then with Davison Gardiner, he sighed and turned his head toward me.

"You know," he said, "I'm really looking forward to two weeks away from your obsession."

"I'm not obsessed," I argued.

"Yes. You are. You're distraught over a job you don't need to be doing, and I'm sorry, but that makes it hard for me to give you much sympathy."

I was anxious to get to work this morning, but I didn't want to leave until he was out the door. I walked over to him. Rested my hand on his arm. "Are we going to make it?" I asked quietly.

He studied me without a smile, then brushed a strand of hair from my cheek. "Not if you insist on putting the needs of other people ahead of your husband's," he said.

I dropped my hand. "I wish you understood."

"Here's my cab." He reached for his suitcases, one in either hand. I opened the door for him and he didn't glance back at me as he headed down the steps.

I drove to work with my foot pressing the gas pedal nearly to the floor. I needed to talk to Charlotte about stopping Ivy's petition as well as my suspicions about Davison Gardiner. But when I got to my office, the door was closed.

"Charlotte's meeting with Ann Laing," Barbara said from her desk.

"Oh good," I said. I knocked on the door, opened it and poked my head inside.

"I'm here," I said to Charlotte. "Sorry I'm late. Can I come in? I need to talk to you about Ivy Hart."

"We're just discussing her now," Charlotte said. "Give us a minute. Why don't you wait for me out there. I'll be right out." Ann didn't even look in my direction. She kept her gaze on Charlotte. Something was going on.

I hesitated. "Well . . . if you're talking about her, can I come in? I have some serious concerns about—"

"Wait for me out there, Jane," Charlotte said. Her tone told me not to argue and I stepped back into the main office.

"We need more space." Barbara smiled at me from her desk. She nodded to the only other chair in the room. It was right next to the cupboards where I'd found the old eugenics pamphlets. "Have a seat," she said.

I sat down and opened my briefcase, pulling out files on some of my other clients. I tried to concentrate on them, but I was too annoyed. Charlotte and Ann were talking about my case in my office, but I wasn't allowed to come in? It was humiliating as well as just plain wrong.

Fifteen minutes passed before my office door opened and Ann came out. She gave me a quick wave, but left the main office without so much as a "hello."

I walked into my office and shut the door behind me. "What's going on?" I asked Charlotte. She was jotting something in a folder on her lap. "Why was Ann here? Why couldn't I come in?"

"You said you have some concerns about Ivy Hart?" she asked.

"I need to stop the petition," I said, still standing in front of the door.

Charlotte shook her head. "You don't stop a petition after it's been approved by the board, Jane."

"She doesn't want it and I think, given what's happened with her sister, we need to—"

"She's fifteen. She's an epileptic. She's pregnant and she didn't even understand that she could *get* pregnant. How long do you think it will be before she's pregnant again? It's not up to her to make the decision. Her grandmother is her guardian and the decision is hers and the board's. Not yours and not a fifteen-year-old girl's."

"I promised her I wouldn't let it happen to her."

Charlotte frowned. "That was very foolish. Now she'll never have faith in a social worker again."

"Well, she *will* if I can stop it. And there's something else going on."

"Davison Gardiner," she said wearily, catching me by surprise. "Sit down, will you?"

I made no move toward my chair. "How do you know?" I asked.

"Because he called me first thing this morning. He told me you're making accusations about him. He called you a 'troublemaker,' and I tend to agree."

"Eli Jordan was very close to Mary Ella and I believe him."

"What really concerns me regarding Mary Ella is that you missed her clinical depression," Charlotte said. "I blame myself for that. You only had three days of training and no background for this sort of work at all."

"What background did Paula have?" I snapped, knowing I should control myself but I was out of patience. "Secretary of her Junior League?"

Charlotte held up her hand like a warning. "Before you say anything else, Jane, I need to tell you that we're letting you go."

"Letting me . . . what do you mean? You mean you're *firing* me?"

She nodded. "I discussed it with Fred and he completely agrees."

"Because . . . why? Because I care too much?"

"Where do I begin?" she said. "I can't count the number of department regulations you've chosen to disregard. We should have let you go right after the beach incident, but I guess our need for one more body in the office clouded our judgment." She frowned up at me. "You get far too personally involved, Jane. It's not good for you *or* your clients. You have no objectivity."

"Who'll take over my cases?" I asked. If it was Gayle, I could reason with her. Explain to her about Ivy.

"Paula will have the Harts, if that's what you're asking."

"Oh no," I said. "Please give Gayle the Harts and the Jordans."

"This is exactly what I mean." She pounded the arm of her chair sharply with her fist. "You can't have favorites. We're all human, of course, but you've neglected other cases to deal with these families, and—"

"Who? Who have I neglected?" I was getting angrier by the minute.

"I'm trying to control my temper, Jane," Charlotte said, "but I'm *furious* that you would approach Davison Gardiner on your own without discussing it with me first. You could set us up for a lawsuit."

"He's the one who should be sued."

"Well, I'm sure Paula will look into your concerns about him, and if she feels there's any merit to them, she'll go through the proper channels."

Which I, clearly, had not done.

"Don't you have to give me two weeks' notice?" I asked.

"We'll pay you for the two weeks."

Was she telling me I had to leave now? *Today?* I walked across the room and sank into my chair. "There must be a way to stop the petition," I said, more to myself than to her.

"Ann saw Ivy early this morning and Winona Hart told her that Ivy may have had a couple of seizures in the last few days. Plus Ann thinks she's going to deliver early, so she's making arrangements to admit her to the hospital this afternoon. I think that's the best and safest place for her until she delivers."

Oh my God. Once she was in the hospital, they wouldn't let her go until she'd had her baby and the surgery. And I wouldn't even be able to talk to her. I was letting her down in the worst way.

"But I'm the one who put the material together for the petition," I argued. "I should be able to withdraw it."

274 | Diane Chamberlain

"I did the early work on it, Jane, and Fred's signature is on it. Mary Ella's suicide just adds credibility to the instability of that family, you must see that, don't you?" She leaned toward me, trying to get me to look her in the eye.

I complied, unhappily.

"Remember what I told you about how you should decide these cases?" she asked. "You ask yourself what chance a child would have growing up in that household."

I shook my head. "I don't want the power to make that decision," I said quietly.

"That's why I'm taking it away from you." She turned back to her desk, and I guessed she was finished with me.

Neither of us spoke as I emptied the few personal items from my desk drawers and put them in my briefcase. When I was finished, I stood up and walked to the door.

"Jane," she said, as I reached for the knob.

I looked down at her.

"You're a very good person," she said. "Just not a very good social worker."

46

Ivy

"You sit," Nonnie said to me when I started to make us tomato sand-wiches for dinner. She took the knife out of my hand and pointed to one of the chairs. She wouldn't hardly let me breathe since Nurse Ann left that morning, telling me I'd have another fit if I lifted a finger. I did what she said, moving around the house slow and careful because I didn't want to go in no hospital. Mary Ella went in the hospital and came out cut open and ruined. I needed Mrs. Forrester to stop that operation.

"I'm okay," I said, but I sat down like she told me.

Nonnie sliced the tomato real thick, the way we both liked it. "If she puts you in the hospital," she said, "I'm gonna be all alone."

"I won't go," I said.

"She said you have to, or that baby might come too early." She got the jar of Duke's out of the refrigerator. "I don't know what to do, Ivy," she said. "When that pee turned orange this morning . . . well, I imag-ine the good Lord is trying to tell me something."

"Like what?"

She spread the mayonnaise near as thick as the tomatoes on the top slice of bread. "Maybe punishing me for not raising you girls up right or something."

Nonnie hadn't been herself since Mary Ella passed. It scared me, her sounding lost like she did.

"It'll be okay," I said. "But you got to be better about what you eat." I wasn't sure the tomato sandwich was exactly right for her.

"Nurse Ann tells me all the things I *can't* eat and not a blessed thing about what I *can*." Nonnie put the sandwiches on two plates and sliced them into halves. "I'm tired, Ivy," she said, handing me one of the plates. "Your daddy would be right unhappy with me to see how bad I took care of you girls." She sat down across from me with her own sandwich, and tears was sitting above her bottom eyelashes. I wished I could do something to keep them from spilling out. *"Mary Ella."* She shook her head, staring into space. *"Mary Ella."*

This was a side to Nonnie I never seen before. This weak, soft side. I knew all of a sudden this was the *real* Nonnie. It got covered up by her yelling and hitting, and it scared me more than anything to know she wasn't as tough as she seemed. I needed somebody in my life to be strong.

"Ain't none of it your fault, Nonnie," I said, though some of it truly was. Wouldn't do no good to point that out to her, though.

I ate a bite of my sandwich, but Nonnie was raising her head high, trying to look out the window. She stood up and grabbed her cane.

"Mrs. Forrester's here," she said, wiping her eyes.

Oh no. I didn't know whether this was good news or bad. I got to my feet and pulled open the door. "Did you stop it?" I hollered. "The operation?"

She climbed the porch steps, out of breath and red in the face, and I wanted to run into her arms at the same time I wanted to punch her. I didn't trust her one bit, but she was all I had.

"You best stay away from here," Nonnie said to her. "You cause a stir wherever you go."

"Ivy." She was so winded, I guessed she'd run all the way from her car. "Come with me. Ann . . . Nurse Ann's coming to take you to the hospital. If you go there, they'll sterilize you. I wasn't able to stop the petition—the order—"

"You said you would!"

"I know, but they fired me. Now I have no authority to do anything." She looked at Nonnie. "Please let her come with me. She doesn't want that surgery. I'll make sure she doesn't get it, but you have to promise me you won't tell that I took her."

Nonnie's eyes bugged out of her head. "You're one crazy girl," she said to her.

I didn't know what to do. How could I believe her? "Maybe *you're* the one taking me to get the operation," I said.

She shook her head, a sad look on her face. "I want to keep you safe," she said. "My husband's out of town. I know you're supposed to take it easy. Rest. You can do that at my house for a few days while I get in touch with a lawyer I know. I'm pretty sure he can help you."

I looked at Nonnie. Her face was so tired. She was fed up with everything, including living.

"Go with her," she said. "I'll say you run off."

I couldn't say nothing right away, I was so shocked. "I can't leave you here alone," I said. And I couldn't leave Henry Allen. At least staying here, I had a chance of seeing him. If I went to Mrs. Forrester's house, how would he find me if he got the money for us to go to California?

"I'll be all right." Nonnie looked at Mrs. Forrester. "When's Nurse Ann coming?" she asked her.

"Sometime this afternoon."

Nonnie reached in the cupboard where we keep the paper grocery bags and handed me one. "Put your things in here and go," she said. "Hurry now!"

I couldn't believe Nonnie was telling me to go. *Pushing* me to go. And as I threw my underwear and one of Nonnie's old dresses and my transistor radio into the bag, I wondered if they was in on it together, all three of them. Nurse Ann and Mrs. Forrester and Nonnie. But I had to pick one person to trust, and I guessed that was going to have to be the lady who took me to the beach and told Mary Ella the truth and cared enough to ask me questions about my daddy.

I didn't say much in the car. We drove down the lane to get to Deaf Mule Road and I guessed she went that way so we didn't have to go past the Gardiners' house. She didn't want nobody to see her car.

I leaned against the car door. If we pulled up someplace that looked like a hospital, I'd get out and run, even if the car was still moving. Where I'd run to, I didn't know, but I'd figure that out later. I should of somehow got word to Lita to tell Henry Allen that I'd be back when I could. When it was safe. But there wasn't no time for that.

We rode quietly for a pretty long while, me watching the whole time for a hospital. After a while, Mrs. Forrester looked over at me.

"Are you okay?" she asked. "Do you feel all right?"

"Well"—I leaned right up against the door—"I don't trust you far as I can throw you."

"I don't blame you." She smiled but it wasn't much of one. "But you're going to have to trust me," she said. "Please believe me, I'm on your side. I feel strongly that you have the right to decide if you should be sterilized or not. It might turn out to be the right choice for you, because of the epilepsy or because . . . just because. But I don't like that the choice has been taken away from you."

"Like they done to Mary Ella."

"Mary Ella was a different case," she said.

I watched her face. She looked angry and not at me. "What do you mean?"

She shook her head. "Now listen. Please. Like I said, my husband is out of town but my maid is at the house, so—"

"You got a maid?"

"I do." We came to a red light and she stopped and looked over at me. "You'll stay in the car while I pay her and tell her to take a few days off." She bit her lip and I could tell she hadn't thought none of this through very well. When she started talking again it was more like she was talking to herself. "I'll pay her for a few days," she said, driving the car again. "Paid vacation. I'll tell her I don't need her as much while Robert's gone." She looked at me for a second. "Then I'll call the lawyer I know. He'll help you." She gave a little laugh. "He'll have to help *both* of us because I'll be in a *lot* of trouble for what I'm doing." She pressed her hand to her cheek. "I can't believe I'm doing it."

"Doing what?"

She shook her head. "Nothing. The important thing for you to do . . . your *job* right now . . . is to rest. That's why Ann wanted you in the hospital. She's afraid you'll deliver early. So when we get to my house, you'll just sit with your feet up and let me wait on you."

"Wait on me?" Either she was crazier than my mama, or she was telling me the truth about going to her house and calling the lawyer. Either way, I stopped worrying she was taking me to a hospital.

"Yes." She sort of smiled again. She reached over and put her cool hand on my arm. "I'll wait on you."

"Nobody ever waited on me in my life," I said, and I started loving her again.

47

Jane

"You live *here*?" Ivy's eyes were huge as I pulled into my driveway. I could only imagine how my house looked to her. Huge. Sparkling clean yellow paint. White trim. A broad porch with hanging ferns and white rockers. My garage alone was larger than her house.

"Yes," I said. Then, as if it explained everything, I added, "My husband's a doctor."

I parked the car in the driveway. "You wait here while I speak to my maid, all right? It's better if I don't introduce you."

She looked past me toward the house. "You'll be right back?"

"No more than five minutes," I promised. I picked up my purse and briefcase from the seat and started toward the house, wondering what in God's name I was doing. Had I just kidnapped Ivy? I felt like a teenager planning a wild party after her parents left for the weekend. Whatever I'd done, there was no turning back, and my legs were rubbery as I crossed the yard. How long before Ann got to the house and discovered Ivy was gone? How many questions could Nonnie endure before she gave in with the truth? I needed to call Gavin right away.

I walked in the front door to the foyer. Angeline peered out from the kitchen, her hand to her throat and her doe eyes round in her face.

"You gave me a start!" she said, then chuckled. "Why you home in the middle of the day? You sick?"

"No, no," I said, setting my briefcase on the floor by the entry table. "I'm fine, but I decided to take some time off. And that means *you're* taking sometime off, too." I put my purse on the table and reached inside for my wallet. "I'll pay you for the rest of the week, but I want you to take it off."

"What do you mean, 'take it off'?"

"You don't need to work the rest of the week. It's just me here, with Dr. Forrester out of town, so it's silly for you to work." I handed her the bills, double what I would have paid her for a week's work, and she gave me a suspicious look.

"What you got planned?" she asked. She was too smart for her own good.

"A long bath followed by a long nap," I said, "and I'm dying to get started, so collect your things and go on home." Her purse was on the table and I handed it to her and guided her toward the door.

"My sweater," she said, pointing to the foyer closet.

"Go ahead," I said, hoping the impatience in my voice wasn't too obvious.

"When you want me back?" she asked as she took her sweater from the hanger, and I realized she was afraid I was letting her go permanently.

"Sometime next week," I said. "I'll call you. You still have a job, Angeline. Don't worry."

She put on her sweater and was finally gone. I waited until she'd walked out of sight in the direction of the bus stop before heading back to my car. I pulled open the rear door where we'd put the grocery bag with Ivy's clothes. "Come in," I said to her, lifting the bag into my arms.

She was slow as she got out of the car, and seeing her now, away from the farm, she suddenly looked enormously pregnant. I rested my free hand across the small of her back as we walked. Once inside, I wouldn't let her lift a finger. I needed to keep her safe and healthy.

She was a little out of breath as we climbed the few stairs to my porch and I kept a careful eye on her, remembering her seizure on the day we walked across the dunes, but she seemed fine. In the foyer, she stood and looked around her.

"I ain't never seen nothing like this house," she said. "It's bigger than the Gardiners' house and it's so empty!"

"Empty?"

"There ain't things everywhere. It's clean, like."

Remembering the Gardiners' house with its knickknacks and quilts on every surface and the deer head on the living room wall, I thought I understood what she meant. The truth was, I didn't spend enough time at home to clutter it up with anything. With Angeline instantly cleaning up any small mess we might make, our house looked like a museum.

"I'll show you around and then we'll get you settled in the guest room. Which is upstairs." I was suddenly worried about my plan. "There are a lot of stairs," I said, pointing to the staircase. "Please go up them very slowly. Nurse Ann said it's important that you rest, so you can stay up there and I'll bring you anything you need."

Ivy was looking all around her. To the right was the living room, with its blue striped wallpaper. To the left the dining room, where we'd yet to entertain Robert's colleagues and their wives around the big table. The cabbage-rose wallpaper was still up in there and I remembered saying to Robert, "That will be the first thing we need to change." We'd changed nothing. I felt a stab of guilt, remembering Robert's dream for our lives in this house and knowing they would not come true because of me. I wasn't the right girl for the lifestyle he wanted. If only I'd realized that before I married him.

"It's so pretty," Ivy said as she took another few steps down the hall and peered into the pine-paneled den. "You have a television!" she said.

"Have you never seen a TV before?"

"Oh, sure I've seen one. I never seen one with a picture, though."

"Why don't you watch it while I call the lawyer?" I pointed to Robert's chair and ottoman. She'd be able to put her feet up. "Have a seat and I'll bring you a Pepsi Cola." I remembered she'd been eating a sandwich when I arrived. "You must be hungry, too. How about a grilled-cheese sandwich?"

She looked up at me as she sat down. "I can make it myself," she said, "but I ain't really hungry. I'm too shook up."

"No, honey, you just sit." I turned on the television. *Guiding Light* was on. "This is a soap opera," I said. "Do you know what that is?"

"Made-up stories about people? I heard of them." She was looking out the window instead of at the television.

"Right. You can change the channel if you want with this knob"—I tapped the knob on the TV to get her attention back—"but it would be best if you didn't get up, okay? I'll be right back."

I walked into the kitchen and stood leaning against the counter, letting out a long anxious breath. I was going to land in jail. *Please, Nonnie, please don't tell.* Even if she did tell, she'd given her permission. That would be my defense, although I thought of Charlotte telling me to leave the office and knew that nothing I'd done in the last couple of hours was defensible.

My hands shook as I sliced the cheese. I smeared butter on the bread and cooked the quickest grilled-cheese sandwich I'd ever made in my life. I put it and a bottle of Pepsi on a tray and carried it back into the den, where I found her nibbling her thumbnail.

"First time I get to see television and I can't pay no mind to it," she said. "Did you call the lawyer?"

"I'm going to do that right now," I said.

"He'll make me do it, though, won't he? Have the operation?"

I shook my head. "He can't make you do anything."

"But he's got to do what the law says if he's a law man."

"He's not . . . that's not what a lawyer does. Don't worry. He's there to help us." I hoped I was telling her the truth.

She looked hard at me. "I'm scared you brung me here to trap me," she said. "You just made up about the lawyer helping me."

I sat down. "Ivy," I said, "I've been honest with you and I'll continue to be honest with you. I promise you that. Mary Ella was sterilized before I got involved and I told her the truth, didn't I? It hurt her and I'm so sorry about that, but I thought she should know the truth, even if it hurt. And I'll tell you the truth, too."

She looked at the TV for a moment and I could tell she was thinking about what I said.

"You took Baby William away," she said. "That was the worst thing you could of done to Mary Ella."

"I know, and I'm sorry about how much that hurt her, but William needed protection."

"I ain't forgiving you for that," she said.

"You don't have to, Ivy." I stood up. "Time to make that call."

Back in the kitchen, I found Gavin's office phone number in the phone book, dialed the number, and sat down on one of the breakfast nook benches.

"Parker and Healy," a receptionist answered.

"I'd like to speak with Gavin Parker, please. This is Mrs. Robert Forrester."

"Mr. Parker is on vacation all week," she said.

I pressed my hand to my mouth to keep from screaming.

"Ma'am?" she said. "Can I take a message to give him when he gets back?"

"I really need to speak to him," I said. "This is an emergency. How can I get in touch with him?"

"Well, I'm afraid you can't. He's out of the country. Mr. Healy is here, though. Would you like to speak to him?"

Did I dare tell a stranger what I'd done? No. I couldn't entrust this to someone I didn't know. I didn't even know Gavin very well. He was nice. He liked me. I was counting on those two facts to get me through this. To get *Ivy* through it.

"Ma'am?" the receptionist said. "Are you still there?"

I felt frozen on the phone. I wanted to call again and have her come up with a different answer. This one felt unreal.

"If you could call Mr. Parker and tell him that Jane Forrester needs to speak with him, I think he'd—"

"He's on a cruise with his parents and daughter, ma'am," she said. "There's no way to reach him. But I'm sure Mr. Healy could help you."

"No," I said. "No, thank you. I'll call back on Monday."

I got to my feet and hung up the phone, staring at it for a moment as though it might tell me what to do. Today was Tuesday. Could I keep Ivy here nearly a whole week? I'd have to. The one thing I wouldn't allow to happen was for Ivy to end up as Paula's client.

"What's wrong?"

I looked up to see Ivy standing in the doorway holding her tray.

I took the tray from her and set it down next to the sink. "Sit down, honey," I said, motioning to the breakfast nook.

She looked at the bench. "I don't think I'll fit," she said. "This belly don't fit too many places no more."

I saw that she was right. The table and benches were built snugly into the small space. "We'll go back in the den," I said.

"You ain't got no color in your face at all," she said as we walked. "What did he say?"

"He's not there," I said. "He's on a cruise."

"Like a ship?"

"Exactly." I guided her back to Robert's chair in the den and turned off the TV. "He won't be back until Monday, so you and I need a plan."

She looked frightened. "If I go back, you said Nurse Ann will come take me away."

"You can't go back," I said. "First, Nurse Ann plans to take you to the hospital, and second, Paula—the caseworker taking over for me—will definitely think you should be sterilized."

"But what do I do?"

"Well, you'll stay here. That's the one thing . . . maybe the only thing . . . we know for sure. You stay here until I can talk to Mr. Parker. The lawyer."

She hugged her arms around her baby. "I'm so scared," she said.

I nodded. "Yes," I said. "I am, too. But we're in this together," I added. "You're not alone."

She watched TV while I made up the guest room bed. I'd have to buy groceries tomorrow. I hadn't planned to shop this week, knowing Robert would be gone. I'd be happy with a bowl of cereal or a can of soup, but now I needed to cook. Maybe I could also buy some games for us to play or a jigsaw puzzle Ivy could put together.

I was rooting around in the refrigerator for something to cook for dinner when I heard a car door slam in the driveway. I looked out the kitchen window to see my mother walking across the yard, carrying a white paper bag.

"Mrs. Forrester!" Ivy called from the den. She sounded afraid, and I guessed she'd heard the car door, too.

"It's all right, Ivy," I said as I walked past the den to the front door. "It's my mother. I won't let her in."

"Hi, Mom," I said when I opened the door. I knew she was on her way home from work. Her reading glasses hung on a chain around her neck and the skirt of her green dress was creased.

"I was at the bakery and saw that bread you like so I picked up a loaf for you," she said, handing me the white bag.

"Thank you," I said.

"I didn't expect to see you home from work this early. I thought I'd have to leave it by the door." She was peering past me, and I knew she expected me to invite her in.

Instead, I walked out onto the porch and shut the door behind me. "My, it's a beautiful day!" I said. "I had the afternoon off so I've been straightening up inside and didn't notice how nice the weather is. Want to sit?" I motioned to the rockers. I couldn't just tell her to go.

She gave me a look that told me I was not behaving exactly like myself, but I ignored it and took a seat in one of the rockers.

She sat down in the rocker next to me. "Where's Angeline?" she asked. "Why are you doing the straightening up? There can't be much to straighten with Robert gone."

"Well, he only just left," I said, "and I decided to give Angeline the week off. I really don't need her with him gone."

"Why don't you have dinner with me all this week?" She looked excited by the suggestion. "I'll cook. The only day I have to work late is Thursday. It's better than both of us eating alone."

If Ivy hadn't been with me, I'd welcome the invitation. My mother was lonely and I was a mess. We needed each other right now. But I couldn't do it. I rarely lied to her, even when I was young. Our parents always listened to Teresa and me without judging. They made it safe to tell the truth. Today, though, I was going to have to lie.

"Mom," I said, "please don't take this the wrong way, but this week I have so much to catch up on. Letter writing and all the things I don't have time to do when Robert's here."

"Hmm." My mother looked out at the sidewalk where a little boy was riding a bicycle with training wheels. "I guess I'm too used to having evenings to myself," she said. "Ever since your father died, I've forgotten what it's like to crave a little time to yourself. I have too much of it."

I reached over to rest my hand on hers. I felt horribly cruel. "I'm sorry, Mom," I said. "How about we pick one night this week to do something together?" Ivy would have to be left on her own one night. I thought I should make it later in the week so she'd be more comfortable and trusting. "How about Friday night?"

"We could go out to dinner and a movie," she said, her eyes lighting up.

"Something to look forward to." I smiled. I loved her so much. I hated that I couldn't tell her what was happening. It would have felt so good to pour it all out to her, but I didn't dare. I'd have to keep everything to myself until I spoke to Gavin.

We chatted a while longer about her day at work and a party her neighbors had thrown, and I was glad she didn't ask me about my work or my marriage. Or, to use my powder room! Halfway through our conversation I started wondering what I would do if she did ask, and my nerves began jangling all over again.

"Well," she said finally, standing up. "I'd better get home and leave you to your straightening up." She kissed my cheek. "Let's talk before Friday night and decide what movie to see," she said.

"Okay, Mom. Thanks for the bread."

I watched her walk to her car and then went back in the house to find Ivy cowering on the sofa.

"You were gone so long!" she said. "I was afraid you weren't coming back."

"It was just my mother," I said. "Nothing to worry about."

I sat down on the sofa to watch the soaps with her, but I knew I wouldn't be able to concentrate. I'd have to do the worrying for both of us.

48

Ivy

At long last, I knew how rich people lived. I was in a palace. Everything was clean and shiny and pretty, like nobody really lived here at all. I had a bathroom upstairs all to myself. The only other bathroom I ever been in was at school, and even that one was a tired old place compared to Mrs. Forrester's. Last night, I had a bath in a real bathtub instead of trying to fit me and my big belly into our galvanized tub, and the hot water came out of a faucet like at school, instead of me having to heat it up on the stovetop.

Mrs. Forrester—she told me I could call her Jane, but it seemed wrong and I couldn't do it—had bubble bath powder she put in the water. She left me alone and told me to relax and take my time. The only problem was I couldn't relax. Every minute, I expected Nurse Ann or that Paula social worker to come busting into Mrs. Forrester's house and take me away, so I was watching for them. The street was right quiet, so any car I heard go by, I was at the window, peeking out real careful so I didn't get seen, making sure it wasn't somebody coming to get me. When Mrs. Forrester's mother showed up yesterday, I was sure it was all over.

I went to bed in her special room for guests after we watched more TV last night. We saw a show called *Twilight Zone* where there was ghosts in the desert and that got me thinking about Mary Ella coming back as a ghost, but I didn't say anything to Mrs. Forrester because I could tell she didn't believe in spirits. Then we watched a funny show with a man named Red Skeleton, but neither one of us laughed. I was thinking too much about Mary Ella and I thought Mrs. Forrester was full of nerves about what we were doing. That made me even more scared.

There was a lock on the bedroom door where I slept, but Mrs. Forrester said she didn't have no key for it so I couldn't lock it. That feeling of not trusting her came back then. This was her own house and she didn't have a key? Did she want the bedroom door unlocked so they could come in and take me away in the middle of the night? I didn't sleep too good. I cried because I thought I'd never see Henry Allen again. Then I cried more, thinking about Nonnie alone at our house, and when I finally did fall asleep I kept dreaming of Mary Ella coming back as a ghost.

The next morning, Mrs. Forrester went to the store and told me to keep the doors locked and stay away from the windows. I watched for her to come home and made a plan. If she had that Paula social worker or Nurse Ann with her when she came back, I'd go out the back door and run away. But when she came home, the only thing she had with her was a bunch of bags full of food. I never saw so much food come from a store. I was going to help her put it away, but she didn't want me to do nothing. She brung a chair from the dining room into the kitchen so I could sit and talk with her while she put everything away.

By suppertime—she called it "dinner" and made tuna noodle casserole—I wasn't feeling too good. I felt like I might even throw up, so I only ate a little.

"Nerves," she said to me, and I reckoned she was right.

After supper, we played cards in the den. We sat on the sofa, me at one end and her at the other and put the cards on the cushion between us. Nonnie taught me and Mary Ella how to play rummy long ago, but Mrs. Forrester had to remind me how to do it. I was bad at it because I didn't have no concentration at all.

I told her I'd been nervous when she went out to the store and she said she didn't think she'd have to leave me again for anything, except Friday night she was going out with her mother. She had to do that, she said, because her mother's feelings would be hurt if she didn't spend time with her. She was a real kindhearted lady and I started feeling really good about her again.

"What about your daddy?" I asked. She talked a lot about her mama but never said nothing about a father.

"He died a few years ago," she said.

"Was it a accident, like with my daddy?"

"Yes." It was her turn to put down a card, but she just stared at the cards in her hand like she wasn't really seeing them. She looked up at me. "I lost both my father and my sister," she said. "Just like you."

I couldn't believe it. I thought of her as a lady with a perfect life, especially now that I seen her house. I felt like anybody could look at me and know I lost too much. I never would of guessed she had, too. "What happened?" I asked.

She held her cards upside down on her knee and leaned back against the arm of the couch. "It was only a couple of years ago," she said. "My father had bought a used convertible . . . do you know what that is?"

"Ain't got no roof?"

"Right. It was early summer, so I was home from college and Teresa—my sister—just graduated high school. We were going for a drive, like we did sometimes on Sunday afternoon. Daddy liked to drive out to the country. Find a farmer's stand and buy some fresh corn or strawberries or whatever was in season. This was a special drive, because of the new car. So we drove out your way. Grace County. Do you know where that KKK billboard is not far from you?"

"I seen a couple," I said, picturing them.

"The one closest to where you live," she said. "We'd just passed it and a deer suddenly ran into the road right in front of us."

"Oh no!" I knew a boy at school who got killed when a buck crashed through the windshield of his car. It was terrible.

"My father swerved and I guess he was going too fast and the car hit one of those ditches along the side of the road and we . . . well, I'm not sure if we hit the trees and then flipped over or vice versa, but the car ended up upside down in the woods and all of us were thrown out."

She turned her cards over again but I knew she wasn't seeing them. I knew exactly how she felt. "I was all right," she said. "I didn't have a scratch on me, though I was sore for days. My mother wasn't badly injured, either, but I didn't know it at the time because she was unconscious. I thought both she and my father were dead. Teresa . . . my sister . . . she was alive, but she was bleeding from a cut on her neck. So when someone's bleeding you're supposed to put pressure on the wound. I knew that, so I took off my shirt and pressed it on the side of her neck to stop the bleeding. But the thing is, we were in the woods and nobody could see us from the road. So I didn't know whether to keep holding pressure on her neck or go out to the road and wave someone down for help." She waved her cards in the air. "It was . . . I don't know, the most horrifying moment of my life. So I stayed with her, holding pressure on her neck and hoping someone could see us, but no one came and my mother and father weren't moving at all. I finally decided I had to run out to the road and get help. I left my sister and ran down to the road, but it was minutes before a car came by. It was a truck, actually. A farmer's wife. She went back into the woods with me, but by then, my sister was gone."

"Gone?" I asked. "You mean . . ."

"Dead," she said. "She bled to death." She looked down at the sofa, running her hand over the cushion. "I blamed myself for the longest time, thinking I made the wrong choice, even though everyone told me I did the only thing I could have. It took me a long time to believe that. I'm still not sure."

I nodded. "I keep thinking I could of grabbed Mary Ella's arm and pulled her back," I said.

"You couldn't have," she said. "She took you completely by surprise."

"I know that's the truth, but it don't change how I feel."

She sort of smiled at me. Then she got up and opened a cupboard by the TV and I could see a big box inside. She moved some things around in the box and then came back to the sofa with a picture in her hand. "Teresa and I were two years apart, like you and Mary Ella, only I was the older sister." She handed me the picture. Mrs. Forrester looked almost like she looked now, but her sister . . . her sister made me think of Mary Ella. The picture didn't have no color, but you could tell Teresa's hair was the same curly blond as Mary Ella's.

I looked up at Mrs. Forrester. "She looks a little like Mary Ella." I said.

"I know," she said.

I looked at the picture another minute. Mrs. Forrester and her sister was both smiling. Both of them happy girls. Maybe happier than me and Mary Ella ever was. "You and me," I said, "we both got the same kind of hurt inside us."

She nodded, and suddenly, just like that, I knew I could trust her with my life.

I thought I'd sleep good that night, feeling safer and all, but as soon as I got into bed the sick feeling came over me again and I started getting a bellyache. I slept for a while, but the pain kept waking me up. Finally I got out of bed to go to the bathroom and when I stood up a puddle of water came out of me like I peed myself, though I knew I didn't. I was so embarrassed, though. It went all over the pretty rug and I had to figure out how to clean it up before Mrs. Forrester seen what I done. I walked real quiet to the bathroom, but on my way back to the bedroom with a towel, I saw her coming out of her room, tying a robe around herself.

"Are you all right?" she asked.

My belly hurt so bad I couldn't stand up straight. "I got a bellyache," I said. "And water come out of me on your rug. I'm sorry. It ain't pee, though, honest."

Her eyes got real big. "Oh no," she said. "I think you're in labor."

I remembered that word from when Mary Ella had Baby William. "No, that ain't it," I said. "It's too soon. I think I just—"

"Come back to bed." She put her arm around me, but a pain gripped my belly so hard I couldn't take a step. I moaned and my face and head felt hot and sweaty. Mrs. Forrester talked to me, but I wasn't really listening. All I could think about was the pain. And then, quick as it came, it left, and I stood up straight.

"It's gone," I said. "I ain't never felt nothing like that before." I didn't want to say that maybe her tuna noodle casserole had gone bad, but that's what I thought. Except I remembered I felt punk before supper, too.

"Okay," she said. "Come back to bed."

She walked me back into the bedroom. "The puddle's there somewhere." I pointed to the rug at the side of the bed but the room was dark and she probably couldn't see.

"Don't worry about the rug," she said. "I need to know if you get that pain again. I'm going to stay here with you for a while and you let me know, all right?" She sat down on the other side of the bed from me. It was like the way me and Mary Ella shared our bed, only I was on the wrong side. Would I ever sleep in that bed again? Could the lawyer make it that I'd be safe at home without always worrying about someone taking me away and cutting me open?

"Was that the first pain you've had?" Mrs. Forrester asked.

"Ever in my life?"

"No, honey. Tonight."

"I felt punk," I said. "And I had a bellyache, but that was the first awful pain. I don't know what's happening to me with all that water coming out. I should mop it up."

"I think your water broke," she said. "That's what they call it when you're going into labor. Getting ready to have the baby. Your water breaks."

I could tell she was scared. She said all them things real calm, but her voice wasn't like it usually sounded. And if *she* was scared, I sure was scared.

"What do we do?" I asked.

She didn't answer right away. My eyes was getting used to the dark and I could see her head leaning back against the headboard. She was looking up at the ceiling. "I'm not sure," she said. "Right now, we just wait to see if you get another pain."

We waited a long time. I slept off and on and when I woke up, my belly felt like it was turning inside out and Mrs. Forrester wasn't in the room. I grabbed fistfuls of the blanket in my hands, trying not to scream, it hurt so bad. Then finally, I had to let it out. "Jane!" I screamed. "Jane! Help me!"

49

Jane

My hand shook as I dialed my mother's number. It was four in the morning and for the past hour I'd been sitting with Ivy while she screamed and cried, and I didn't know which one of us was more terrified. I kept hoping the pains would stop, but instead they came closer and closer together, and I knew I had no choice but to call Mom. How would I ever explain what I'd done? Right now, though, I couldn't worry about myself. Ivy was in agony down the hall. I didn't think it would happen like this, so soon and so quickly. I hoped that didn't mean something terrible was wrong. I'd never forgive myself if I'd hurt her or her baby by taking her away.

"Hello?" My mother's voice sounded muffled and worried.

"Mom?" I said. "I'm all right, but I need your help. I'm sorry to—"

"What's wrong?" She sounded suddenly alert. She was going to be angry with me, but I felt certain she'd help me.

"It's one of my clients," I said. "I . . . it's hard to explain, but she's here. At my house. And she's pregnant and going into labor. And I don't know what to do."

There was silence on my mother's end of the line as she took that in. "Why did she come to you?" she said.

"She didn't. I brought her here. I was fired this morning. Yesterday morning, I mean. It's—"

"You were *fired*?"

"Yes. It's too long to go into right now. This girl . . . she's only fifteen and I can't take her to the hospital. I'll explain when you get here. She wasn't supposed to have the baby yet and I thought I could get this attorney I know to help us, but—" My voice suddenly caught, surprising me. I was so overwhelmed with frustration at things not going according to my plan! I heard Ivy scream from the other room. "I don't know what to do, Mom!"

"Call an ambulance," she said.

"I can't let her go to the hospital! Can you come over? Please? I'll explain it then, but right now I'm scared."

Again, that silence, and I waited, clutching the phone.

"I'll be over in a few minutes," she said, and I breathed out a sigh of relief. I wouldn't be handling this mess alone any longer.

"Thank you," I said, but she'd already hung up the phone.

I went back in the guest room with a cool, damp washcloth and I pressed it to Ivy's forehead. She barely had time to catch her breath between the pains now.

"My mother's coming over," I said.

"No! She'll—"

"We need some help," I said.

"She'll make me go to the hospital!"

I shook my head. "I won't let that happen," I said, although I knew if Mom and I couldn't handle this, we'd have no choice but to call an ambulance. "I'll make sure—"

"They fired you! You can't make sure of anything! I don't want your mother to come."

"Ivy, just concentrate on having your baby, please. She'll help us, honey. I promise."

She clapped her hands over her ears. "Shut up, shut up, shut up!" she cried.

I did. I wiped her forehead and let her squeeze my hand when the next pain came, but I didn't say a word. Instead, I listened for the sound of my mother's car in the driveway. I prayed she would hurry up. I knew next to nothing about childbirth, but my mother'd had two babies. At least that was something.

She must have driven up while Ivy was screaming, because I didn't hear another sound until she called "Hello!" from downstairs.

"We're up here!" I shouted. "In the guest room!"

"*No,*" Ivy pleaded. "I'm afraid."

"It'll be all right," I said, listening to my mother climb the stairs.

She reached the doorway and stood there a moment, taking in the scene. She looked wide awake. The only sign that I'd awakened her a few short minutes ago was her lack of rouge and lipstick and her uncombed graying hair. Still, she was a beautiful sight.

"This is Ivy," I said to her. "Ivy, this is—"

"I don't trust her," Ivy whispered in a voice my mother couldn't possibly miss.

My mother glanced at me, then back at Ivy. "You can trust me," she said as she walked into the room. She had the large first-aid kit with her, the one we'd kept in our pantry all my life for our cuts and scraped knees. I wondered what was in there that could possibly help us deliver a baby.

Ivy let out a long groan and I knew she'd begin screaming again any second. My mother touched my shoulder. "I need to talk to you, Jane," she said.

"No!" Ivy grabbed my hand. "Don't leave me."

I'd been sitting on the edge of the bed, but now got to my feet. "Let me explain everything to her," I said to Ivy. "I'll be right outside the door. Two minutes. I promise." I had to pry her hand from mine, while she whimpered, too tired to fight me.

Mom and I walked into the hallway and I shut the door behind me.

"We need to call an ambulance right now," my mother said firmly. She started toward my bedroom and the phone, but I grabbed her arm.

"No!" I said. "We can't."

She stopped walking and gave me a quizzical look. "What's going on, Jane?" she asked. "What does this have to do with you being fired . . . and why were you fired? And why on earth haven't you taken her to the hospital? She can't have a baby here!"

"They plan to sterilize her after the baby is born, and she doesn't want to be sterilized, so I brought her here," I said. "I know a lawyer I thought could help, but he's out of town. I didn't think she'd have the baby this early."

My mother stared at me for a moment. "They wouldn't sterilize her," she said. "Not a fifteen-year-old girl. That's ridiculous."

"Yes they would. I know it for a fact. They did it to her sister at fifteen, and she's not the only one I've seen. Please, Mom. Please help me. You've had babies. You must—"

"I had twilight sleep with both you and Teresa," she said. "I went to sleep and when I woke up, there was a baby. I have no more idea how to deliver a baby than you do."

"*Mom,*" I pleaded. "Please. We have to try."

"This is crazy, Jane."

"I promised her I wouldn't let anything happen to her." I could hear Ivy crying through the door. "She's so scared."

My mother looked at the door of the guest room as if she could see Ivy inside it, and I knew she was giving in. "Well," she said with a sigh, "they always say to boil water, so you go do that while I get to know her. Does Robert have any medical books here?"

"Yes! In the den. I'll go look." I gave her a quick hug. "Thank you!" I said, as I headed for the stairs.

"We'll need scissors or a sharp knife to cut the cord," she called after me. "Put them in the boiling water. And we'll need towels. Do you have a plastic shower curtain in your bathroom up here?"

"Yes!" I called over my shoulder.

"I'll put that under her."

"Okay." I turned to look up at her. "Thank you, Mom," I said again, but she shook her head.

"I'm as big a fool as you are," she said.

I ran downstairs, my heart thumping hard. What if Ivy died because she wasn't in the hospital? What if one more girl died because of my mistake? I didn't dare think about that now.

In the kitchen, I pulled a pot from the cupboard and dropped it on the floor, my hands were trembling so hard. I picked the pot up and started filling it with water, marveling that my mother was able to think clearly at a time like this. I was so glad she was here.

I put the water on to boil, then ran into the den and scanned the titles of Robert's medical books until I found one on obstetrics. Back in the kitchen, I set the book on the counter and paged through it, trying to make sense of the technical language. It was full of all the things that could go wrong, and scanning the book did nothing to calm my nerves. We needed to tie off the cord, the book said, so I cut two lengths of kitchen string and added them to the pot of water with the knife. We also needed a syringe, and while the water heated, I checked Robert's medical bag in the foyer closet. I found two syringes in the bag and carried the tiny blue one back to the kitchen. From upstairs, Ivy's agonized cries were so close together that they became one long extended scream and I was afraid something was going terribly wrong. I knew labor could be excruciating, but I'd had no idea it was this bad. I thought of that twilight sleep she could have if she was in the hospital, and I felt guilty I was depriving her of that.

I wasn't sure how long to boil the knife and string. I wanted to boil them for hours because I was scared to go back upstairs, but I couldn't let my mother handle this alone. I left everything in the water for fifteen minutes, then lifted them out with tongs and put them in a bowl—that hadn't been sterilized, I realized too late—and carried them and the book upstairs.

I walked into the room to find Ivy red-faced and sweaty. She moaned and cried, barely noticing me as she focused on what was happening to her body. Her nightgown was hiked to her waist, her knees wide apart, and my mother sat on the bed at her feet, coaching her to push. Mom looked up at me.

"I can see the baby's head," she said quietly. The anxiety in her voice was impossible to miss. "It looks like it's coming, but then it goes back in."

I handed the bowl to her, afraid to look at what was happening between Ivy's legs. I'd always been squeamish, and my mother knew it.

"Maybe I can find something about that in this book." I started to open the book with my trembling fingers.

"No time for that," my mother said, nodding toward the head of the bed. "Help her push, Jane. Encourage her."

I put the book on the dresser, then moved to the head of the bed and sat on the very edge. Ivy was raising her head and shoulders as if she were trying to put more force into her pushing, and I put my arm beneath her shoulders to help.

"Don't touch me!" she shouted, and I quickly pulled my arm away. She looked up at the ceiling, droplets of sweat on her forehead. "Help!" she cried. "Please, somebody help!"

I had the feeling she didn't know what she was saying, she was in such distress. So I tried again, putting my arm beneath her shoulders, and this time she didn't fight me. "You're doing really well, Ivy," I said, my cheek against her damp temple. She made ragged, primal sounds—grunts and moans that came from some part of her I never knew existed.

"I see the head again," my mother said. "Push, Ivy!"

Ivy tried her hardest, but I could tell she was exhausted. I looked at my mother, who gave me a small shake of her head. "Disappeared," she said. Then she mouthed the word to me: *ambulance.*

As if Ivy heard the word, she gave a sudden, ferocious push.

"Yes!" my mother said excitedly. "Yes, Ivy! Like that!"

I propped Ivy up as she pushed and pushed. I was sweaty and winded myself after a few minutes. I could only imagine her exhaustion. But it was working.

"The baby's head is coming!" my mother said. "I think it's going to . . . the head is out!"

Ivy let out a long wail—half scream, half groan—and her baby nearly flew into my mother's hands.

"Oh my God!" I started to cry, awestruck and relieved.

"It's a girl!" my mother said.

Ivy lay back against the pillow, sobbing and shaking, and I watched while my mother used a towel to wipe blood from the limp little baby girl, who was a horrible, sickly pale blue. *Oh God.* We weren't out of the woods yet. I watched my mother's lips move in a silent prayer as she reached for the syringe and pressed it to the baby's nose. I held my breath, waiting, waiting.

"Where is she?" Ivy tried to raise her head to look, but she seemed too tired to manage and I didn't help her, afraid for her to see her life-less daughter.

Suddenly, though, the baby gave a sharp cry. My mother gasped, and she and I looked at each other, both of us letting out our breath in relief. Already, I could see the baby's skin was beginning to lose its bluish hue, and she batted one of her arms against the towel. Her tiny, perfect fingers put a lump in my throat.

I leaned over to whisper to Ivy. "She's all right," I said. "She's beautiful."

My mother wrapped the baby, still attached to the umbilical cord, in a fresh towel, then leaned over to rest her in Ivy's arms. Ivy was trembling all over, and I helped her hold the tiny bundle. The baby's face peeked out, eyes open and searching, pale little eyebrows raised, lips so perfect they looked as if they belonged on a porcelain doll.

"I love you," Ivy said to her. "I love you so much."

I looked up to see my mother using another of the towels to wipe tears from her own eyes. I smiled at her, full to overflowing with gratitude and admiration. This long, long night was over, and as the sunrise painted the sky outside pink, I knew that every one of us in that room had been forever changed.

50

Ivy

"Happy five-hour birthday to your sweet baby," Jane said, handing my baby to me across the bed. "Got her?"

"Uh-huh." I pulled the baby to me. She was wrapped in another towel and light as air. I was so tired I was dizzy, but I didn't want to sleep no more. I fell asleep off and on all morning since she was born. Now all I wanted was to stare at her. She was teeny tiny and wrinkly and bald and she didn't open her eyes but a few times, but I loved her more than anything. She was my Mary. I knew when Jane's mother said it was a girl, that would be her name. A close enough name to remember my sister by, but not so close it would always make people think of the terrible thing my sister done to herself.

I put little kisses all over Mary's head, then looked up at Jane. "Your mama is real nice," I said.

"She really is wonderful." Jane sat down on the other side of the bed.

"She said I was brave." I laughed, but real quiet so I wouldn't wake up Mary. "Bet you ain't never heard a brave person scream the whole night through."

"Mom said that when I was born, they gave her some medicine that let her sort of sleep through the labor," Jane said, "so you really *were* brave to do it without anything to help the pain."

Mary Ella said she didn't remember nothing about having Baby

William, so I guessed she got some of that medicine, too. I wished I had it, but now it didn't matter. It was over and I had my baby girl and didn't have no surgery, neither. Jane's mama'd washed my baby and asked me if I wanted to nurse her or give her the bottle. Baby William had trouble with the bottle because he didn't suck right, and I remembered Nurse Ann saying he never would of made it at the breast. Besides, I didn't know nobody who ever did that breast nursing, so I said bottle. So, right now Jane's mama was out buying diapers and formula and bottles, and Mary was wearing one of the diapers Jane cut up from a towel.

"You're going to be an excellent mother," Jane said to me now.

I looked down at Mary's pale eyelashes where they fluttered on her cheeks. She wasn't going to look a thing like Henry Allen, I didn't think. I wished he could see her. "I want to be a good mama more than anything," I said, "but I want my baby to have her daddy, too." I got choked up, saying that.

"Don't think about that right now." Jane patted my arm. "Just think about Mary. About how beautiful and perfect she is. We'll have time to worry about her father later." She stood up from the bed. "Are you all right for now?" she asked.

"Yes," I said. "We're fine."

She went downstairs and I sat watching Mary and thinking about her future. It looked pretty bad, I had to admit. I just didn't want anything to hurt her. I wondered if my own mama'd felt this way, watching me after I was born. Did she think about how she'd never let anything hurt me? I only hoped I did a better job of it than she did.

51

Jane

At two in the afternoon, I made my exhausted mother a late lunch. I sat across the breakfast nook table from her and watched her eat the eggs and bacon in silence. Her eyelids were heavy and she chewed slowly. She'd called the library that morning to say she wasn't feeling well and wouldn't be in and I was grateful. I felt bad about dragging her into this turmoil I'd created, but I needed her here. Taking care of Ivy had been one thing. Taking care of Ivy and a newborn baby, quite another.

"You need to sleep," I said to her now. "You can nap in my bed."

"Well," she said, sipping her coffee, "first we need to talk."

"All right." I owed her an explanation. Several, actually. I'd only had a chance to tell her bits and pieces of what was going on.

"You've essentially . . . kidnapped this girl?"

"Her grandmother told her she could come with me. But, I'd say she gave her permission . . . under duress."

"But you were already fired when you took her?"

I nodded.

"Why?"

I reached for her pack of Salems on the table. "May I?" I asked.

She nodded, and I lit one of the cigarettes and inhaled deeply, the menthol like ice in my throat. "I wasn't following the rules," I said. "And I got too involved with my clients. That's what they said, anyway."

I told her about Ivy's petition and how I'd tried to fight it. "They do this to girls and women who aren't smart enough or healthy enough or rich enough . . . or *white* enough . . . to fight it. They say it's for women who are mentally retarded or mentally ill or epileptic. Ivy's epileptic, but—"

"She is?"

"Yes, but her seizures are very rare." I'd honestly forgotten about her epilepsy during her labor, and now I was relieved she'd had no problems with it. "She mostly had them when she was younger, although I've seen her have a small one."

"That doesn't seem like a good enough reason to sterilize her," my mother said. "She came through this fine, and she seems like a sweet girl."

"She *is* a sweet girl. But she's poor. Very poor. So maybe her children won't have the best chance at a future, but still . . . it should be her right to say yes or no to having more kids."

"So, you argued for her and they fired you?"

"Exactly." I took another drag on the cigarette and blew the smoke away from us. "I also did some other things they didn't like. I took Ivy and her sister to the beach one day. Against the rules, though I honestly didn't know it."

My mother couldn't hide her smile. "You were never good at following the rules," she said. "Even as a little girl, you insisted on coloring outside the lines. You said it was prettier that way."

"Robert calls it 'stubbornness.'"

"Yes, you are that." She pushed her half-eaten lunch to the side and lit a cigarette from mine. "So, your department . . . Won't they realize you took Ivy?"

"It depends on what the grandmother says. She told me she'd say Ivy ran away."

"What do you plan to do with her, though? You mentioned an attorney?"

I told her about Gavin and my hope he could help us. "But it turns out he's on a cruise until Monday," I said, tamping out my cigarette, "so nothing quite went according to my plan."

"Oh, Jane." She shook her head. "I can't believe you did this. You could be in so much trouble."

"I know, Mom. But I had to. I needed to *save* her."

She studied the tip of her cigarette. "Sweetie," she said slowly, "after the accident . . . you did what you thought was right, leaving Teresa to go for help. I hope you've never doubted that."

My cheeks felt hot. I couldn't look her in the eye. "Of course I've doubted it." I ran my fingertips over the edge of the ashtray.

"I think I would have done the same thing you did. I've never held that against you. You know that, don't you?"

"I think you would have stayed with her."

"Well, even if I did, I believe she would have died anyway. I don't think anyone or anything could have saved her."

"Ivy lost her sister, too." I looked at her. "It's only been two weeks."

"Oh no."

"The department lied to her—to Ivy's sister—about her sterilization," I said. "I thought that was cruel, so I told her the truth. And then I had to take her little boy away from her for neglect after he got into the grandmother's medicine." I started to cry. "And then she killed herself."

"Oh, Jane." My mother stubbed out her cigarette and moved to my side of the breakfast nook, her arms around me.

"I feel like that was my fault, too," I said.

"You were doing your job."

"But I should have realized how depressed she was and helped her."

She let me cry for a minute, rocking me like I was her little girl again. Then she picked up a napkin and dried my cheeks. "You threw yourself into this social work job with your whole heart, Jane," she said. "But maybe it wasn't meant for you."

"I thought I was doing some good until everything fell apart."

"There are other jobs," she said. "There's other rewarding work."

"And there are other *Ivies*, too," I said. "Now that I know they exist, I can't just forget about them."

"Can your marriage handle it if you don't?"

I shook my head.

"Sometimes coloring outside the lines can cost you," she said. "Only you can figure out if it's worth it."

She went upstairs to say good-bye to Ivy, then came back into the kitchen and gave me another hug. "I have off tomorrow, so I'll come back in the morning," she said.

"I hate for you to go," I said. "I know nothing about taking care of a baby."

"I'm five minutes away," she said.

"You won't say anything to anyone, will you?" I knotted my hands in front of me. "I know this puts you in a terrible position. I'll say I delivered the baby myself when I speak to Gavin. The attorney. I won't bring your name—"

"Don't lie," she said, patting my hands. "If the attorney can get you out of this mess, I'll assume he can get me out of it, too."

52

Ivy

It was Monday morning, the day the lawyer was supposed to be back. My nerves was on edge, waiting for Jane to call him. I had a dream last night he didn't come back and I woke up in a sweat. I wasn't sleeping so good since Mary was born because she was always hungry. Until yesterday, Jane had to get up every time Mary needed the bottle, because she didn't want me to go downstairs to heat it up. But yesterday, Jane's mama said she thought it was time I got up and moved around, so now it was all up to me. So far, except for being sleepy all the time, it was going fine.

Mary was done eating and I put the bottle on the table and raised her to my shoulder to burp her. I heard Jane on the stairs and saw her through the open door carrying my breakfast tray. I told her she didn't have to wait on me no more, but she said this one last time. Someday I'll pay her back for everything she done for me.

"Hi, honey," she said. "You ready to put Mary in her basket and have some breakfast?" We'd made up the laundry basket with a soft blanket for Mary and she loved it, except for the colic. Jane's mama said that's why she got fussy sometimes and to burp her good. She said Jane had colic when she was a baby, too.

"I'm still burping her," I said.

"How about I do that while you eat?" Jane put the tray on my lap and took Mary from me. Jane loved holding her. The baby crinkled up

308 | Diane Chamberlain

her face like she was going to holler but once she was on Jane's shoulder she settled right down. Jane sat next to me on the bed and patted Mary's back. I found out Jane was only seven years older than me. I always thought she was so much older because she seemed like it, but here in her house it was more like we was friends almost the same age. We done this a few times, the past couple of days, sitting next to each other, leaning against the headboard and talking about one thing or the other. Mostly about what she'd tell the lawyer this morning. She was real nervous about that.

I started eating. She'd made me fried eggs and grits and sausage and a cup of fruit. She was always making me more food than I could eat.

"Sweet little baby," Jane whispered against Mary's ear while she patted her back.

"Your mama said don't be afraid to do it harder." I cut the sausage with the side of my fork. "Helps with the colic."

Jane patted a little harder. "Mom agrees with me that you're going to be a good mother," she said.

"She did?" That made me happy. I liked Jane's mama so much.

"Uh-huh. She said you have a natural feel for how to handle Mary," she said. "A 'natural confidence,' she called it."

I liked the sound of that. *A natural confidence.*

"I noticed that about you from when I first met you, Ivy," Jane said. "You were the one running your household. Making sure everyone was taken care of."

"I didn't do such a good job of that," I said, thinking of Baby William and my sister.

"You were up against too much."

Mary made chirpy sounds against Jane's shoulder and I reached over to touch her cheek. She wasn't wrinkly no more. Her skin was smooth as butter under my fingertips. She still didn't have a hair on her head, though.

"I keep wondering about my own mama," I said. "Did she ever love me like I love Mary? I wish I remembered her better. Or I could see her."

Jane didn't say nothing right away. "I don't think it's fair you never got to visit her," she said finally.

"She's still alive, ain't she?"

"As far as I know."

"Did they do it to her, too? The operation?"

Jane nodded. "They do it to most patients in institutions," she said.

"Why?" I asked. "Who'd she have a baby with if she's locked away?"

Jane let out a long sigh. "Hard to say," she said, and I could tell she wasn't going to talk no more about it.

"They're trying to erase us," I said. "Erase my whole family. Like we was never born." I thought of sweet Baby William, wherever he was, maybe getting the operation, too, 'cause Jane told me they done it to some boys. That put tears in my eyes. "If you didn't come get me, I'd of had the operation by now, wouldn't I?" That kilt my appetite and I put down my fork.

Jane nodded. "I think so, honey."

I felt like screaming, it made me so mad. By now they would of cut me open and got rid of my chance to have a family. Mrs. Werkman! I thought she was wonderful. If Jane didn't take over for her, I'd be cut open right now and everybody would of told me they took out my appendix.

"Thank you for coming along when you did," I said.

Jane stood up. She kissed Mary on her forehead before putting her down in the basket. Mary let out a cry, but then went quiet. Jane looked at me.

"We're not out of the woods yet, Ivy," she said, looking at her watch. "I don't know what Gavin's going to say when I talk to him. I'm sure he'll try to help us, but even though you and I think I did the right thing, it wasn't legal and I'm not sure what will happen."

"Cutting girls open without them having a say-so shouldn't be legal, either," I said.

Jane smiled. "I agree with you there." She looked at my plate, hardly touched. "You want to hold on to that a while?"

I wasn't hungry no longer, but I knew I had to eat for Mary's sake. "I'll keep it," I said.

"After breakfast, I'll help you bring Mary downstairs and we can play cards or watch TV," she said.

"All right." It seemed like months ago that we watched them

programs on her television. So much happened since then. My whole life was different now. I was a mama. Television didn't hold a candle to that. "How long till you call the lawyer?"

She looked at her watch again. "It's eight-thirty," she said. "I'll call at nine. I hope he gets to his office by then."

Jane went downstairs and I was picking at my breakfast again when I heard a car door slam outside. I stopped chewing to listen. Jane's mother already came over this morning on her way to her job, so it couldn't be her. I was scared Jane's husband would come home early from Atlanta. She didn't talk much about him, but I was sure he didn't want to find no strange girl and baby in his house. Real quick, two more car doors slammed. I nearly knocked over my tray getting out of the bed and running to the window.

Police cars! Two of them, one in the driveway, one parked out front. I saw a lady and two policemen walking up the sidewalk. I lifted Mary out of the basket and put her against my shoulder. Then I grabbed the fork from my tray and looked for a place to hide. The closet. It was my only choice.

It was black in there. The only light came through the keyhole. There was some coats or something hanging up, but not too much, and nothing on the floor. I sat down as easy as I could so Mary wouldn't wake up. She was being real good. She settled into the crook of my arm and I rocked her a little. I held the fork in my fist, the sharp part pointing out, and if a policeman opened the closet door I was going to stab him in the face or the legs or wherever I could reach. I wasn't going without a fight! I just hoped Jane could say something that would make them go away. That lady with them . . . who was she? Maybe they had nothing to do with me? But I knew better. Policemen didn't come to your house for no good reason, and I was the only good reason around.

I'd left the bedroom door open. *Dumb.* I heard the doorbell. Then thumping on the door, like Jane wasn't fast enough opening it. Maybe she wouldn't open it at all if she saw it was the police. But then I heard voices and knew they was inside and I started to cry. They was going to take me and cut me open. And when Mary got old enough, they'd do the same thing to her. They'd erase us. Right now, though, me and Mary was alive and together. I took the fork and dug our names into the wall of the closet. *"Ivy and Mary was here,"* I wrote. I dug so deep into the wall, no one would ever be able to erase the words. Not ever.

53

Jane

It was a minute before nine o'clock and I was ready to dial Gavin's office number when the doorbell rang. I was afraid I knew who it was without looking and I dialed quickly, but only made it through four turns of the dial before the pounding started. I hung up and walked into the foyer. Through the sidelight, I could see a blue uniform.

I opened the door and feigned a look of utter surprise at seeing two policemen and Paula standing on my porch.

"Paula!" I said. "What are you doing here?" I glanced from her to the policemen, one young and feminine looking, the other much older, gray hair at his temples beneath his hat. "What's going on?" I asked.

"Are you Jane Forrester?" the younger one asked.

"That's her," Paula said.

I nodded. "How can I help you?" My hand shook and I hung on to the doorknob to keep the tremor from showing.

"We'd like to come in and speak with you a moment," the older policeman said.

"All right," I said. "Why don't we sit out here?" I motioned to the rockers on the porch, although there were only two of them. "It's such a pretty day."

"We need to come in, ma'am," said the younger policeman.

"Where is Ivy Hart?" Paula asked.

"At home, I assume," I said, blocking the doorway.

NECESSARY LIES | 313

"You need to let us in, ma'am," the older policeman said. "Step aside, now."

I did. What else could I do? They walked into the foyer, looking left and right into the living room and dining room.

"Your former client, Miss Ivy Hart, has gone missing," the older policeman said. "Mrs. Jorgen, here, has reason to believe you might know where she is."

I hadn't out-and-out lied yet. I wondered how long I could evade the truth. "Why would you think that?" I frowned at Paula.

"She just coincidentally disappeared the day you're fired?" Paula asked, although it wasn't really a question.

"She probably ran away," I said, wondering what Winona had told them.

"The grandmother believes you have her," the young policeman said.

"She's not here," I said. My first—and I hoped my only—actual lie. "And I was just on my way to the grocery store, so I'd appreciate it if you'd let me get on with—"

"Listen!" Paula held her hand in the air to stop my chatter.

"Listen to what?" I said. I thought I'd heard it, too. The small but distinct cry of a baby. "I don't hear anything."

The three of them cocked their heads, waiting. I looked at my watch.

"I really need to go," I said. Just then, Mary let out a full-blown wail and I shut my eyes.

"She had her baby already?" Paula asked, but she didn't wait for an answer as she took a step toward the stairs.

I grabbed Paula's arm. "You can't just walk in here and—"

"We have a warrant," the young officer said.

"Please!" I said to Paula as she jerked free of my grasp. "Please leave her alone. She just had a baby."

Paula marched across the foyer toward the stairs, the younger policeman close behind her. "You are in so much trouble," Paula said to me over her shoulder.

I looked at the policeman in front of me. "She needs to rest," I pleaded. "Let her stay here and—"

"You're under arrest for the kidnapping of a minor." He pulled handcuffs from his belt, and I panicked at the sight of them. I raised my arms out to my sides to keep my hands away from him.

"No, please!" I said. "Don't do that. I'll do whatever you say. You don't need to—"

"*Two* minors!" Paula corrected the older officer as she climbed the stairs. The younger man was close on her heels. "She kidnapped *two* of them."

"Give me your hands," the policeman said, and there was something about the authority in his voice that made me give in. I lowered my hands in front of me, fighting panic as he snapped the cuffs into place. Bile rose in my throat. I'd failed Ivy and her baby, once again. And Robert! Oh my God. How long before everyone knew his out-of-control wife was under arrest?

"Don't hurt her!" I shouted after Paula as she and the younger police officer disappeared into the upstairs hallway. "Please!"

But my last word was drowned out by the shouts of a panicky fifteen-year-old girl, the cries of her baby . . . and the scream of a full-grown woman.

54

Ivy

The lady yanked me to my feet and pulled Mary out of my arms before I could stop her. I never been so furious in my life. I stabbed her in the face with the fork. I wasn't thinking about what I was doing. She had my baby and I wanted my baby back. I would of killed the lady if I could and I tried to stab her again, but the policeman grabbed me by my arms, holding them behind my back and twisting my fingers until the fork dropped out of my hand. The lady slapped me across my face, she was so mad. Four trickles of blood ran down her cheek. I wished I hurt her worse. I tried to get away from the policeman to get Mary back, but he wasn't letting me go, and the only thing I could do was kick the air. The lady held Mary way too tight and halfway upside down, and Mary was crying and crying.

"Jane!" I screamed. "Help!"

The lady turned and walked out of the room toward the stairs, carrying my baby. "No!" I hollered. "No! Come back!" I was crying and trying to kick the policeman to make him let go of me, but he was like a dog with a bone and I couldn't get free no matter how hard I fought.

"She'll keep the baby safe," he said. He had a calm voice I hated. "That's what this is all about, miss. Keeping both of you safe and sound."

"Let go of me!" I pictured the lady walking down the stairs with

Mary in her arms. I thought of the blood running down her cheek, and then I remembered my mama—how she cut Mrs. Gardiner. For the first time, I understood how you could get crazy enough to do something like that. They locked my mama up for all time. They locked her up and then they cut her open. Was that going to happen to me now?

"I want my *baby*!" I shouted.

"Now, now," the policeman said, and he must of loosened his hold on me because I suddenly got one arm free. I flung my elbow into his face and heard the crack of his nose. He yelped and let go of me, and I ran out the door and flew down the stairs, hanging on to the railing and jumping over half the steps. Nobody was in the big hallway, but I heard car doors slamming and voices shouting in the front yard and I just kept running and running.

I needed to get to my Mary.

55

Jane

The older officer had pushed me into the backseat of the police car parked in my driveway and he was now getting in the front.

"If you let me go to her, I can persuade her to cooperate," I said, trying to sound reasonable and rational when I felt anything but. The younger policeman and Paula were still inside my house with Ivy and the baby, and I had no idea what was going on. "She's terrified," I said. "She's just a child herself. Please." The officer acted as though he didn't hear me, and I wondered if he was deaf. "You can keep me handcuffed if you have to, but just let me talk to her." The police car parked at the curb made me nervous. "You'll let them ride with *me*, won't you?" I fought hard to keep my voice from breaking. He wouldn't even turn to look at me, much less answer me.

But then he said something I didn't understand.

"What?" I leaned forward to hear better, but realized he wasn't speaking to me but to his radio. I kicked the back of his seat. "Damn it!" I shouted. "Listen to me! We have a lawyer. You have to let us speak to—"

A *third* police car pulled up to the curb, and I suddenly spotted Paula rushing across the yard toward it, Mary in her arms. The policeman in the third car got out and opened the rear door for her.

"No!" I shouted as Paula climbed into the car with the baby. I turned in my seat to look back at my house through the rear window. "Where's Ivy?" I shouted. "Let them ride with me!"

The officer sitting in front of me started the car.

"What are you doing!" I kicked his seat one more time. "Wait for Ivy!"

I turned to look out the rear window again and saw Ivy running down my porch steps. "*Please* wait!" I said to my deaf driver. "She's right there. Please let her come with us!"

But as the car her baby was in drove away from the curb, and the car I was in pulled out of my driveway, Ivy stood alone in my front yard in my blue robe, her hands pressed to her pale cheeks. Not screaming. Maybe not even crying. She turned her head toward the car I was in, and I pressed my cuffed hands to the window. *Be strong,* I wanted to shout to her, though I'd never felt so weak and powerless myself. I watched her standing there, looking small and dazed, until I couldn't see her anymore.

56

Jane

I was sitting on the cot in my small, wretched cell, leaning against the cold concrete wall and hugging my knees, when the guard appeared on the other side of the bars. "Your lawyer's back," he said. "They're checking him in, so he'll be here in a minute."

Finally! I jumped up from my cot and held on to the bars of my cell, trying to see the heavy door at the end of the hall, just out of my sight. I'd been cut off from everyone and everything for the last twenty-four hours. I had no idea what was happening, and I'd spent a sleepless night, imagining the worst.

They'd allowed me a few phone calls when they first brought me in the day before. I'd called Gavin first, of course, then tried unsuccessfully to reach Robert at his parents' and my mother at the library. Gavin came over right away and I nearly attacked him when he walked into my cell, trying to tell him everything as quickly as I could because I needed him to find Ivy and prevent them from sterilizing her. After all she'd been through, after all I'd done to try to prevent the worst from happening, I couldn't bear the thought that we'd lost the battle. I cried every time I thought about it.

Once Gavin got over the shock of what I'd done, he was agonizingly methodical, taking notes as he sat on the chair in my cell while I paced. He talked about trying to get me out on bail, explaining why it was going to be difficult, and I had to stop him. "I don't *care* about that right now!" I said. "Find Ivy first!" I'm sure I sounded hysterical to him. He asked so many questions, and I rushed through my answers. The only time I slowed down was when he asked me about the baby's birth. I hesitated before telling him about my mother. It would come out eventually, I knew, and I needed him to be able to trust me and my word.

When he'd gathered as much information as I was willing to take the time to give, I literally pushed him out of my cell. "Go!" I said, pushing his arm. The guard holding the door open eyed me like I was a crazy woman. "Hurry, Gavin, please!" I said.

Then he was gone, and I'd spent the loneliest night of my life, my overactive imagination my only company.

Now, I heard the door at the end of the hall creak open and fall shut with a thud, and in a moment the guard appeared again, Gavin two steps behind him. I tried to read his face, but it was impassive. He looked at the back of the guard's head rather than at me, and I clutched the bars tighter. *Please,* I thought. *Please let her be all right.*

"Morning, Jane," he said, as the guard unlocked my cell door.

I didn't answer. I wasn't interested in niceties. I waited until he was locked inside with me and then grabbed his arm. "Is she okay?"

He motioned toward the cot. "Sit," he said, sitting down himself on the small wooden chair.

I sat on the edge of the cot, leaning forward, my hands locked around my knees and my feet jiggling impatiently on the floor. "Tell me," I pleaded.

"Ivy and the baby were taken into custody by DPW and placed in two separate foster homes," he said. "They—"

"Oh, that's crazy!" I stood up again. "They need to be together. Ivy adores her. She's responsible. That baby's in no danger from—"

"Please sit, Jane," Gavin said again, and I did so, reluctantly. "They had to do it that way while they evaluate the situation. You worked for the department. You must understand they have to determine what's in the best interest of the child. Or in this case, two children."

"Yes, but—"

"They planned to have Ivy examined by a physician today, but—"

"Oh no. I'm afraid once they—"

"Jane!" he said. "Let me finish. This is a quickly changing picture, all right? Ivy's gone."

"What do you mean?"

"She took off from the foster home in the middle of the night."

"Took off? She ran away?"

He nodded.

I sat down on the cot again, taking that in. She'd given birth only a few days ago and had nothing with her but one of my nightgowns and my robe and whatever clothes DPW had given her.

"Is there any way she could have found out where Mary . . . where her baby was?" I asked.

"The baby's still safe in another foster home," he said, "but some-one else is missing." He looked at his notes. "The son of the farmer who owns the place where she used to live. Henry Allen Gardiner."

Both my hands flew to my mouth. "Oh my God, Gavin!" I said. "He must be the baby's father!"

"You know him?"

"Not well, but I've met him. I had no idea." No wonder Davison Gardiner was so anxious to have Ivy sterilized. "I know Ivy loved him . . . she loved the baby's father. I don't know *his* feelings . . . although if he took off with her last night, they must be mutual." I hoped he could keep her safe. Maybe, just maybe, we didn't need to find her. Maybe her life would be better at this point if no one ever did. But her *baby*, I thought. Ivy would die without her Mary.

"So, of course they're looking for her," Gavin said, "and I'll see what I can do about getting a hold put on that sterilization order for when they find her, but it'll be hard with her gone. Meanwhile, we need to focus on getting you out of here. I managed to reach Robert. He's on his way home from Atlanta."

I cringed. "Was he furious? This was supposed to be his time away from me."

Gavin smiled for the first time since walking in my cell. "He honestly didn't sound all that shocked," he said.

"What did he say when you told him I was in jail?"

"Nothing right away. He didn't say anything for so long, in fact, that I thought we'd lost the connection. Then he said, 'Why couldn't she take up knitting, like normal wives?' "

I groaned. "That sounds like Robert," I said.

"Well, I don't think he'll have to worry about you being a working girl any longer," Gavin said. "It's not easy to find a job when you have a record."

"A record," I repeated. They were words I'd never expected to hear in relation to myself.

"You'll have to do some time," he said, "but I'll do my best to make sure it's as little as possible."

I nodded. He'd warned me about that yesterday, so it wasn't a surprise.

"My mother?" I asked. "Were you able to speak to her?"

"Yes, and she's understandably very upset. I'm trying to work it out so she can see you. Be careful what you say when she's here."

"Will she"—I lowered my voice to a whisper—"is she in trouble?"

He shook his head. "Not yet, anyway. I think she'll be all right. I'm going to talk to her after I leave here." He stood up.

"Thank you, Gavin," I said, shaking his hand. Looking into his blue eyes made me remember Lois's funeral, not even a month ago. "I'm sorry to drag you into this," I said. "I know this has been a hard month for you. How is Brenna doing?"

"Adjusting." His smile was sad. "She's more resilient than I am." He looked through the bars thoughtfully, then back at me. "I'll never forget how she went to you after Lois's funeral that day," he said. "She's a very intuitive little girl, and that moment told me something about you."

"It did?" I asked.

He nodded. "It told me you're someone worth fighting for," he said.

After Gavin left, I lay down on my cot, my imagination once more on fire. Ivy and Henry Allen Gardiner. My God. I pictured their faces on my ceiling and smiled to myself.

Run, Ivy! I thought. *Just keep going.*

I remembered her dream of living in California with her baby's father. They'd looked at picture books. I would imagine them there, sitting on a palm-tree-lined beach, holding hands. They would long for the baby they had to leave behind, but they would have more children, and grandchildren, and great-grandchildren.

I smiled at the ceiling, tears running from the corners of my eyes. I'd hold on to that dream for her as long as I lived.

57

Brenna

The last time I'd felt this crazed had been three years ago, when I'd planned the surprise party for Mom's seventieth birthday. Driving back to the hotel after visiting her old house in Hayes Barton, I reminded myself that the birthday party had come off without a hitch. This was different, though. Until two days ago, I wasn't sure if my plan for this morning was going to happen at all, but now it looked good. Very good.

I parked in the front lot of the hotel, since I wouldn't be long. We had to get to the Eaddy Building for the hearing by nine-thirty. I stopped in my own room to run a comb through my hair, then crossed the hall and knocked on my parents' door.

My mother opened the door, and I could tell by the lines between her eyebrows that I wasn't the only anxious one this morning. "Was it still there?" she asked, instead of saying hello.

"It is," I said, walking into the room, "but wow! Let me get a good look at you! It's been a while since I've seen you in your power suit." I took a step back to check her out. My mother lived in yoga pants and T-shirts. I learned early on that buying her clothes or jewelry was pointless. She'd prefer a good book or a new smartphone or dinner out at one of the ethnic restaurants she and Daddy could walk to in their Washington, D.C., neighborhood.

"You're right," she said. "I haven't worn this suit in years. How does it look?" She turned to give me a three-hundred-sixty-degree view of the awesomely tailored pantsuit. With the blond bob she'd worn her whole life, she always had a sort of timeless look about her.

"You look seriously amazing, Mom," I said, and I meant it. I was a size fourteen and I sometimes wished I had her genes. "How do you stay that skinny, the way you eat?"

"Tell me about the house!" She was getting impatient.

"Were you able to see the closet?" Daddy walked into the room from the bathroom, straightening his tie. At eighty-three, he had the slightest limp from a knee replacement that hadn't gone according to plan and that had scared Mom and me into a stupor, but other than that, he was as fit as my mother and I was glad. So many of my friends had lost their parents already or were busy investigating nursing homes. Mom and Dad claimed they were just lucky, but I knew it was more than that. It was their marriage. It was the way they took care of each other.

"I have a picture," I said, pulling my phone from my purse.

"Oh." Mom sat down on the edge of one of the queen-sized beds. "I'm not sure I want to see it," she said. "Gavin, you look."

Daddy took the phone from me. "That's something," he said. "Amazing no one ever painted over it."

"Every owner told the next one not to," I said.

"We should get a print of this, Jane, don't you think?" He handed the phone to my mother, and she looked at the picture, gnawing her lower lip.

"My," she said quietly. "My." She stared at the phone, shaking her head, and I wondered what she was remembering. "That poor girl," she said after a moment. "What ever happened to her?" She handed the phone back to me. "I wonder if she has any idea about the hearing today."

Daddy sat down and put his arm around her. "Maybe it's time we searched for her again," he said. "It's so much easier to find people these days."

"Oh, I Google her name at least once a month," Mom admitted. "Ivy Hart, or Ivy Gardiner, in case she did marry the boy she ran off with. I don't think, if she's still alive, that she'd be the Internet type, though. I can't see it."

"Yeah, well, she probably wouldn't guess you're the Internet type, either." I laughed. My mother was so on top of things. She'd been a freelance journalist for decades. She'd covered every type of story imaginable and even wrote about the Eugenics Program way before it was on the public radar. No one paid much attention to the program, though, until the *Winston-Salem Journal* ran a series of articles about it in 2002. Then, all hell broke loose, and at the hearing today, the victims would finally get to tell their side of the story.

I straightened the collar on my mother's blouse. "We should get going," I said.

"Let's stop at the concierge desk and see if they can make a print from the picture on your phone," Daddy suggested.

I looked at my watch. "If they can do it quickly," I said.

"Why are you so insistent we leave this early?" Mom asked. "It's not like you."

She was right. I ran late for everything. My poli-sci students at Georgetown were ever hopeful I wouldn't show up for class so they could leave. They'd groan when I'd walk in the door twenty minutes late.

"The hearing's going to be a media circus," I said. "We want to be sure to get a seat."

"We have reserved seats, honey," my father reminded me. "Mom's already on that sign-up sheet to testify."

"Oh, I know. But I need my latte first or I won't last the morning."

They exchanged a "what's with Brenna?" look, but got to their feet.

We took the elevator to the first floor. The guy at the concierge desk was not only quick printing the picture from my phone, but he also put it in a manila folder so it wouldn't bend. Then we walked out to my car.

"You two sit in the backseat," I said. Driving down from D.C., Daddy'd sat in the front with me so he'd have more legroom, but this morning I thought he should sit next to Mom. Give her some moral support.

They didn't fight me. They got in the backseat and I started the car and headed out of the parking lot, thinking that I was not only the driver this morning. I was the master of ceremonies.

58

Jane

I slipped my arm through Gavin's as we waited in line at Starbucks. I'd never known Brenna to be a big Starbucks fan, but on the drive to Raleigh yesterday, she told us she knew she'd need a latte this morning, so here we were. I thought Gavin would have preferred bacon and eggs, but really, it didn't matter. Brenna was usually unflappable and I was surprised my plan to testify at the hearing today seemed to have shaken her up so much. I'd been speaking in public most of my life. I still did whenever some women's club or Rotary wanted to dust me off and trot me out. Give me almost any topic and I could find plenty to say about it. But I wasn't crazy about revisiting my own past, which was why, when I woke up this morning, I decided not to go over to my old Hayes Barton house with Brenna. It wasn't the closet, though that was certainly part of it. It was the reminders of a time I'd tried to forget. My marriage to Robert that never should have been. A job I had not been cut out for. Just coming back to Raleigh after living happily—I could even say *joyously*—in Washington, D.C., for forty years was hard enough. So my trepidation made sense. Maybe Brenna picked up on it.

"Oh, that's cool," she said now, pointing to a room at the side of the Starbucks. It had a glass wall, so we could see inside to ten comfortable-looking upholstered chairs. "Let's take our coffee in there."

"It might be reserved for a meeting," Gavin said.

"They can kick us out, then," she said. "Why don't you guys go sit in there and I'll bring our coffee. You want scones or muffins or . . ."

"You pick something out for us, honey." I thought getting Gavin off his feet was probably a good idea. He could walk a few blocks most days, but standing like this often bothered his knee.

He and I went into the room and sat in a couple of chairs next to each other. The music was much quieter in here. Brenna looked at us through the glass wall and we waved.

"She has ants in her pants this morning," Gavin said.

"I was thinking the same thing."

We watched as she walked toward the room balancing a cardboard cup carrier and pastry bags. Gavin got up and opened the door for her.

"We really don't need this big space," he said.

"I feel like stretching out." She handed each of us our cups and pastries. "Now we're all set." She sat down across from us. "Do you know exactly what you're going to say this morning?" she asked me.

She said something else, but I didn't hear it. Through the glass wall, I spotted a woman leaning against the back of a chair, watching the main door of Starbucks as if she were waiting for someone. She made me think of Teresa. Oh, she was close to Brenna's age, but I thought, *I bet that's what Teresa would have looked like if she'd lived.* I had trouble taking my eyes off her. Her blond hair was in a high short ponytail, an explosion of fuzzy curls on the top of her head. She wore a sleeveless blue tank top and white capris.

"Mom?" Brenna said. "Did you hear me?"

"What?" I turned to my daughter, but only for a moment before looking back at the woman. I didn't want to lose the grown-up Teresa. The woman glanced at me and I looked away quickly and laughed.

"What's so funny?" Brenna asked.

"I was staring at a woman out there and she caught me," I said, pulling the scone from the pastry bag.

"Who?" Gavin asked.

"Don't look," I said. "Just someone who reminded me of my sister." I couldn't help myself—I had to look again, and now another woman was greeting her. They hugged and when they separated, I saw her friend's face and gasped. "I think I'm cracking up," I said. "First I thought I saw someone who looked like a grown-up Teresa and now I see someone who looks like a grown-up Ivy. I'm sure it's because of today. She's on my mind."

"Mom." Brenna moved to the chair next to mine and rested her hand on my knee. "It *is* Ivy."

I stared at my daughter, her words not quite sinking in. Brenna looked away from me to wave to the two women, and I turned to see them walking toward the room. *Oh my God.* She had Ivy's eyes. Ivy's smile. I was suddenly back in the police car, unable to help the terrified girl who stood alone in my yard. I had wanted to reach her, hold her back then. And I couldn't.

But now I could.

"What's going on, Brenna?" Gavin asked, but I didn't wait to hear her answer. I raced out of the room, my scone flying off my lap, and in a moment I had Ivy in my arms. I didn't know which of us was crying harder.

We sat in the private room, which *had* been reserved—by Brenna. I couldn't take my eyes off Ivy, who sat next to me, holding my hand. "I can't believe it," I said, over and over again. "I just can't believe you're here in front of me!"

"I know," she said. "I feel like I stepped into a time machine. Yesterday, I was fifteen and you were twenty-two, and now, suddenly, here we are—senior citizens. And you look beautiful."

"Oh, you too, Ivy!" I said sincerely. She did. Her highlighted short blond hair was simply styled, her skin was tan but not weathered. She wore a white and gold striped top and khaki pants. The farm girl was gone.

The younger woman sat on Ivy's other side. She'd introduced herself to us as "Rose," but with her lithe build and wild hair, she reminded me so much of Mary Ella that I knew she had Hart blood in her. There was an edginess to her. A depth to her voice that made me think she smoked. Close up, I could see silver scattered through her wild blond hair. She was so sweet with Ivy, rubbing her shoulder, touching her hand. She loved her. That much was clear.

"I'm no speaker," Ivy said. "But when Brenna told me you were going to testify on Mary Ella's behalf, I knew I couldn't let you do it alone."

"I've thought of you so often!" I said. "I've looked for you for fifty years, do you know that? What happened? You and Henry Allen must have taken off together. That much I figured out."

"We did," she said. "It was terrible in a way. I didn't want to leave Mary"—she squeezed the hand of the younger woman sitting next to her—"but we had no way of knowing where she was."

"Is this Mary?" I had to know.

Ivy nodded with a smile. "The first foster home named her Rose, and she was nearly five when we finally found her, so we kept the name. We didn't want to confuse her any more than she already was. I call her Rose Mary, but I'm the only one who does."

"Thank God." Rose laughed.

"How did you find her? Where did you go? Tell me everything!"

"Me and Henry Allen knew we had to get out of North Carolina because everyone was looking for us. You were locked up or I knew you would have helped me find her, but we had to leave. So we hitched our way to California."

"That was your dream," I remembered.

She nodded. "Our *real* dream was Monterey, but we didn't make it as far as the coast. We found an olive grove where they needed help, and—"

"An olive grove!" I said.

"Far cry from tobacco, huh?" She smiled. "We worked for the owners for years. They gave us a little house on their property." Now she laughed. "That probably sounds familiar—like the Gardiner farm, right? But believe me, it was nothing like it. Indoor plumbing for one thing. Two bedrooms. We couldn't get married till I turned eighteen, but the family that owned the grove didn't care. They were happy to have hard workers."

"Who spoke English," Rose added.

"True," Ivy said, "though we both picked up Spanish pretty quick. Then Henry Allen went to night school to learn more about the business, and the boys were born."

"Boys?" I asked.

"Here." Rose handed her mother a phone, and Ivy touched the screen and leaned over to show me.

"They're holding down the fort while me and Rose are here," Ivy said.

I looked at the photograph of Ivy's three children—Rose flanked by two brown-haired men who appeared to be in their early forties. Brenna and Gavin, who'd been sitting on the other side of the room, crowded close to peer at the phone.

"That's Henry Allen junior on the left and Steven on the right," Ivy said.

"How wonderful," I said. "We have two sons and a daughter, too." I smiled at Brenna.

I didn't think Ivy heard me. She was lost in the picture of her children. She raised her gaze to mine. "I wouldn't have the boys—and my three grandkids—if it wasn't for you," she said. "I think about that all the time, Jane. About what you did for me. I can't imagine life without my boys."

I pressed my fist to my mouth, overwhelmed by the stark truth in her words.

"What did you mean, 'they're holding down the fort'?" Gavin asked, as Brenna pulled her chair and his closer to ours so that we formed a tight little circle. "What's the fort?"

"The grove," Rose said. "We all work there."

"And the tasting room," Ivy added. "This is tourist season."

"Tasting room?" Brenna asked. "Wine?"

"No, no. Olive oil." Ivy smiled. "To make a long story short, we kept working on that farm and the couple who owned it treated us like their kids, since they had none of their own. When they retired, they sold the farm to us. I was about . . . oh, I guess forty then."

I sat back in the chair and shook my head in wonder. "I never pictured this future for you," I said. "Ivy, I searched and searched. I looked for Ivy Hart. Ivy Gardiner. If you owned a farm . . . a grove . . . wouldn't your name have shown up somewhere?"

"Henry Allen died twenty years ago," she said.

"Oh, I'm sorry."

She nodded. "He was way too young, but we had thirty great years together," she said. "A few years later, I got married again. A good man. I'm Ivy Lopez now. That's why I didn't show up in your searches."

I looked at my daughter. "How did *you* ever find her?"

Brenna let out her breath as if she'd run a mile. "It wasn't easy," she said. "It took a private detective and a long conversation with a retired—and really distrustful—Wilmington cop named Eli Jordan."

"Oh!" I looked at Ivy. "Eli!" I said.

Ivy nodded. "We stayed in touch with him," she said. "Him and Lita looked after Nonnie until she died."

The Jordan family came back to me in a rush. "How are the Jordans?" I asked. "I guess Lita is . . ." I let my voice trail off.

"She's still alive," Ivy said. "She lives with Eli and his family."

"She was such an interesting woman, wasn't she?" I asked. "And how about the boys? Devil and Avery and—"

"Devil lived up to his name," Ivy said with a shake of her head. "He's been in prison a long time, I don't even remember what for. All I know is it broke Lita's heart."

"Oh dear," I said. "And Avery?" I remembered our drives to the Braille teacher, filled with his nonstop chatter.

"He taught at a school for the blind in Raleigh," Ivy said. "He's retired now."

"Really!" I loved that he'd become a teacher. "Did he ever have the surgery?" I almost whispered the question, as though I weren't sure I wanted the answer.

"He has kids," Ivy said, "and I believe they're his."

"Oh, that's wonderful to hear!" I said.

Ivy nodded. "Sheena was a teacher, too, but she died a couple of years ago."

"I remember you wanted to teach," I said.

"The closest I got to that was volunteering in my kids' classrooms," she said.

Rose groaned. "My friends loved her, but my brothers and I hated having her there," she said. "We couldn't get away with anything."

"That was my plan." Ivy smiled. "Little Rodney . . . do you remember him?" she asked me.

I nodded, picturing the little boy the first time I saw him, running through the Jordans' house wearing a cardboard carton decked out as a car.

"He's a cop, too," Ivy said.

"Probation officer," Rose corrected.

"Close enough." Ivy shrugged.

My mind had shifted to the other little boy on the Gardiners' farm. "Do you know whatever became of William?" I asked. "He was so darling, and I never stopped feeling terrible about that night in the emergency room when I—"

"You did what you had to do," Ivy said firmly. She touched my knee. "Jane, I never blamed you for anything. Maybe a little back then, but the more I grew up, the more I could see why you had to do it. It turns out William got adopted out of the residential school he was in."

"Adopted!"

"They couldn't tell me who adopted him. It's not like today, when all that's so open and everything, so we never were able to track him down."

"That's a goal of mine," Rose said. "He's my cousin. Maybe he'd like to know who his family is."

"It's good he was adopted, though," I said. "I'd pictured the worst for him." I turned to Brenna. "Why didn't you tell me you found her?" I asked.

"I thought I was going to fail," she said. "We only connected a few days ago, so I didn't want to get your hopes up."

I looked at Rose. "How did Ivy and Henry Allen . . . your parents . . . find you?" I asked.

"They just never gave up," Rose said.

"We always talked about finding Mary," Ivy said. "She was our daughter. How could we not look for her? But we knew we didn't stand a chance of getting her until we got married. Then we told Dan—the owner of the olive grove—everything. He hired a lawyer who tracked down Rose and helped us to get her. He's the one who found out about William, too. Rose had been shuffled from foster home to foster home."

"I don't remember much about that time at all," Rose said. "I've blocked it, I guess. My earliest memory is running around in the grove with my little brothers. They were annoying, but all in all, it was a pretty cool childhood."

I smiled. Watching this mother and daughter who both seemed so content with their lives, I thought of how you could look at people and never know what had come before. What trials. What horrors. You couldn't see Ivy's impoverished roots, or how close she'd come to having no family at all. You couldn't see the loss of her sister—a loss that would haunt both of us forever. The wounds were deep, and yet they didn't show. It was hard to imagine that in a few minutes, we'd be reopening those wounds, revisiting one of the worst times in either of our lives. I felt like saying, "Forget the hearing! Let's all go out for a nice brunch instead." But we needed to do this, if not for ourselves, then for Mary Ella and thousands of others like her.

"Mom," Brenna asked, "can I show them the picture?" She held up the manila folder.

I hesitated, feeling protective of Ivy. I didn't want to introduce more pain into her life when she'd worked hard to put that pain behind her. And yet she was here, wasn't she, facing the past head-on. "If she wants to see it," I said.

"A picture of what?" Ivy asked.

"I went to Mom's old house today," Brenna said. "I took a picture of the bedroom closet where you hid when the police came."

Ivy's hand rushed to her throat and her eyes widened. "That closet! Why would you take a picture of—"

"The names are still there," I said. "The names you carved into the wall."

"They are?" she whispered.

"What names?" Rose asked.

Brenna handed Ivy the folder. She hesitated a moment before opening it, and I watched as tears filled her eyes.

"You wrote that?" Rose leaned close, touching the corner of the photograph.

Ivy nodded. "I carved it with a fork while the police were coming for us. I wanted to write our names so deep in the wall they'd never be erased." A look of anger flashed across her face, but only for a second.

"I never dreamed . . . all these years later . . ." She looked at me, one tear falling over her lower lashes. "I wish I could talk to that girl in the closet right now," she said. "I wish I could tell her everything would work out all right. She was so scared."

"She *made* everything work out all right." I put my hand on hers. "You were so strong, Ivy," I said. "That day the police drove me away while you stood all alone in my front yard . . . that image of you will be in my mind forever and I—" My voice broke and Ivy turned her hand to link tightly with mine.

"I survived it," she reassured me quietly, and I nodded, unable to trust my voice.

"Ladies," Gavin said, ever so gently, "I think we'd better get going."

I looked at Ivy as she let go of my hand to brush a tear from her cheek. "Are you certain you want to do this?" I asked. I thought I'd be able to get through my testimony today dry-eyed; now I wasn't so sure. I could only imagine what this would be like for her.

Ivy looked at the picture in her lap once more, then closed the folder. "More sure than ever," she said.

"All right then." I got to my feet with a sense of determination, then held my hand out to her. "Let's go tell our story."

AUTHOR'S NOTE

Although the characters in *Necessary Lies* are fictional (as is Grace County), the Eugenics Sterilization Program was not. From 1929 until 1975, North Carolina sterilized over seven thousand of its citizens. The program targeted the "mentally defective," the "feebleminded," inmates in mental institutions and training schools, those suffering with epilepsy, and others whose sterilization was considered "for the public good."

While other states had similar programs, most of them stopped performing state-mandated sterilizations after World War II, uncomfortable over comparisons to the eugenics experiments in Nazi Germany. North Carolina, however, actually increased its rate of sterilizations after the war.

In the early years of the program, the focus was on institutionalized individuals, but in the fifties, it shifted to women on welfare. Around the same time, the Human Betterment League, an organization founded by hosiery magnate James Hanes and Clarence Gamble of the Procter and Gamble dynasty, spread sterilization propaganda to the public through pamphlets and articles, such as the ones Jane discovers in her office. Sterilization of "morons" was touted as both a way to improve the population, prevent the conception of children who would live "wasted lives," and make life easier for the "mental defectives" who would have to raise those children.

North Carolina was the only state to give social workers the power to petition for the sterilization of individuals—in all other states, eugenic sterilization was limited to institutional populations. As a former social worker myself (although I was never a welfare worker), I can't imagine having that much control over my clients' lives. I believe the vast majority of social workers had their clients' best interests at heart, and in a time when there were very few choices in contraception, many women—like Lita Jordan—were desperate for help. I'm sure many social workers viewed their ability to recommend sterilization for their clients as something of a blessing, yet that power could easily be abused. A misunderstanding of genetics, moral judgments about sexual behavior, and concern about the burgeoning welfare rolls led to many unnecessary and unwanted sterilizations.

In later years of the program, more African Americans than Caucasians were sterilized, but the program did not set out to target a specific race. In the thirties and forties, only 23 percent of those sterilized under the program were African American, but this is almost certainly due to the fact that they were excluded from the welfare rolls during that time. In the late fifties, 59 percent of those sterilized were African American and the number grew to 64 percent in the mid-sixties.

The last sterilization took place in 1974. The records of the Eugenics Board were sealed until 1996, when researcher Dr. Johanna Schoen, currently an associate professor at Rutgers University, was given access to the board's redacted records. Her research inspired a series of articles titled "Against Their Will" in the *Winston-Salem Journal*, bringing the Eugenics Program back into public awareness. The values of the past suddenly collided with those of the present.

While many of the victims had died by that time, as many as two thousand were still living, prompting a public apology from then governor Mike Easley. An apology, however, was not enough, and when Governor Bev Perdue took office in 2008, she created the North Carolina Justice for Sterilization Victims Foundation, which on June 22, 2011, held a hearing where victims or their loved ones could tell their stories. It's at this hearing that Ivy and Jane are preparing to testify in the final chapter of *Necessary Lies*. You can watch the actual hearing

on the Internet at http://www.wral.com/news/video/9755940/#/
vid9755940.

After the hearing, the foundation recommended compensation of
fifty thousand dollars per living victim. Governor Perdue announced
she would put $10.3 million in her proposed budget to fund this com-
pensation and the other work of the foundation, stating: "We cannot
change the terrible things that happened to so many of our most vulnerable citizens, but we can take responsibility for our state's mistakes
and show that we do not tolerate violations of basic human rights. We
must provide meaningful assistance to victims, so I am including this
funding in my budget." The bill providing for compensation was easily approved by the North Carolina House, but the Senate refused to
support the plan. In 2013, however, under the administration of Governor Pat McCrory, both the state Senate and House approved allocating
$10 million for compensation. Victims who came forward by the June 30,
2014, deadline are expected to receive compensation on June 30, 2015.

It's estimated that about 1,800 victims are still living. Reaching
them has been difficult. Many have hidden the fact that they were sterilized from their loved ones, and many others may still be unaware that
they were ever sterilized. As I write this on the day after the deadline,
630 people have applied for compensation. If their claims are verified,
each will receive approximately sixteen thousand dollars of the $10 mil-
lion total.

I chose not to sensationalize the Eugenics Program in *Necessary
Lies*. I easily could have. Many of the cases border on the incompre-
hensible, such as a twelve-year-old girl sterilized because she was
overly interested in boys and hard to control at home, or the teenaged
girl who was molested by her father, who signed his consent for her
sterilization himself. Instead, Ivy's and Mary Ella's and Lita's cases
were more the norm, and I think by making that point, all the more
horrific.

Diane Chamberlain
Raleigh, North Carolina
July 1, 2014

Acknowledgments

As you can imagine, *Necessary Lies* was a research-heavy novel and I have many people to thank for their various contributions.

I'll be forever grateful that I stumbled across the book *Choice and Coercion: Birth Control, Sterilization, and Abortion in Public Health and Welfare* by Johanna Schoen, Ph.D. Not only was the book itself enlightening and helpful, but Johanna proved to be most generous with her time and research as well, sharing records from the Eugenics Board meetings and transcripts from her interviews with social workers and other professionals involved in the program. Johanna's work helped me understand both the mechanics of the sterilization program as well as the toll it took on its victims.

In 1960, I was a kid in suburban New Jersey, so the rural South and tobacco farming were not even on my radar. Once I moved to North Carolina, however, I quickly discovered that I couldn't walk into a party without meeting at least a few people who had "worked to-bacca" as kids. I was grateful to be able to gather information from all of them, but I'm particularly indebted to my friend, mystery author Margaret Maron, for sharing her memories of growing up on a to-bacco farm. Margaret read the entire manuscript of *Necessary Lies* for accuracy, and she and her friend Ann Stephenson drove me all over their rural county—the inspiration for my fictional Grace County—

regaling me with tales of how life used to be. Ann also gave me a tour of her family's old tobacco farm and I'm indebted to both of them for answering my endless questions with patience and enthusiasm.

For brainstorming help and constant support, I'm grateful to the six other writers of the "Weymouth Seven": Mary Kay Andrews, Brynn Bonner, Katy Munger, Sarah Shaber, Alexandra Sokoloff, and again, Margaret Maron. We retreat a couple of times each year to the Weymouth Center for the Arts in Southern Pines, North Carolina, to write and commiserate, and I pinch myself every time I head up that long driveway to the mansion for a solid week of writing. Thank you to the Weymouth Center for its generous support of North Carolina writers.

Retired psychologist Mary Kilburn and retired social worker Mel Adair both worked in North Carolina during the era of the Eugenics Program and both were generous in sharing their experiences with me.

I'm grateful to Kathy Williamson, who proved to be a skillful researcher as she helped me track down even the most esoteric bits of information I needed for my story.

For various contributions, thank you to the late Sterling Bryson, Patricia McLinn, Glen Pierce, Helen Ramsey, and Eleanor Smith.

It was my lucky day when I joined forces with my agent, Susan Ginsburg. Her knowledge of the publishing world is surpassed only by her genuine warmth. Thanks for everything you do, Susan. I'm also grateful to my agent in the United Kingdom, Angharad Kowal, for all the work she's done on my behalf, and to Wayne Brookes, publishing director at Pan Macmillan in the UK for his faith in *Necessary Lies* and his endless enthusiasm.

I've wanted to work with editor Jen Enderlin since I was a newbie author way back when, and Jen has certainly been worth the wait! Thank you, Jen, for being such an insightful editor and good friend. I'm grateful to the entire team at St. Martin's Press, particularly Sally Richardson, Matthew Shear, Jeff Dodes, Paul Hochman, Dori Weintraub, Lisa Senz, Sarah Goldstein, and the entire Broadway and Fifth Avenue sales forces. I couldn't ask for better people to work with.

Finally, thank you to John Pagliuca, my significant other, muse, critic, brainstorming partner, resident photographer, and first reader. Thanks, John, for helping me think out loud, for letting me know when I've gone way off track, and for once again putting up with all those take-out meals.

Reading
Group
Gold

NECESSARY LIES
by Diane Chamberlain

About the Author

- A Conversation with Diane Chamberlain

Behind the Novel

- "From Shi##y First Draft to Real Book:
  Words of Wisdom for Newbie Authors"
  An Original Essay by the Author

Historical Perspective

- A Selection of Images

Keep on Reading

- Recommended Reading

- Reading Group Questions

A
Reading
Group Gold
Selection

For more reading group suggestions,
visit www.readinggroupgold.com.

ST. MARTIN'S GRIFFIN

A Conversation with Diane Chamberlain

Did you always know you wanted to write? Were there always characters in your head?

I knew I wanted to write when I was in the first grade and our teacher read us E. B. White's *Charlotte's Web*, a chapter each day. What excitement and pathos and heroism in that story! Even now, I remember being struck by the realization that a human being could write something amazing and that since I was a human being, maybe I could do it too. I became much more practical when it came time to pick a career (social work), so even though I had that very early yearning, I set it aside for a long, long time.

Yes, there were always characters in my head. If I'd allowed anyone into my six-year-old brain back then, I probably would have been rushed into therapy. I loved going to bed at night so I could spend a couple of hours thinking up stories before drifting off to sleep. My parents probably wondered why I was always so tired in the morning after eight hours of "sleep."

The other thing I did constantly as a kid was narrate my life. You know: "Diane reluctantly climbed the stairs to her room. Peering out the window, she thought longingly of the puppy she wanted for her birthday." Et cetera. I think I may have read way too much as a kid. Is that possible?

Is there a book that most influenced your life or inspired you to become a writer?

This is a two-part answer. (I also address this issue in the essay that follows.)

Part 1. If you have a passion for writing, do all you can to learn how to write well (take a class, for example) and just do it. I hear all the time from people who say they have an idea for a book but can't get started. I know how scary that blank page is, believe me. If you want to write a book, there is no way around putting the words on the paper.

"I'd like to continue writing entertaining stories for as long as I'm having fun and my readers want more."

A page a day equals a book in a year, or at least it will equal a draft for you to revise—please never think that once you've written a draft, you're finished. But go for it! Start writing.

Part 2. I am personally glad that I didn't major in writing in college. I do wish I had the skills I might have learned while getting a master's in fine arts, but working in the real world has given me experiences that influence everything I write. I always suggest that kids interested in writing go into a field that puts them in contact with people. The creative well needs to be constantly replenished.

What's your favorite book you have written?

I have so many! I'd say *Necessary Lies* is at the top of my list of favorites because I'd wanted to write this book for so many years. I knew the story had the potential to be controversial and uncomfortable and was a bit different from many of my other books. I loved the research—learning about something I knew nothing about (tobacco farming) as well as something I could all too easily imagine—a social worker having ultimate power over her clients—since I'd been a social worker for many years myself. I'm glad I was never in Jane's position.

If we judged Jane by today's standards, her use of such phrases as "my husband allowed me to work" would seem downright subservient. How did you manage to characterize Jane so perfectly—and so uncommonly progressive—for her era?

In so many different aspects of this novel, I tried to strive for the middle ground because I wanted the story to feel realistic. For that reason, I didn't want to make Jane a flaming feminist. At the same time, she's not a meek, little housewife. She was raised in a household that valued helping those less fortunate and that was a huge part of who she was. When she married and found herself with money and a comfortable lifestyle, she didn't forget her roots. I think the fact that she does still have traditional values common to women in 1960 made her actions in helping Ivy that much more dramatic.

What do you still hope to do in life, both personally and professionally?

Yikes, there's no way to answer that question in a few sentences, but I'll try.

Professionally: I'd like to continue writing entertaining stories for as long as I'm having fun and my readers want more. After that, I'd like to write a memoir, and I also have a few ideas for novels that are different from my usual. I hope I'll be writing my crazy time travel novel when I'm in my eighties!

Personally: I want to spend more time with my family and friends. I'd love to fly around the country visiting all the people I miss.

Problem: My personal and professional longings don't mesh together very well, as one doesn't allow much time for the other. I imagine that's true for most of us.

"Ivy is one of my all-time favorite characters."

Brittany Bailey

The author (with Cole and Keeper)

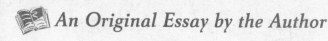

An Original Essay by the Author

"From Shi##y First Draft to Real Book: Words of Wisdom for Newbie Authors"

"I want to write a book, but I can't get started."

I hear that over and over again, so I'd like to give wannabe writers some encouragement. I think a big part of their problem is that they expect the first words they put on paper to glow with perfection. I'm a big believer in what Anne Lamott calls "The Shi##y First Draft," so I thought I'd share my first draft attempt at a few paragraphs from *Necessary Lies*.

Necessary Lies is my twenty-second novel, and I've been using the Shi##y First Draft method a very long time. The book is set in 1960s rural North Carolina and is the story of a young, green social worker named Jane and her fifteen-year-old client, Ivy. As Jane discovers the secrets in Ivy's life, she's thrown into a moral dilemma that jeopardizes both her job and her marriage. Ivy is one of my all-time favorite characters and it was immense fun writing from her point of view.

I keep all the drafts of my novels as I write. Below I'm going to show you a paragraph and the road it traveled from Shi##y First Draft to the final form you'll find in the book. I hope it encourages those of you who think you need perfection right off the bat.

In this scene, Nurse Ann, the public health nurse, is visiting Ivy. Ann is concerned that Ivy might be having sex (she is) and she wants to give her contraception. Ivy's seventeen-year-old sister, Mary Ella, already has a child. The scene is written from Ivy's first-person point of view.

Behind the Novel

Nurse Ann showed up with contraceptives. "Open this bag."

I opened it up and pulled out a box of spermicidal jelly.

"This kills sperm. Sperm comes from the boy and makes babies."

"I know that."

"And this is what you use to get it inside you." She pulled a long tube from the bag.

"I need to sweep the yard," I said.

"You need to stay right here," she said.

She opened the bag again and brought out Trojans. "These are rubbers," she said. "The boy wears these. They're even more protective than the jelly."

"You mean protection from having a baby?"

"That's right."

"I don't need these things. You should talk to Mary Ella. She's gonna get pregnant again any day."

"Mary Ella's not your business. These things are for you and you can have more if you need them."

Why was she giving me this stuff instead of Mary Ella. I'd told Mary Ella the boy should pull out to have no babies, but she ignored me as usual.

Pretty shi##y, huh?

Okay, here's a draft about halfway to the final.

Nurse Ann opened her bag in her lap. "I have some things here for you," she said, handing me a paper bag.

I opened it up and pulled out a box that said spermicidal

jelly on the side.

"You don't eat this kind of jelly," she said. "It kills sperm. Sperm comes from the boy and that's what makes babies."

"I know that."

"Now here"—she opened the box and pulled out a long tube—"you use this to put the jelly inside you." She said how to do that and I knew my cheeks was red.

She reached in the bag one more time and brought out little packages that said Trojan on them. "These are rubbers," she said. "The boy puts these on. They're more protective than the jelly."

"You mean protection from having a baby?"

"That's right."

I handed the bag back to her. "I don't need none of this. Mary Ella's the one you should be talkin' to."

"I'm not worried about Mary Ella right now. I'm worried about you."

"I ain't doing nothing."

"Well, just in case, I want you to have these things and I can bring you more if you ever need more."

I didn't know why she wasn't giving these things to Mary Ella. I'd give them to her myself. I'd told Mary Ella about pulling out to have no more babies, but she ignored me as usual.

And the final draft, where I show more of Ivy's emotions.

Nurse Ann opened the medical bag in her lap. "I have some things here for you," she said, handing me a paper bag. "Look inside and I'll explain how you use them."

I opened it up and pulled out a box that said spermicidal jelly on the side.

"This is not the kind of jelly you eat," she said. "It kills sperm. Sperm comes from the boy and that's what makes babies."

"I know that." I wished I was someplace else.

"Now here"—she opened the box and pulled out a long tube—"is the applicator you use to insert the jelly in your vagina." She went into a long description of how to do that and I knew my cheeks was red, listening to her. This talk was turning out worse than I expected.

She reached in the bag one more time and brought out little packages that said Trojan on them. "These are rubbers," she said. "The boy puts these on. They're more protective than the jelly. And the best protection is using both of them together."

"You mean protection from having a baby?" I wished she'd speak plain.

"That's right."

I handed the bag back to her. "I don't need none of this. Mary Ella's the one you should be talkin' to. She already got herself a baby and any day she's gonna end up with another for sure."

"I'm not worried about Mary Ella right now. I'm worried about you."

"No need to be. I ain't doing nothing."

"Well, just in case, I want you to have these things and I can bring you more if you ever need more."

I didn't know why she wasn't giving these things to Mary Ella. I'd give them to her myself. I'd told Mary Ella about

*the pulling out to be a way to have no more babies,
and she just looked off into the blue yonder the way
she always did, like she didn't hear a word I said.*

So, there you have it, from first draft to actual book. I
hope it encourages you to put your story on paper.

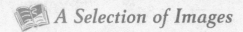 *A Selection of Images*

The following settings and historical markers
served as inspiration for *Necessary Lies*.

An old tobacco barn in rural North Carolina.

A Southern red-roofed farmhouse.

This plaque appears in Raleigh, NC, near the building
where the Eugenics Board met.

Historical
Perspective

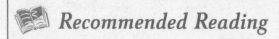

Recommended Reading

Choice and Coercion: Birth Control, Sterilization, and Abortion in Public Health and Welfare by Johanna Schoen

When I decided to write about the Eugenics Program, I purchased this book and it became my bible as I did my research. Johanna Schoen shines a light on North Carolina's approach to reproductive health care for poor women during the last century. She helped me understand not only the plight of young women who were about to be sterilized without their knowledge, but that of women who wanted sterilization but had to fight for it as well.

The Wayward Girls of Samarcand by Melton McLaurin and Anne Russell

McLaurin and Russell tell the true story of sixteen teenaged girls who set fire to their North Carolina reform school in 1931 and faced the death penalty as a result. I read this book after *Necessary Lies* was published, and in spite of all I knew about the Eugenics Program, I was still stunned by the way the legal system dealt with these young girls. An eye-opener.

Bootlegger's Daughter (along with the rest of the Deborah Knott series) by Margaret Maron

Margaret is a friend of mine who was raised on a North Carolina tobacco farm. Her popular Deborah Knott mysteries are set in her fictionalized rural Colleton County (spookily similar to my fictionalized Grace County). Margaret told me much of what I needed to know to flesh out my setting, but her novels told me even more while keeping me thoroughly entertained at the same time.

The Secrets She Carried by Barbara Davis

This debut novel set on an old North Carolina tobacco plantation has the sort of gothic feel that I love in a story. If you enjoy my books, I think you'll enjoy this novel as well.

A Long and Happy Life by **Reynolds Price**

As I wrote *Necessary Lies*, I sought out novels set in
North Carolina during the '50s and '60s, the time frame
for my own novel. This story of a teenaged girl and the
noncommittal boy she loves was one of my favorites.
I've been a fan of the late Reynolds Price since reading
his *Kate Vaiden* years ago. *A Long and Happy Life* was
published in 1961, and the details of the setting and
language of the characters fed my imagination as I read.

A Land More Kind Than Home by **Wiley Cash**

You'll love this book. It's a beautifully told story of a
young boy who knows more about the tragedy that
befalls his family than he should. Once again, it has that
gothic North Carolina feel that I adore.

Reading
Group
Gold

*Keep on
Reading*

Reading Group Questions

1. Did the truth about Mr. Gardiner's involvement with Mary Ella surprise you? If not, at what point did you begin to suspect it?

2. Charlotte gives Jane a lot of reasons for why the Eugenics Sterilization Program is a good thing for both individuals and society. What are the reasons she gives and what were your reactions to them?

3. Various people throughout the story tell Jane that she is too emotionally invested in her clients, and Fred refers to her as "a loose cannon." Have you ever been in a situation where you had to balance emotional investment with professionalism?

4. Jane picks up on a lot of subtle but important details about the Harts during the extra time she spends with them. What key pieces of information does she glean from these interactions that she doesn't get from her formal interviews?

5. At one point Ivy observes that, "It was like the whole world was moving forward, taking Henry Allen with it, while I was holding still." How are the lives and actions of the various female characters influenced or restricted by their role in society as women?

6. Jane knows Lois for a short time, but it is a time when Jane most needs a friend, and Lois has a profound effect on her. Has there been someone who was only in your life briefly, but had a big impact on you?

7. How much of a role do you think the loss of Jane's sister played in her determination to help Ivy?

8. Jane's mother tells her: "Sometimes coloring outside the lines can cost you. Only you can figure out if it's worth it." Can you think of a situation from your own life to which this applies? Did coloring outside the lines cost you, and was it worth it?

9. How did you feel about the way the different characters' lives turned out, as revealed by Ivy at the end of the story?

10. What do you think you would have done if you were in Jane's position? Would you have put Baby William in foster care sooner, or not at all? Would you have told Mary Ella about her sterilization? Would you have gone as far as hiding Ivy in your home?

11. What would you have done in Ivy's position? Would you have gone with Jane? Would you have taken a different path?

Keep on Reading

12. Jane realizes that whether or not a person is perceived as intelligent has a lot to do with whether or not he or she is in a familiar environment. What examples of this do we see?

13. How do racial prejudices play a role in different people's assumptions, including Jane's, about what is happening between the residents at the Gardiners' farm?

14. Ivy realizes that she and Jane have more in common than she ever imagined. What are some similarities between them?

15. The social services system as depicted in this novel displays a hierarchy of power that trickles all the way from Jane's boss, Fred, through the different levels in the office and the different people on the Gardiners' farm all the way down to Baby William. What different levels of power do we see, and how are people at each level restricted in the power they have over their own actions and the actions of others?

I was an insatiable reader as a child, and that fact, combined with a vivid imagination, inspired me to write. I penned a few truly terrible "novellas" at age twelve, then put fiction aside for many years as I pursued my education.

I grew up in Plainfield, New Jersey, and spent my summers at the Jersey Shore, two settings that have found their way into my novels. In high school, my favorite authors were the unlikely combination of Victoria Holt and Sinclair Lewis. I loved Holt's flair for romantic suspense and Lewis's character studies as well as his exploration of social values, and both those authors influenced the writer I am today.

I attended Glassboro State College in New Jersey before moving to San Diego, where I received both my bachelor's and master's degrees in social work from San Diego State University. After graduating, I worked in a couple of youth counseling agencies and then focused on medical social work, which I adored. I worked in hospitals in San Diego and Washington, DC, before opening a private psychotherapy practice in Alexandria, Virginia, specializing in adolescents. I reluctantly closed my practice when I realized that I could no longer split my time between two careers and be effective at both of them.

It was while I was working in San Diego that I started writing. I'd had a story in my mind since I was a young adolescent about a group of people living together at the Jersey Shore. While waiting for a doctor's appointment one day, I pulled out a pen and pad began putting that story on paper.

Once I started, I couldn't stop. I took a class in fiction writing, but for the most part, I "learned by doing." That story, *Private Relations*, took me four years to complete. I sold it in 1986, but it wasn't published until 1989 (three very long years!), when it earned me the RITA Award for Best Single Title Contemporary Novel. Except for a brief stint writing for daytime TV (*One Life to Live*) and a few miscellaneous articles for newspapers and magazines, I've focused my efforts on book-length fiction and have written twenty-one novels.

My stories are often filled with twists and surprises and—I hope—they also tug at the emotions. Relationships—between men and women, parents and children, sisters and brothers—are always the primary focus of my books. I can't think of anything more fascinating than the way people struggle with life's trials and tribulations, both together and alone.

I now live and write in North Carolina, the state which has become my true home and has also spawned many settings for my stories. I live with my significant other, John, a photographer, and two sweet Shetland Sheepdogs, Keeper and Cole. I have three grown stepdaughters, a couple of sons-in-law and four grandbabies. For me, the real joy of writing is having the opportunity to touch readers with my words. I hope that my stories move you in some way and give you hours of enjoyable reading.

Read on for a sneak peek at
Diane Chamberlain's next novel

The Silent Sister

Available October 2014

JANUARY 1990

PROLOGUE

Alexandria, Virginia

All day long, people stopped along the path that ran through the woods by the Potomac River. Bundled in their parkas and wool scarves, they stood close to one another for warmth and clutched the mittened hands of their children or the leashes of their dogs as they stared at the one splash of color in the winter-gray landscape. The yellow kayak sat in the middle of the river, surrounded by ice. The water had been rough the night before, buffeted by snowy winds, rising into swirling whitecaps as the temperature plummeted, and the waves froze in jagged crests, trapping the kayak many yards from shore.

The walkers had seen the kayak on the morning news, but they still needed to see it in person. It marked the end of a saga that had gripped them for months. They'd looked forward to the trial that would never happen now, because the seventeen-year-old girl—the seventeen-year-old murderer, most were sure—now rested somewhere beneath that rocky expanse of ice.

She took the easy way out, *some of them whispered to one another.*

But what a terrible way to die, *others said.*

They looked at the rocky bank of the river and wondered if she'd put some of those rocks in her pockets to make herself sink. They wondered if she'd cried as she paddled the kayak into the water, knowing the end was near. She'd cried on TV, for certain. Faking it, *some of them said now as they moved on down the path. It was too cold to stand in one spot for very long.*

But there was one woman, bundled warm, gloved hands in her pockets, who stood at the side of the path for hours. She watched as the news chopper collected fresh aerial images, its blades a deafening dark blur against the gray sky. She watched as the police milled along the banks of the river, pointing in one direction and then the other as they considered how they'd retrieve the kayak from the ice . . . and how they would search for the girl's body beneath it.

The woman looked at the police again. They stood with their hands on their hips now, as though they were giving up. This case was closed. She pulled her jacket more tightly around herself. Let them give up, *she thought, pleased, as she watched a police officer shrug his shoulders in what looked like defeat.* Let them wrest that kayak from the river and call it a day.

Although a yellow kayak stranded in ice proved nothing.

They were fools if they thought it did.

PART ONE

JUNE 2013

1.

Riley

I'd never expected to lose nearly everyone I loved by the time I was twenty-five.

I felt the grief rise again as I parked in front of the small, nondescript post office in Pollocksville. The three-hour drive from my apartment in Durham had seemed more like six as I made a mental list of all the things I needed to do once I reached New Bern, and that list segued into thinking of how alone I felt. But I didn't have time to dwell on my sadness.

The first thing I had to do was stop at this post office, ten miles outside of New Bern. I'd get that out of the way and cross one thing off my list. Digging the flimsy white postcard from my purse, I went inside the building. I was the only customer, and my tennis shoes squeaked on the floor as I walked up to the counter where a clerk waited for me. With her dark skin and perfect cornrows, she reminded me of my friend Sherise, so I liked her instantly.

"How can I help you?" she asked.

I handed her the postcard. "I'm confused about this card," I said. "My father died a month ago. I've been getting his mail at my address in Durham and this card came and—"

"We send these out when someone hasn't paid their bill for their post office box," she said, looking at the card. "It's a warning. They don't pay it in two months, we close the box and change the lock."

"Well, I understand that, but see"—I turned the card over—"this isn't my father's name. I don't know who Fred Marcus is. My father was Frank MacPherson, so I think this came to me by mistake. I don't even think my father *had* a post office box. I don't know why he would. Especially not in Pollocksville when he lives—*lived*—in New Bern." It would take me a long time to learn to speak about my father in the past tense.

"Let me check." She disappeared into the rear of the building and came back a moment later holding a thin purple envelope and a white index-type card. "This is the only thing in the box," she said, handing the envelope to me. "Addressed to Fred Marcus. I checked the records and the box is assigned to that name at this street address." She held the index card out to me. The signature did look like my father's handwriting, but his handwriting was hardly unique. And besides, it wasn't his name.

"That's the right street address, but whoever this guy is, he must have written his address down wrong," I said, slipping the purple envelope into my purse.

"You want me to close the box or you want to pay to keep it open?" the clerk asked.

"I don't feel like it's mine to close, but I'm not going to pay for it, so . . ." I shrugged.

"I'll close it then," she said.

"All right." I was glad she'd made the decision for me. I smiled. "I hope Fred Marcus doesn't mind, whoever he is." I turned toward the door.

"Sorry about your daddy," she said.

"Thanks," I said over my shoulder, and my eyes stung by the time I got to my car.

Driving into New Bern, I passed through the historic district. Old houses were packed close together on the tree-lined streets and gigantic painted bears the town's iconic symbol, stood here and there among the shops. A pair of bicycle cops pedaled down the street in front of me, lightening my mood ever so slightly. Although I hadn't lived in New Bern since I went away to college, it still had a hometown pull on me. It was such a unique little place.

I turned onto Craven Street and pulled into our driveway. Daddy's car was in the garage. I could see its roof through the glass windows—one of them broken—of the garage door. I hadn't thought about his car. Was it better to sell it or donate it? I had an appointment with his attorney in the morning and I'd add that question to my ever-growing list. The car should really go to my brother Danny to replace his ancient junker, but I had the feeling he'd turn it down.

My old house was a two-story pastel yellow Victorian in need of fresh paint, with a broad front porch adorned with delicate white railings and pillars. It was the only house I could remember living in, and I loved it. Once I sold it, I'd have no reason to come to New Bern again. I'd taken those visits home to see my father for granted. After Daddy's sudden death, I came back for two days to arrange for his cremation and attend to other details that were now a blur in my memory. Had he wanted to be cremated? We'd never talked about that sort of thing and I'd been in such a state of shock and confusion that I couldn't think straight. Bryan had been with me then, a calming, loving presence. He'd pointed out that my mother'd been cremated, so that would most likely be my father's wish as well. I hoped he was right.

Sitting in my car in the driveway, I wondered if I'd been too hasty in ending it with Bryan. I could use his support right now. With Daddy gone and Sherise doing mission work in Haiti for the summer, the timing couldn't have been worse. There was no good time, though, for ending a two-year-old relationship.

The loneliness weighed on my shoulders as I got out of my car and looked up at the house. My plan had been to take two weeks to clean it out and then put it—and the nearby RV park my father owned—on the market. Suddenly, as I looked at all the windows and remembered how many things were in need of repair and how little my father liked to throw things away, I knew my time frame was unrealistic. Daddy hadn't been a hoarder, exactly, but he was a collector. He had cases full of vintage lighters and pipes and old musical instruments, among zillions of other things I would have to get rid of. Bryan said our house was more like a dusty old museum than a home, and he'd been right. I tried not to panic as I pulled my duffel bag from the backseat of my car. I had no one waiting for me in Durham and the summer off. I could take as much time as I needed to get the house ready to sell. I wondered if there was any chance of getting Danny to help me.

I climbed the broad front steps to the porch and unlocked the door. It squeaked open with a sound as familiar to me as my father's voice. I'd pulled the living room shades before I'd left back in May and I could barely see across the living room to the kitchen beyond. I breathed in the hot musty smell of a house closed up too long as I raised the shades to let in the midday light. Turning the thermostat to seventy-two, I heard the welcome sound of the old air conditioner kicking to life. Then I stood in the middle of the room, hands on my hips, as I examined the space from the perspective of someone tasked with cleaning it out.

Daddy had used the spacious living room as something of an office, even though he had a good-sized office upstairs as well. He loved desks and cubbies and display cases. The desk in the living room was a beautiful old rolltop. Against the far wall, custom-built shelves surrounding the door to the kitchen held his classical music collection, nearly all of it vinyl, and a turntable sat in a special cabinet he'd had built into the wall. On the north side of the room, a wide glass-fronted display case contained his pipe collection. The room always had a faint smell of tobacco to me, even though he'd told me that was my imagination. Against the opposite wall, there was a couch at least as old as I was along with an upholstered armchair. The rest of the space was taken up by the baby grand piano I'd never learned to play. Danny and I had both taken lessons, but neither of us had any interest and our parents let us quit. People would say, *They're Lisa's siblings. Surely they have talent. Why don't you push them?* But they never did and I was grateful.

Walking into the dining room, I was struck by how neat and orderly it appeared to be compared to the rest of the house. My father had no need for that room and I was sure he rarely set foot in it. The dining room had been my mother's territory. The wide curio cabinet was full of china and vases and cut-glass bowls that had been handed down through her family for generations. Things she'd treasured that I was going to have to figure out how to get rid of. I ran my fingers over the dusty sideboard. Everywhere I turned in the house, I'd be confronted by memories I would need to dismantle.

I carried my duffel bag upstairs, where a wide hallway opened to four rooms. The first was my father's bedroom with its quilt-covered queen-sized bed. The second room had been Danny's, and although he hadn't slept in our house since leaving at eighteen—*escaping,* he would call it—it would always be "Danny's room" to me. The third room was mine, though in the years since I'd lived in the house, the room had developed an austere air about it. I'd cleaned out my personal possessions bit by bit after college. The memorabilia from my high school and college years—pictures of old boyfriends, yearbooks, CDs, that sort of thing—were in a box in the storage unit of my Durham apartment waiting for the day I got around to sorting through them.

I dropped my duffel bag on my bed, then walked into the fourth room—my father's office. Daddy's bulky old computer monitor rested on a small desk by the window, and glass-fronted curio cabinets filled with Zippo lighters and antique compasses lined two of the walls. My grandfather had been a collector, too, so Daddy'd inherited many of the items, then added to them by searching through Craigslist and eBay and flea markets. The collections had been his obsession. I knew the sliding glass doors to the cabinets were locked and hoped I'd be able to find where my father had squirreled away the keys.

Propped against the fourth wall of the room were five violin cases. Daddy hadn't played, but he'd collected stringed instruments for as long as I could remember. One of the cases had an ID tag hanging from the handle, and I knelt next to it, lifting the tag in my hand. It had been a long time since I'd looked at that tag, but I knew what was on it: a drawing of a violet on one side and on the other side, my sister's name—*Lisa MacPherson*—and our old Alexandria, Virginia, address. Lisa had never lived in this house.

My mother died shortly after I graduated from high school, so although I would never stop missing her, I was used to her being gone. It was strange to be in the house without Daddy, though. As I put my clothes in my dresser, I kept expecting him to walk into the room and I had trouble accepting the fact that it was impossible. I missed our weekly phone calls and knowing he was only a few hours away. He'd been so easy to talk to and I'd always felt his unconditional love. It was a terrible feeling to know that there wasn't a soul in the world now who loved me that deeply.

He'd been a quiet man. Maybe one of the quietest people to ever walk the earth. He questioned rather than told. He'd ask me all about my own life, but rarely shared anything about his own. As a middle school counselor, I was the one always asking the questions and I'd enjoyed being asked for a change, knowing that the man doing the asking cared deeply about my answers. He was a loner, though. He'd died on the floor of the Food Lion after a massive heart attack. He'd been alone and that bothered me more than anything.

Bryan had suggested I have a memorial service for him, but I wouldn't have known who to invite. If he had any friends, I didn't know about them. Unlike most people in New Bern, my father hadn't belonged to a church or any community organization, and I was certain my brother wouldn't show up at a service for him. His relationship with our father had been very different from mine. I hadn't even been able to *find* Danny when I got to New Bern after Daddy's death. His cop friend Harry Washington told me he'd gone to Danny's trailer to give him the news, and I guess Danny just took off. He'd left his car parked next to the trailer, and Bryan and I hiked through the forest looking for him, but Danny knew those woods better than anyone. He had his hiding places. Now, though, he had no idea I was in town, so this time I'd surprise him. I'd plead with him to help me with the house. I knew better than to hope he'd say yes.

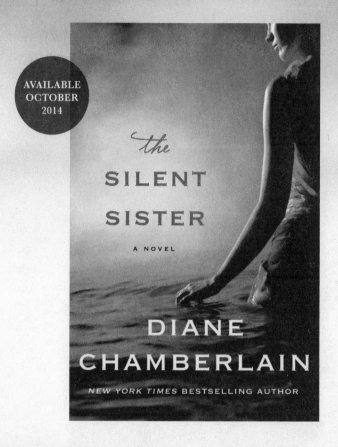